PRAISE FOR *DANCING ON THE BRINK OF THE WORLD*

"Marianne T. Rafter writes with a historian's authority and a romantic's heart—a perfect combination for historical fiction. She brings to life early California in the days of the Spanish dons, real events rich with authentic characters and period detail interwoven with the sweeping story of William Richardson and María Antonia Martinez. *Dancing on the Brink of the World* is a welcome addition to the lore of the often-gritty world of the Californios in an era of profound change."

—Wayne Bonnett, author of *Sausalito Moments in Time*

"Rafter's imaginative narrative weaves fact and fiction with scenes and dialogue that immerse readers in the daily lives of people who lived during this time. The book will captivate fans of both fiction and history."

—*Panorama*, San Francisco Historical Society newsletter

"Marianne Rafter has brought the charismatic settler William Richardson to life in her novel *Dancing on the Brink of the World*. History buffs will be intrigued to follow Richardson's dealings with legendary characters such as Mariano Vallejo, John Sutter, John Fremont, Kit Carson, and more. It's tough to tell when history leaves off and Rafter's imagination takes over—it all has a convincing ring of authenticity."

—Larry Clinton, past president of the Sausalito Historical Society

DANCING ON THE BRINK OF THE WORLD

DANCING ON THE BRINK OF THE WORLD

A Novel of Alta California

MARIANNE T. RAFTER

SWP

SHE WRITES PRESS

Published in 2026 by
She Writes Press, an imprint of The Stable Book Group

32 Court Street, Suite 2109
Brooklyn, NY 11201
https://shewritespress.com
Library of Congress Control Number: 2025915419
Print ISBN: 979-8-89636-034-6
eISBN: 979-8-89636-035-3

Interior Designer: Tabitha Lahr
Hand-drawn maps by Linda Beeman

Printed in the United States of America

Names and identifying characteristics have been changed to protect the privacy of certain individuals.

For Peter, Chris, and Jennifer
With love and thanks

"It is not in the stars to hold our destiny but in ourselves."

—William Shakespeare

From *The Tragedy of Julius Caesar*

CONTENTS

Book 1: Seduction

1822–1829

San Francisco Bay

Book 2: Life on Land and Sea

1829–1835

Misión San Gabriel Arcángel and El Pueblo de Los Angeles

Book 3: Staking a Claim

1835–1846

El Pueblo de Yerba Buena and Rancho Saucelito

BOOK 1

SEDUCTION

1822–1829

SAN FRANCISCO BAY

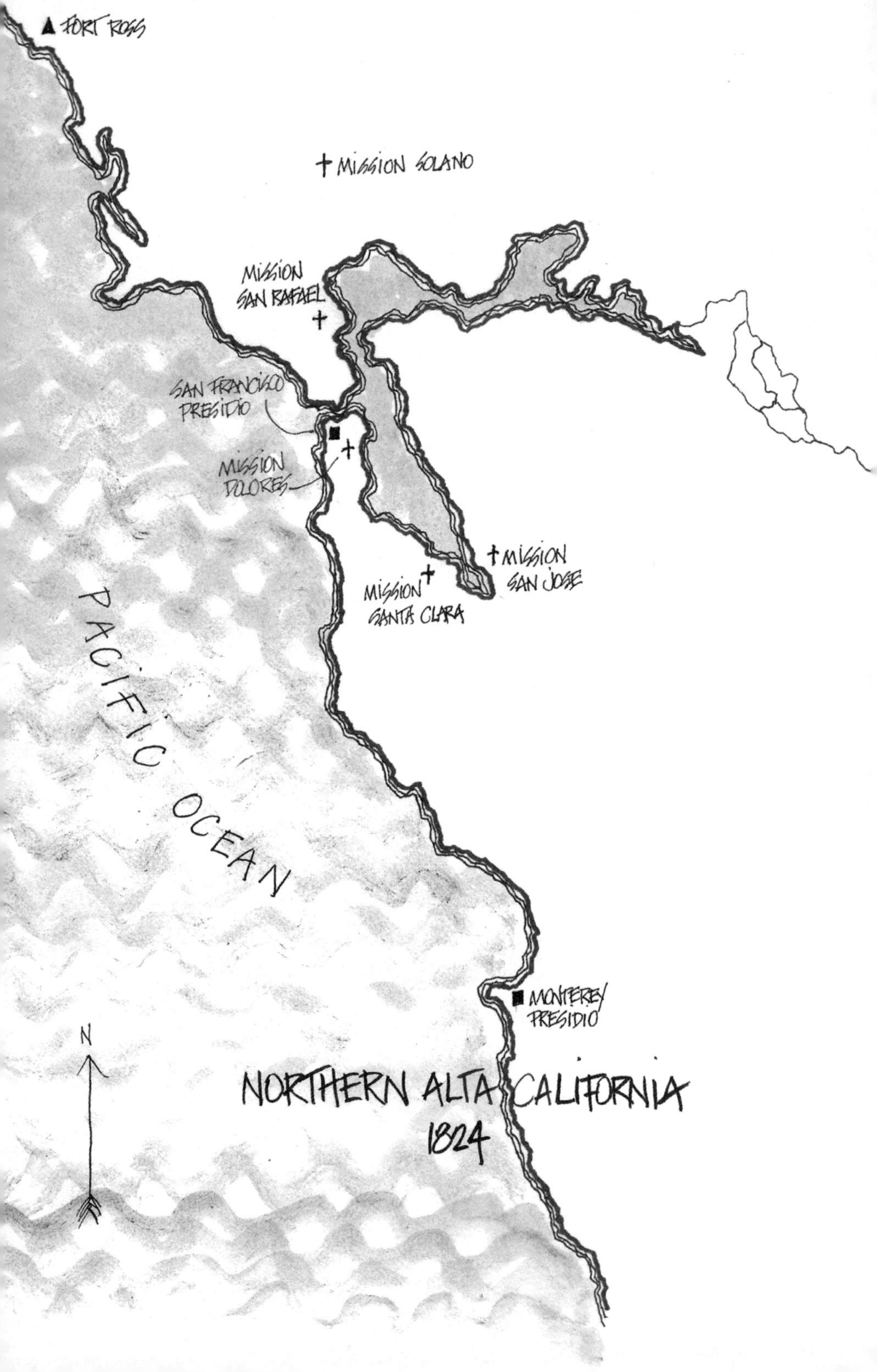
FORT ROSS
MISSION SOLANO
MISSION SAN RAFAEL
SAN FRANCISCO PRESIDIO
MISSION DOLORES
MISSION SAN JOSE
MISSION SANTA CLARA
PACIFIC OCEAN
MONTEREY PRESIDIO
N
NORTHERN ALTA CALIFORNIA
1824

CHAPTER 1

THE BAY

August 1822

An ocean breeze filled *Orion's* sails, and like an aggressive swan, the British whaler glided toward the bay. Onboard, sailors tensed, ready for fight or flight, unsure of their reception on a foreign shore. The eerie creaking of the ship's rigging and seabird calls made them even edgier.

Nothing, however, suited First Mate William Richardson better than life at sea and exploring new lands. After two years' confinement aboard a filthy whaling ship with a merciless captain, he was ready to take his chances ashore. He was sick of the nauseating stench of rotting whale, boiling blubber, and sailors' piss. His belly churned, and his mind raged with anger whenever Captain Barney ordered him to punish intoxicated sailors with a flogging or to keelhaul a man through icy seas if caught stealing food.

William yearned for a safe harbor where he could go ashore alone and explore a new land while the crew filled the ship's empty water barrels. He lifted his head and took a deep breath. He could smell the land surrounding them. Sun-dried grasses, something like cedar or pine, and something sweet like flowers or mint. With hope, he guided the helmsman away from the shoals into deeper waters toward the bay entrance.

Rocky points of land stretched straight up to the cloudless sky. A little farther into the bay, to starboard, sandy beaches promised an easy landing spot. William searched the shore for signs of life.

There! A small group of men and women.

And a puff of smoke drifting from the mouth of a cannon near them.

A deafening boom and a loud splash broke the silence. Was that cannon shot a greeting?

Or was it a warning?

His heart pounding, William focused his spyglass on the group. Grim-faced men wearing leather-jacket uniforms and grasping metal-tipped lances stood at attention. Nearby, a uniformed man on a black horse snapped orders at the soldiers. One of the men turned toward the ship and bellowed something in Spanish.

Captain Barney gruffly asked his first mate, "You jabber their lingo, don't you? What's the bloke saying?"

"Heave to. We're in Mexican territory," William translated. "He wants us to send a boat ashore with a representative to state our intentions."

"Give the order then, Mr. Richardson."

William directed the crew to set the ship's anchor. Two sailors then lowered a longboat over the side. The captain stepped to the rail, the ship's papers in hand, and paused.

Was Barney worried about the cannon shot they'd heard from shore? William wondered. Before he could express his own concern, the captain turned and handed the ship's documents to him.

"Since you speak Spanish, Mr. Richardson, you should be the one to go." William pursed his lips together and grasped the papers. The captain stepped back, clasped his hands behind his back, and said, "Explain what we need and get back here as quick as you can."

William darted below deck to wash up. He threw on a fresh shirt and put on his uniform jacket before returning topside to board the longboat. Two sailors rowed while William thought about the supplies the ship needed. Meat, vegetables, and fruit. Fresh bread! Permission to go ashore to gather firewood and fill their empty barrels with fresh water. Mentally, he prepared his request in Spanish.

When the boat neared the beach, they leaped out, sloshed through the water, and hauled the boat onto the sand. William heard indistinct whispering among the señoritas.

One particular young woman with a long braid of raven black hair and luminous dark eyes gazed at him intently. She murmured something to her friends who stared at her, then at him. He locked eyes with the woman and an intense rush of excitement stirred within him.

Attend to business, William chided himself and turned away from this stunning woman to concentrate on what the man on horseback was saying.

He seemed to be the leader. His worn uniform was made from deerskin. The unsheathed burnished broadsword he held radiated distrust and caution. William felt the hair on his neck rise.

"Identify yourself," the mounted soldier demanded in Spanish. "What is your ship's business in our bay?"

In his best Spanish, William introduced himself and explained the *Orion's* peaceful mission. "We've been chasing whales up north but are now low on food. I'm here to ask for provisions and permission to send men ashore for wood and fresh water. We mean no harm to anyone and can pay in gold coin." The soldier studied William's face. Then a broad smile broke under his dark mustache, and he sheathed his sword.

"Señor, I am Sergeant Sánchez. You and your men are welcome, but you must make your request to Lieutenant Ignacio Martínez, the *comandante*. Please ride with us to the Presidio," he said, motioning to a soldier to hand the reins of a saddled horse to William. "You will present your ship's papers to the comandante and give him more detail about what you need."

The sergeant ordered three men to stay with the cannons and watch the *Orion*. The two oarsmen remained at the shore with the longboat. Then the sergeant and the first mate led the march to the Presidio.

As they moved out of sight of the *Orion*, William recalled tales he had heard of the spirited, though rugged, life in California. He grew more eager for a taste of this new land and its society, no matter how short his stay. The captivating señoritas trailed behind the soldiers, and William wondered whether he would see more of the one with the mesmerizing eyes.

Watch your step, he thought. *This stop is serious business, not pleasure.*

The sergeant told William he had been at the Presidio for three years. William knew that Mexico, until recently called New Spain, had been a Spanish New World colony and had just won its independence. Troops in the outlying forts were probably more cautious with strangers in their newly won territory although he sensed no hostility from the soldiers.

The riders approached the fort's substantial adobe walls, and the sergeant led the group through the north-facing gates. As was common for all Spanish presidios, the adobe buildings within formed a square. Barracks, a stable, a jail, and workshops served as one wall. Along another side ranged several low adobe buildings with red tile roofs and a small, whitewashed chapel with a cross on the peak. To the left, part of an adobe wall was crumbling. William could see over the pile of broken bricks to the field beyond. Clearly, this fort wasn't getting attention from the Mexican government.

In the center of the Presidio, on a well-packed dirt parade ground, a soldier on horseback raced at a full gallop and flung his lance into a dummy target of a bear. He reined in his horse and wheeled it around in a tight circle to charge back. William had never seen such superb control of a horse. Since he spent all his time at sea, riding was a skill he'd never perfected.

When the sergeant and William dismounted at the stable, several barefoot workers in plain, coarse clothing passed by carrying baskets of firewood, vegetables, and laundry. The tattooed brown faces of the women and men reminded William of the tattooed faces of people he had seen in the Sandwich Islands and in the South Seas. As he and the soldiers walked to a long, low adobe building, whitewashed like the chapel next to it, he heard music drift out its open doors. The sergeant dismissed the men and directed William to come with him. The Englishman brought his long strides into step with the soldier. They entered the building, and Sergeant Sánchez approached a large dark wood door and knocked.

"*Entrar*!"

The sergeant opened the door, escorted William in, and saluted his superior. "Comandante Martínez, Sailor William Richardson wishes to make a request. His whaling ship is in our bay."

Still wary, William bowed slightly and said, "Lieutenant Martínez, I am first mate on the ship *Orion*, out of England." He presented his ship's roll listing the seamen on board and the ship's identification papers to the officer behind the desk. "We're requesting water and provisions for the ship's crew."

The lieutenant, a lithe man with graying hair at his temples and a military bearing, accepted the documents gravely and examined them thoroughly. *What is he checking?* William wondered. England and Mexico aren't at war. The comandante scrutinized the first mate's face as if looking for a trace of malice or deception. William held his gaze.

Returning the documents, the lieutenant said, "Yes, yes, everything is in order. I am sure we can fulfill your needs and secure a safe mooring for your ship. But I also have a request."

William tensed.

"Tonight, you must join us for evening entertainment, Señor Richardson. A fresh face with news from abroad is always an agreeable addition to our nightly dances."

William hesitated, thinking of his captain waiting for his report. But not wishing to refuse this generous invitation, William smiled and agreed to stay. All thoughts of his filthy whaling ship and surly captain floated from his mind.

✠ ✠ ✠

The comandante and William paused at the open double doors of the ballroom and watched dancers swirl around the floor to the music from two guitars and a violin. William rose on his toes and bounced in time to the lively tune. Then he saw her, the señorita who had locked eyes with him on the beach. Holding his breath, he felt a flush of heat rush through his body. She was wearing a white silk dress with a crimson sash. Her dark eyes sparkled as she clapped in time to the music and laughed with her friends.

The comandante stepped into the room, and William, breathing again, followed. The music stopped and the company turned to greet Lieutenant Martínez and stared at the stranger with him. Ships seldom stopped at their remote Presidio. The comandante handed William a glass of brandy and began introducing him. William turned his attention to meeting the older *dons* and *doñas*, young *caballeros*, and the señoritas. There were no homespun clothes here. Everyone was dressed in the latest European fashions made from expensive velvets, French satins, and Italian silks. While the older women wore dark silk dresses, the señoritas blossomed in flowered or white silks with lace or lawn scarves wrapped around their shoulders and tucked modestly into the dresses' necklines. Dainty shoes adorned their feet. The men wore white shirts with lacy cuffs flowing from the sleeves of their short, fitted jackets. Silver buckles clasped at the knees of their tight trousers. Their knee-high leather boots were highly polished.

When William turned from meeting a señora, the comandante finally introduced him to the woman he ached to meet, the beautiful, bold señorita who had stared at him. Her eyes fringed with long, dark lashes arrested his attention, but he managed to murmur a greeting in Spanish. Lieutenant Martínez kissed her hand and said, "Señor Richardson, my daughter María Antonia."

Stunned, William couldn't believe he was meeting the comandante's daughter!

"I'm pleased to make your acquaintance, Señor," María said. "I saw you come ashore today and hoped you would join our dance." Looking at his daughter, the comandante raised one eyebrow.

William took in every inch of María's shiny dark hair and lovely face. When she sweetly smiled, feelings stirred in him that were more than those from a man who had been too long at sea.

Bewildered by this strong attraction, his British reserve kicked in. He bowed and said, "I'm honored to meet you."

She gazed into his blue eyes and made a comment in Spanish that William didn't understand but assumed was witty since everyone else laughed.

"Perhaps we can enjoy some refreshments and watch the next dance together," María said.

He felt awkward towering over the petite María, but recalled his manners and extended his arm with a slight bow. She rested her hand on his arm as he guided her to the table where wine was served. While they sipped their wine, the music began again, this time with a lively beat.

"This old folk song 'La Bamba' comes from Veracruz," María said. "The dancer is my sister, Juana."

Juana glided to the center of the dance floor, and the guitar player began to sing.

María smiled. "The singer insists he isn't just a sailor, he is a captain." William glanced at María's profile, but she had turned her attention to the dancer. He did also.

Juana placed a glass of water on her head, balancing it while she performed complicated steps, and *caballeros* tossed coins at her feet as she danced without spilling a drop. After the graceful Juana finished her dance to cheers and applause, two servants plucked the coins from the floor and delivered them to her.

María sighed, "I'm not as nimble as Juana. But I love to dance. Perhaps we can try the next dance for couples?"

William grinned and stepped onto the dance floor with María, thrilled to have her hand on his arm.

✠ ✠ ✠

They spent the evening drinking, dancing, and eating. After months at sea eating the ship's slop and wormy hardtack, William's reserve broke down at the feast spread out on the banquet table. He recharged his plate several times with succulent beef, roasted venison, and rich chicken stew. The strong wine warmed him from head to toe. Turning loose his pent-up energy in an explosion of merriment, he danced with every woman in the room and more than once with the enchanting María. He talked and joked with the men, relaxing in their company.

Late in the evening, when there was a lull in the dancing, William worked his way through the crowd to María's side but found himself at a loss for words. Growing up in the company of men in the British merchant marine, he'd had little experience conversing with refined ladies. What should he say to this well-bred young woman? What could he say that would amuse her? María tucked her hand under his arm and led the way toward the open door.

"Do you know much about California, Señor?" she asked. "I was born in Alta California, which makes me a Californio. But I am a descendent of an old Spanish family and proud of our heritage." More nervous with this beautiful, confident woman than he was on a ship in a gale, he searched his mind for something to say in response.

María bit her lip and peered across the parade grounds with the chilly bay fog drifting over it, obscuring the view. "Presidio life must feel strange to you. Why are you here?"

And William was launched. They wandered onto the veranda where he told her about his life as a sailor.

"I have my captain's certificate," he said, "but a whaling ship under my command became icebound when anchored in the Arctic overnight. Low rations and hot tempers threatened the crew's survival. Fortunately, another British whaler rescued us days later. I returned to England for a naval hearing about the incident and was cleared of all charges of neglect."

Although exonerated, he had to serve again as chief mate before he could get a new command. William spoke bitterly about this ruling, thinking of the bully captain he served under on the *Orion*. He paused, shook off the feeling, and lightened his mood with talk about places he'd visited and about life aboard a whaler.

"It's tedious," he said, "until a whale is sighted. Then the chase is on!"

Enthralled, María reacted to every turn in his story. "What exciting adventures you've had! So much traveling around the world! I've never traveled. I've lived in Alta California all my life."

Suddenly aware that he was jabbering, William broke off his tale and took one of María's hands in both of his. She looked surprised and stepped back but didn't pull her hand away. After spending fifteen years in the British navy with unruly, uncouth sailors, he lacked experience in society and with women. No, not with women. He'd had experience with women, ever since he was fifteen. This was a lady, and he had to treat her as such, not as a female companion for a night.

Though confused by his emotions, William realized he wanted to forget his past and his dull days aboard the whaler, obeying the orders of a bad-tempered captain. All he wanted was to think about this señorita and get to know more about her, but when a quiet female cough told him they were not alone, his thoughts burst like soap bubbles.

María slipped her hand from William's tender grasp while whispering, "My *dueña*, my guardian. It isn't seemly for an unmarried woman to be alone with a man, even a married man. My father might be dismayed."

Worried that he'd made a social blunder, William stiffened and stepped back. "I'm not married, but I'm sorry if I might have caused you any trouble."

Smiling, María dipped her head and laid her hand on his arm, saying loud enough for her *dueña* to hear, "I would enjoy another dance with you, Señor. Let us join the rest." They strolled into the crowded room, followed by the watchful *dueña*.

William floated around the dance floor with María in his arms, never sparing a thought to his mission or to the anxious sailors waiting for him on the beach.

CHAPTER 2

THE DECISION

Shivering in the night fog, the two sailors from *Orion* trotted back and forth on the cold beach sand to stay warm. It was past midnight. The first mate should have been back by now, and the lack of communication was unlike him. The boatswain and his shipmate worried he'd been arrested.

The Mexican soldiers who'd been guarding the sailors left hours ago for their evening meal. They must not have been too concerned about them or the ship.

What should they do? the boatswain wondered. *Return to the ship?* He decided it was up to him to find their wandering first mate.

He left his shipmate on shore with the longboat and plodded uphill in the general direction William and the soldiers had disappeared. When he heard music, he walked through the fort's unguarded gates and slipped silently across the square to peer in the lighted windows of an adobe building. His eyes widened. There in the middle of the dance floor, encircled by the Presidio residents, First Mate Richardson was dancing an Irish jig.

Moments later, the boatswain felt a hand on his shoulder and was escorted into the *sala*.

✠ ✠ ✠

Since no one had said anything about William's indiscretion of being alone with María and holding her hand, he was carrying on joyfully until the music stopped. Face red from exertion, he bowed to the applause from the company but came up short when he spotted the boatswain's serious face.

William nodded sheepishly to the boatswain. Realizing he'd been having a grand time while his sailors shivered in the cold waiting for him, he grabbed a glass of wine and gave it to the chilled sailor, who gulped it gratefully. William gazed sadly at María and then approached the comandante.

"I must beg your pardon, Señor. I have enjoyed your company so much that I almost forgot my reason for coming. I must leave for my ship and inform the captain of our arrangements. Thank you for your warm hospitality."

"Tell your captain that I would say he has an admirable first mate. I will send some men in the morning to direct you to a place for fresh water and dry wood. We will also supply provisions for your ship."

María rushed to her father's side, and her sad eyes begged William to stay. He looked longingly at her but said his final farewell to the comandante and turned to go. He signaled to the boatswain and trudged through the doors. María caught up to him at the front steps of the adobe, a worried look on her face.

"Must you leave tonight? Will I see you again?"

William's chest tightened as he whispered in her ear, "I pray it will be so. You have captured my heart."

María looked into his eyes and answered, "And you mine."

✠ ✠ ✠

As the longboat plowed over the dark waters of the bay to the *Orion*, William knew he had a dilemma. He had spoken words of love to a beautiful young woman in California, yet he was an officer of the British merchant marine and had signed on as first mate with this ship. He was duty bound to stay with the whaler until the end of the voyage, as unpleasant as it might be. It would be treasonous not to. But María's dark eyes, ruby lips, and soft voice haunted his thoughts and roused his desires. He had never felt this way about a woman.

So, he would have to return to England on his ship, then resign from the merchant marines and catch a ship to the east coast of Mexico. From there, he would have to travel across Mexico by mule and wait on the Pacific coast for a ship to Alta California. That might take years! He could endure the delay, but would María wait for him?

By the ship's lantern lights, William could see the red-faced captain, standing on deck with his arms folded across his chest, waiting for him. As soon as William climbed aboard, Captain Barney lashed into him.

"Where the hell have you been? Were you under arrest? What the devil were you doing all night?"

William explained as quickly as possible what had happened, sliding over details, and never mentioning the sweet María. He finished by saying, "I felt if I left too soon, the comandante and the rest of the guests would be insulted. It was their party, and they were the ones to say when it was over. I slipped away as soon as I could. The comandante has given us permission to anchor in a safe cove nearby and to come ashore for provisions."

The captain wasn't satisfied. "So you left us bumping around in this chop because you were too busy dancing at a damned *fandango* to let me know I could anchor in calmer waters in this frigging bay? Blast your eyes, if you weren't once a captain, I'd spread-eagle you and clamp you in irons 'til we rounded Cape Horn. You're a disgrace to the British service."

Captain Barney started tearing off his captain's coat and shirt. "Still, you're not going to get away so easy. Strip down, you selfish rotter," he said grinding his teeth. "No one makes a fool of me. I'm the captain, not you! We're going to settle our personal differences. Put up your props!"

Since every British merchant marine was a pugilist, William wasn't too concerned about fighting the captain. If anything, he looked forward to it and so did the crew. As he stripped down for the fight, the entire crew of twenty gathered around on deck, eager for some excitement. William knew they looked up to him like an older brother because he often protected them from the bad-tempered captain. He was sure they wanted him to win. But if he did, what would the humiliated captain do then?

His thoughts were still muddled as he prepared to face the captain. He was confident he could beat the man, but should he?

Captain Barney was barrel-chested with muscular arms and legs. Although the extra weight made his movements ponderous, he could pack plenty of power behind any punch that connected. The wiry William with a body hardened from his seaman's life eyed his opponent as they circled around, each looking for an opening for the first punch.

Unsure of what he should do, William danced around and ducked a few punches. The captain took the opportunity to land a few jabs. William was quick and deflected the blows with his left or dodged enough so he didn't feel the full impact.

The roar of the crew rose to a more fevered pitch with each punch.

"Go in, man!"

"Quit dancing, Bill!"

"Mix it up!"

The excited voices seemed louder in the still, early morning. Seamen were always eager to see a good fight, especially a fight between a captain and his first mate.

As William continued to avoid blows, never striking back, the captain took a chance. He gave a half-hearted swing at William's chin, which missed its mark, but then put all his might into a jab in his ribs. William staggered sideways, his ribs aching from the heavy blow.

Fury in his voice, the captain yelled, "Now how does that feel, you blackguard! Leaving us to freeze on this damn bay. I should discharge you right now! You can then wait with your Spanish friends 'til another whaler takes you from this god-forsaken place."

The pain shook William's thoughts like a gambler would a pair of dice. When his head cleared, he saw his future was in

California, not on this filthy whaler or any other whaler that might come into the bay. Whether he won or lost, Barney might discharge him and maroon him. Maybe he could build a new life here. With María. At least he could try. So he sailed into the captain with his head and his heart aimed at victory.

His first punch drew blood from the captain's upper lip. The crew roared their approval. William continued to bob around the deck. He was beginning to enjoy the fight. His next blow struck the captain on the right side of the forehead. The bleeding man growled and came lashing back.

"That's it, Bill!"

"Go get him, Captain!"

The crew was yelling with delight, thumping each other on their backs, swinging their rights and lefts as much as the two fighters.

To avoid the captain's next punch, William slipped to one side but didn't move fast enough. The swinging fist clipped him on the ear, making it ring. Both men showed signs of tiring. Their bodies glistened with sweat. Their hands were bleeding. Knuckles raw from flesh and bone smashing into flesh and bone. Their arms hung a little lower, a little heavier, as the fight dragged on. There were no rounds in this ring. No breaks to recover breath and strength.

William's final blow came unexpectedly. The captain's sides were heaving like a horse's after a race. His guard drooped. William swung with his right.

His fist connected with the point of the captain's jaw. The blow was straight and hard, with all the power of his back put into it. The captain dropped to the deck, laid flat, his fall causing the ship to shudder. The crew's screams and shouts were deafening. William understood he had won as well as lost. His old life was gone. He looked south to the shore. What would his new life bring? Would they even allow him to stay?

The captain raised himself on one elbow, looked William in the eye, and snarled, "Get off my ship!"

✠ ✠ ✠

"Why, Señor Richardson! We thought you went back to your ship." The comandante took in William's bruised face and disheveled appearance when he stumbled into the nearly empty *sala*. The lieutenant waited without comment for William to speak. María quickly crossed the room to her father's side, and bit her bottom lip when she saw his injuries.

William bowed stiffly to them and asked, "Comandante Martínez, do you think there would be a place for me in this roomy country of yours?" He glanced at María's concerned face. "After my introduction to your society last night, I feel a strong desire to live among you. I think I could become a worthwhile addition to the people of Alta California."

María's eyes widened in surprise. She put a hand on her father's shoulder and squeezed it.

"Certainly," Lieutenant Martínez agreed. "But, Señor, what happened to your head?"

William self-consciously touched his bruised chin. "The captain and I had a disagreement on procedure. I didn't come out too badly. In fact, I think I won the argument. The captain, though, won't be able to appear for a week."

"Oh, he could have killed you! That beast!" María blushed after she said this.

Chuckling, Lieutenant Martínez clasped William on the shoulder and drew him into the room. "*La casa es la suya*—make yourself at home. We'll decide over the next few days what you can do for us. And if you can stay."

A room in the comandante's headquarters was prepared for William. The furnishings were sparse but tidy: a narrow, rough-hewn bedstead, a crucifix, wood clothing pegs on the wall, a wooden bench, and a small table with a filled water pitcher and bowl. After William tucked his meager sack of belongings under the bench and washed up, he stretched out his aching limbs on the bed for a few hours of sleep.

"If you can stay," the comandante had said.

Feeling uneasy now about his decision, William realized he could never return to England, never see his mother or father again. He swore to himself he would do whatever he could to make this country—and María—his. Certainly something to do with this fine bay and the sea. María's perfect face floated into his mind's eye. Rest, he thought. The time for more decisions will come soon enough.

CHAPTER 3

CALIFORNIO RIDING GAMES

While residing at the Presidio headquarters, William began to search for some means of livelihood in his new life on the brink of the world.

He had seen and spoken with María only briefly since he'd decided to stay. The comandante monopolized his time by escorting him around the Presidio and introducing him to the officers. After supper, the two retreated to the comandante's office where they discussed the wars Spain fought with other European nations and New Spain's rebellion.

"All those foreign wars," William said, "yet Spain managed to hold onto its vast New World colonies. And to search here for the gold she needed to pay for those wars."

"True," the comandante said. "However, New Spain had been ignored, except as a colony forced to buy Spanish goods and help pay for Spain's war debts. That's why the people threw off the Spanish yoke."

"So now," William said, "after eleven years of war, New Spain has its independence."

Lieutenant Martínez reached for a cigar and offered one to William. "It has not been easy. New Spain is now the Republic of Mexico, but most Californios feel more allied with Spain because their ancestors came from there. Things have changed though. The Mexican government opened our ports to foreign trade, reversing Spanish trading policy. Customs duties collected from foreign merchant vessels now remain in the Mexican government's hands."

"Isn't that better for Mexico and you?"

"The California presidios are still waiting to benefit. So far, the new government has not sent money for officers' or soldiers' wages." The lieutenant frowned at his cigar. "They do manage to send cigars and tobacco. We depend on the nearby mission for food. The padres grow crops and raise cattle, using the *Costeños*, coastal native people, as laborers. The Presidio must pay for its meat and grain with drafts, and the Mexican government promises to send money—eventually—to cover them."

✠ ✠ ✠

One morning, María approached her father while he and William finished breakfast.

"*Papá*, you have bored Señor Richardson enough with military and government talk. My sisters and I would like to take him to the *carrera del gallo,* the race for the rooster. Doña Sánchez and her daughters will accompany us."

The comandante patted María on her arm. "Fine, fine, I'm sure Señor Richardson would prefer the company of young ladies and to see some excellent horsemanship as well."

"Good," María said. "Everyone is waiting for us." She flashed William an impish grin and led him quickly outside before her father changed his mind. Here was her chance to learn more about this handsome man who had occupied her thoughts since the night they had met. She had been enchanted with William's tales and watched his face glow as his story grew livelier. His tales revealed his cleverness, but his sapphire-blue eyes showed kindness and gentleness.

During the short walk to the field where the contest would take place, María alerted William that Doña Sánchez was watching. The doña made it clear by her formal greeting that morning that she wouldn't tolerate any nonsense from him or any young man.

María and William talked together constantly. He was an extraordinary man, unlike anyone she had met before. She admired the way he walked, smiled, and was at ease speaking Spanish. He listened when she described her life at the Presidio, and she encouraged him to elaborate on his life in England and on ships. She wanted to know everything about him.

María's sisters giggled at the exchange. Doña Sánchez cuffed one of her daughters who joined in the laughter.

✠ ✠ ✠

Doña Sanchez led the way past the crowd, many on horseback, along the sides of the field to a spot near a scrawny tree. Her daughters spread out coarse woolen blankets on the ground, and everyone sat down to await the start of the contest. A small group of riders stood next to their horses at one end of the field, talking among themselves, checking their saddle cinches. Some were in uniform. A few young men in shirtsleeves and trousers wore black silk handkerchiefs knotted around their heads.

"They are the sons of the *rancheros,*" María explained to William, "and are exceptionally good at the sport. Those men," she pointed, "are Doña Sánchez's sons."

They watched a young man carrying a wriggling sack in one hand ride midway down the field and jump off his horse. He proceeded, with some difficulty, to draw out from the sack a squawking, flapping cock and bury it with its head sticking out above the sandy ground. The rider leaped on his horse again and galloped back to the contestants.

"For this contest, each rider must try to pluck the cock from the ground," María explained.

The first rider mounted his horse and waited until one of the Presidio lieutenants gave the signal to start. The horseman galloped sixty yards down the field, leaned far over the left side of his horse, and swiped at the head of the cock. All he had in his hand were a few feathers.

Everyone at the sidelines hissed and laughed. The next two riders did no better, and both were greeted with laughter. William said he was amazed at their riding skills, but María observed that he soon joined the others in laughing at the unsuccessful competitors.

When the fourth rider tried to mount, his horse danced around in a circle, and the noise from the rooster and the crowd increased. The horseman finally got his mount under control and started his run down the field. Gracefully and smoothly, as if making a bow, he leaned out of his saddle and swooped the squawking cock from the ground. Cheers and applause thundered across the field.

For the next event, a length of rawhide was laid on the ground. The riders galloped full speed toward the strip and attempted to rein in their horses before their forefeet touched the leather. Several of the Presidio soldiers and the rancheros' sons performed this trick neatly. The spectators laughed at those who failed, and a few dragged their friends from their horses in fun.

"Are most of your people so skilled in riding?" William asked.

"Many people say we are born in the saddle," María said with pride. "The rancheros spend a good part of the day riding to check on their herds. Cattle and well-trained horses are important in our world. I am an experienced rider. Anyone who lives here must ride." María looked at him. "Do you ride, William?"

He laughed. "After a fashion. I'm sure I will improve with practice, but I'll never be as expert as your soldiers or rancheros. I'm not a land animal." He looked away, across the wide field, and beyond, to a glimpse of the bay. "The sea is my natural home."

María stared down for a moment to hide the frown that came with her first real understanding of this man's passion for the sea. Would she be able to share a life with him if he was always at sea? Would he ever fit into the Californio way of life?

CHAPTER 4

MISSION DOLORES

A week after William's arrival, the comandante accompanied him to the nearby mission to talk to the padre. Lieutenant Martínez was naturally at ease in the saddle. William bumped along on his horse as best he could.

They paused at the top of a low hill and gazed at the sparkling bay that stretched far to the north and the south.

"I was going to suggest that you become a rancher, Señor," the lieutenant said. "I could help you gather some cattle and petition the governor for land. After you become a Mexican citizen, that is. But you don't appear comfortable in the saddle."

Becoming a Mexican citizen didn't bother William much, but giving up the sea would. William studied the breathtaking view and said, "With a strong harbor like this, there must be some way to arrange my plans around it."

"Well, let's see what Padre Altimira can suggest," the lieutenant said.

"Do you know much about the California missions?" the comandante asked as they rode on.

"Not much," William admitted. "Knowing more might help my future decisions."

"*Misión San Francisco de Asis* is our destination. It was named for St. Francis of Assisi, the founder of the Franciscan Order. Franciscan friars started the mission in October 1776."

"That was the year the British colonies on the eastern coast of the continent declared themselves a new nation," William said.

"Earlier that year, in April, Lieutenant Colonel Juan Bautista de Anza was exploring Alta California, a province of Spain's New World colony. He selected the site for the mission on the Friday before Palm Sunday, the feast day of our Lady of Sorrows. Anza chose the spot on the bank of a small stream he named *Arroyo de los Dolores*, Stream of the Sorrows, in honor of Christ's mother Mary. So, we know it as Mission Dolores."

William and Lieutenant Martínez approached the mission, and two young boys wearing long, coarse shirts, belted at the waist, rushed to meet them. The boys held their horses while the men dismounted. A friar dressed in a gray robe and sandals strode toward them from the open mission doors. Smiling, he held out his arms to the comandante and embraced him. To show his respect, the comandante bent to kiss the padre's hand.

"I am honored to have you visit the mission, Lieutenant." Turning to William, the padre said, "You are also most welcome, Señor."

"I hope we are not disturbing your work, Padre," the comandante said. "May I introduce you to Señor William Richardson, a new resident of Alta California. William, this is Padre José Altimira."

"I have heard about you, Señor. In a small community, news travels quickly. I'm pleased to make your acquaintance."

William held himself stiffly. Not sure what to do, he nodded to the friar. Being brought up in the Church of England, he looked unfavorably on Catholic clergy.

The lieutenant filled the awkward silence. "We came to discuss Señor Richardson's future. We hoped you might have some suggestions about how his skills might be used in our province."

"And what are your skills, Señor?"

"You probably know I'm a seaman by trade. But I've picked up a few other talents along the way. I'm a fair carpenter, good with figures, and—"

"But don't ask him to ride a horse!" the comandante said.

"I think I'll have to improve that skill if I remain in Alta California!" William said, feeling more at ease.

"Well, let's walk around the mission and perhaps have a drink in the shade. I already have some thoughts of how to use your skills."

The padre shepherded them through a pair of large wooden doors that gave William the impression he was entering a fortress. Ahead was a dark, cool passage that opened onto a busy, domestic scene in the central courtyard. The mission's buildings formed a quadrangle with the church its cornerstone on the left. To the right was the storehouse. In the center were small garden patches of herbs. Small groups of Ohlone women sat cross-legged on the ground weaving baskets. Others made candles from melted tallow. All wore simple white blouses and skirts. The aroma of baking bread drifted from beehive-shaped adobe ovens.

"Our mission was established more than forty years ago," Padre Altimira began. "We rescued these *Costeños* from their uncivilized, crude lives. Now we feed them three times a day, clothe them, and introduce them to Christ. Everyone works. Even the children. They weed gardens and chase away birds in the fields. We teach the women and men skills and encourage those who do well to specialize in certain tasks. Come. I will show you our workshops."

William and Lieutenant Martínez walked with Padre Altimira along the outdoor arcade that bordered the square. They stopped near the first open doorway to watch several women spinning wool. The women paused in their work to murmur greetings to the padre and his guests.

"These women are adept at spinning and the men at weaving cloth," the friar said. "However, we still cannot produce fabric of the same quality as that from foreign traders."

They peered in a storeroom door, where a few leather bags made from cattle hides were leaning against the walls.

"To support themselves, most of the missions grow grain and fruits, and they herd cattle, sheep, and goats," Padre Altimira explained. "Tallow, melted cattle fat, is stored in the bags you see here. We use it to make the mission's candles and soap. We trade tanned cattle hides and excess tallow with supply ships for tools, nails, cloth, and whatever other goods we cannot make in the mission. Unfortunately, Mission Dolores doesn't have large herds so we don't have many hides or bags of tallow to trade. But a few nearby ranchos do."

"What do you offer in trade instead?" William asked.

"Dry firewood, food, and fresh water," Padre Altimira said.

"Just like we arranged for your ship," the comandante said. "Some of the mission neophytes ferry the food and water to the ships in our small boat. The Presidio provides the safe harbor and directs the ships to missions farther down the bay. There they can trade for grain, wine, and fruits grown at those missions as well as cowhides and tallow. Most of the hides end up in Boston for the manufacture of shoes, belts, and such. The tallow goes to South America where it's made into candles and soap."

The men continued their tour around the square. "Most of the men tend our cattle, horses, sheep, and goats or make pottery and adobe bricks in a separate building," the friar said. "My associate, Padre Tomás Esténega, and several lay assistants are with them. It's a strange thing with the people here. They behave like children. We must watch them and direct them in their work. They aren't accustomed to working in fields or watching animals. They would lie in the fields and sleep face down all day if Padre Esténega or I or a soldier were not there." *Just like some seamen I know*, William thought. Most sailors stayed engaged when assigned work they enjoyed.

Padre Altimira paused before the next door that opened onto the arcade. "The contents of this room may interest you, Señor Richardson." With that preamble, the padre led them through the doorway.

When his eyes adjusted to the dim light, William gazed at hammers, hatchets, two-man saws, planes, chisels, and other woodworking tools hanging on the walls and littering a few crude benches.

"We have trained men to be blacksmiths and cobblers," the friar said. "But at this time we have no carpenters, no one to train the workers. Although, as you can see, we have tools."

Lieutenant Martínez clapped William on the shoulder. "You may have found your livelihood!"

Just then a younger friar rushed up to them. "Excuse me, Padre Altimira," he said. "Another of our charges is sick. I think it's the same problem with the lungs. I would like to take him immediately to Padre Amorós at Mission San Rafael."

Padre Altimira sighed. "Señor Richardson, this is Padre Esténega. Señor Richardson is hoping to help us in our work at the mission, Tomás."

"If we can manage to stay in this damp hole," the younger friar said. "Most of these *Costeños* either get sick or run away, tempted by their friends across the bay."

Padre Altimira held up his hand. "Tomás, no one has decided to abandon the mission yet. We will continue to do our work here until given other directives. As to your question, yes, take the sick man to Padre Amorós as quickly as possible."

The young priest gave a short bow to Padre Altimira and the visitors and left. Padre Altimira sighed again. "Padre Esténega swears Mission Dolores was a mistake. I am pressing Governor Solá to move this mission north across the bay to the Sonoma valley, where a new mission could be constructed. There is also a small church in San Rafael, truly only a hospital for the sick. They seem to recuperate more quickly in the sunny climate there than here. The cold fog that surrounds Mission Dolores gets in the bones." He looked around the room. "Well, Señor, I think we could use your carpentry skills. And we might be able to include your sailing skills as well."

William's eyebrows shot up. "What did you have in mind, Padre?"

"Let us have some refreshment and I will explain."

The three men walked along the arcade to the kitchen where Padre Altimira requested three glasses of brandy, some cake, and cheese, and then seated themselves comfortably on benches under a tree. The brandy arrived, and Padre Altimira made a toast.

"To your new life in Alta California, Señor. May it be happy and prosperous and blessed by God!" After a sip of the brandy, he smiled. "Ah, such a civilized drink! I am just sorry our supply is more limited than that of the southern missions."

"Where do you get such excellent brandy?" William asked.

"From *Misión San Fernando Rey de Espana*. I serve it sparingly since Providence does not often smile on us with an abundant shipment."

The comandante frowned. "Providence and Mexico forget to send many things to this outpost." He looked directly at William. "It's a full day's march just to the next mission south of here. And several days to Monterey, where there are better supplies. Even worse is the lack of information in this distant spot."

"How many supply ships do you see each year?" William asked.

"We have seen only one government vessel this year," Padre Altimira said. "We've had about fifteen foreign ships, but almost half, including your ship, Señor, were whalers seeking provisions. And this leads me to my thoughts about your future.

"When these ships enter our bay, the traders hire the small mission boats to ferry the rancheros and their families to the ships for trading. Because our boats aren't large, the mission men must make many trips, carrying the rancheros as well as wood and barrels of food to the whalers and trading ships. I think the *Costeños* can build larger, sturdier boats if someone like you directs them in their labors. Are you willing to help us?"

William leaned forward, clasping his hands and resting his elbows on his knees. "I saw you had most of the tools I would need. Do you also have the lumber nearby?"

The padre smiled. "All the lumber you will need."

"When can I meet my pupils?"

Lieutenant Martínez and Padre Altimira laughed. "I can help there," the comandante said. "I'll choose several civilized men to assist you in your work."

"There are many suitable young men," the padre said. "One in particular. Diego. He is eager to work on the bay rather than in the fields. Tonight, I will write to Governor Solá and recommend that you be allowed to remain in Alta California because your skill as a carpenter will be of great use to the Church."

The comandante added, "Then you will have to write a petition to Governor Solá yourself, asking to become a resident of our Province."

"You've spoken of Governor Solá before," William said. "In what way does he control what happens in Alta California?"

"When we became free from the yoke of Spain this year," the lieutenant explained, "Solá was appointed to his post as governor in Monterey. He reports to the Mexican Congress and settles disputes if necessary. He is a fair man, Señor. With Padre's recommendation and mine, Solá will grant you residency. But Solá is not well so we must act quickly."

✠ ✠ ✠

In early October, William borrowed a horse from the Presidio stable and rode south with three Presidio soldiers on *El Camino Real,* the Royal Highway, which stretched from San Francisco Bay to Mexico City. The stable hand had chosen a calm horse for him, and no charging wild hog or irritated bear challenged his riding skills. At Monterey, he presented his petition to the governor in his Presidio headquarters:

> William Richardson, a native of Great Britain, and a resident of this Province, hereby respectfully represents that he arrived at this port of San Francisco on the second day of August last, as mate of the British whaleship Orion, and it be my intention to remain permanently and become domiciled in this Province at some place with suitable climate, I most humbly pray that your Worship be pleased to grant me this privilege and favor.
>
> William Richardson
>
> San Francisco Presidio, October 7, 1822

The governor studied the sailor standing before him and then read the petition again and the letters of recommendation from Padre Altimira and Lieutenant Martínez. The governor picked up his pen, wrote something on the petition, and slid the paper across his desk to William who was then escorted from the governor's office.

Standing in the brilliant sunshine, he read Governor Pablo Vicente de Solá's decree, written in the margin:

> *Being aware that the petitioner, besides being a navigator, is conversant with and engaged in the occupation of a carpenter, I hereby grant the privilege he asks for with the obligation that he shall receive and teach such young men as may be placed in his charge.*
>
> *Solá*

He could stay in California. With a satisfied smile, William rolled up the document and leaped on his horse for his journey back to the Presidio, eager to fulfill his obligation to Governor Solá and the Mexican government.

CHAPTER 5

NEW LAND, NEW LIFE

William rode four miles to the mission every day to supervise and train six Ohlones assigned to work with him. For his first project, the comandante asked him to rebuild two small boats the Mexican government owned into one sturdy longboat. Since all mission neophytes had been taught Spanish, William had no trouble instructing his workers. Because he respected their exhaustive knowledge of the bay and the land, he began to learn the Ohlone language to acquire more extensive information about the new world where he had settled.

The Ohlones were enthusiastic students, and soon the mission's carpentry tools were no longer lying about unused. Diego, Padre Altimira's first recommendation, happily ditched his hoe and the cornfield for a chance to be on the bay.

After William taught the men how to use the adze, chisels, and other woodworking tools, he had them remodel the longboat as the comandante requested. Next, he worked with his crew to construct a large single-masted launch they could sail around San Francisco Bay. He taught the men how to navigate and sail. They soon became skillful sailors and called him captain. He appreciated their quiet deference to him and admired their abilities.

Curious about all sea vessels, William was game to try paddling an Ohlone tule craft, and Diego was eager to be his teacher. Although the Ohlones knelt in their tule boats as they paddled, Diego had William dangle his long legs over the sides in the chilly water, riding the narrow canoe-shaped boat like a horse, as they paddled across the bay and back.

✠ ✠ ✠

The Ohlones had traveled on the bay in tule boats for much of their lives and could swim well, a skill many European sailors, excluding William, lacked. The men quickly learned to sail the launch and used the longboat and small mission boats to transport food, household goods, and rancho customers to and from the trading ships anchored in the bay near the Presidio.

William used the launch to fetch provisions from the Missions San José and Santa Clara de Asís, both located at the southern end of the bay. These missions supplied the Presidio and Mission Dolores with wheat, corn, apples, olives, and fine olive oil. Both missions had large herds of cattle and grew abundant grapes, which the padres shared with Mission Dolores to add to its small grape harvest to crush and ferment into wine.

Besides showing his Ohlone crew how to steer and handle the lines and sails, William taught them to use the currents, tides, and winds to their advantage. He spent days sailing the bay, sounding the water depth to ensure the safe passage of trading vessels inside the bay as well as a mile outside the entrance. To measure the depth, he cast overboard a chunk of lead attached to a line marked in fathoms with cloth strips knotted at intervals. In some places, the water was so crystal clear William could see a pebble thirty feet below. He marked his findings on his hand-drawn nautical charts, identifying all submerged rocks, shoals, and cross currents.

In recognition of his contributions to the continued success of their northern outpost and the opening of the harbor to trade, the Mexican government agreed to pay him for his work. However, William had to buy everything he needed on credit since the young government had no money to spare. *This won't do*, he thought. *Without money in my pocket, Lieutenant Martínez will never allow me to court María.*

✠ ✠ ✠

During the winter, a twenty-foot whaleboat drifted into the bay, a sign of some unknown tragedy at sea. William splashed into the frigid bay water and swam to the boat with Diego, who matched him stroke for stroke. Using a frayed rope trailing in the water from its bow, they tugged the abandoned boat toward the beach where sailors hauled it ashore. Soon after it was overhauled and repaired, the boat was put into service.

One clear morning, two cannon shots from the Presidio announced the arrival of a trading ship waiting to be piloted safely into the bay.

William and four of his new sailors slid the restored whaleboat over the sandy shore into the ripples breaking at the water's edge and jumped in to row out to the ship. At the bay's entrance, the men pulled lustily on the oars against the strong incoming tide. Sea foam spouted over the boat's gunwales.

William called instructions from the prow. "Pull to port away from the rocks! Slow down! Sandbar ahead."

Wind-bent scraggly oaks clung to the rocky cliffs that towered over them near the narrow gateway to the sea. An English ship, anchored in deeper water outside the entrance, bucked like a wild horse with a rider on its back. The Ohlone crew eased the whaleboat alongside; William grabbed the Jacob's ladder and climbed aboard. A ruddy-faced man with a full beard stepped up to meet him.

"Good morning, Captain," William said shaking the ship captain's hand. "Permission to come aboard. I'm Captain Richardson."

"Captain Wilson, sir. Mighty glad you're here to help us. The custom house at Monterey told us you can steer us through to safe harbor. My ship is riding low with all this cargo, and I'd hate to lose her now that we've finally arrived!"

"Glad to help. Now is a good time. Conditions are favorable. Shall we proceed?"

Captain Wilson nodded.

William took the helm and called out instructions to the first mate who relayed them to the ship's crew. Sails were unfurled, and the anchor weighed. The ship shot ahead before the wind, propelled through the gateway on the tide. William steered the ship midway between the lofty cliffs and the sharp black rocks that threatened to rip open the ship's bottom like a bear's claws through a salmon's belly.

Once the ship was anchored in the deep, calm waters of Yerba Buena Cove, the grateful captain encouraged William to select anything he wanted when he inspected their cargo. With no coins in his pockets, William cheerfully accepted his offer as suitable payment for his piloting work.

"Well, that is extremely generous of you, Captain. Tobacco and tea would be welcome," William said. "And perhaps a string of pearls if you have them. A certain lady at the Presidio would be most appreciative."

Chuckling, Captain Wilson clapped William on his shoulder. "I'll introduce you to my supercargo, the man in charge of all the trading goods we have aboard. He'll show you around below deck."

After William reviewed the ship's roll and customs' documents as required by the Mexican government, the supercargo took him below to survey the trade goods. Then he met with Captain Wilson to discuss the provisions the mission could offer.

"We can also supply your ship with fresh spring water, the best water there is along this coast, Captain. Let me know what you need, and my men will have it available in a day or two. We can provide excellent beef as well as onions, peppers, potatoes, beans, and other produce."

"I thank you kindly. We'll require all of those items," Captain Wilson replied.

"I have a launch for hire and can deliver whatever you want to your ship. I'll be happy to arrange the transport for you."

"I appreciate your offer," Captain Wilson said. "And I would like to extend an invitation to you and the comandante,

Lieutenant Martínez, for dinner on board tomorrow evening. Please carry my regards and invitation to the lieutenant."

By the time William returned to shore with a few goods from the ship, the rest of his crew was preparing the launch to sail rancheros and their families across to choose purchases from the ship's cargo. Men, women, and children crowded around small bonfires on the beach to keep warm while they waited for their turns to board the ship. Stacks of cured hides and bags of tallow sat on the sand, ready to trade in exchange for bolts of cloth, shawls, jewelry, tables, chairs, and tools, as well as flour, sugar, tea, and coffee. Horsemen raced along the well-worn trail between the mission and the Presidio to relay tidings of the ship's arrival.

William and the crew were now a team working smoothly together, prepared for almost anything. He was accumulating valuable gifts as payments from sea captains. To be truly successful, however, he knew he must be captain of his own ship, not the mission's or the Presidio's.

CHAPTER 6

BUILDING A FLEET

Trading life on the bay began to follow a pattern. Whenever a ship entered the port, the captains hired the Presidio and mission boats to transport supplies from the shore to their ships and to load the empty boats with trade goods for the ranchos, the mission, and the Presidio. The merchant ships also traded their cargo for grain, fruits, and olives from the San José and Santa Clara missions.

William developed strong friendships with these sea captains and enjoyed hearty meals aboard their ships while at anchor. To repay William for his services, they encouraged him to select whatever he wished from their cargo. He tactfully asked for items he knew the comandante and his family would welcome. The traders did well selling their cargo to the Californios who were prudent buyers but happy to pay for quality goods.

The captains became familiar with Marino, too. Marino was one of William's sailors who proved to be especially reliable and quick to learn to sail the launch. He was almost as tall as William, strong, and like Diego, an excellent swimmer. He and a few of the other sailors learned to pilot the trading vessels into the bay if William was unavailable. When William and a few crew members sounded the bay, he discovered Marino knew the currents and dangerous shoals that could founder a ship or a tule boat.

During one of their conversations, Marino told William the boatmen preferred to be called Ohlones or Miwoks, not the Spanish name *Costeños*. He was a Miwok, born in a village across the bay in the shadow of Mount Tamalpais. When the Spanish soldiers on horseback arrived to force Miwoks to live at the mission, Marino led his people in many skirmishes against them. Even after most of his people were killed or caught, he eluded the soldiers but eventually was captured. After spending time in the Presidio jail, he entered Mission Dolores.

Diego also shared stories of his past life with William. He described how he and his father would sit in a sweat house to be purified before they hunted for deer, how his mother and sisters gathered herbs and wild berries where the mission's cornfield was now, and how he fished for salmon with his friends. Then Spanish soldiers had rounded up his family like cattle and kept them captive at Mission Dolores.

Many Ohlones were herded to the mission in the same way, Diego said. Sometimes the padres lured them there with food and blankets. Like Marino and the Miwoks, some Ohlones resisted or fled. Many fought the Spanish, but were overwhelmed, their bows and arrows no match against men on horseback armed with pistols, flintlock rifles, and lances.

William sympathized with these men. The friars had no qualms about capturing them, taking away their names, their languages, their land. They lost their identities, their beliefs, and their freedom. Even though the mission system was an accepted practice, William hoped he could give back to his crew some of their freedom.

✠ ✠ ✠

While William and the crew rested one day in a shady spot overlooking the bay, he looked at the perfect blue sky, felt the warm breeze. He was beginning to fall in love with Alta California as well as its people. He was eager to discover everything he could about his crew and this land where they and their ancestors had lived for so long.

Admiring the boat they had built together, William said to Marino, "This is such a splendid bay for trade. Did Miwoks always use tule boats to trade with others living across the bay?"

Marino replied, "My father's father told me that many, many years ago, the sea did not come in through the gap at the west of the bay. We didn't need tule boats to cross the bay. Our people could walk across on a land bridge to get here, and we traded with the Ohlones. But at some time, long, long ago, the earth rocked and shook, and the land bridge collapsed. The sea rolled in. Ever since, my people and the Ohlones have had to cross the water in tule boats."

"I'm glad that bridge is gone," William said. "If the earthquake hadn't happened, I might not be here working with you. And we would not have such an immense bay and safe harbor for trade ships to enter."

Marino gazed at the bay and said, "Yet I grieve for my people and what might have been."

Soberly, William wondered what life might have been like here if the Spaniards had never arrived. Or if they had lived peacefully side by side with the Ohlones, Miwoks, and others. He might have continued sailing British ships and become a captain again.

"I too wonder about my previous life. But since I'll never return to my old life, I'm satisfied with my new one. More than satisfied."

He wanted more, though. He wanted María. Although he still stayed in the Presidio headquarters and ate supper with the Martínez family, he yearned for the chance to be alone with her, to talk with her. Without her, life would be meaningless. Without money, he wasn't worthy of her.

✠ ✠ ✠

During one trip in the launch to Mission Santa Clara, William spied an old fifteen-ton sloop. Torn sails drooped from the spars, and seabirds rested on the railing. Curious about why it wasn't sailing on the bay, he approached one of the padres serving at the mission. The friar explained he no longer had people trained to repair or sail it. William asked permission to inspect the ship. When he climbed aboard and found the vessel sound, he decided it would be a good purchase and offered to buy it.

The padre hooked his thumbs in his rope belt and smiled. "I think we can come to an agreement on an acceptable trade. Our mission has always had close ties with Mission Dolores and the Presidio, providing them with wine and foods they lack. Your piloting work brings trading ships safely into the bay, and that benefits all the missions. We all need their foreign trade goods. Let's see what you can bring us to trade for our ship. She's called *El Rey del Mar,* the King of the Sea."

✠ ✠ ✠

William became indispensable to the missions and the Presidio. By sailing *El Rey del Mar* to Santa Clara and San José, the missions no longer spent days waiting for goods to be hauled by lumbering oxcart over the hilly terrain. Whenever a ship arrived, William served as translator during trade negotiations since he spoke fluent Spanish now and scraped by in several other languages. To maintain safe navigation, he continued to sound the depths and trace on his charts the rivers, sloughs, and creeks as well as the locations of islands. The missions paid him in cattle hides—known as *California dollars*. William's confidence swelled. He could survive here and thrive.

As for winning María's heart and being worthy of her love, he felt he was still on rocky ground. What more did he have to do to be a Californio?

CHAPTER 7

RODEO

Spring was the time for rodeos.

When Don José Vicente Peralta invited Lieutenant Martínez and his wife to the roundup at the Peraltas' rancho, Doña Martina told her husband she regretted she was unable to accompany him and suggested María go in her place. She also coaxed him into asking William to attend.

"After all," she reasoned with him, "if he is to become a Mexican citizen, he should be acquainted with this California custom."

✠ ✠ ✠

It was a bright day, a cornflower blue sky overhead, when William sailed them across the bay. During the crossing, William sensed María and the comandante's excitement. He was eager to learn more about what would occur.

"Throughout the year," the lieutenant explained, "thousands of cattle from the East Bay ranchos mingle and roam the unfenced valleys and hills. During the spring rodeo, *vaqueros* separate and count the cattle and brand the calves. They slaughter a few cattle for hides and tallow, which are stored and later traded.

"The vaqueros ride over the land for many days rounding up the wild cattle, driving them toward the rodeo ground. This chore requires trained horses and expert riders. Many riders are Ohlones who grew up at the missions and trained as vaqueros from a young age. The vaqueros, the only neophytes allowed to ride horses at the missions, now work on ranchos around the bay."

"Does Don José Vicente own Rancho San Antonio?" William asked.

"Oh, no, his father, Don Luis María Peralta, does," the comandante said. "He is a good friend of mine. A retired soldier. The government granted him eleven square leagues of land for his forty years of military service. His four sons are in charge of the rancho while Don Luis enjoys his retirement in the San José Pueblo. This year, his youngest son, José Vicente, is the host for the rodeo. Vicente is also the *juez de campo,* the judge in case of quarrels or disputes of ownership."

William anchored near an East Bay beach, where a Peralta vaquero met them with saddle horses. On the ride to the rodeo ground, William admired María's skillful horsemanship. Even riding sidesaddle, she was as comfortable on a horse as her father or any *caballero*. Because of William's long work days dealing with trade ships and sailing the bay, he had not had a chance to see much of María in the past few weeks except at evening suppers. She now wore the usual riding costume that most Californio women sported—a short brimmed hat with leather ties under the chin, a short jacket that showed off her slender waist, and fine leather gloves. Her long raven hair hung down her back in a thick braid. He wished he had the right to touch it, to unbraid it and run his fingers through that glossy hair. Delighted they would finally have a whole day together, he felt even more excited about the day's event. He could tell María was thrilled as well by the secret looks she cast his way.

At the rodeo site, vaqueros had penned six *cabestros* in a corral.

"These tame cattle calm the unruly steers when they are separated from the herd and driven into the corral," Lieutenant Martínez explained to William.

Men and women sat on their horses outside the corral to survey the wild steers milling about on the rodeo grounds. Children sat in *carretas*, carts, or stood on fence rails.

Straddling his horse beside María, William watched with fascination as each horse and rider worked as one to keep the cattle placid while herding them together on the open rodeo ground. Cattle with brands from other ranchos mingled with the Peralta cattle. The vaqueros rode slowly among the cattle to separate those to another area. They would later drive them to those ranchos. From the remaining cattle, the Peraltas selected about fifty steers for slaughter, the ones most fattened on the abundant grasses and wild oats. Again and again, the vaqueros rode quietly among the milling cattle, one rider coming up on each side of a chosen steer to edge it toward the corral. At just the right moment, the vaqueros shouted "*Hora!*" or "Now!" The startled steer would run at top speed to join the *cabestros* in the corral. Finding itself among these tame cattle, the newcomer soon calmed down and became docile.

✠ ✠ ✠

Culling the herd raised huge clouds of dust. Horses whinnied and frightened calves bawled. Shaking their great horned heads, steers crashed into each other. María grabbed William's arm and pointed when one beast broke from the herd on the rodeo ground. A horse and rider dashed after the maverick. William stood in his saddle to watch. The steer tried to dodge the rider, but the horse smoothly swerved next to it and guided it back to the herd.

When another steer escaped from the group and an alert rider followed, Lieutenant Martínez pointed it out to William and said, "Watch this vaquero."

The rider galloped alongside the runaway steer, leaned from his saddle, grabbed its tail, and by urging his horse to move faster, jerked the steer's tail, flipping the animal off its feet and causing it to roll over several times on the ground. The steer regained its feet, shook its great head, and trotted back to the herd with the vaquero at its heels.

"That was a neat trick," William said.

"Mastered by only the best riders," said the lieutenant.

A young man, smiling broadly, trotted up on his tall black horse, swept his sombrero off his curly brown hair, and greeted Lieutenant Martínez. "Welcome, Comandante, . . . Señorita. You have arrived at just the right time."

"A glorious day for your rodeo, Don Vicente!" Lieutenant Martínez said. "Señor Peralta, I'd like to introduce Captain William Richardson, who now works with Padre Altimira building boats and handling trade with the foreign vessels visiting our bay."

"Welcome, Señor! Is this your first rodeo? It may seem very confusing, but we have it quite organized, I assure you."

"I'm pleased to meet you, Señor Peralta. Being new to this country, I'm unfamiliar with rodeos. I'm enjoying the activity immensely!"

"We hold roundups for branding in the spring. Each rancho has a *fierro*, a brand, to identify its cattle. You will soon see the vaqueros ride in among the cattle and move those wearing the same rancho brand to one side."

As they watched the action, one man on horseback lassoed a calf and pulled it out of the group. "That calf will be marked with the same brand as its mother," said Vicente.

✠ ✠ ✠

Don Vicente and the comandante continued talking while William and María observed the noisy scene near the corral. María explained what would happen and how important the branding was, all the while watching William's reaction to the scene. If William wanted to live among her people, as her husband, he would have to take on the responsibility of a rancho eventually and all the work that went with it. María wondered whether he would be willing. She had observed how adaptable he was on many things, but rancho work would take away his time from his ships.

María pointed out a bawling calf following its mother to a place near a branding iron fire. A vaquero lassoed the calf, dismounted to tie its rear legs to one front leg with a leather strip, and then expertly tossed the calf off its feet onto its right side. After a man with a red-hot branding iron marked the calf's left hip, the vaquero loosened the nooses from its legs and neck, and it jumped up and stumbled away calling for its mother.

Mixed with the smell of cattle, horses, and dry grass was the pleasing aroma of roasting beef. Long, wooden planked tables had been set under shade trees, and beef was roasting in barbecue pits dug earlier that morning.

"They are roasting the beef for the mid-day meal," María said.

Ohlone women working on the rancho had made tall stacks of tortillas. Others gathered and prepared baskets of vegetables from the rancho garden for the workers. Many meals would be provided for all the rodeo participants.

"After we eat, everyone will rest. Brush shelters for sleeping have been built for the riders, the men, and the boys who help with the branding. You may join my father to rest with the men. The branding will continue all day today, and some cattle will be slaughtered for their hides."

"I'm amazed at the amount of work. Although the vaqueros are excellent horsemen and handle the branding well, the number of cattle is astounding! I can see why it might take a week to finish.

✠ ✠ ✠

After their midday meal and siestas, everyone gathered for the branding and the slaughter of more cattle. William, María, and Lieutenant Martínez watched from horseback.

Don Vicente had chosen fifty of his cattle to be slaughtered. One of his vaqueros rode into the corral, lassoed a husky steer by the horns with his reata, and led it away from the corral. Another man on horseback looped his reata around one of the steer's hind legs, and his horse quickly backed up so that the steer was thrown on its side. Each horseman attached the tail of his reata to his saddle. The well-trained horses, their ears weaving forward and back, alertly watched the steer and backed up until the reatas were taut and the steer lay stretched out on the ground. A vaquero roped the steer's forelegs and hind legs together. He pulled out a long knife and quickly stabbed the animal in the back of its neck, killing it. Two men cut the hide from the huge beast, careful not to nick or scratch the skin. Ohlone women took away the hide, scraped it clean, stretched it out, and pegged it to the ground to dry in the sun.

Thick fat found just under the skin of the carcass was melted in huge caldrons to make tallow. William recognized the caldrons. They were the same as ones used on whaling ships when boiling whale blubber. Whalers often left the heavy pots at a rancho in trade for produce when they no longer needed them and didn't want the extra weight on their return voyages home. The melted tallow was poured from the caldrons into *botas*, leather bags made from cowhide.

"Ohlones working at the rodeo will get some of the meat from the slaughtered animals," María explained. "The ranchero claims the choicest parts for his family. The rest is thrown away for coyotes, vultures, and other wild predators to devour."

✠ ✠ ✠

The blood-red sun slid from the sky and the air cooled. Lanterns were lit and all rodeo participants came together for the evening meal after a hard day of work. Everyone told stories about the day's events—a runaway calf, a lost child who was found, a near miss from the deadly horns of an angry bull. William sat with Lieutenant Martínez, Vicente, and his two brothers, Domingo and Antonio. He enjoyed the camaraderie of the men while María ate and talked with the women.

"I have never tasted such sweet beef!" William said to Vicente.

"It's all in the way the steer is slaughtered," the don said. "Because we stretch out the animal on the ground when we kill it, less blood drains and more is preserved in the meat. We think it is more delicious. Some foreigners object to our way of slaughtering, but I think the meat is more nutritious. Look how healthy we Californios are! Notice my brother's good teeth!" Vicente turned to his brother Domingo who gave a huge grin to show off his teeth, causing William and others at the table to laugh.

William raised his glass of wine and said, "A glass to our generous hosts and their healthy teeth!"

All the guests laughed and drank to his toast. Domingo put his glass down and turned to William. "When we were boys, my father told us to plant the land and reap. 'Don't search for gold like the conquistadors did,' he said. 'These are your gold fields as all must eat!' So we enjoy our wine and our cattle. And our families! What more in life can we beg from God?"

William nodded his head in agreement, gazing at the joyful gathering and the grassy hills dotted with gay, dancing orange poppies. *Indeed*, he thought, *what more can a man ask?*

Obtaining a land grant from the Mexican governor would be the wisest move he could make to assure his future in California. But first he had to earn it, as Don Luis María Peralta did for his family. His service would be through his navigation and shipbuilding skills though, not the military. After his day at the rodeo, he felt overwhelmed by the amount of work and skills needed to run a rancho. William looked down the table at María's happy face, as she conversed with her friends. Even if he was married to the sea and developed a steady income from his shipping business, he needed a home port for his lovely bride-to-be, and in the future, their family. Yerba Buena Cove could become a fine port, he thought. A plot of land there, with a house overlooking the harbor. Would that be enough for María?

A few notes from a guitar told the party that music and dancing would commence. All rose from the tables and strolled to the *enramada,* a brush shelter decorated with flower garlands, for the evening entertainment. The older women perched on chairs and benches, while everyone else stood or rested upon the ground to watch the dancers. Several *caballeros* and señoritas were already on the dance floor. The young women stood ramrod straight with their arms at their sides, gently tapping their feet in time to the music. Since the skirt hems touched the ground, each woman seemed to glide over the dance floor while her partner clapped his hands and stomped his heels, taking graceful steps in a circle around her.

María slipped next to William as he clapped in time to the spirited music. He stopped, smiled into her dark eyes, and knew the next dance was theirs. Would it always be so? William felt his future—their future—was still uncertain. He knew he was in love with her, but there were still obstacles in his way. Joining the Catholic Church was one.

CHAPTER 8

SURRENDERING

When William approached the mission to continue working on a new longboat, he heard shouts and wailing. A crowd had gathered in front of the church, and at the center of the circle of onlookers stood a young Ohlone stripped to his waist, his wrists tied to a post. Padre Altimira stood next to him, addressing the throng of reserved but curious mission neophytes and soldiers assigned to the mission as guards.

"This foolish man was caught gambling with two others," the padre shouted over the noise of the throng. "The other sinners escaped, but we will catch them and bring them back for their punishment. They know the rules. Gambling is an abomination in the eyes of God. It causes laziness, distracting you from your work. You are now children of God and must obey mission rules. This man will get twelve lashes, one for each of the Apostles who were offended by his actions."

The friar stretched out the short leather strap he held and proceeded with the punishment. The youth grunted with each vicious lash, arching his reddened back in pain. Blood oozed from the deep cuts. Appalled by the padre's cruel actions, William dismounted and pushed his way through the watching mob to Padre Altimira. He grabbed the wrist of the hand holding the strap.

"I've seen many sailors tied up spread-eagle and punished this way, Padre," William said in a low voice, his blue eyes boring into the friar's surprised face. "None reformed due to their punishment. Rather, they hated the captain more and then spread dissent and anger among the other sailors. I've heard priests sometimes whip sinners. Frankly, it would seem such a beating would be hateful to God."

Padre Altimira glared at William. "Do not interfere in God's work, Señor Richardson. These people must obey the rules. All are like children and must be punished for wrongdoing. Now step back or the guards will restrain you." Two soldiers stepped forward, lances in hand, ready to comply with the friar's request, but William moved back. The rest continued to watch, grumbling but trying to show no emotion.

Rolling up his sleeve, the padre resumed the punishment. After half a dozen heavy lashes, the young man slumped to his knees, his tender flesh slashed and bleeding, but Padre Altimira continued. When he finished, the friar directed two men to untie the man and help him to his feet. Freed from his restraints, the bleeding man kneeled before the friar and kissed his hand in submission, the very hand holding the whip dripping with his blood. Head down, the beaten Ohlone staggered into the mission courtyard toward a woman healer who would apply a poultice to his wounds.

"All of you get back to your work," the padre said. "And remember what will happen if you bend to the Devil's will."

Gritting his teeth, William shoved through the ghoulish onlookers, away from the sickening scene, and led his horse to the corral. The British navy condoned flogging so he had witnessed many during his years of service. Usually, beatings were meted out for violations that endangered the ship. He didn't believe the man deserved a severe whipping for gambling. Still scowling, he joined his workers but could not focus on the longboat they were building.

Diego had also witnessed the scene and now approached William. "The Spanish soldiers took my family and me to the mission when I was younger, Señor. The friars forced my people to become farmers and vaqueros. They taught us the Catholic catechism to prepare us for salvation. They told us we must worship only one god, their God, not our animal spirits.

"Over the years, I have seen many beatings. That's how the padres force us to do as they say. Farm work, no other gods, no gambling. The padres say it is God's will. We heard a story about a man at another mission who took his punishment but said to the padre, 'If this is how your God treats his people, I want no more to do with him.' A few days later, he ran away from the mission. Soldiers searched but never found him. Padre is afraid some of us will do the same and lose our souls and places in Heaven. Others have tried to leave, but not me." He looked across the water. "I have work on the bay. My family is here. I am willing to stay." Though he didn't say he truly believed in the padres' God, William didn't press him.

William liked many things about the missions such as how the friars provided the Ohlones with food, shelter, and clothing and cared for them when they were sick. He acknowledged that the friars spent little money on themselves. They wore plain clothes and had austere furnishings even within the mission church itself. Born and raised in the Church of England, he despised the gold and silver adornments of the Catholic churches and cathedrals in Europe, riches better spent on feeding and caring for starving or sickly people. These friars had turned away from the accumulation of wealth and lived as simply as their charges did. He liked Padre Altimira but hated his harsh disciplinary actions, which Diego said other friars accepted and also employed. They showed no respect for the native people and their ways.

William had traveled to many countries on whaling ships and had worked with people of various cultures, each with their own traditions and customs. Through his experiences, he had learned to accept them, even admire some, and had never found a need for violence or dominance when he was captain of his ships. His Ohlone and Miwok men were trustworthy and loyal, and he respected them. William made a silent vow never to treat his workers as cruelly as the padre did.

He turned and clasped Diego on the shoulder. He liked this man and found him clever with his tools as well as a competent sailor unafraid of the sea.

"I believe incentives work better than punishment. Let's finish our work on this boat and then have something to eat."

✠ ✠ ✠

Although William was pleased with his occupation as instructor of carpentry and sailing, he knew in his heart that he would only be allowed to remain in California as a citizen of Mexico and marry María if he were baptized a Catholic. After dinner one evening, María asked William to talk with her about his future. Her mother Doña Martina accompanied them into the sitting room as chaperone. While her mother settled in a comfortable chair with her embroidery, the two of them sat on the settee to discuss his reluctance to become a Catholic, a major hurdle to their happiness. They spoke in low voices so Doña Martina wouldn't hear.

"It is simple. Padre Altimira will teach you our beliefs, you will pledge yourself to Christ, and the Padre will baptize you into the Church. It does not take long. Maybe a few months," María explained.

"María, I have been thinking about this a lot, ever since I was in Monterey meeting with the new governor. That's when I found out that I must enter the Church. However, I was raised in the Church of England. The English King and Church have not looked favorably on the Pope and all the Catholic Church's wealth and fancy gold trappings. I've been at sea most of my life and haven't stepped in any church since I left home. My spiritual dealings have been strictly between my God and me."

María glanced at her mother, who was softly snoring in her chair, and whispered anxiously, "William, you have seen our mission. We don't have gold or much wealth in our Church. The padres have little yet do so much for their people. You will be able to continue to deal with God personally, especially when at sea."

William rested his arms on his knees and looked out the window. "I've also heard stories and seen punishments that I can't abide. The Costeños are captives, forced to work with the friars' tools for building, to tend sheep and cattle, to till the mission's fields. I've seen one whipped, treated like an animal."

Putting a gentle hand on his sleeve, María said, "The friars are educated men. They live simple lives and are full of ambition. On fire with the love of God. They see the Costeños as ignorant beings, lost in the wilderness, who must be saved body, mind, and soul. They believe the Costeños labor, not as slaves, but for an education. To learn to help themselves when they are given land and farm animals for their families. That was Padre Serra's plan for the missions." María sat back then and looked down at the floor. "More importantly, please remember that I am Catholic. My father and my mother would never permit me to marry anyone who is not."

William looked into María's pleading eyes and kissed her hand. "I feel I'm making a good start in my life here. I'll think about what you said. Because my life must be in California with you."

✠ ✠ ✠

When William attended the wedding of María's younger sister Juana and a Presidio soldier, José Joaquin Estudillo, he witnessed the joy the ceremony blessed by the Church brought to the Martínez family. William was conflicted. He wanted to make María and her family just as happy through their union, but he felt as reluctant as a horse balking at jumping a fallen log. Finally, he made up his mind to capitulate and clear this obstacle to his life in California. Brutal punishments were accepted in many places, but as long as he wasn't forced to carry them out, he would overlook Padre Altimira's actions.

William commenced his studies in Christian doctrine with Padre Altimira at Mission Dolores and later was examined in these beliefs. On a June evening in 1823, with the comandante as his godfather and Doña Martina as his godmother, he became a Catholic and was baptized Guillermo Antonio Richardson.

As a Catholic, William was required to attend Sunday Mass as well as Masses on holy days. All Presidio residents and soldiers who were not on duty rose early Sunday morning and rode their horses or traveled in ox carts to Mission Dolores. After his baptism, William made the journey in the company of María and her family.

CHAPTER 9

THE BULL AND THE BEAR

The ringing of the mission bell summoned the worshippers to Sunday Mass. The neophytes gathered in front of the mission and filed in after the *gente de razón,* the Californios from the Presidio and nearby ranchos, who entered the church first and stood close to the altar. According to Spanish tradition, the *gente de razón* were the civilized, educated people of reason who had been baptized into the one true faith. The neophytes stood at the back of the church with Presidio guards among them who poked sharp pointed sticks into any who seemed to be dozing.

The first Sunday William accompanied María to Mass, all attendees left the church, after the final hymn was sung, to gather around a corral set up a short distance from the church entrance. Shouting and laughing, the crowd clamored for the event to start. Children stood up in oxcarts next to their mothers ready to view the contest. William was curious about the drama to take place in the corral.

"Oh, have you never seen the bear and the bull fight?" María asked him. "Let us sit on our horses to watch near Papá and Mamá. We will get a better view from the saddle."

While waiting for the entertainment to start, María explained to William how a bear is captured.

"During the dry season, two skillful vaqueros ride into the hills and hunt for a bear on a Saturday. When they discover one rummaging in the bushes for berries or digging for grubs in a rotten tree, one man throws his reata's noose around its neck and backs up his horse until the loop tightens. The second rider then flings his reata so a second noose drops over the bear's head."

"The bear must be furious," William said.

"Oh, yes," María said. "It growls, shakes its head, and swipes at the leather ties. The vaqueros drag their captive to the Mission and secure it to a post overnight. Look, here come the vaqueros. The contest is about to start."

Two men on horseback dragged a bear to the center of the corral. One vaquero snaked a long reata with a loop onto the bear's rear left leg. Then the bull was brought into the ring, and the other end of the reata was looped around the bull's right front leg. The reatas were released from the animals' necks, and the fight began.

The noise was deafening. People around the outside of the corral jeered, yelled, and whooped at the wild animals. Several vaqueros sat attentively on their horses, ready with reatas in case the bear tried to leap, or the bull to ram, the corral fence. The beasts growled and snorted.

The spectators roared. Clouds of dust rose from the animals' feet as each beast jerked the reata on its leg and scrabbled to get away from its enemy.

The bull pawed the ground fiercely, flinging dirt over its back. Then lowering its great head, it charged, attacking the bear, goring its leg with its horn even as the bear's claws raked the bull's head. Blood poured from each animal's wounds, soaking the ground. Growls and grunts of pain spurred on the cheers and screams of the onlookers.

The bear dodged an attack from the deadly horns and put the bull on the defensive, scraping its long claws across the bull's face and drawing blood. Finally, the bear managed to grab the bull's front knee. As the bull lowered its head and bellowed, the bear swiped at its tongue, trying to grab it. Immediately, two vaqueros intervened and separated the two exhausted, frightened animals.

"I'm relieved that contest ended," William said, shaking his head in disbelief, "but the crowd isn't. Why did they stop the fight?"

"A bull is a valuable animal, even though we have many. The bear would have killed it and tried to eat it. Instead, the men will kill the bear and butcher the bull for beef."

William furrowed his brow. "This is a cruel sport." He looked around at the rowdy crowd enjoying the spectacle and shook his head in disgust.

Although María had grown up with this bloody entertainment and didn't question it, he disapproved. Another grisly contest was about to follow. "María, I'd rather not remain here."

"The mission people will be dancing soon," she said. "Let's watch them." They, along with Doña Martína, walked their horses from the brutal scene in the corral to watch the dance.

The Ohlone men danced first. Although they usually wore long, loose shirts the padres had given them, today they wore only breechclouts. Broad stripes of red, black, and white body paint made from clay, charcoal, and chalk encircled their bare arms, legs, and chests. Wearing feathers in their hair, woven bands of flicker feather shafts tied around their foreheads, and necklaces of bear teeth, they danced and sang to the steady beat of drums, heads and bodies bent forward. After the men finished, a few women danced, also stooped forward, stomping on the hard ground, swaying heads, arms, and hips, and singing in their own tongue. Wearing their usual white blouses and long skirts that swept the ground, the women danced alone and moved freely, their tattooed faces still, as if in a trance, unconscious of the surrounding onlookers.

"Dancing is more to my liking than a bloody fight," William said. María raised her eyebrows.

"I seem to remember a fight is what determined your fate to live here in Alta California."

William smiled at her. "True, but it was a fight between two willing men with fists, not the claws and horns of wild animals that didn't seek such a match."

He mulled over the consequences of what he had just said. Although he had lived in the comandante's headquarters for more than a year and was now a Catholic, he fretted his connection with María was more tenuous than he'd thought. *Was I right to denounce that bull and bear fight*, William mused. *Was she disappointed in me because I criticized and won't accept one of her customs as entertainment?*

They moved away from the dancers to return to the fort, and William noticed the eyes of several caballeros following María. Would he have to compete with the rancheros' sons and Presidio soldiers for her attention?

CHAPTER 10

COURTING MARÍA

In the winter of 1823, the Russian frigate *Kreiser* sailed into San Francisco Bay for a cordial two-month visit. Years before, the Russians had established their settlement of Fort Ross farther north to hunt seals and otters for their valuable fur. With the otter and seal numbers diminishing, they arranged with Spain, and later the Mexican government, for a yearly hunt in the San Francisco Bay. The navy paid a fee for every fur pelt and duties for anchorage. They also traded for wine, grain, and beef.

Nineteen-year-old Dimitry Zavalashin was the officer in charge of supplies for the *Kreiser* and its crew. Because his duties called for him to spend most of his time ashore, the comandante provided a room in his Presidio quarters for Dimitry's business dealings. The frigate's craftsmen remodeled the room with wooden floors, glass windows, and fashionable European furniture for his comfort. Dimitry tallied daily hunting records in his room and dined with the Martínez family.

✠ ✠ ✠

The Mexican government paid William in furs to keep track of the number of otter and seal pelts taken and to collect the fees for the government. He welcomed the arrangement, another chance to add to his income. With this deal and the gifts and tidy profits he amassed helping trade ship captains avoid duties by smuggling their cargo into hidden coves, William's livelihood seemed assured. However, in his personal affairs, especially every night at dinner, the young, fascinating Dimitry pricked him like a thorn. Although he and Dimitry lived under the same roof as María at the Presidio headquarters, the Russian had more opportunities to see her than William did.

William had arranged to meet Dimitry at the Presidio daily to count the number of furs acquired before Russian sailors loaded the pelts onto the *Kreiser*. One afternoon as he rode to the comandante's headquarters, he spied María beaming a charming smile while she spoke with Dimitry, who held a basket of fragrant bread, but whose dark eyes never strayed from María. A kitchen servant stood nearby carrying another basket.

"Señor, you're early," Dimitry said to William, looking surprised and perhaps a bit annoyed.

"Good afternoon, María," William said nodding his head. "Dimitry . . . I'm here to count the pelts taken today. There seemed to be a hefty haul so I came sooner than usual. I hope I'm not . . . intruding."

María smiled up at him. "Not at all, William. We were bringing in provisions for tonight's dinner, and Dimitry gallantly stepped out to help me with this heavy basket. He will be at your service as soon as we take the bread to the kitchen."

The two men nodded to each other, and as he watched Dimitry and María disappear into the Presidio headquarters, William's tight smile disappeared. He wondered how often Dimitry was meeting María by chance. Yet despite his concern about Dimitry's interest in María, he had grown to like the man as much as the Martínez family did.

✠ ✠ ✠

In the evening when William joined the Martínez family for supper, the handsome Russian officer was entertaining all with exciting tales of naval life. Not one to be eclipsed, William added his own humorous stories about past sailing adventures and the day's events.

Doña Martina's blue eyes darted back and forth, looking at the faces of the two young men at her dinner table, who tried to catch María's eye as soon as she entered the room. Knowing her daughter harbored a passionate attraction for William, Doña Martina decided to encourage him to acknowledge his feelings for María. A little rivalry always helped.

"Dimitry," Doña Martina said, "I hope you and the other officers will join us in the Presidio *sala* tomorrow evening. The room will be arranged for dancing, and we'll have food and drink, as is customary. I pray it will not interfere with your duties."

"I thank you for the invitation and will inform my comrades. I'm sure they will attend if possible. I will definitely be there."

"And William, will you be available too?"

William glanced at María. "Oh, yes, I'll be there."

✠ ✠ ✠

The next evening, Russian officers in their dark dress uniforms mingled with the caballeros in their fitted velvet jackets and eyed the señoritas in their fashionable silk dresses. When William arrived at the *sala's* main doors, he spotted Dimitry dancing the Contradanza with María. Dimitry stood in one line with the men, opposite María and the other señoritas. Starting at the head of the lines, a gentleman danced beside his partner as she pirouetted down the aisle created by two lines of swaying dancers. While dancing, the couple sang a verse of a popular folk song to the accompaniment of guitars and violins. Another couple followed them and sang the same verse, harmonizing with the first couple. When the two couples returned to the end of each line, the next two couples progressed down the aisle. During every step, Dimitry's gaze never wavered from María's radiant face, her cheeks flushed with excitement, her black hair loose and flowing down her back.

Several young Russian officers standing at the edge of the dance floor stared at her and murmured among themselves about the enchanting "Madonna" and her bewitching dark eyes. When William entered the circle of Russian admirers, the whispers stopped. Dressed in his own officer's uniform of a navy wool jacket with brass buttons, nankeen trousers, and polished black boots, he stood out among the others. María stared at him and smiled, making Dimitry look up and stumble in the last step.

At the end of the dance, he led María to the crowd of officers surrounding William.

"Gentlemen," María said, "have you met Señor Richardson? He has been our savior, guiding trade ships safely into our bay. It's now a haven for trade vessels that bring us fine wines, wonderful cheeses, and precious goods."

William bowed to María to kiss the warm, soft hand she extended to him. Dimitry and William nodded to each other. William greeted the other officers cordially in Russian, but his mind was focused on asking María for the next dance. She readily accepted when he did.

The music started, and María and William joined the other dancers in the middle of the room. Except for one or two dances with Dimitry, María spent the entire evening with William. He knew her heart and her future lay with him.

✠ ✠ ✠

As William and María became more certain of each other's love, they searched for occasions to be together. Often, they meandered in the early evening on the Presidio grounds along a straight path, later known as Lover's Walk. A *dueña* always accompanied them, strolling behind at a discreet distance, her duty to protect María's virtue. Knowing their desire for each other, the *dueña* sometimes looked away, allowing them time for a lingering kiss.

During their strolls, William taught María English and more about the English way of life. She taught him Spanish customs and acceptable deportment in her culture. He started wearing the Mexican style of clothing to fit in with his new life. The two also talked about William's promising future in shipping and trade. William was afraid to ask, however, whether María understood how much he would be away at sea. Was she truly willing to make that sacrifice for a life with him?

After the evening meal with the family, William and María were permitted to sit side by side on a settee while Doña Martina sat on the opposite side of the room with her embroidery to keep an eye on them. As an excuse for being together, William continued to teach María English. Frequently, Doña Martina interrupted them with a cough or a rustle of her skirts when they held hands and leaned their heads too close to each other, whispering.

After drinking a little too much wine one evening, Doña Martina's eyes grew heavy. When she nodded off and William heard her light snoring, he dared to brush María's soft cheek with his fingertips and tuck a stray lock of her dark hair behind her delicate ear. He moved closer and slowly pulled her shawl away from her neck. When he kissed her warm skin, María closed her eyes and shivered. William drew her to him and pressed his lips to hers. She responded with longing.

When the señora roused herself, she was startled to see her daughter in a passionate kiss, enveloped in the arms of this handsome young sailor.

"My heavens, young people," she exclaimed, "this is something my husband must know about at once."

CHAPTER 11

MARÍA ANTONIA

While William stayed at the Presidio as a guest of María's parents, he courted María. She harbored no shred of doubt about their love for each other. One night after supper, he asked her to stroll with him outside. An old *dueña*, a friend of María's mother, accompanied them, walking a few paces behind, watchful as always. Several other couples meandered around the Presidio grounds, enjoying the mild evening. Although it was the rainy season, the past week had been dry. The air was clear, and stars winked in the heavens.

William pointed out the Pole Star, the guiding light for sailors. Then he turned her gently by the shoulders to look at him and gazed into her eyes. "I feel I've settled into a satisfying life here in California," he murmured, "but there is one thing missing."

María's heart beat harder, but she did not dare assume what he would say next. She looked at him wide-eyed and asked, "What could that be, William? You are a busy man now, building boats, teaching young men at the Mission carpentry and sailing. The padres think you are a fine teacher. Your students admire you. And you are now a Catholic and can become a Mexican citizen. What do you feel is missing?"

"You. I want you to be my wife. You are already my heart and soul. I have feared asking you because of my life as a sailor. Could you be patient and content with a man who often must be away at sea?"

María trembled with delight and love, placing her hand on his cheek. She could not live without this man. He was gentle yet strong. She felt safe with him. He had a few rough edges, but she could smooth them. "I have been waiting for you to speak. I can be patient. And I will always pray and wait for your return."

William sighed. "I intend to talk with your father tonight."

"Yes, yes, *mi amore*, my love, speak with him tonight!"

✠ ✠ ✠

After the comandante granted permission for them to marry, months of preparation followed, with servants sewing and embroidering six of every garment for María's bridal trousseau. William was also busy, applying to the governor for permission to marry, acquiring pearl necklaces to adorn María's hair and neck, and buying the most desirable horse, a palomino, and the best saddle he could find for his wedding.

At last the joyous wedding day, May 15, 1825, arrived. Early in the morning, William, dressed in his captain's coat, nankeen trousers, and polished black boots, paced the veranda in front of the comandante's quarters. The wedding cavalcade assembled on the Presidio parade ground. Impatient horses shook their heads and stamped, making their silver trappings jingle merrily. All the wedding participants awaited the appearance of the bride. Officers and soldiers, smartly dressed in short, blue wool uniform jackets and breeches, stood next to their horses. Caballeros from surrounding ranchos wore their finest clothes, jackets and breeches trimmed in braid and silver. Senoritas and señoras, dressed in silks and satins, wore over their heads and shoulders expensive mantillas and embroidered shawls purchased on trade ships from China, Europe, or Boston.

When María stepped through the door, her hand on her father's arm, William stopped pacing and drew in his breath, astounded by this vision of perfection. A lacy white mantilla floated over her glossy black hair from a high tortoiseshell comb. Her pale yellow satin dress gave her an other-worldly appearance, an angel without wings. And today this heavenly beauty would become his wife.

The comandante mounted his horse and settled himself on a bear-skin-covered tailpiece behind the saddle. A servant lifted the bride into her seat so she could sit side-saddle in front of her father. Then William rushed forward to help María place her white satin shoe in the silver braid loop hanging from the saddle horn.

Looking up at María, he said in a husky voice, "I am the luckiest man on earth!"

"But it is Heaven that is smiling on us today," María whispered to her husband-to-be.

The comandante gathered the reins and called out, "Let's go! This is my daughter's wedding day!"

The rest of the party climbed into the oxen-drawn *carretas*. William mounted his palomino and the other men climbed on their gaily decorated horses to parade through the Presidio gate and on to Mission Dolores, where the mission's bell joyously rang to announce their arrival. Padre Esténega greeted the bride and her father at the Mission's steps and led the wedding party into the church. There, during the Mass, the friar blessed the couple, draped a long, white satin sash around their necks and shoulders and over their joined hands to signify they were bound together as husband and wife forever. William and María declared their love and promised their devotion to one another for the rest of their lives.

✠ ✠ ✠

The officers, their families, and the families of surrounding ranchos attended the evening banquet on the wedding day. Dozens of Ohlone servants had prepared the feast and were ready to serve the guests roasted haunches of beef and elk, platters of steelhead, crispy duck and chicken, followed by a final course of sweet desserts. Wine and brandy flowed all night.

Before supper was served, the musicians tuned their guitars and violins, and couples of all ages stepped onto the dance floor. The dancers formed two lines, each gentleman facing his lady, to dance the *jota*. William spun María onto the dance floor and joined the dancers at the head of the lines as the guitars, violins, and singers began. William had learned this dance but unabashedly improvised adding leaps, hops, and kicks, which made María laugh. On the refrain, the men and women formed two circles, the men in the outside circle holding hands and facing the women in the inner circle. The men stepped smoothly clockwise, and the women, silk skirts swinging, danced gracefully in the reverse direction until they were opposite their partners once again. William pulled his wife to him and gave her a long, passionate kiss while the wedding guests applauded and cheered.

A frisson of happiness slid through him. "We were made for each other," he murmured in her ear.

The wedding celebration continued for two more days. Music, dancing, feasting, horse races, and contests of riding skills entertained the guests, many who had traveled far to honor the comandante and share in his family's joy.

✠ ✠ ✠

Late on the third evening of the festivities, after María changed from her party finery into a traveling dress and shawl, she and William slipped away from the feasting. At the beach, two of William's sailors were ready with a small boat to row them across the bay to Saucelito. There, near a sheltered cove, a honeymoon camp had been arranged, a pastoral paradise where the young couple could spend their time alone learning about each other. Although she had no intimate experience with men, María had overheard frank talk from family servants and her sister Juana. She trusted her husband would be tender and understanding.

When the boat touched the Saucelito sands, William leaped out and turned to carry his bride to shore. They clung to each other, two lovers now husband and wife.

"Forever, *mi amore*," María declared to William.

After he set her down gently, he took her face in his hands and kissed her eyes and lips, and whispered back, "Forever!"

William slipped his arm around María's slim waist, and they stood side by side gazing over the bay at the full moon, a silver orb in the clear night sky sprinkled with stars. His warm hand on her cool, bare arm sent a tingling sensation through her. They turned from the shore, and hand in hand, strolled from the beach, the moon behind them, rising over the *Isla de Nuestra Señora de Los Angeles,* Angel Island, lighting their way to their wedding bower, where instinct and passion pulled them, as insistent as the tide.

Even in paradise, however, time does not stand still. After two days, the honeymoon was over. William and María reluctantly returned to the Presidio so he could take command of the schooner to carry a longed-for bell to Mission San Francisco Solano.

CHAPTER 12

THE LAST MISSION AND A BRIGANTINE

When the schooner arrived in Sonoma with the new mission bell, a parade of Miwok men leading saddle horses and driving a creaking oxcart greeted the visitors. A wiry, dark-haired friar in a gray robe followed them and dismounted from his donkey at the water's edge. Seeing the familiar face, William leaped from the launch to shore and approached the friar.

"Good day, Padre Altimira! Here is your bell!"

"Welcome, William! And God bless you for bringing it to us," Padre Altimira said as William bent to kiss his hand. The two men watched the sailors and mission workers transfer the heavy bronze bell from the launch to the oxcart. "I have brought horses for you to ride to the Mission," the padre continued. "You will be pleased when you see our fine church."

At Mission Dolores, William had worked with Padre Altimira on building plans for this new and last mission in the chain of California missions. He looked forward to seeing the friar's progress. Although he and the friar had their differences, especially about disciplining the Ohlone, he tried to be cordial and on good terms with this influential, dogmatic man. It was Padre Altimira's idea to abandon Mission Dolores and establish a mission in the

Sonoma Valley, a warm, sunny place away from the chill of the San Francisco Bay. The governor, as well as the California Territorial Assembly, readily agreed with the new mission site because they viewed it as another outpost to protect the northern Mexican territory from foreign encroachment. Although the Father Prelate opposed the idea at first, he and the governor finally compromised by keeping Mission Dolores as well as building Mission San Francisco Solano, named for St. Francis Solano, a canonized Franciscan missionary from Peru.

When the precious bell arrived at the mission, the friar showed William around. Similar to the layout of other missions, the new mission's workshops, dormitories, storerooms, and a guard tower were built around an open quadrangle. After a walk around the fields and pasture grounds surrounding the church, the men settled under a shady oak tree where two native women served them refreshments of cheese, roasted quail, toasted tortillas, beans, and wine.

"I am sorry I could not officiate at your wedding," Padre Altimira said. "But of course, I wish you and María much happiness and contentment. How is your lovely bride?"

"Well, and I thank you for your good wishes, Padre. María is now with her family at the Presidio, but was sad I had to leave so soon."

Padre Altimira poured two glasses of wine. "I'm sorry your time together was so short. You will be back in a few days." Handing William a glass, he said, "A toast to you and María Antonia. God bless you both."

After a sip of the soothing wine, the friar continued. "We have waited a long time for the arrival of our bell to call our flock to Mass. We'll use it for emergencies also, to warn of dangers, such as attacks from uncivilized heathens or Russians."

"I don't think you need to worry about the Russians. They seem content with their current arrangements with the Mexican government. Their hunters have come into the bay many times, and always pay for the privilege."

After a few more sips of the mellow wine, William relaxed and surveyed the valley of Sonoma and its surrounding green hills. He breathed in the sweet smell of the tall grass. "You have some wonderful country here. I wouldn't mind staking a claim to some land near here for myself. With all this sunny weather, it's no wonder everyone is so healthy."

"Not all are, I'm afraid. God has been generous with our crops. Our grape vines and fruit trees are growing well, and we have baptized more *Costaños* to praise and honor God. Some have run away, though, because so many died a few months ago. Of those that remain, not all are well. I pray they are not infected with the dreadful pox disease. But we can discuss that later. Come! If you have finished eating and rested enough, I can show you where I want to place the bell."

Within two days, the wooden frame for the bell was constructed and raised in place. Using ropes, wooden pulleys, and horsepower, the men hung the bell from a thick redwood crossbeam. With a small group of neophytes gathered around, the priest blessed the bell and grinned as he rang it for the first time.

"Ah, the voice of our mission! Thank you again, William! And now I think we had better move inside. These darkening skies portend rain."

The rain pounded all evening and into the night. Sailing to the Presidio was impossible. With nothing to do, William paced up and down the veranda. He went to bed, grumbling to himself. "Confound this blasted storm! It's keeping me from my bride!"

✠ ✠ ✠

Concerned about new cases of illness among the Miwok and Pomo people, Padre Altimira visited them at the mission's *rancheria* in the morning. Both groups were native to the Sonoma Valley and had lived there long before the Spanish arrived.

The neophyte families lived in circular tule huts. The sick, young and old, lay on tule mats on the ground in their huts, coughing and tossing with fever. He spoke with them, observed their condition, and assured them he would return with help. He stepped outside the last hut, breathed in some fresh air deeply, and set out to talk with William about a different pestilence.

"I don't think smallpox is the cause of this fever, praise the Lord," the friar said. "I can treat this sickness with blackberry syrup and some of the *Costaños*' remedies, which I will let their shaman give them. The neophytes believe so strongly in their medicine man that I must let him care for them, too. But I do have a request for your help with the pox.

"Several men who milk the cows have developed cowpox. I have been told the scabs and ooze from their weeping sores can protect uninfected adults and children from smallpox. The ooze is scratched into a healthy person's skin. I haven't done it myself. The smallpox vaccine would be better, but we haven't had a shipment of vaccine from Mexico nor from the Russians at Fort Ross for many years."

William offered to help the friar immediately. "Because I had the pox when I was a child, I can't get it again. I know about variolation, the technique you described. I've seen it done. And I know how contagious and dangerous smallpox is. Even if a person survives that scourge, the pox sores can leave hideous scars all over the body."

✠ ✠ ✠

Padre Altimira ground fresh weeping pox scabs scraped from the cowpox-infected men into a bowl. He and William gathered the healthy children and proceeded to scratch a wrist or arm with a needle they had touched to the crushed pox scabs. They bound each wound with a clean bandage.

"I know these children will get sick with the cowpox, but it'll be mild, and they won't get the deadly smallpox when older," said Padre Altimira as he clasped William's hand in both of his. "Thank you for your kind assistance, William. I'll be sure to inform the comandante and the governor about your willingness to help me save these poor children from such suffering."

✠ ✠ ✠

The first Mexican governor of Alta California, Luis Argüello, wrote to Padre Altimira about a French brigantine anchored at Monterey, its captain and crew dead from scurvy. The governor wanted the padre to ask Captain Richardson whether he would be interested in commandeering a crew to return the ship to its home port in Panama. William was busy with transporting cargo on the bay and declined with regrets.

Now that Mexico, a republic free of Spain, encouraged foreign trade, Governor Argüello had thrown aside old Spanish rules and welcomed foreign vessels. He looked favorably on the skilled foreigners settling in California. The governor had heard about William's ambitious effort to provide safe passage for trading ships into the San Francisco Bay, which fostered more trade. Lieutenant Martínez's reports praised William's work sailing launches around the bay to gather hides and mission crops. Keeping in mind his desire to dispose of the brig cluttering Monterey Bay, the governor wrote William and asked him about his progress with new launches and navigation instruction. Not wishing to bite the hand of authority, William graciously replied that he and his crew would sail one to Monterey for his inspection.

The governor was so pleased with the launch that he made William an offer. "Would you be interested in buying the abandoned brig in my harbor?"

William jumped at the chance to claim it. His credit had improved over the past year; he was sure he could afford it. The rancheros paid him generously in California "dollars," some of the hides William transported for them to the trading ships. Satisfied sea captains handed him a bit extra as well. Even though Comandante Martínez knew about the payoffs and graft, he was happy to look the other way since he benefitted also with gifts from the same sources.

After thoroughly inspecting the ship for damage and knowing that no one else was bidding on the ship, William bargained with Governor Argüello for a lower price. When they completed their negotiations, his crew cleaned above deck and below and loaded the ship with provisions. A few days later, they secured the launch to the brig, and William piloted his new ship out of Monterey Bay and sailed to San Francisco Bay. He hugged the shore, making short tacks, sailing away from the coast and back toward it, with every sail set and the mainsail and foresails free. The ship picked up winds from the sea by day and from the land at night, six or seven knots strong. In this way, William sailed the brig home in record time.

When he landed, he sought out María to tell her of his windfall and his plans. "Once she's fully repaired, I'll christen her the *María Antonia*. I must see your father to tell him about our good fortune." He took both of María's hands and kissed them. "Now that I've met the governor, I'll petition him for some land. With good reports from your father and Padre Altimira, I think he'll approve. Yerba Buena Cove is a perfect place for a home and a secure harbor for ships."

✠ ✠ ✠

María Antonia sat on a small barrel at the prow of her husband's ship, *El Rey del Mar*. She was mending a shirt, but now and then, she looked up to watch William as he worked. If her husband was happy, she was content. He now owned another ship and had named it after her. Whenever she saw it, her heart surged with love for her ambitious man. Every day she thanked God that he had remained with her in Alta California. Every day his work and successes proved her instincts and leap for love were right.

During their sail on the bay that day, he dropped a chunk of lead attached to a line over the side of the sloop. When the line grew taut, he marked figures in a book and on his charts. María learned this work was called sounding the bay and marking the depths on his charts made navigation safer for small boats and ships.

William had been sounding the cove opposite the little island called Yerba Buena. At the edge of the beach, the water was shallow, and an ebb tide exposed mud flats that extended into the cove for about a quarter of a mile. William seemed pleased as he took his soundings. "A full five fathoms! Even foreign ships can find safe harbor a stone's throw from the mud flats. It's a snug harbor. The government should build a trading center here."

María gazed out over the water, north to the hill *Loma Alta* and south toward *Punta del Rincon* past the drifting sand dunes. Lonely and cold, she thought and tightened her shawl around her shoulders.

She and William had talked about building a home here near the cove. But he was also considering land north of the bay entrance, where they had spent their all-too-brief honeymoon. The Mexicans called the place "Saucelito," meaning "little grove of willows," for the cluster of willow trees growing there. Plenty of land was available for raising cattle and grain. He knew it was a good harbor, too, and had directed ships there to sell them fresh water.

Even though cold winds blew here, María thought Yerba Buena Cove should be their first choice for a home, a spot close to the Presidio and her family. William said he'd bet money this cove would grow into a town, a city, a trading center. He told her his first priority, though, was to sail *María Antonia* to Sitka to procure much needed merchandise for the Presidio and missions. María hugged her belly and prayed William would be safe and the sea voyage short.

CHAPTER 13

WAITING

Winter, 1825–1826

The *María Antonia* held a cargo of grain, hides, and tallow to trade for tools, glassware, bolts of cloth, and other supplies in Sitka, a city in the Russian territory of Alaska. William also hoped to secure the vital smallpox vaccine for his family and for Padre Altimira. While William was gone, Diego and Marino would handle port duties and pilot ships into the bay.

William had assured María he would be gone only a few months. She was a sensible woman who accepted his life as a seaman, but she was disappointed. She had pressed her lips together and looked away when he told her he wouldn't be back until after their child was born. He had thought of bringing her with him but knew it was impossible. She was much better off in the capable hands of her family. *What did he know about birthing babies?* he mused. *What did he know about being a father?* He brushed that doubt aside, confident he would learn.

The longboat crew carried William to the brig. He put impending fatherhood out of his mind and scrutinized the ship's two tall masts and rigging. This was the life he knew. His ship was strong, seaworthy, and he had checked every inch of her. His crew had followed his instructions to refit her, their repair work precise. He had sailed her many times up and down the bay, but this would be her first long ocean voyage under his command. When he climbed the Jacob's ladder from the longboat and stepped onto the deck of the *María Antonia*, his sailors cheerfully greeted him, and William felt excitement swell through his belly. His passion for the sea was overpowering. He had mastered a mariner's craft and was prepared to do whatever he had to, under any conditions—storms, unfriendly foreign ships, even possible rebellion among the crew. But like all true seamen, he returned to the sea with pleasure.

"Prepare to weigh anchor and set sail!" he called to his first mate.

The ship groaned as the anchor rose, the square sails flapped and then billowed with the breeze, and the *María Antonia* glided from the harbor to the entrance of the bay and out to the Pacific. She appeared to be as eager as her captain to get moving. "Only a few months, María," William whispered to himself. Then he turned his attention to his ship, delighted to be under stretched canvas again.

✠ ✠ ✠

While awaiting the baby's arrival and William's return, María looked for things to do to occupy her hands and her mind. Though she had yearned to go with William on this voyage to a new place, a foreign territory, her daydream of exploring the Russian outpost floated away with him. Another time, perhaps. Her duty was here. She must stay safe and prepare for the new life within her. Giving birth was dangerous enough in familiar surroundings with knowledgeable people. María was aware of the risks and had witnessed difficult births. She wouldn't be so foolish as to travel to a foreign land and give birth with the help of strangers.

Ohlone women living at the Presidio handled many of the household chores, under the direction of María and her mother Doña Martina. They cared for Doña Martina's young children also, though María helped keep them in line. Her younger sisters caused as much mischief as her brothers, squabbling, teasing each other, annoying pets, ignoring chores. María's caregiving responsibilities helped prepare her for rearing her own children.

After the servants finished daily duties of making tortillas and hearty stews, baking bread in the outdoor adobe ovens, sweeping, and washing dishes and pots, Doña Martina would ask two young girls to pull chairs near the windows, or if the day was fine, onto the veranda, so they would have good light for sewing. María, her mother, and several servants sewed baby clothes every day. Many were needed because Doña Martina was pregnant with her seventh child, María with her first, and both children were due in the spring. Every bit of baby clothing was handmade—soft swaddling cloths, the baptismal dresses and caps, sewn with fine stitches and trimmed with delicate lace. Everything must be ready for the new family members. Everything must be new because used baby clothes were usually given away or thrown out.

"What will you name your *niño,* Señora Richardson?" asked a ten-year-old girl who was sitting on the floor rolling balls of wool that would be woven into soft blankets for the babies.

"I won't choose a name until she is born," María said. Her mother nodded in agreement. "I feel sure this baby will be a girl."

"Oh, that is too bad! A boy would be better, to help his father and protect his family," said one old woman.

"I will be pleased with a girl . . . or boy," Maria said. "She will grow up healthy and strong, and I will teach her to be capable of caring for herself and her family."

"Like her mother," Doña Martina said, smiling at her daughter.

And like her father, Maria thought. She wondered whether William would be as pleased with a daughter as a son. What kind of father would he be? She was sure his patience and kindness would carry him through. He was at ease dealing with many types of people. *He'll get used to children, too.* She had witnessed him playing with the Presidio children, running races, giving them rides on his shoulders, even teaching them to defend themselves fairly with their fists. Yes, he would do fine.

✠ ✠ ✠

Pounding early winter rains turned the brown California hills green again, lush pastures for the mission cattle, horses, and sheep. But muddy trails made travel impossible and indoor confinement dragged on as María waited for her child.

Holy days offered a welcome distraction with everyone putting their pent-up energy into decorating the church and the comandante's headquarters. For Christmas, walls and windowsills were draped with bright green ivy, toyon branches heavy with red berries, fragrant redwood and pine cuttings, and colorful ribbons. To chase away the darkness, clay bowls with candles were set out, ready to be lit for Christmas.

On Christmas Eve, Presidio residents attended High Mass at Mission Dolores. The church bells called all believers to celebrate the birth of Christ. The church choir of Ohlone and Miwok boys, whom the padre had trained, sang joyful hymns, accompanied by musicians on flutes, guitars, violins, and drums. On Christmas Day, feasting, music, and dancing cheered everyone.

At the beginning of the new year, María and Doña Martina had their clothing adjusted to accommodate the baby each was carrying. María felt fine and energetic but impatient for her child to be born so that she could hold her—or him—and look into her eyes, eyes she imagined would be as blue as her husband's.

✠ ✠ ✠

The days and weeks of rain that followed the holidays did not help María's disposition. Everyone in the house seemed to be gloomy and restless. The Presidio parade grounds and the dirt roads streamed with the rainwater that no longer seeped into the soaked earth. One morning a torrent of rain drummed on the tile roof. María halted her pacing, stared out the window at the leaden skies, frowned, and stamped her foot.

"When will it stop raining!"

"Patience, *cariño,* sweetie," said Doña Martina, her head bent over her sewing. Since the first year after her marriage to Lieutenant Martínez, when she was fourteen, she had carried six babies to term and was used to waiting.

María paced the room again, picked up her embroidery from the table, and then plunked down in a chair next to her mother.

"Even though I can't go riding, I want to go out to walk and breathe in the sweet, clean air." *And what was William doing now?* she worried. *Was he hurt, sick, or in danger? Was he enjoying himself in the Russian society in Sitka, with dinners, balls, and slender young women in elegant dresses? Did he even think about her?* Other Presidio wives had told her about wandering, drunken husbands. She was sure William had intimate experiences with women in the past. He might dance with women in Sitka, but he wouldn't bring them to his bed. She would never believe William could be unfaithful. She shook her head to banish these thoughts.

"I too long to be outside," Doña Martina said. "Like you, these endless wet days make me as nervous as a cat. Dry days will come soon. But let us pray those days will not be too soon or too long. We need the rain or else the cattle and sheep will be lean and hungry during our dry summer."

✠ ✠ ✠

Lent arrived, the season for repentance and preparation for the Easter holy days. Fasting and lighter meals reminded the Californios how Christ suffered for mankind's sins. The days preparing for the Easter Sunday celebration were as busy as the days before Christmas. María, Juana, and the women of the Presidio gathered at tables to gossip and to make *cascarones*. They poked small holes in the ends of many eggs, blew out the insides into bowls, let the shells dry, then filled the empty eggshells with perfume or small pieces of bright paper, and sealed the holes with wax. The *cascarones* were laid in baskets ready for dancers at the Easter ball to pick up and crack over their partners' heads.

As they worked, the women revealed whom they hoped to surprise with a *cascarón*. María daydreamed about teaching her unborn daughter how to make them. She smiled, imagining her little girl giggling and cracking a *cascarón* on her father's head.

On Easter Sunday, María dressed in her finest black dress, adjusted to her wider girth, braided her long black hair, and covered her head and shoulders with a black lace mantilla, as all married women did. When they were ready, Doña Martina and María rode to the Mission for Easter services in a clumsy ox-drawn *carreta*. The Mission women had decorated the altar with calla lilies and wildflower garlands, and the boy choir sang with joy for Christ the Savior's resurrection.

In the evening, the Presidio families arrived at the comandante's house for a dinner and the dance that followed. The doñas wore fancy dresses with ruffled skirts while the dons were decked out in black velvet jackets and knee-length trousers trimmed at the edge with gold braid. Upon arrival, each guest picked up a *cascarón* from the baskets near the door, ready to surprise his or her partner during the first dance. Señoritas cracked eggs on their partners' heads, drenching them with perfume. The men reciprocated with *cascarones* filled with bits of multicolored paper that flew out over their señoritas' hair. The Easter *cascarón* ball had begun! Although María wished William were with her as he was last year, she glided onto the dance floor with her father. Slyly smiling at him, she raised her hand quickly over his head and cracked a *cascarón* on it, perfume dampening his hair. Her pregnancy was not going to stop her from enjoying this ball even if she would dance only with her father.

✠ ✠ ✠

Sunny days soon outnumbered the rainy ones. Dry weather meant other chores that had been neglected were now possible. Wash day, a priority, required a major expedition and careful planning. The night before, servants gathered bedclothes, towels, shirts, petticoats, and underclothing. In the morning, the bundles would be loaded into a *carreta* that had been washed and its heavy wooden wheels greased. María woke before dawn, had a light breakfast, and supervised the packing of lunch baskets.

"María, you are going to the lagoon, too?" Doña Martína frowned at her daughter.

"I feel fine, Mamá, and the day is so fair. I will ride in the cart. All will be well."

"I'd rather you didn't go. Sometimes babies are born early, you know. I'm not sure you'll be safe."

Ignoring her mother's warning, María threw a shawl over her shoulders and said, "I'll ask Papá."

Her father overheard his daughter and went into his office, returning with a pistol. "Bears have been sighted near the shore, and panther prints were in the sand near the lagoon. I know you are a fine shot, but I'll send a guard also to watch for danger." María took the gun from her father, kissed his cheek, and put the heavy pistol in her skirt pocket.

"Thank you, Papá. Your grandchild will be safe." She patted her pocket, confident in her ability to defend herself.

"Return to the Presidio immediately if you feel any pain!" her mother warned.

María and older Ohlone women, who would be washing the laundry, climbed into the oxcart with the laundry bundles. Young children clambered in to ride on top of the bundles, but the younger women and older children walked. One servant handed her young son, Felipe, to María who made room for him next to her. He was a quiet boy who preferred his own company but liked being with her if his mother was busy.

More bundles of dirty linen were tied onto the backs of pack horses, each led by a mounted servant. The Presidio soldier guarding the party climbed on his horse to follow the group. A gray-haired Ohlone man started the parade, using a pointy stick to prod the oxen into a walk.

Progress was slow and took several hours even though it was only a few miles from the fort to *Laguna Pequeña.* Clear spring water flowed into the lagoon, and low-growing bushes and scrub oak trees clung to the banks. When the women arrived at the lagoon's edge, a herd of deer stopped drinking, flicked their tails, and daintily trotted away from the noisy party of humans. The children jumped from the carts and scattered to play hide and seek and pick wildflowers. The women unloaded the laundry bundles to begin their washing duties. They sang and laughed as they scrubbed each article of linen with soap until it was as white as snow again, and then flung the clean, wet laundry over fragrant bushes to dry. María strolled along the lagoon's bank, breathing in the clean, fresh air tinged with fragrance from the minty herb underfoot. Pausing, she tilted her head and closed her eyes, enjoying the warmth of the sun on her face.

At midday, the women placed blankets and cowhides on the ground and opened baskets of food. Mothers called their children to stop their games and come eat.

When they trailed in, one mother cried out, "Where is Felipe?" No answer.

María and a few of the women spread out to search for the missing boy. Moving deeper into the underbrush, away from the lagoon, María looked under the thick bushes. When she rounded a tall bush, she spotted the boy looking into the branches of a scrub oak. She followed his gaze and found herself staring into the golden eyes of a mountain lion crouching on a limb.

Carefully drawing her pistol from her pocket, her eyes never leaving the big cat, she hissed to Felipe, "Don't turn around. Slowly, walk backward to me."

The mountain lion growled and stood up on the branch. Tail thrashing, it opened its mouth wide, showing all its savage teeth, and let out a wild, chilling screech of fury when it saw its prey escaping. It gathered itself, ready to pounce.

María had only one shot, one chance. If she missed, the beast would spring for her and the boy. She would have no time to reload. Heart thumping, she steadied the heavy pistol with both hands, aimed, and fired.

The big cat shuddered and tumbled to the ground. Hearing the shot, women screamed in the distance. María released her breath. Her hand grasping the heavy pistol dropped to her side.

The soldier assigned to guard the women dashed around the bush with his rifle ready. Warily, he approached the still animal, kicked it, and said, "Dead. Shot between the eyes."

Felipe tucked his dark head into María and clung to her skirt. Looking up at her, he said, "You saved my life! I've never been so scared!"

María smoothed his hair and spoke softly to calm him. "You're safe now. All's well." Silently, she thanked her father for teaching her to shoot.

Felipe's mother and several women hurried toward the sound. They marveled at the panther's size. Felipe's mother knelt to hug him and check for injuries.

"He was very brave," María said. She gave a great sigh as she felt a pain in her belly. "Oof, my little one did not like all that excitement."

On the walk back to the lagoon and the picnic site, María stopped in her tracks and bent over, holding her belly.

"Another pain?" asked one woman coming to María's side and holding her arm to steady her.

"I must return to the Presidio." *Not yet, little one,* she thought, *please, not yet. Oh, Mamá, you were right. This outing was too strenuous. But I must make it home. This child will not be born here.*

CHAPTER 14

A CHILD IS BORN

The contractions started the next morning. Two servant women hastened to ready the birthing room. An old Ohlone woman, who had attended many births, helped María undress and slip on a loose chemise. María's mother and sister Juana held onto her arms to help her walk back and forth across the room. The pains became more intense and closer together.

"Oh, William," María groaned, bending over a sharp contraction. Even though men didn't enter birthing rooms, she wished he were there to hold her hand, to give her his strength.

"He couldn't help you even if he were here," Doña Martina said. "He most likely is fine and on his way back. You are strong! You can do this with us. Breathe slowly between the pains."

All the women in the room had families of their own and knew how to comfort a laboring woman. When María sat on a cushioned birthing chair, two women took turns massaging her back and arms, murmuring that everything was good, as it should be. Juana held a cup of cold water to her lips.

"Don't drink. Just moisten your lips," the old woman advised.

Tendrils of María's shiny black hair clung to her perspiring forehead and neck as the pains continued and became more severe. She wasn't conscious of what the others did, only of her own body. Minutes, hours passed, she was unaware of time. As the Ohlone women crooned a chant, María felt the overwhelming need to push.

The old woman said, "Yes, yes, you are ready. Push!" María clenched her teeth and grunted aloud. She panted and then grunted again as she pushed.

"I see the babe's head!" exclaimed Juana.

"Another push!" the old woman said. She then knelt on the floor and caught the baby as it slid out into the chilly room with a protesting cry. "A beautiful girl!"

One woman gently bathed the child and wrapped her in a blanket while the others washed and cared for the new mother who cried and laughed with joy.

As María nursed her precious baby for the first time, she looked down at her and whispered, "I will call her Mariana." She felt a strong surge of tenderness and protectiveness for this physical affirmation of William's and her love. With tearful eyes, María looked at her mother and held out her hand to grasp hers, grateful for her support in the birth of her first child.

✠ ✠ ✠

Two booms from a ship's cannon announced the arrival of a trading vessel. A month earlier, a ship had delivered a letter to María from William saying he would return in a few weeks. It had been six months since he was home. Was the arriving ship the *María Antonia*? María swayed gently with Mariana in her arms as she waited on the veranda for the boy she'd sent to find out the ship's name. If it was William's ship, she'd tell the women in the kitchen to begin preparations for a feast to celebrate his return.

Doña Martina, carrying her baby Rafaela, her fifth daughter, born a week after Mariana, joined María. "Is it William's ship?" María's mother asked.

The boy came running through the Presidio gate and up to the veranda. Out of breath, he gasped, "It's the *María Antonia!*"

María whirled around in a circle with her baby and looked into her clear gray eyes as she waved her little fists. How would

William react to his little daughter? Would he be able to recognize her? She turned to face her mother. "Let's play a trick on William. We'll switch babies and ask him to tell us which is his child!" Doña Martina smiled and agreed.

After María checked on the kitchen, she and her mother sat on the veranda, holding each other's child. Soon they heard horses and men's voices at the Presidio gate. Comandante Martínez stepped onto the veranda to greet the returning men. William broke away from the soldiers and sailors and galloped to the veranda. He sprang from the saddle, embraced María, and kissed her with the baby between them.

"Be careful of baby Rafaela!" she scolded.

The comandante and Doña Martina smiled at the young couple as William examined the baby's face. Her eyes were closed, and she sported soft tufts of hair as dark as Maria's. He then gazed at the babe in Doña Martina's arms, gray eyes wide open, taking in the world, and a small head with fine wisps of brunette hair, as light as his own.

"Are they not beautiful?" asked María. "Now you must tell us which one is yours."

William looked at both children again. "What is the name of your baby?" he asked Doña Martina.

"We named her Mariana," she said.

"You mean María named her because I believe you are holding your grandchild!"

All of them laughed as Doña Martina handed William his child and took Rafaela from her daughter.

María hugged William again, and said, "I will have to be cleverer in the future if I want to fool you!"

✠ ✠ ✠

Baby Mariana was christened in her handsewn white christening dress and bonnet at Mission Dolores. William carried her to the mission on horseback, followed by a procession of relatives, friends, and Presidio soldiers who carried lanterns to light their way. At the mission doors, he and María dismounted with the comandante and Doña Martina who would be Mariana's godparents. Padre Altimira greeted them and led them to the baptismal font. All others who had come to celebrate Mariana's baptism and entrance into the Catholic faith waited outside.

When the baptismal party emerged, the troops lined up and fired a salute for the first child born in the San Francisco Presidio of foreign parentage. The church bells tolled and fireworks lit up the night sky. When the musicians began to play again, all the guests including the friar mounted their horses to ride to the San Francisco Presidio for the festivities.

At the Presidio, refreshments were served and music and dancing began. María lifted baby Mariana from Doña Martina's arms and said to William, "This little one is yawning. I think she should join her Aunt Rafaela who is already asleep. Mariana has had enough of this celebration even though it is in her honor."

"She'll have the chance to attend many balls in the future," William said. "But will you come back to the party?" He didn't relish entertaining all the guests by himself.

"Of course, *mi alma*! I have no desire to retire early and miss this fiesta with you!"

While María was gone, William talked with the guests, but his mind was distracted. Being at home again with María and their child made him realize he must focus on his quest for land and a home for them. He had accomplished so much for the missions and the Presidio, but had heard nothing from the governor about his request for land. What could be the matter?

CHAPTER 15

YERBA BUENA COVE

Soon after William and María married, he had prepared a petition to the governor of Alta California to request land at Yerba Buena Cove and the tract known as Saucelito. Padre Altimira had written a letter of recommendation, verifying that William was teaching mission neophytes carpentry and navigation as well as helping with the smallpox vaccinations of numerous Costaños at Mission Solano and Mission Dolores. William provided written proof of his baptism into the Catholic faith and stated that he had resided in Alta California for three years, married the daughter of the Presidio's comandante, collected a regular income, and amassed enough savings to support himself and his wife.

He had felt confident Governor Argüello would grant his petition for land and his naturalization as a Mexican citizen, but two years later, no word had come from Monterey, and a new governor was in office. William became apprehensive about his petition as reports about enforcement of secularization drifted north from Mexico City.

"You should apply again," María said to her husband. "To the new governor. What else can we do, *mi amore*? It's likely that your first petition was lost."

When Spain ruled Mexico and the territories of Tejas (Texas) and Alta California, the Franciscan friars' avowed goal was to baptize the indigenous people, civilize them, and give land and farm stock to each mission neophyte after ten years. Governor Argüello's replacement, Governor José Maria de Echeandía, supported the Mexican Congress's decision to secularize the missions, transferring the lands to the mission neophytes in Alta California. But even now, forty years later, the friars were unconvinced their flock was ready. They were unwilling to surrender the flourishing mission lands they had worked so hard to make productive.

María looked at her husband with sad eyes. "I worry your petition is buried under mounds of government papers. The land we desire might be awarded to another person, one of the mission neophytes. Or one of the new governor's friends!"

"I've heard Governor Echeandía is a grim military man. He's most likely distracted with enforcing the laws and the secularization decree," William reasoned.

"I long for a home of our own, William," María pleaded. "My parents' family is growing, too, and they need room."

William squeezed María's small hand. "I'll talk with your father. He can advise me." He looked at his beautiful wife, pregnant with their second child.

✠ ✠ ✠

In the evening the next day, the headlands across the bay shone like a beacon in the setting sun, distracting William from his work. While his sailors tidied the launch on the beach, William was deep in thought. His memories of Saucelito flashed in his mind. During his brief honeymoon, the lush green glens, sweet spring water, the dense forest of madrone and redwoods, and the abundant elk, deer, songbirds, and other wildlife had captivated María and William on their picnics and strolls. The governor must grant him a rancho there. But with another child arriving soon, perhaps a home at Yerba Buena Cove would be the best choice right now.

After dinner that night, he broached the subject with his father-in-law in the comandante's office.

"I know you have a lot on your mind lately," William began, "but I would like your advice, Comandante, about something María Antonia and I have been ruminating on for some time."

The lieutenant poured two tumblers of brandy and offered one glass to William. "I think I know what is on your mind," the comandante said, as he sipped his brandy. "You're interested in petitioning the new governor for the title to some land for a home. And a rancho, perhaps?" William's jaw dropped. "Don't be surprised! And don't be angry with your wife. She can hide nothing from her mother, who sees all and can draw secrets out of the most reluctant child or servant."

William smiled and rubbed his neck. Even his strong-minded wife was no match for Doña Martina. "Well, it's true. I sent the governor my petition for land but had no response. My work is evidence that I'm worthy of becoming a Mexican citizen and the recipient of a land request. I have been patient and kept quiet until now because news travels slowly. But I fear my first petition has gone astray. So, I plan to prepare another petition to request a land grant from Governor Echeandía, for the headlands north of here because of the deep, safe harbor near Saucelito."

The comandante nodded in agreement. "Ship captains can use it as a natural stopping place for their ships to be refitted and repaired before they conclude their trading around the bay."

William looked down and swirled his brandy. "It's also fine country for a rancho with a small herd of cattle and some horses. Maybe even a sawmill in time. For the present, land near Yerba Buena Cove would suit María and the children more because they'd be near you and Doña Martina. For me also since my livelihood is in trade and shipping." He paused and looked directly at Lieutenant Martínez. "However, I think both Saucelito and Yerba Buena will someday be great ports, great cities, on this bay."

Lieutenant Martínez put a hand on his son-in-law's shoulder. "You have vision, William," the comandante said. "But troubles are brewing in Alta California and here in our Presidio. I hope to retire soon and procure land across the bay, but the Mexican government is in turmoil. It has neglected its soldiers and isn't sending any pay. Although Governor Argüello assured us we'd be reimbursed for our expenses, we're still buying everything on credit. I haven't been paid a peso for many years! The soldiers and officers are angry. Their uniforms are in tatters!"

The comandante paced across the room to a window and with a furrowed brow looked out across the empty parade ground. "Spain neglected us before and now the Mexican government does, ignoring her loyal soldiers, especially those at this northern outpost. This Presidio was built to secure the border. But the walls of the battery and the Presidio are crumbling. My requests for masons and carpenters are met with official silence."

He faced William. "Our defenses are weak. As you remember, our recent Russian visitors noticed. The *Castillo de San Joaquin* was built on the headlands to defend the bay. That battery was once the strongest in Alta California. How can we guard the bay with rusting cannons? We have to beg foreign ships for cannon balls and gunpowder just to return their salute from our one serviceable cannon!"

William had witnessed firsthand Lieutenant Martínez's struggles with unruly soldiers and a government that ignored him. He was glad he and the lieutenant had agreed to collect and keep a few extra pesos from the trade ship captains grateful for the safe harbor. They needed the cash to provide for their families. The small fees and a bit of smuggling helped them avoid destitution. These slight misdeeds enabled the comandante to afford the courtesy of dinners and entertainment to ship captains and Russian naval officers.

"I'm aware of some of these problems, Comandante, but I must get my oar in for land near Yerba Buena Cove and Saucelito before Governor Echeandía grants it to someone else."

William's father-in-law shook his head slowly. "I'm afraid requests for land grants will be ignored. But I'll support your petition. María said you are a restless man, always looking ahead, striving for more. And persistent. Because of that, I'll never worry that your family will ever suffer.

"Go to Saucelito and mark off the boundaries for a rancho. I'll order two vaqueros and one of my corporals to go with you. Send your petition for the rancho again, and we'll hope the governor answers this time. We'll worry about a land grant at Yerba Buena Cove later. Meanwhile, continue directing foreign ships to the Saucelito shores to fill their water kegs."

✠ ✠ ✠

The vaqueros led the horses down the ramp from the launch to the Saucelito shore. The corporal and William mounted their horses and walked them to the first marker, a deer skull atop a stake William had pounded into the ground.

"Start measuring the land boundaries from here," he instructed the two vaqueros. One man held the end of the fifty-*vara* long reata above the deer skull while his partner rode ahead unwinding and stretching the braided leather rope its full fifty-yard length along the shoreline. William marked off the first measurement on his *diseño*, a crude map showing the bay and points of land, which he would send to Governor Echeandía with his application for the land. The corporal cleared the way through the brush, and at each stopping point, used another sun-bleached skull, notched a tree, or built a pile of stones to act as a marker for each stretch of the land grant.

"The game here is so plentiful!" the corporal said as they rode past a herd of antelope and elk grazing on a small hill.

"The land will support a herd of cattle and horses, too," William said, dismounting his horse. He knelt and dipped his cupped hand for a drink of the cold, clear water trickling from a ground spring. "Plenty of good water as well."

The survey group completed what they could that day and prepared to camp for the night. At ease with sleeping outdoors in the mild California climate, the group rolled themselves in their blankets on the ground and slept. In the morning, the men woke to the noise of hundreds of otters diving and chattering as they floated on the bay close to the shore. *Yes,* thought William, *this land will be a wonderful home for my family.*

With his survey finished, William returned to the Presidio and sent his petition to Governor Echeandía, and at the same time, he applied for naturalization to become a Mexican citizen. Again, there was no response.

BOOK 2

LIFE ON LAND AND SEA

1829–1835

Misión San Gabriel Arcángel and

El Pueblo de Los Angeles

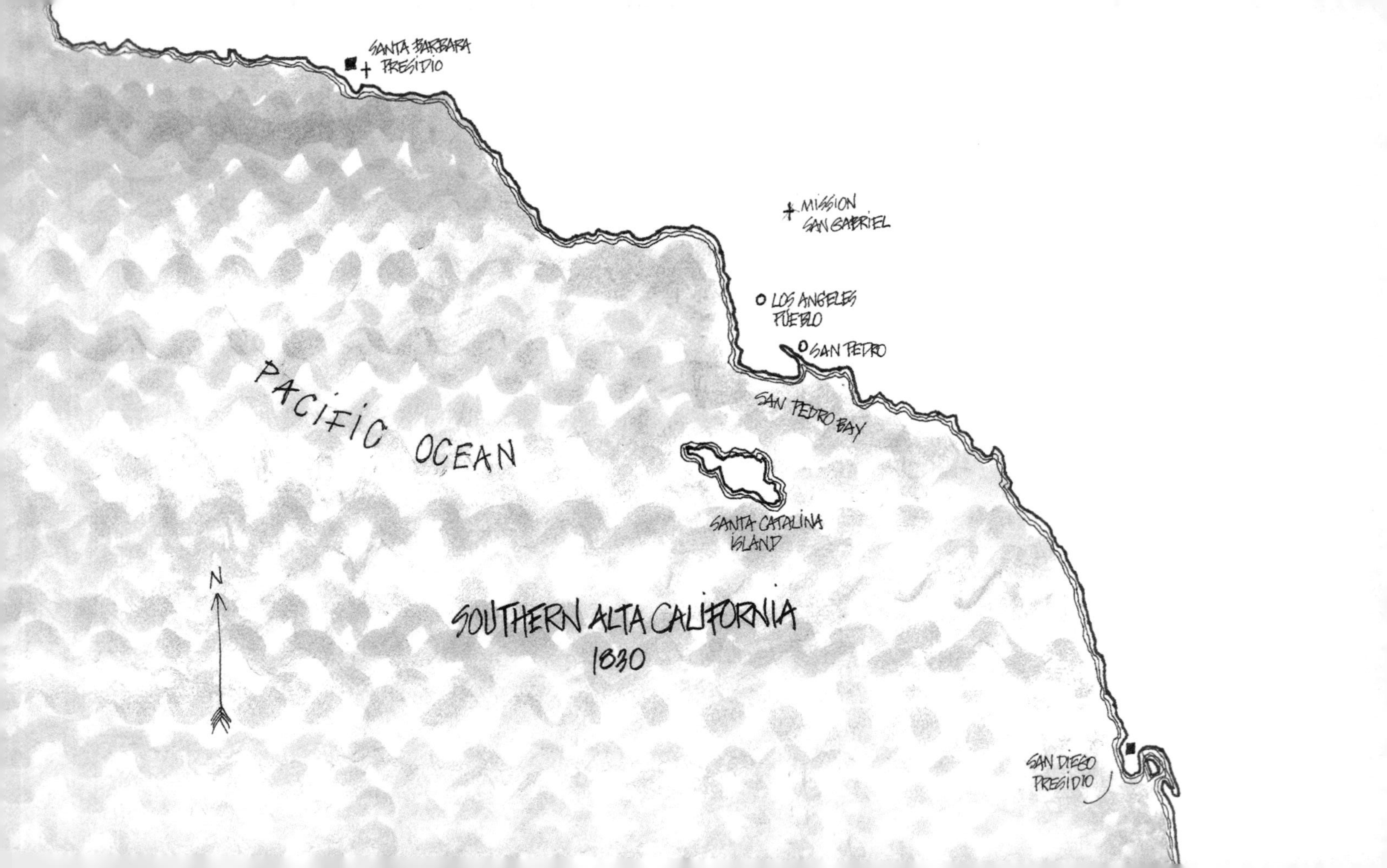
SANTA BARBARA
PRESIDIO
MISSION
SAN GABRIEL
LOS ANGELES
PUEBLO
SAN PEDRO
SAN PEDRO BAY
PACIFIC OCEAN
SANTA CATALINA
ISLAND
N
SOUTHERN ALTA CALIFORNIA
1830
SAN DIEGO
PRESIDIO

CHAPTER 16

LEAVING THE PRESIDIO

December 1829

María Antonia trudged onto the veranda at Presidio headquarters and handed a servant a bundle of children's clothing to put in the waiting oxcart. She pushed back a lock of dark hair that had escaped from her long thick braid and stared at the main gates wishing William would appear. They were sailing on the *María Antonia* today, leaving the only home she knew. She felt a hollowness inside knowing she would not see her father and her mother for several years, but she agreed with William that she and the children must move with him to southern California. She encouraged her husband to make the arrangements quickly. If they were to have a home of their own at Yerba Buena Cove, and perhaps a rancho, then they must petition the governor in person.

It would take time to arrange a meeting with Governor Echeandía. In addition to his official duties, the governor was likely preoccupied with numerous greedy Californio rancheros, hoping to acquire portions of the valuable mission lands even though they had thousands of acres already. Some mission land was supposed to be dispersed first to neophytes who worked at the missions. The rancheros' demands may have diverted the governor's attention from them as well as from William's claim, which he'd sent a year ago. Even after the governor approved his request, William would have to appear in Mexico City to finalize his petition before he acquired the land, another time-consuming process.

María shaded her eyes and she surveyed the muddy parade ground. Two of the Presidio's defensive walls surrounding the square were crumbling. One section of a collapsed wall was a trash heap of broken adobe bricks, beef bones, and rubble where dogs, fearless coyotes, and turkey vultures gathered and fought over the bones. María shook her head, doubting the Presidio, in such a neglected condition, could protect the northern border and intimidate encroaching interests of visiting foreign ships. A tattered Mexican flag that someone occasionally took the trouble to hoist, or the few ancient rusted cannons lying on decaying wooden gun carriages, or the disinterested guards in worn-out uniforms would not impress any visitor. Her father had told her he was ordered to build a guardhouse and a barracks at Yerba Buena Cove as well as a training center at the Presidio. However, since the Mexican government delivered no funds and no trained laborers, only promises, nothing was built, and the Presidio continued to deteriorate.

María looked west to the top of *Punta del Cantil Blanco* and watched another small boulder roll down the hill. Even the once mighty battery at the top seemed to be slipping as one rock at a time tumbled down the slope into the bay. One severe earthquake might carry the battery and its cannons to the knees of the high, white cliff.

María sighed and wandered inside to finish packing her family's traveling trunks. She worried about leaving her parents and her siblings. A few months before in Monterey, soldiers had staged a rebellion with the intent of overthrowing the Mexican government. They stormed the governor's offices, demanding back pay and overdue rations. Then in November, her father's life had been threatened when the rebels headed north and seized control of the San Francisco Presidio. A few officers and fifty disgruntled enlisted men had joined the rebellion and imprisoned the comandante for a time. Loyal soldiers released him and ended the uprising. María's father assured her the government would prevail. In a year or two, she would return to a rebuilt fort as strong as it had been a decade ago. Even with these reassurances, she feared for the safety of her parents and her sisters and brother.

Still, her father had urged her and William to move to Los Angeles and advised them to settle near *Misión San Gabriel Arcángel* where María's aunt Doña María Rafaela Arellano (her mother's younger sister) and other Arellano relatives lived. From there, William could easily journey from Los Angeles to San Diego, where the governor lived, and press the governor for an audience and approval of his petition for land. William agreed.

Returning to the veranda with another traveling case, María scanned the fort again and saw William galloping through the gate on his palomino.

He reined in and dismounted. "María, the tide is turning. We must set sail soon."

She hurried into the house to say a tearful goodbye to her mother and father.

✠ ✠ ✠

Over the whoosh of the wind that swelled the ship's sails, María heard her husband's commands to the crew to weigh anchor, but she didn't watch the action on deck. Standing at the ship's rail, she stared at the shore with tears in her eyes. She held her youngest child, fifteen-month-old Francisco, in her arms and hugged him. Three-year-old Mariana stood at her mother's side, clutching her skirt. They listened to the gulls' mournful crying as the ship passed between the rocky headlands at the bay's entrance. María remembered her father had said, "in two years." But when would they truly return? And would they possess their dream when they did?

✠ ✠ ✠

The sail down the Alta California coast on the *María Antonia* was uneventful. No early December storms caused delays, and they arrived in good time to disembark at San Pedro. The so-called port was just a roadstead with a few wood-planked shacks and adobes clinging together against the prevailing winds along a rocky shore.

"It doesn't seem like much now," William told María, "but with time I believe San Pedro will grow into the principal loading port for *El Pueblo de Los Angeles* and the ranchos. Someday, trading ships from Europe, New England, Peru, and Chile will anchor here."

Since the harbor was shallow, the *María Antonia* had to anchor quite a distance offshore. A small launch was sent to unload the passengers and goods from the ship. Sailors carried the children ashore and helped María pick her way over slimy, green rocks and stones slick with kelp and seaweed. While the crew unloaded trunks, chests, and bundles from the ship, William rode to a nearby rancho and purchased two horses and an oxcart for the twenty-six-mile trek north to Los Angeles. Toddler Francisco rode with María, and Mariana sat astride before William. The chests of clothing and other possessions would follow on the lumbering oxcart.

✠ ✠ ✠

The church *Nuestra Señora de los Angeles,* Our Lady of the Angels, dominated one side of the treeless plaza of *El Pueblo de Los Angeles.* The population of about 770 *gente de razón* lived in single-story adobe brick houses with flat roofs coated with tar from Rancho La Brea's tar pits. Like all Spanish pueblos, the dwellings were scattered around the plaza with several mean, unpaved streets rolling up to its edges from all directions. During the dry summers, horses and oxcarts whipped up choking, red dust clouds from the dirt streets. But now, during the wet winter, horses and carts splashed mud on pedestrians' boots and skirt hems.

The roads may have been dreary, but the little three-room houses were not. Windows alight with bright candles welcomed the Christ Child, and within green boughs and gay red berry clusters decorated each adobe.

William had arranged for his family to stay at Nathaniel Pryor's boardinghouse. Nathaniel, a silversmith and clockmaker from Kentucky, had settled in Los Angeles the previous year. A bachelor, he lived in one room of his house and rented the extra rooms to travelers since there were no hotels in the pueblo nor anywhere in Alta California. The tired children and María tumbled from their horses into Nathaniel's home, a welcome rest stop before they continued the journey to Mission San Gabriel.

The children and María ate supper and retired for the night, but William met his host in the main room to smoke cigars and talk about the mission.

"I plan to be involved in the mission's shipping business," he said to Nathaniel. "I've heard the San Gabriel herds are more abundant than those of the northern missions. There should be lots of hides and tallow to transport."

"That was true in the past," Nathaniel said. "At one time, San Gabriel owned 25,000 head of cattle, about 15,000 sheep, and more than 2,000 horses and mules, according to the friars. During the recent dry years, they slaughtered thousands of starving cattle on the overstocked land and shipped the hides from San Pedro harbor for trading in other countries. I don't know what the situation will be this year. You'll find out from the padres."

They continued talking about the growth of Los Angeles and trading ships, and then William bid goodnight to his host and trundled to bed. His thoughts whirled about his future occupation at Mission San Gabriel, hoping he hadn't misjudged his opportunity for success.

CHAPTER 17

MISIÓN SAN GABRÍEL ARCÁNGEL

After a few days of rest in the pueblo and the arrival of their trunks, William and María began the family's journey on *El Camino Real* (the Royal Road) to *Misión San Gabriel Arcángel*. Also known as "The King's Highway," it followed the route the Spaniards established to link the missions from San Diego to San Francisco Bay. The road also led south to Mexico City with offshoots into Tejas. Although government messengers, rancheros, and traders frequently traveled *El Camino*, the road was deserted that day.

Mariana chatted constantly to her father as they rode his black horse, and María restrained a wriggling Francisco on her mount. The road to Mission San Gabriel led northeast across low hills and valleys where new grass and wild mustard shoots were responding to the winter rains, covering the brown land with a faint green carpet.

Because life-giving rains had been sparse the previous two years, the animals still suffered. Bands of thin wild horses scattered as the riders approached. Horned cattle roamed freely over the hills, just as untamed as the cattle in the north. Countless long-horned skulls were strewn across the bare land, testifying to years of drought.

Near the mission, the scenery changed. The Richardsons rode past vineyards, olive trees, an orange grove, and apple and pear orchards. Snow-dusted San Gabriel and San Bernardino Mountains loomed beyond the church and mission buildings. Nathaniel had told William that during the spring, winter rains and melting mountain snow fed the *Rio San Gabriel*, the river that flowed through the valley and provided irrigation for the vast mission orchards, vineyards, and fields of grain.

The mission church, named for the Archangel Gabriel, was impressive. William and María reined in their horses and marveled at the size of the building as compared to small Mission Dolores. Stone and brick walls climbed to thirty feet high; the massive wooden front doors faced the rising sun. Buttresses supported the mission's walls, and long narrow windows manifested Spain's Moorish influences. Mariana clung to her father and looked up wide-eyed.

"Tongva people from this area built the mission. They're called Gabrielinos now. My father told me an earthquake in 1812 toppled the original bell wall," said María. "The padres had the Gabrielinos rebuild the wall as a separate *Campanario* with arched openings to hold the mission's six bells."

The Richardsons dismounted their horses at a side gate. Several neophytes hurried out to greet them and escorted them into the large, serene garden hidden behind the high surrounding walls. Birds trilled and chirped, and water trickled in a nearby fountain. Even at this time of year, pomegranate and lemon tree branches bowed down with fruit, and herbs flourished. Camellias were bursting with red buds and white blooms. Inside the mission walls, the extensive square included a military guardhouse, the padres' living quarters, guest rooms, kitchens, granaries, a whiskey distillery, and many workshops. A tiled path beneath a grapevine-covered colonnade led to the friars' quarters. A guide led the family past the blacksmith, the weaving rooms, and other workshops and then along the colonnade to the padres' rooms. The friar who sat writing at a polished mahogany desk stood as they entered. María reached for the padre's hand and kissed it in greeting. The children followed her example, as did William reluctantly.

"Captain Richardson, praise to God that you arrived safely!" the padre said. "Welcome, welcome, to you and your wife! And your beautiful children. I am Padre Sánchez. Come in and sit. Luis, refreshments for our guests."

The neophyte rushed off to fulfill the padre's request while William and María sat on two high-backed chairs at a small round table, and the children settled on a rug.

Fifty-year-old Padre José Bernardo Sánchez, a Franciscan missionary from Spain, planted himself in his desk chair. A husky man of medium height with graying hair and a light complexion, the friar was known for his successful management of Mission San Gabriel. As a result, he had been named Father-*Presidente* of the Alta California missions, the latest in the line of *Presidentes* leading back to Padre Junípero Serra. In this position, he was responsible for procuring funding for all the California missions and advising the friars in charge of them.

"Thank you for your warm welcome, Padre," William said. "After we landed at San Pedro, we rested a few days in the pueblo. But as you know, we would like to make our home here, near the mission."

María spoke up. "My aunt is Doña María Rafaela Arellano, Padre."

"Ah, yes, yes, I remember. Padre Altimira mentioned her in his letter of introduction. I'm pleased to have you resettle here and join our mission family, Señora, especially now, in time to celebrate Christ's birth. You are welcome to stay here at the mission as our guests for as long as you like. We have rooms prepared for you and your family."

Padre Sánchez turned to William. "Padre Altimira informed me of your good work, Señor, at Mission Dolores and the San Francisco Presidio. We are happy to welcome a man with your skills. This week, I'll introduce you to Señor Joseph Chapman, a talented carpenter. He plans to build a schooner for our mission with help from our neophytes. Your shipbuilding skills will be most appreciated."

The neophyte Luis carried a tray into the room, and Padre Sánchez said, "Ah, now let's have the chocolate drinks, cakes, and the fruit Luis brought and then go into the church to thank God for your safe journey."

✠ ✠ ✠

After offering prayers of thanks in the church and washing up in their guest rooms, the family mounted their horses again to ride to the Arellano adobe. Although María's aunt expected them but couldn't be sure of the exact day they would arrive, María knew her aunt would happily embrace her, William, and their two children. As with all *gente de razón* in Alta California, the Arellanos were generous hosts and enjoyed entertaining guests, family or strangers.

With directions from Padre Sánchez, María and William found the Arellano adobe. The front door flew open at William's knock. María's aunt, with three curious children clinging to her black silk skirt, stepped out the door and hugged María.

"Welcome, welcome, my dear child! I prayed you would arrive before Christmas Day. We are so excited to see you. It has been years, you a mere girl when your parents left the Santa Barbara Presidio. And now you are grown. With your own delightful family. So come in, come in! We have much to talk about."

Her aunt pulled her into the house. Between kisses and hugs, María introduced William and their children.

"And this is Cristobal, Joaquín, and Sophia." Her aunt placed her hand in turn on the head of each of the three children peeking around her. "The rest of your cousins are here, somewhere. You will meet them later. Cristobal, find your mother. Quickly!"

Doña María Rafaela turned to María and William, "Now come in, sit down, and tell us the news about the San Francisco Presidio. But more importantly, how are my sister and your father?"

✠ ✠ ✠

On Christmas Eve, María dressed herself and Mariana in their best clothes to attend High Mass and to see the Christmas pageant at the Mission. They would celebrate Christmas Day with their cousins.

"Stop wiggling so much, Mariana! I can't braid your hair!" María said to her impatient daughter.

"What will we see, Mamá? When will we eat the sweet *buñuelos,* the honey cakes?"

María tied a ribbon in Mariana's second braid. "There!" She turned her daughter to inspect her. "What will we see? There'll be a play and fireworks. Dancing and music. But first, Mass, so let's meet your father and your brother to go to church."

María took Mariana's hand, and they joined her husband and Francisco outside for the short walk to the church entrance, where they met their cousins. When joyful church bells rang at midnight for the Christmas Mass, they and the rest of the worshippers proceeded into the church, which glowed with dozens of lighted candles and was fragrant with the sweetness of incense.

At the end of the solemn service, everyone pressed back against the church nave's walls to make room for the Christmas play "*Los Pastores,*" The Shepherds. The drama began with the shepherds singing a Christmas carol while they watched their imaginary flocks of sheep. The archangel Michael appeared to announce Christ's birth and commanded the shepherds to hurry to the stable and adore Him. A boy, wearing a blue tunic and a pair of large feathered wings attached to his shoulders, acted the part of the Archangel. A gilded paper crown sat on his head, and a small sword hung from his waist.

"One day you will play the angel, Francisco," whispered María to her son. María cuddled him in her arms so that he could see the actors. She brushed back his dark hair and imagined her son as the glorious archangel brandishing his sword. He would grow up as brave and as confident as her husband, she was sure.

The crowd murmured when the Devil showed up dressed in black with a red sash draped across his chest and tied at the waist. A fierce-looking mask, horns, a pointy tail, and a sword added to his evil appearance. The Devil tried to convince the hermit, wearing a sheepskin mask with the wool shaved off except for the beard, not to go to the stable. A lazy clown in a sheepskin mask, called Old Bartholomew, stepped forward. He carried a staff with clanking tin pots tied to the top and made wisecracks while Satan and the hermit argued. Mariana, in William's arms, laughed and clapped along with the audience, even though she didn't understand the bawdy jokes.

Of course, the Devil didn't deter the shepherds from going to see the Christ Child. The last act was in the manger in Bethlehem although the Holy Family was unseen, left to the audience's imagination.

After the shepherds sang more hymns, they and the audience streamed out the huge church doors into the plaza to watch the archangel Michael and the Devil duel with their swords. Everyone applauded at the end when the Devil was defeated.

Many residents held lanterns and candles to chase away the dark while several men at one side of the plaza played guitars and violins and sang Christmas hymns. María helped Doña Rafaela and other women distribute the delicious fried sweet cakes Mariana craved. The audience as well as the troupe of actors capered about the plaza, drunk with holiday joy. Fireworks exploded, sparks scattering like glowing dandelion seeds blown across the pitch-black sky. Everyone cheered and the church bells chimed merrily. Francisco's cheeks were flushed with the night chill, and Mariana's eyes gleamed while the two children gazed at the bright fireworks. William hugged and kissed María. "A joyous omen to the beginning of our life here," he said.

✠ ✠ ✠

A few days after Christmas, Padre Sánchez, true to his word, arranged for William to meet with Joseph Chapman while María and her aunt searched for the Richardsons' permanent lodgings.

CHAPTER 18

BECOMING NEIGHBORS

On the ride to the Chapman adobe, the padre told William about Joseph.

"He's an American sailor who has lived in Alta California for ten years. Joseph married Guadalupe Ortega, the daughter of a fine Spanish family. They now have four children. You and Joseph have some similarities. He solidified his citizenship with the Mexican government by working as a carpenter, blacksmith, and jack-of-all-trades, repairing and building anything the Mission needed. His first project, a gristmill, now grinds our grain. Joseph has many skills and is always willing to help. He is very well liked.

"Now that Señor Chapman has been baptized a Roman Catholic, I view him as a model of true Catholic piety, even though he had been steeped in the Baptist faith. He follows all Church rules and readily does whatever I ask of him. Some wouldn't be so agreeable."

William stared straight ahead between his horse's ears, smiling to himself. *This friar misses nothing,* he thought, remembering his hesitation before kissing the padre's hand when they met. *I'll have to watch my tongue and show respect. And try to follow his rules.*

✠ ✠ ✠

When William and Padre Sánchez arrived at a low, whitewashed adobe with a fenced-in garden, a slim man with a full dark beard stepped out of his house to greet them. They dismounted their horses and shook hands with Joseph. The padre introduced the men.

"Joseph," the friar said, "we've come to talk with you about your plans for the new ship."

"Come inside," Joseph said, opening the door wider.

The men entered the house and greeted Guadalupe, Joseph's wife, who had set out refreshments. She invited them to sit at the large pine table in the center of the room.

"William is an experienced captain and carpenter," Padre Sánchez said, "and is interested in possibly helping you."

"It's a big job, a ninety-nine-ton top-sail schooner," Joseph said, "the first ship of its size to be built in California. We have many Gabrielino men to build her, but I welcome someone with your skills, Captain, to help me supervise their work. I have some sketches I can show you."

"The mission will pay you for your labor, of course," Padre Sánchez said.

"Always pleased to work on anything to do with the sea," William said, his voice exuding excitement at the prospect of building a schooner.

As they sipped their tea, they looked over the ship sketches laid out on the table.

"The Gabrielinos and I built the gristmill," Joseph said. "But carpentry for this ship will be a different matter for us. We'll build her at the mission, and upon completion, we'll disassemble her and move the parts by oxcarts to San Pedro Bay. There, we'll reassemble the ship and launch her."

William studied the sketches, noted a few improvements he might suggest later, but decided the plans were sound. "I'd be glad to work with you," he said.

"Excellent!" Padre Sánchez said. "A fine start to the new year."

"And where will we obtain the timber for this ship?" William asked.

"In the past, we felled in the mountains and cañons to the east and north," Padre Sánchez said. "The lumber from these trees was used in the mission's construction and to build a small ship some years ago. With our neophytes' help, we will do so again.

"I can't emphasize enough how important this ship will be for our mission as well as for the other missions in Alta California. Instead of paying foreign trade vessels to carry our goods, we'll send our mission products on our own ship along the coast, and the mission will keep all the profits. It'll be useful for another reason as well. The sea otters are plentiful near San Clemente and Santa Catalina Islands now. But the Russians, the British, and other foreigners are trapping them heavily up north and may soon ask permission to take ours. We must fill our warehouse with otter pelts before the foreigners seize them. The otter supply will not last long if they do."

✠ ✠ ✠

Although the mission servants and the friars were kind and attentive, María Antonia was impatient to move from the mission into a house of their own. Within a few weeks, she and Doña María Rafaela located an empty one-story adobe the Richardsons could rent. After a thorough cleaning and a few repairs, the house was ready to become their first home. The walls were whitewashed with a lime and water mixture, and cowhides and woven grass mats were laid on the earthen floors. William promised to install a wood floor later. Because of the mild weather in southern California, a brazier of hot coals in the main room instead of a fireplace provided warmth when needed. The Richardsons purchased a few pieces of furniture from trading vessels that called at San Pedro, and William built some furniture with Joseph's help. María unpacked the chests of clothing, china, and linens they had brought from the San Francisco Presidio, and soon she and William felt like *vecinos,* residents, of the mission community.

While María handled the household duties and the children's needs, William organized a trading voyage for the *María Antonia*. No ship can remain idle bumping around in a port for too long. She had to be on the seas, sailing to the next harbor and earning the owner money.

William arranged with Padre Sánchez to take time away from shipbuilding duties to transport a cargo of mission products. He and his crew sailed along the California coast to the other missions and the presidios, taking with them San Gabriel's fine brandy, olive oil, citrus fruits, and the mission's soap.

María included a long letter to her parents in the ship's mailbag for delivery to the San Francisco Presidio. William was confident that in his absence María and the children would be safe in their new adobe home near the *Misión San Gabriel Arcángel* and with so many family members nearby.

✠ ✠ ✠

When William returned a few months later, he threw himself into his occupation at the mission—shipbuilder. He met with Joseph, the master carpenter and architect of the project, and with another carpenter, Miguel Blanco, a tall, weathered American sea captain. At the mission carpentry workshop, they drew up lists of what was needed. Nails, tools, and canvas for sails were purchased from foreign trading ships. Timber would be cut in nearby hills and canyons. For that arduous logging job, more than a hundred laborers were needed, strong men for felling trees and sawing logs into countless board feet of lumber with two-man handsaws.

When the logging was completed and the lumber stacked at the mission site, the shipbuilding began in earnest. Joseph's prior apprenticeship with a Boston shipbuilder ensured construction proceeded smoothly. The Gabrielinos who had been trained at the mission as blacksmiths and carpenters worked on the keel, ribs, and deck beams. Gradually, the ship's skeleton arose on dry land.

✠ ✠ ✠

On Sundays, in the spring, when the sun warmed the land, people attended Mass and then socialized outdoors at *meriendas,* picnics, that Padre Sánchez hosted.

The Richardsons joined their relatives, the Chapman family, and other neighbors at the padre's favorite picnic site near the mission's gristmill. Known for his tenor voice, William entertained everyone with rollicking sailor songs as well as romantic ballads. Skillful guitarists accompanied him and provided music for dancing. Everyone danced, from babies to grandparents. Francisco stomped around in a circle in his own solo dance. Mariana clapped her hands excitedly when her father pulled her mother from the ground to dance.

"Are you happy?" William whispered in María's ear.

She smiled and said, "Very happy, *mi amore*! We have loving, generous relatives and friendly neighbors here. And I have you, little Francisco, and Mariana."

A feeling of satisfaction mixed with relief washed over William. He smiled and kissed María lightly, then whirled her around, her long black braid flying out behind her. Mariana jumped up and down begging to dance with them. William and María each took one of her hands, and the three of them waltzed through the grass together. When little Francisco cried out, "Mamá! Papá!" they circled over to him, grasped his little hands, and the four of them danced round and round together.

When the adults sat down, the children continued their fun, running freely in the grass, screeching and laughing. They played tag, hide-and-seek, and blind man's bluff with their young cousins and with the Chapman children until the smoky aroma of barbecued beef roasting on an open fire distracted them. They rejoined their parents to eat the juicy San Gabriel heifer and the fresh vegetables and ripe fruits from the mission's gardens. Families shared tortillas and baked treats with neighbors. Mission wine and chocolate drinks were available for all. Sated, the adults and children stretched out for a siesta on blankets in the sweet-smelling dry grass.

María settled her children for their naps with their cousins. Joseph's wife, Guadalupe, spread a blanket next to them for her four children, and then she began to tell a story her mother had told her and her siblings.

"The Tongva lived in this valley for a long time," Guadalupe said. "They survived many earthquakes. This story explains how Great Spirit made the land for the people to live on and why the land quakes."

María tensed and thought she should object since she and the children, and even Guadalupe herself, were members of the Catholic Church. The Bible told how God created the heavens and earth and all the creatures. Then she calmed down, reasoning that this was just a story the Tongva people told about how the world began. And that was before the missionaries introduced them to the Catholic faith. The tale would entertain the children and get them to rest.

The children listened and their restless little bodies relaxed until gradually they fell asleep. María and Guadalupe smiled at each other and lay down to rest.

All the indigenous Gabrielinos—mission workers, servants, field hands, and vaqueros—enjoyed the Sunday picnics as much as the *gente de razón*. During the long afternoon, the Gabrielinos played field hockey and competed in foot races, which the *vecinos* loved to watch. The most thrilling entertainment was the horse race.

After the siesta, William and María strolled with their children and the Chapman family to an open field of trampled grass for the horse race. Although the friars frowned on gambling, William and Joseph quietly wagered a small barrel of brandy on their favorite riders.

Likewise, the Gabrielinos secretly made bets among themselves, wildly risking most of their basic possessions—beads, knives, clothes. These items were of little importance to them, and they couldn't fathom why white men valued things when they lived in a land of such plenty.

"I can't see! Papá, lift me up so I can see the race!" said Mariana, tugging on William's trouser leg. He hoisted her onto his shoulders, and María stood next to them holding Francisco, who clapped his hands with excitement.

All the riders were Gabrielinos and dressed in lightweight shirts and trousers. They grabbed handfuls of manes and leaped onto the backs of spirited horses, twisting their bare feet through ropes tied around the horses' bellies. Stirred by the rowdy crowd, the animals danced nervously, but the skillful riders tightened the reins and brought them under control. At a signal, the horses charged forward, dust and dry grass flying from their hooves into the air. Each onlooker whooped for a favorite. Mariana cheered with her father for his chosen horse and rider.

In the end, Joseph's rider was victorious, holding onto his title from last year. William groaned but smiled as he and Joseph shook hands.

"It seems I owe you some brandy," William said in a low voice.

✠ ✠ ✠

Before dawn the next day, a thunderstorm rolled in over the Mission lands. No rain fell, but bright flashes cut through dark, heavy clouds and lit the gray sky. Lightning bolts zigzagged to the ground. One bolt found the patch of dry grass it needed to spark a fire. From that small thatch, the fire jumped to the next and the next, forming a line of flames that devoured those patches and crept forward greedily, leaving smoldering black destruction behind.

One tremendous thunderclap woke William and María from a deep sleep. William leaped out of bed and opened the window shutter to look out over the fields. The mission bells were clanging.

"What is it?" María asked.

William yanked on his trousers and boots. "I don't know. It must be an emergency."

María rose from bed. "I'm going to the children in case they are frightened."

William grabbed his hat and said, "I'm riding to the mission to find out what happened."

CHAPTER 19

LIGHTNING AND FIRE

William galloped up to the mission gates, passing soldiers and Gabrielino men mounting horses, with rakes, scythes, and shovels in their hands.

Reining in his horse and dismounting, he called to the padre, "I'm here to help. What happened?" William smelled smoke in the air.

Padre Sánchez climbed on his donkey and explained, "A lightning strike. Smoke is coming from the direction of the mill. If the fire spreads, it could consume the mill and the fields. Take an ax and shovel from the workshop."

He shouted orders to the mounted soldiers and Gabrielinos, "You men, cross the river and go up the bank to the left to keep the fire back. You know what to do! Corporal, follow them, but have your soldiers clear the grass to the right. Dig down to the soil. Make it a wide firebreak. The rest of us will tackle the middle and cut down the undergrowth near the water."

The waiting soldiers and Gabrielinos charged to the gristmill, where the Richardsons and their neighbors had picnicked the day before.

William grabbed an ax and shovel from the workshop, ready to follow the padre's crew, when Joseph and Michael White who worked with them on the ship galloped up. "How can we help?" called Joseph.

"The fire is near the mill," William said handing Joseph the shovel. "The Gabrielinos are digging a firebreak. Let's clear the undergrowth across the river in case the fire jumps it." The three friends rushed to the mill, covered their faces with wet bandanas, and waded across the river.

With no rain for the last two weeks, the river was shallow. Across the river from the gristmill, a wall of flames was spreading through the dead vegetation. If the grass fire jumped the river, the vineyards and crops, as well as the mill, would burn to cinders.

The dry, brittle grass had turned gold. It stretched out in all directions until it met the small trees and brush at the river's edge. Now bright, orange flames flicked their tongues at the dead grass, readily consuming the fuel. The vegetation snapped and sparks flew like fireworks. Smoke turned the early morning sky a murky gray.

Following the padre's orders, the Gabrielinos and soldiers spread out along the fire's perimeter, pulled up bandanas to cover their noses, and disappeared into the choking haze. With scythes and shovels, they slashed at the unburnt grass and smothered the flames with dirt. Dozens of mission neophytes scraped down to the soil with hoes and rakes. Others hacked with iron picks through the tough grass roots to widen the firebreak and rob the fire of fuel.

Padre Sánchez formed bucket brigades. Men stood shoulder to shoulder down to the riverbank. The first man filled wood buckets in the stream and passed them hand to hand to the last man who threw the water on hot spots.

Michael used a scythe, and William wielded the ax to chop down brambles and the thicket at the riverbank. Joseph tossed the debris into the water. Thick, drifting smoke made their eyes burn and water. No one spoke, saving their air just to breathe.

Hours later, the fire was defeated. Weary men dragged themselves across the river, splashing themselves to wash ash and soot from their faces and arms. Near the mill, men collapsed on the ground, gasping for breath and spitting black mucus from their throats. They pinched their noses and sneezed to clear them. Padre Sánchez, his face as smudged as any of them, thumped several men on their backs, thanking all for their courageous actions.

William, Joseph, and Michael shook hands and went home to rest. They agreed to meet later that day to work on the new schooner. William gathered his horse's trailing reins and thought how fortunate he was to have dependable neighbors willing to risk their lives if necessary. He knew they would step in to protect his family even when he was at sea.

CHAPTER 20

THE FITCH AFFAIR

While William arranged trading voyages for the *María Antonia* and built the ship with Joseph Chapman, María Antonia organized her household. Following Padre Sánchez's recommendations, she hired young Gabrielino women from the mission for housekeeping chores and cooking. Trained by her mother, she instructed the new servants in her preferences for her home. Each servant excelled in a particular job, such as sewing, washing, making tortillas, or preparing meals. María taught the new cook her favorite family recipes—empanadas, tamales, stuffed chicken, and sugary *buñuelos.*

Through her aunt, she met many of the women living near the mission and formed strong bonds with them. She became acquainted with Doña Eulalia Pérez, a short, hunched woman with sun-dried skin and frizzy gray hair worn in a tidy bun on her neck. Doña Eulalia lived close to the mission with her husband in their own adobe home, but for many years, she had served as the padre's housekeeper, residing at the mission. Her duties as housekeeper included overseeing the sleeping quarters where all the young mission girls were locked in every night as protection from molestation. However, customs were changing. Ever since the Mexican government ordered the missions to secularize, fewer Gabrielinos were staying at Mission San Gabriel *rancheria,* and fewer children were living under the mission roof.

The remaining young girls were encouraged to work for the *gente de razón* households. With advice from Doña Eulalia and María's Aunt Rafaela, María hired Lucia, a young Gabrielino, as a nanny for Mariana and Francisco. Grateful for the doña's advice, María soon returned the favor when her aunt told her about the predicament of a particular young woman under Doña Eulalia's care.

With her own home under control, María had more time to spend with her aunt and cousins. The children accompanied María, with their nanny Lucia, on her visits. María and Rafaela often sewed and gossiped about local people and life at the mission while the children played with their Arellano cousins under the attentive eyes of mission girls and women hired to keep trouble among them to a minimum. Their older cousins thought of games for them to play together and places to explore near their adobe. María encouraged Mariana to follow the example of her cousins, even helping with simple chores. They hauled water from a well and filled large barrels near the kitchen for the Arellano's cook. The strongest of them carried wood logs for the kitchen fire while Mariana, only four years old, carried small bundles of branches.

During one visit in July, the children played follow-the-leader, jumping, trotting, and balancing on a log, with Lucia's help. María settled beside her aunt in the shade on the veranda to embroider poppies on a blouse for Mariana. Curious about a new couple who had landed in San Diego, she asked her aunt if she knew them.

"Ah, yes, the Fitches." Doña María Rafaela lowered her embroidery into her lap, and as she stared into the orchard where the children were now chasing one another, her blue eyes, so like María's mother's, filled with tears. "What a romance Josefa has had! And so much heartache!"

María searched her aunt's face with concern. "Why? What happened?"

"Captain Henry Delano Fitch," Rafaela said, picking up her embroidery again and poking her needle through, "a handsome young man. An American sea captain. He and Josefa met in San Diego at her father's house and fell in love. Her father is Don Joaquin Carrillo, a retired soldier. He agreed the two could be married after Captain Fitch was baptized. Their wedding day was set for a day in April a year ago. I remember the Carrillo house was decorated with lilies and fragrant orange blossoms. Family guests had arrived, and the padre was dressed in his elegant vestments, ready to celebrate the marriage. But the ceremony never took place."

María was puzzled. "But all seemed to be in order. Her father had agreed to the marriage, and Captain Fitch was baptized. What prevented the union?"

"The governor. First, as the ceremony began, Josefa's uncle strode into the room and demanded the padre to stop by order of Governor Echeandía. The friar himself was threatened with military and ecclesiastical punishment if he did not desist! The entire assembly was shocked. The poor padre was frightened and embarrassed. He quickly took off his vestments and left."

"How distressing and sad! Why was there an objection to this marriage?"

"According to His Excellency, several formalities were disregarded. For instance, no banns of marriage were announced at the parish church."

"That is scandalous, but surely that is a church matter, not the governor's."

"People are used to obeying authority. The governor speaks and all bend to his will. No one wants to face this governor's wrath."

"What did Josefa and Captain Fitch do?"

Doña María Rafaela laid her embroidery in her lap again and sighed as she looked at María. "They eloped. Soon after this embarrassing scene in her home, Josefa secretly boarded a ship bound for Valparaíso, Chile, with Captain Fitch. They married there last July. Josefa knew the governor would oppose her marriage to anyone. You see, Governor Echeandía had wanted

Josefa for himself and had courted her." Doña Rafaela shook her head. "What a thin, soulless man he is! Spiteful! He detested Captain Fitch ever since Josefa chose the captain, not him. He was furious at their escape, claiming Josefa was abducted. Even today, a year later, he still holds this grudge. That's why the captain, Josefa, and their child might be arrested soon."

María looked out at the children, playing freely in the sun, and thought about the Fitches' difficulty, wondering what she and William would have done had they faced such opposition to their marriage. "What will happen to them now?"

"There might be an ecclesiastical trial," her aunt said. "Padre Sánchez is the President of the missions. He will decide what will be done." Then her aunt glanced at her niece's anxious face and smiled, putting her hand on María's. "I have hope that all will be well."

✠ ✠ ✠

As with any momentous event in Alta California, the homecoming of Josefa and her husband Henry Fitch, even though under a threatening cloud, called for a celebration. Everyone in the area was invited to a ball at the Carrillo home, but people gossiped among themselves, astonished this celebration would happen. Wasn't Josefa's elopement scandalous and their marriage suspect? Governor Echeandía will be furious. However, the governor was in Monterey at present so nothing would prevent the Californios from having a merry dance.

✠ ✠ ✠

María wore a splendid silk dress and her favorite pearl earrings and necklace William had given her when they were married. Mariana wriggled with excitement while her nanny Lucia tried to dress her.

The Richardsons were in San Diego for the Carrillo's ball. They were staying with friends of the Arellano family for several nights, except young Francisco who had recently recovered from a fever. To avoid overexcitement and as a precaution against a relapse, he remained with his cousins near the San Gabriel Mission.

Everyone was dressed in their finest. William and the other men in the household mounted their horses. Mariana rode to the Carrillo house with her mother, her great-aunt Doña Maria Rafaela, and several other family members in a gaily decorated *carreta*. The young girl grew more and more restless in the slow oxcart because she heard the music long before they arrived.

Dozens of candles lit up the Carrillo house, and fragrant orange tree boughs decorated the interior. Musicians played a lively tune on their violins and guitars. The caballeros in velvet jackets and señoritas in voluminous silk gowns whirled around the great room and sang old Spanish folk songs while watchful dueñas observed them from the edges of the dance floor. Servants had prepared a supper of freshly roasted beef, olives, cheeses, delicious cakes, and rich wines, a lavish spread to ensure a warm welcome for Don Carrillo's guests and to honor his daughter and her husband.

Although María and William had not yet met them, they were sympathetic to the young couple's plight. They knew from their own experience how difficult it was to obey all the Church rules for marriage but also the government's rigid laws for immigrants.

When they walked through the door to the Carrillo *sala*, Mariana squealed with delight when she saw her cousins and skipped over to join them.

Doña Rafaela guided María and William over to the Fitches, where she introduced them to Josefa, who wore a dark wine silk dress, and to her husband, Henry, in his captain's coat.

"María and Captain Richardson reside near Mission San Gabriel and are eager to make your acquaintance."

María gently touched Josefa's arm and said, "We are so pleased you returned but are upset to hear of your difficult situation. Both William and I are ready to aid you in any way we can."

Henry Fitch shook William's hand, two sea captains at instant rapport with one another. The women moved away to greet other friends, and then the men discussed the Fitches' year in Valparaíso. William summarized his current work on the Mission's schooner, as well as his decision to remain in California and his luck in courting his beautiful wife.

"Ah, so you had to face the same challenges I did to be accepted by the Mexican government and marry," Henry said. "But converting to their religion stuck in my craw. I almost persuaded the San Diego Presidio friar to skip the baptism."

William chuckled. "I had similar misgivings. But my father-in-law, the San Francisco Presidio comandante, convinced me that when his daughter was ready to give me her whole heart, such a triviality as religion shouldn't stand in my way. I made the right decision."

"In my case, the governor was the major blockade," Henry said. "After I had bowed to all their requirements, the governor put his oar in and stopped the marriage. I was furious! But my brave Josefa agreed to sail with me secretly to Chile and marry there. My gallant friend Pío Pico, in sympathy with my heart's desire, agreed to help. After I bid *adios* to my Presidio *amigos* and my beloved, I boarded my vessel for South America. On land that night, as soon as it was dusk, Josefa crept out of her house to meet Pío, and together they galloped to the beach on his horse. He helped her into the boat I had arranged to carry her to my ship, which was anchored just offshore." Henry smiled ruefully and gazed across the room at his wife deep in conversation with several friends. "We were married in Valparaíso in July, soon after we arrived. We now have a handsome son. But I might have the devil to pay. I will send the good padre our marriage certificate when we reach San Pedro harbor and pray that will settle things. My ship *Leonor* carries an excellent cargo from Chile, which I hope will also pour oil on these rough waters."

"So you will continue up the coast?" William asked.

"After San Pedro, we stop in Santa Bárbara and then Monterey."

"I wish you luck and calm seas, Señor, but also offer you my services if you need them."

When the two men turned to survey the dance floor, William spied María and Josefa approaching them with a regal young woman unknown to him but almost a twin to Josefa.

After introducing her, María said, "Doña Francesca is Josefa's sister and the wife of Lieutenant Mariano Guadalupe Vallejo, now serving at the San Francisco Presidio."

"I have heard of the many successful military actions your husband has had recently with the *Costeños*, Señora," William said. He didn't mention how courageously the native people had fought to remain free or how the well-armed soldiers overwhelmed them in vicious, bloody attacks. William detested the bloodshed. "I hope the conditions in the North will be more peaceful soon."

"As do I," Francesca said. "I have not heard when it might be safe to join him. I remain in San Diego until then."

Josefa, Francesca, and Henry Fitch turned to greet other guests. The musicians struck up a new tune. William bowed to his wife and kissed the back of her hand.

"May I have this dance, *mi amore*?" He guided her onto the dance floor, and the Chapmans and the Fitches joined them. He wondered about the Fitches and their future. Would they be as happy in a few weeks if there was a trial contesting their marriage?

✠ ✠ ✠

The day after the ball, Henry Fitch and his family sailed north on the *Leonor*, stopping at San Pedro to send their marriage documents to Padre Sánchez and then continuing up the coast. When the padre reviewed their marriage certificate, he wasn't satisfied and sent word to Monterey to arrest Captain Fitch. Henry and his family returned to Los Angeles and guards escorted him to guest quarters at Mission San Gabriel, essentially under house arrest. Josefa and her infant son moved into Doña Eulalia Pérez's small adobe to await her husband's trial.

When María visited Josefa soon after, Doña Eulalia met her outside to speak with her before they entered the house.

"Padre Sánchez told me the governor is displeased with the living arrangement for Doña Josefa," the old woman said to María. "He claims because she lives in my adobe so close to the mission, she's able to see her husband daily. This is no punishment at all, according to him. Also, my humble home is too small for my family as well as the Fitches. Do you think you might find it in your heart to lodge Doña Josefa and her son with you?"

María agreed to speak with William but assured the kind woman that she was sure new arrangements could be made. She had not forgotten Doña Eulalia's kindness and advice and was eager to do her this service.

After dinner that evening, when the children were settled in bed, María sat next to William as he sipped a brandy.

"I have been asked to do a favor for the Fitches, *mi amore*." She explained Doña Eulalia's request.

"So, our temperamental governor is still jealous and wants to inflict more punishment on Fitch. I suppose we can make room for Josefa and her son. It might be good for you to have the company of another woman."

Within a few days, a room was prepared, and Josefa and her son moved in. Mariana and Francisco were happy to have a new baby to fuss over. Lucia helped with the infant as well. With William at sea on the *María Antonia* or working at the mission shipyard on the *Guadalupe* from dawn to dusk, María was pleased to have Josefa in the house as a companion.

✠ ✠ ✠

Josefa's move to the Richardsons' adobe did not satisfy Governor Echeandía. After the governor returned from Monterey to the San Diego Presidio, he heard about the ball welcoming the Fitches back to California. He seethed with anger. Clearly, he detested Henry. Unable to turn the *gente de razón* against the Fitches, he was determined to punish them in some other way, so he announced that Josefa was no longer allowed to visit Henry at the mission. Since Padre Sánchez did not wish to anger the governor further, he agreed to this proclamation.

"The man has no heart. He is punishing my son and me as much as Henry!" moaned Josefa to María as she paced the floor in the Richardson's adobe. "What can I do?"

María had been sitting at the table writing a letter to her parents while the children napped. She folded her letter and then turned to her friend. "Why don't you write letters to Henry? I'll deliver your messages to him secretly when I visit the mission on some errand or other. Tell him what your son is doing and what is in your heart."

Josefa bent down and hugged María. "You would do this for us? And maybe Henry can write also. Will you be allowed to see him?"

"The governor said nothing about visitors. We will not mention this to anyone."

They were taking a risk, but María knew how lonely and worried she felt when William was on a trading voyage. However, her husband would have to agree to this plan. After supper, she spoke with him as they walked arm in arm in the cool evening garden while Josefa helped Lucia prepare the children for bed.

"You and Josefa seem to be getting along well, like sisters. Is she happy here?" he asked.

María pulled her shawl tightly around her shoulders and looked up at the starry night sky. "How can she be happy when separated from her husband? She can no longer even see him. I know her heart is breaking. I talked with her today about writing to Henry and he to her. I offered to carry their messages secretly. You could too."

"Is that wise, María? The governor is furious that the *gente de razón* are so sympathetic. If he finds out we're carrying clandestine missives, I fear our actions will ruin our petition for our land." William stopped and faced his wife. "I've been working hard to get Padre Sánchez on our side, too. He knew I helped immunize the people at the northern missions against smallpox, so he pressed me to do the same at Mission San Gabriel. Because of that and my shipbuilding work, the padre trusts me now. I don't want to break that trust."

"Helping Padre Sanchez is the right thing to do, *mi amore*. Helping the Fitches might be risky and may not be wise, but it also is the right thing to do," María said, looking up into her husband's concerned face. "I will tell the padre when I see him."

✠ ✠ ✠

At the beginning of the ecclesiastical trial, Henry was charged with abduction and adultery. The church's prosecutor alleged that the Fitch marriage ceremony in Chile was invalid because neither of them were a member of that parish in Valparaíso. Also, Josefa had not received permission from her own parish priest in California to marry there. In his defense, Henry produced their marriage certificate signed by a Chilean priest and a notary, but the prosecutor found it faulty. If these claims were accepted, Henry and Josefa realized their son would be considered illegitimate. They both swore they did not know the canon law and believed their marriage was legal. They pleaded with the court and with Padre Sánchez to accept their marriage.

The court proceedings were held in a room at the mission, and María attended when she could to support Josefa. Her heart ached for her new friend, knowing herself what people in love will do. She had carried many letters to Henry from Josefa, aware of how much the couple longed for each other.

At the end of December, Padre Sánchez delivered his verdict. "I am declaring that the marriage was valid but irregular," the padre said. "You have caused a great scandal in the Church. In atonement, you must perform this penance: when you attend Mass on three festival days, you will carry lighted candles to signify to others your contrition for your sin and you must recite the rosary together for thirty days. You are also ordered to supply a bronze bell for the pueblo's church *Nuestra Señora de los Angeles.* It must be a fifty-pound bell, to be hung in the church's belfry."

Josefa hugged her father and her sister Francesca who sat next to her, and with tears streaming down her face, rushed to the front of the room to embrace her husband.

✠ ✠ ✠

After Padre Sánchez absolved the Fitches, they were reunited as a family. Josefa and her son moved from the Richardsons' home, and María and William were again alone in their snug adobe with their children. Though the Gabrielino servants carried out numerous household duties during the day, they returned to their families and their own homes at night.

William stayed with María and the children throughout the winter while he was occupied with the new schooner, the *Guadalupe,* but when spring arrived, María faced months on her own while William was at sea. Bears, coyotes, and wolves prowled close to the scattered adobes at night. Often a distant gunshot from one of the houses was heard. María loaded her pistol as well as a rifle, prepared to protect her children when she was alone.

CHAPTER 21

LIFE WITHOUT WILLIAM

In the spring, William prepared the *María Antonia* for a trading voyage. María had washed and mended his shirts, and on the day he was to sail, packed them into his seaman's bag.

"It will probably be only a month or so," William said, tenderly stroking María's swelling belly. "I don't want to leave you too long with our next child on the way." María had told him she wasn't pleased with his long absences. He gently squeezed her hand. "I'm also worried because Francisco seems to get ill more frequently during these wet months. I don't like the high fevers he runs."

"I can take care of everything," María assured him caressing his face. "The children and I will be fine. My relatives are nearby, my women are well trained and competent. I'll have few problems. Even Mariana is beginning to help me with Francisco. Don't worry about us."

William threw back his head and laughed. "That's like telling the rain to stop! Of course I'll worry. I'll be thinking of you every day."

William took María in his arms and kissed her and then knelt on one knee to hug Mariana and Francisco. "I'll bring you special treats when I return." He reached for María again to give her a long, lingering kiss before he picked up his bag and stepped out the door.

✠ ✠ ✠

The next day was sunny but still cool. Fruit trees in the family garden had sprouted leaves so María decided it was warm enough to plant early vegetables. She hired one of the Gabrielino men to turn over the soil and prepare it for sowing. After he finished his work, María, with the help of her kitchen servant Marguerite, dug furrows for pea and bean seeds. She could hear the children playing in the house with Lucia. The chickens murmured contented clucks and wandered over the newly turned soil, pecking for grubs.

"Marguerite, please fetch two buckets of water for the garden. I'll start sowing the seeds." Though a little awkward with the growing child, María knelt to begin her job. Alone in the garden, she became absorbed in her work.

A horse snorted, startling her, and a soldier's black boots appeared at her side. Taken by surprise, María tipped over sideways onto her backside when she twisted to face him. Towering over her stood a muscular man, with curly dark hair, a mustache, and a small scar on his chin. His horse stood outside the garden gate, which Marguerite had left open when she dashed out for the water.

"My dear lady, are you all right?" he politely inquired. Offering her his hand, he pulled her to her feet. "When I saw you on the ground, I thought you were in distress."

Taken off guard but at ease in her own garden, María brushed dirt off her skirt, feeling slightly embarrassed. "Thank you for your concern, Señor. I was sowing seeds and waiting for my servant to return with water for them." She stared at him and said, "Your face is not familiar to me. I thought I knew all the soldiers stationed at the Mission."

"Ah, I have recently come to San Gabriel. Sergeant Juan Luis Feliz. At your service." He bowed his head but continued firmly holding her hand, his eyes boring into hers. The soldier's closeness and familiarity made her apprehensive. And irritated. How dare he, a stranger, enter her garden without warning!

María tugged her hand from his grasp just as Marguerite entered by the gate lugging two buckets of water. Feliz stepped back and asked, "And your name, Señora?"

Still irked, María held her chin up and answered, "María Antonia Martínez Richardson, Señor. I am grateful for your concern, but as you can see, all is well."

"I hope to see you again soon," he said, giving a short bow. Although he smiled, his bold eyes did not. Whistling, he sauntered away through the open garden gate, mounted his horse, and rode toward the mission.

María stared in the direction of the sound of the retreating horse. Disturbed by the encounter, she asked, "Marguerite, have you ever seen that soldier before?" Marguerite shook her head.

"Well, if I see him at Mass, I'll ask the padre about him." Pushing the impertinent Sergeant Feliz from her mind, María brushed her skirt again and turned to her garden. "Now let's finish our work here so we can go in to help the cook prepare supper."

✠ ✠ ✠

María never saw Feliz in church and thought nothing more of her rude visitor. One soldier was insignificant since so many soldiers were assigned to the mission guardhouse. María grew up around soldiers and usually felt at ease with them. She didn't even think to mention the incident to William when he returned home weeks later. Besides, a more important distraction occupied everyone at this time.

The *Guadalupe,* the first vessel of her size built in California, was ready for her maiden voyage. Many people flocked to San Pedro from near and far to see her launched. The finished ship was dismantled at the mission and hauled overland in a parade of *carretas* to the San Pedro harbor, where it was reassembled and waiting to be launched.

Invitations to the launching were sent to government officials, rancheros, and other prominent Californios. María and the children, the Chapman family, and many others made the long trip to the harbor to witness the event. People lined the steep bluffs above the beach, sitting around bonfires to keep warm. Others raced their horses in nearby fields while waiting. Some people climbed into canoes and other watercraft to view the spectacle from the bay. Everyone cheered when the ship slid down the hill and into the water.

✠ ✠ ✠

William, the first master of the *Guadalupe*, sailed the schooner on a short trip to Santa Bárbara. In July, he made a longer voyage to San Blas, Mexico, and planned another voyage for the fall.

The mission built another smaller ship, a 30-ton schooner named the *Refugio*, that year, prompting William to sell his sailing vessel *María Antonia* and eliminate the financial liability for owning a ship. Instead, he rented cargo space on the mission's schooners for his small loads of hides and otter pelts for trade, which supplemented his income earned from his navigation duties.

On August 3, 1831, while William was at sea, María gave birth to their second son. Her aunt and other relatives, as well as the competent Doña Eulalia Pérez, fussed over her and helped ease the birth. María and William had chosen the name Esteban Jesús for their third child, if he was a boy.

"He is perfect, María," Doña Eulalia said, as she laid the child in her arms for the first time. "God has blessed you with three beautiful children."

Although Mariana and Francisco were eager to see their new brother, Lucia made sure their hands and clothes were clean before they were allowed to approach their mother's bed. Mariana clasped her hands and squealed in delight at her tiny brother. But when Esteban bawled, Francisco put his hands over his ears and cried in sympathy.

The women laughed and Doña María Rafaela picked him up, clucking at him. "It's all right, Francisco! Esteban can't speak words yet like you. Crying is his way of saying he is hungry." María stretched out one hand to Francisco as she began to nurse the baby. Rafaela then said, "See, your mama knows what he wants. Her milk."

Francisco quieted and Mariana took his hand. "When Esteban is older, we will have such fun together, the three of us," she said. "Let's play hide and seek now in the garden with Lucia. Mamá and our baby brother need to rest."

Rafaela and María watched the two children walk out the door hand in hand. "She knows just what to say to him even though she is only five," María murmured. "He adores her. I'm pleased I can depend on her."

✠ ✠ ✠

When William returned from Mexico on the *Guadalupe*, Padre Sánchez baptized Esteban at Mission San Gabriel, and the Richardsons held a feast to celebrate his birth. María's aunts and uncles and her many new friends made a great fuss over her and the boy. William whispered in María's ear that he was pleased he had a healthy son and that she was fine. The only thing that marred María's happiness was that her parents weren't present.

A few months later William was packing his bag again. "I must leave you alone once more, my love. A longer trip I'm afraid, down to Mazatlán and San Blas. Miguel Blanco will be master of the *Guadalupe* this time, but I'm in charge of the cargo. The mission gave us a valuable load—dried beef, olives, wine, casks of San Gabriel's famous brandy, and its fine soap. We'll be paid well for our services."

María struggled to smile. She knew these trips were necessary, but she still missed her husband. Like most Californio wives, the husband's business was all important. María grew up understanding that wives had little control over a husband's decisions. Because María's father was a soldier, her mother had even less influence on their family's life than María had.

Sighing, María said, "I understand, William. I'll be patient. The children and I will be praying for your safe return."

At least she felt secure near Mission San Gabriel with her new friends and relatives, people she could depend on, but quiet nights could be lonely. Her life here was so different from her life at the Presidio under the protection of her mother and father. She ached to live near them.

✠ ✠ ✠

Life at San Gabriel continued much as before, but María was busier now with three children. Lucia helped by caring for Mariana and Francisco, and Mariana tried to help her mother, carrying food or drinks to her as she nursed little Esteban. María's attention was fully consumed with her children's needs and household duties.

One evening, after William had been gone a few weeks, the servants left for the night, and María tucked the children in bed. Smelling smoke, she stepped into the dark garden. Thoughts of another grass fire troubled her. She sniffed again. No, that was cigar smoke.

The moon shed enough light for her to see a shadowy figure standing near the garden wall. When he saw her, he tossed his cigar to the ground and crushed it under his boot.

"Who's there?" she called loudly and sternly.

Sergeant Feliz stepped forward and identified himself. "Such a lovely night, I decided to take a ride."

"What are you doing hiding in my garden? Leave at once!"

Feliz stepped closer to María, stared at her outraged face, and shifted his gaze downwards. "I'm not hiding. I've been admiring you. And I see you are no longer with child." He locked eyes with her. "And you're alone."

María stepped back, now fearful of this man.

"Perhaps you would be interested in a man's comfort. I'm certain no one will hear us."

He was right. No one could hear them, even if she screamed. The adobes were too far apart. Feliz advanced slowly toward her. Her eyes darted, looking for an escape or weapon. Then the door squeaked. Her head and Feliz's swiveled. Mariana in her nightdress slid to her mother's side.

Feliz leered at María. "Ah, your daughter! Well, never too soon for her to learn what men enjoy."

Horrified about what might happen, María knew she was ready to die to defend herself and her daughter.

Trembling, Mariana edged closer to her mother. María felt something heavy bump against her leg. It was the loaded pistol. Quickly she reached for it and aimed it at the intruder. Rage and anger surged over her.

"And you will learn what your Maker thinks of your intentions, Sergeant, if you do not leave now." The pistol held only one bullet. She couldn't miss, she must not miss.

Moonlight glinted on the muzzle of the pistol. Feliz held up his hands and backed away. "*Caramba*! I merely thought you might be lonely and in need of company. But—I see you are not interested. I will go." Step by step, he backed up to the wall, his eyes fixed on the pistol María held. Then he turned and hoisted himself over the wall. María heard his horse gallop away into the night.

She lowered the gun and embraced Mariana. "Thank goodness you knew what to do. You are a brave girl!"

"I heard a stranger's voice and you sounded angry. So, I got up to bring you the pistol. You're not angry that I touched it, are you? I carried it like you and Papá do."

"You did exactly the right thing, *cariño*, sweet one. I am so proud of you." She hugged her daughter again and squeezed her eyes shut to prevent tears from falling. "Now let's go inside and get you back in bed. You are shaking from the cold. All is now well. We are safe."

Once again in bed, Mariana drifted into a child's deep secure sleep, but María stayed up listening for any creak, any rustling, her pistol and loaded rifle nearby.

✠ ✠ ✠

The next day María galloped to the mission. Although no one could identify Sergeant Feliz, Padre Sánchez fumed to hear this stranger had threatened María. Several Presidio soldiers who had been at the Mission had left early that morning to return to the San Diego Presidio. Because soldiers report to the governor, the padre explained, he couldn't demand any of them return to answer for an indiscretion. Friars were powerless over military matters.

Furious with the friar for doing nothing, María returned home and took out the pistol and bullets. She had been naive about their safety. They were isolated in this adobe, no other adults, her husband often away. She regretted having to rely on her daughter. So young! But she remembered learning to fire a pistol and a rifle when she was not much older than Mariana. Because of her skill, she had saved Felipe from the mountain lion. Mariana must learn to protect herself and others in this wilderness from beasts, both wild animals and menacing men.

She directed Marguerite to stand small, fat logs on top of tree stumps near the rear garden wall. Then she called Mariana to her side.

"I'm going to teach you how to shoot."

✠ ✠ ✠

After his four-month trip on the *Guadalupe* to Mazatlán and San Blas, Mexico, William returned in February of 1832 to many surprises at home. Francisco and Mariana were learning to ride, and his daughter could now shoot a pistol.

When María explained why she had taught Mariana to shoot, William's eyes turned stormy blue, his face clouded with anger and fear for his family's safety. He pulled her to him, encircling her protectively, grateful she and Mariana were unharmed. How could he possibly safeguard them when he was away on trading voyages so often? María tried to soothe his worries and had Mariana shoot at a paper target in the garden to demonstrate her skill.

"The San Diego soldiers are gone from the mission guardhouse," said María. "I'm not afraid but will be more cautious, prepared for wolves and bears, but also for strangers."

"If I had been here, I would have shot the bastard!" William growled, clenching his fists. "Or at least beaten him senseless."

His young daughter shouldn't be the one to protect her mother and brothers. Mexican troops protected the mission and the rancheros from violent Gabrielinos. But some soldiers who were sent to serve in Alta California had been imprisoned in Mexico. They couldn't be trusted.

Was it possible the former governor, Echeandía, recently replaced by Manual Victoria, was behind the incident? Was he encouraging harassment of his family in revenge for their help with the Fitches?

Having served in the British navy, William was intimately familiar with violence and the worst side of men, their unquenchable thirst for revenge. He knew the cruelty they were capable of to satisfy their raw appetites if given the opportunity.

As master or supercargo of mission ships, he had to sail the brigs down the coast and to Mexico. During those trading voyages, William brooded constantly. How could he be in two places at once, sailing a ship for the Mission and at home guarding his family?

CHAPTER 22

AN EDUCATION

Because Mariana had watched her older cousins ride everywhere, she had begged her mother to teach her. María explained that she and Francisco would learn the same way all Californio children learned to ride.

Every sunny day, Lucia took the children to the mission orchards for riding lessons. Aunt Rafaela and the children's cousins accompanied them to help. They placed Mariana and Francisco on young calves and led them around the fenced orchard. Later, when the children were allowed to ride their small steeds alone, they didn't have too far to fall if the calves acted up. When their father came home, the children eagerly showed off their riding skills.

"Oh! Oh!" Mariana yelled as her calf took off at a gallop. She clung to the reins, her little legs gripping the animal's sides. When the calf came to a sudden stop, she pitched forward onto its neck and slid off to the soft ground under the fruit trees. She sucked in her lower lip and pouted in frustration. While her cousin Cristobal chased after the runaway calf, she picked herself up and dusted off her dress.

María was nursing baby Esteban and watching her daughter and her son from a chair under a shade tree. William, next to her, jumped up, but María put her hand on his arm to restrain him.

Mariana heard her mother call, "Don't be discouraged, Mariana! Everyone falls off a few times. You can do this."

William sat down. Mariana gritted her teeth, walked over to her calf, and mounted with Cristobal's help. She spent the next half hour riding the calf and falling off, until the poor animal was worn out. Francisco had already quit. But they would try again the next day, and the next, until their mother judged they were skilled enough to try a saddle horse.

✠ ✠ ✠

William held bitter feelings for former Governor Echeandía, who now claimed to be governor *pro tem*, but after returning home from sea, he learned Californios reviled Manual Victoria, the governor of the past year. Victoria was known for his cruelty in the name of law and order. In previous years, Governor Echeandía had tried—unsuccessfully—to secularize the missions by giving land to the Gabrielinos and other mission neophytes in Alta California. His edict to give away the Church's lands infuriated the friars who had put their souls into building the missions, winning converts, yes, but also making profits. They would not meekly turn the missions over to others to run.

The Congress had replaced Echeandía in January 1831 with Manuel Victoria, who sided with the Church. While William was at sea during the last few months, Governor Victoria's politics and severe punishments had stirred up an angry backlash and finally a confrontation.

✠ ✠ ✠

María encouraged William to invite Nathaniel Pryor and Joseph Chapman for supper to hear the full story about Mexican politics and what happened in November and December, the incident at Cahuenga Pass.

His friends arrived a few days later, eager to hear news from William about the rest of the world and to relate the unsettling tale about the shaky Mexican government.

With the children settled in bed, María covered the table with a fresh white linen tablecloth, set out a fine meal for her husband and his friends, and sat at the table with them to hear about the battle at Cahuenga Pass.

Joseph began. "To my mind, Echeandía was always a mean-spirited, pompous man, thinking only of himself and his health," Joseph said. "But the newcomer, Victoria, I think you'd agree, was the worst governor yet! Besides reversing all the secularization efforts, he willfully changed the criminal laws. He declared California must be crime-free."

"He ordered many severe punishments for minor crimes," Maria added. "We learned of two neophytes who stole food from a mission. Usually the priest dispenses the punishment, such as extra work for a week. But this brute of a governor ordered the death penalty for both! They were shot! All the people as well as the padres were shocked."

"But this was only the beginning," Joseph said. "Victoria declared the members of the Alta California legislature, the *diputación*, were illegally elected, so he would not call for a convention. No meeting meant he could rule without them."

"That egotistical bastard!" William said. "Thinking he could administer justice as he did in the military and take away our representation. He might be a courageous soldier, but he knows nothing about ruling as a governor."

"While you were gone, several of our leading citizens objected too," Nathaniel said. "Don Pío Pico, as a senior speaker of the *diputación,* and Joseph Bandini, José Carrillo, and Abel Stearns."

"I'm not surprised Abel joined in," William said as he poured each man a glass of brandy. "I've done some trading with him. A shrewd businessman. Supporting the Californios would support his interests."

"These men urged Echeandía not to return to Mexico but to stay in San Diego," continued Nathaniel, "thinking that Victoria wouldn't be governor for long. Of course, Victoria, sitting up in Monterey, was furious when he heard this. He declared Carrillo and Stearns guilty of treason and banished them from Alta California."

"No trial, of course!" Joseph said. "And this led to the revolt and battle.

"Though banished, José Carrillo and Abel Stearns raised an army of discontents in Baja California, planning to depose Victoria. They marched north over *El Camino Real* and easily seized San Diego since the Presidio soldiers supported Echeandía. The rebels persuaded Echeandía to re-assume command of the territory. They pressed on to Los Angeles, where everyone who despised the new governor joined the rebellion against the tyrant. By November, when the rebel leaders learned Victoria was marching south from Monterey, they resolved to march north to engage him and his army. Victoria's troops included Captain Pacheco and soldiers from San Francisco and the Monterey Presidio.

"The two forces met head on at Cahuenga Pass on December fifth. Victoria had about thirty trained soldiers facing the undisciplined rebel army of about one hundred fifty. At first the two sides glared at each other from their positions. The rebels were on the high ground above the valley floor.

"Victoria commanded the rebels to surrender. They refused.

"He ordered his soldiers to shoot. The rebels fired a return volley. Nobody was hurt, but no one retreated either.

"Victoria then shouted a command, and Captain Pacheco, expecting to lead a charge, raised his six-foot-long lance and galloped onto the field. However, none of the soldiers followed him! Realizing his mistake, he reined in his horse.

"Enraged by this show of aggression, a rebel leader Captain José María Ávila charged. He leveled his lance to meet Pacheco. The two fought like feudal knights, Pacheco on his black stallion and Ávila on his white steed."

Slapping his hand on the table, Nathaniel said, "And that was the battle. No one else on either side came forward. They just watched both riders charge each other and turn to charge again several times. Finally, Pacheco caused Ávila to drop his lance. When Ávila turned, he drew his pistol and shot Pacheco in the heart."

"Oh, my Lord!" María gasped. She hadn't heard these details.

"What happened next isn't clear. Most say Ávila picked up his lance, charged Victoria, and was shot dead. Then another rebel charged the governor and ran his lance in Victoria's face. Ripped off a good part of one side!"

María's eyes widened, and she held her hand over her mouth.

Nathaniel took a sip of his brandy to avoid looking at his hosts. "Pardon me, Doña María, for being so descriptive."

"Both sides retreated," Joseph said, "and the governor was taken to the Mission San Gabriel to see to his wounds. The man was in agony. I tended him as best as I could. Doña Eulalia Pérez assisted me. His face was terrible to see, but the lance wound in his chest was just as serious. The upshot was that Victoria met with Echeandía at the mission and agreed to step down as governor. He asked Echeandía to act as temporary governor. After a few weeks at the mission, Victoria returned to Mexico. The *diputación* is now back in session, and Echeandía claims to be in charge."

"*Claims* to be," Nathaniel said. "Don Pío Pico here in Los Angeles challenged that claim. And in Monterey the citizens appointed the governor's secretary Agustin Zamorano as their acting governor. So, nothing is settled."

William frowned and looked at María's troubled face. This chain of events made their future and their plans for land in Yerba Buena and Saucelito all the more uncertain.

✠ ✠ ✠

After their guests left, María lit two tallow candles, and she and William sat across from each other at the table to discuss what their path might be if Echeandía were ultimately in charge. They would be facing a governor who undoubtedly held a grudge against them for their support of the Fitches.

The missions as well as the Mexican government teetered on the verge of collapse. Through trade, foreign countries entered California's door at its ports and poked and prodded secretively to find the Mexican government's weaknesses. During the past few years, American fur trappers and explorers also swarmed into California over its mountain threshold, following the Old Spanish Trail from Santa Fe. Such government instability in upholding the law threatened William's dream.

"As you know, *mi amore*, I wish we could move back north," María said. "I miss my father and my mother, as well as all my sisters and my brother. There are even some new members of the family I haven't met. I'm trying to be patient."

"Echeandía is no friend of ours, María. He'll dismiss our petition with a wave of his hand as he has done before. But his position seems weak. Let's wait a bit longer. I'm hopeful things will calm down."

María searched William's face and reached across the table for his hand, unshed tears in her eyes. "I will pray that you are right. I trust you to know what is best."

"I know how difficult life here is for you," William said, kissing her hand. "But I must continue working for the mission, filling ships with its cargo. More and more foreign vessels are competing with our shipping. I'll talk with Padre Esténega tomorrow. And with our friend Abel Stearns. The success of his store in the pueblo proves he's a smart businessman. He'll give sound advice."

He rose from his seat and came to her side of the table to help her to her feet. As he hugged her, he murmured into her ear, "Though I hate to leave you alone again, sailing a new ship is the best way for me to care for our family right now."

✠ ✠ ✠

To keep Mission San Gabriel functioning, the padres had purchased a brig, a two-masted square-rigged vessel called the *Crusader.* They rechristened her the *Cruzador* and asked William to be her master. The ship was loaded with cargo from the mission and Abel Stearns's *tienda,* the retail store he established on the plaza in Los Angeles. The brig also carried William's own cowhides and furs, payment for his services. Earnings for his services and profit from his meager cargo, though, couldn't match what he could gain from sailing his own ship.

CHAPTER 23

LIFE AS BEFORE

1832–1833

Echeandía insisted he was Alta California's governor, ruling from San Diego, although temporarily. After he convened the *diputación* in Pueblo de Los Angeles, the members declared Don Pío Pico should be the temporary governor. This action infuriated citizens of Monterey who then elected Agustín Vicente Zamorano, Echeandía's former secretary, as governor. These *pro tem* governors, Pico in Los Angeles, Zamorano in Monterey, and Echeandía in San Diego, caused an uproar in Alta California for the entire year with all three men claiming the title and the right to issue rulings. The threat of secularization was a whisper in the background but very much on the minds of the friars as well as the rancheros who craved the mission lands.

✠ ✠ ✠

To reap more earnings than he ever could sailing Mission San Gabriel's ship, William jumped at the chance to purchase a schooner of his own, the *Josephine*. He rehired his former crew from the *María Antonia* and sailed the *Josephine* up and down the coast to Santa Bárbara, Monterey, and Yerba Buena, transporting his cargo and that of the other missions. As sole owner of this ship, however, he assumed all the risk if she was wrecked or if he couldn't sell his cargo for a profit.

In October 1832 the *Josephine* bobbed on gentle waves in San Pedro harbor. William stood on the shore admiring her lines as he watched his sailors load her for their next voyage. He would be transporting cargo to San Diego and ferrying local sea otter hunters to Santa Catalina Island. The governor encouraged Californios to take the sea otters and seals before foreigners diminished the population. Successful hunters traded the prized furs with Abel Stearns and other merchants who in turn sold the pelts for cash or traded them with British and American vessels for precious silk and other valuable goods from China.

On a fine autumn day, William sailed the *Josephine* to Santa Catalina Island to drop off the hunters. After a smooth and swift voyage to the island, where the passengers disembarked with all their gear, the first mate turned the ship south to San Diego, a two-day voyage with a favorable wind.

When they arrived, the crew anchored the schooner as close as a pistol shot from the beach. William oversaw the unloading of items for the San Diego Presidio and supervised the transfer of cowhides, which would be cured and then locked in a nearby storehouse, ready to ship and sell in Peru. He visited friends in the pueblo and arranged to load the *Josephine* with local rancheros' cargo for trade in *El Pueblo de Los Angeles*.

Within a few days he weighed anchor heading to Santa Catalina to pick up the hunters, who had intended to stay on the island for only a week. Although strong, hot seasonal winds blew from the land at this time of year, the first day at sea was trouble free. The following day the ship's barometer reading dropped, a sure warning of severe weather ahead. William and his first mate became uneasy when they spied dark clouds building on the western horizon.

"Might be a bad storm, Captain," his first mate warned, his voice tight, his face grim.

"I don't want us caught in open water when the winds strengthen and this weather worsens," said William.

"Something in these *diablo* winds tells me evil will happen. The men feel it too."

William wasn't as superstitious as other sailors, but experience warned him these warm, dry winds signaled danger. "Put on more sail," he said. "As much as the masts will take. Let's outrun this storm."

✠ ✠ ✠

The *Josephine* raced to its destination, but the storm swept in faster.

"All hands on deck!" roared the first mate. "Shorten sail!"

Men scrambled out of the hatch like ants from an anthill, joining the crew on deck in the wind and driving rain. The schooner bucked and lunged through gray and white-capped waves, up on watery mountains to the crest and down deep valleys to the trough.

Sailors on deck loosened the sheets and eased the sails, which snapped with explosion-like thunderclaps in the wild wind. Men scampered up ratlines and hung over spars, precariously balanced on their stomachs, while gathering in the flapping sails and reefing them, tying them to the spars. The crew below jumped to grab lifelines when booming waves of seawater flooded the deck and sent them sprawling.

William's blood surged as the threatened ship strained to plunge ahead. From the helm he watched fifteen-foot waves soar high over the ship's rail and break across the deck. Torrents of seawater tugged on barrels and crates tied down on the deck, loosened the ropes, and swept away cargo. Terrified sailors dangled from swinging pulleys or clung to lifelines to avoid being washed overboard on the rolling ship.

An angry wind howled and wailed in the rigging. Cold rain slashed William's face and ran down his collar soaking his clothes under his foul-weather coat. He shouted orders to the helmsman beside him. The two of them worked together to maintain their course. Tacking in a powerful wind would put sails and spars at risk.

William and the first mate strained to see. Was there land ahead? All was a ghostly gray. Even the sailors appeared as ghoulish shadows when cascades of waves crashed on the schooner's deck.

The ship was stretched out for the island, so close to safe harbor and anchorage, when the current elbowed it aside like a toy boat. A crunching and scraping to the port side told the tale's end.

Caught on a submerged rock, the ship's side ripped open. The schooner shuddered and lurched to a dead stop. With the sudden halt, the main mast broke in two with an earsplitting crack, pitching the vessel over on her slashed side. Sea water filled the hold. Monstrous waves continued to pound and prod the doomed ship.

The race was over, the ship was breaking up, its valuable cargo lost. The triumphant sea had won.

Resigning himself to the bruising defeat, William cursed and then shouted, "Abandon ship!" The safety of his crew was now foremost in his mind. He and the men scrambled into longboats to save themselves and row to Santa Catalina Island.

CHAPTER 24

LIFE AT SEA

Weeks after the wreck of his *Josephine*, William and his crew were sailing to South America on the mission's *Cruzador* loaded with cargo from the mission and local rancheros. Some of the cargo was his which he would trade in Peru.

Discouraged and frustrated, he knew he would have to make many voyages like this one to recover the financial loss of his schooner. Although the wreck of the *Josephine* had thwarted his plans, he thanked God no lives had been lost. He might manage to buy another ship, but how long would that take? He yearned for land up north and for his own trading ships, so he wouldn't have to work for the missions.

✠ ✠ ✠

In the morning, William rose before dawn and appeared on deck while the crew roused from their hammocks below. He swung himself onto the ratlines secured to the shrouds of the mainmast and scrambled up to the mainsail yard. Hooking his arm over the platform, he hauled himself onto it. The ship rolled on a swell, and he clung to the mast as tightly as a barnacle. Glancing down, he saw the deck seventy feet below and then nothing but sea as the ship heeled, suspending the mast over the gray water.

Lazily, the mast swung back in an arc to starboard. William stood on the platform and looked east, where the dark was lifting. On the horizon, the sun teased with a sliver of lemon yellow. Its blinding brilliance lit the top of the mast and next William, chasing away the night. He peered through his pocket spyglass and saw clear skies for ten to twelve miles. Not a sail nor dark bar of land broke the smooth horizon.

The thrill of being on the open sea, in command of a sailing ship, bewitched him.

The forenoon watch—the crew expected on deck—had stowed their hammocks, breakfasted, and gathered topside for the captain's orders. The sailors on morning watch had gone below for their meal by the time William climbed down the rigging. He trusted his sailors to know what was expected of them and to do their jobs well for the safety of the ship. He had trained all of them except two shipwrecked seamen who had readily signed on to sail for Mission San Gabriel.

Thankful he did not have to discipline any crew this morning for infractions such as drunkenness or fighting, he gave his daily orders to his first mate to relay to the ship's company. Then, satisfied with conditions on deck, he rubbed his hands together and went to the captain's cabin to have his first meal of the day—corned beef and eggs, his favorite dish—and to write the day's report in the ship's log: *5th January 1834. Strong warm breeze, calm sea, overall fair weather. All sails set, expecting strong trade winds . . .*

He recorded the distance covered from the last port, Mazatlán, Mexico. So far on this trip, he had no reports of illnesses, accidents, or injuries to add to the log.

The *Cruzador* had weighed anchor from San Pedro harbor with the ship's hold full of hides, barrels of brandy, crates of oranges, lemons, and figs, and bags of grain. But most of the cargo was *botas* of tallow, which provided excellent ballast and ensured the ship's stability at sea.

Early in the journey, they stopped at San Blas and Mazatlán where the supercargo sold brandy, fruits, and grain to merchants for a sizable profit. More importantly, at these stops the ship took on fresh water, flour, chocolate, vegetables, and whatever else might be required for the long voyage to Callao, Peru. The hides and tallow would be sold at Callao to British and Yankee trading vessels headed for London and Boston. William planned to return to California with a full cargo of American and European furniture, carpeting, tools, mirrors, silverware, glassware, and other manufactured goods, which would rake in a tidy profit with a markup of 200 to 300 percent when sold to the *gente de razón*.

This day at sea, the *Cruzador* seemed to enjoy the voyage as much as her captain. The foresail and mainsail billowed out before the wind, straining the shrouds as though eager to reach Callao. William had sailed the ship several times along the coast and knew her well. She dipped daintily into the troughs and rose on the swells without a shudder. He compared his thoughts with his first mate, saying, "How fast do you say she's moving? Six knots?"

"Yes, Captain," said his mate. "The cargo weight is holding her back. But it's still a good clip for the day. She'll glide through the Trade Winds soon. We're close to North 30 degrees by my reckoning. More pleasant days ahead. We'll make up any delay with fair weather and all sails set."

William leaned on the railing lost in thought, hypnotized by the ship's wake at the stern.

"There she blows!" cried a man aloft.

William turned and spied a jet of heart-shaped mist spouting from twin blowholes. A humpback whale passed the ship to starboard, swimming north to its winter feeding grounds. William watched the wide black backs of two more humpbacks that followed the first. They slipped through the water and then dove deep into the sea, flipping up the flukes of their huge tails before they disappeared below the waterline. Recalling his early life on whalers, he thanked God he had decided to remain on this side of the world. His wife, his children, and his life as captain of a trading vessel suited him just fine.

Although the work on a long sailing voyage was demanding and unpredictable, the crew relished being at sea as much as their captain. They were a mix of cultures but spoke the common seaman's language and followed the customs of a ship, working as a team. They liked the routine and their home on the sea.

The sails were set and trimmed to take advantage of the fine weather, and the first mate steered a course to make use of the currents and sea winds as they headed to Peru. The lookout aloft maintained a continuous watch for navigational hazards and other potential dangers. Men swabbed the decks. A few sailors used the pleasant day to sit on deck and patch a sail. No one remained idle.

Ship maintenance tasks were done every day, leaving a few hours in the late afternoon for leisure or personal chores. Two crew members aboard the *Cruzador* often played their guitars while the others sang along and carved wood, repaired clothing, or plaited ropes or their long hair. On Sunday afternoons, William, a Roman Catholic sailing a mission ship, read aloud a passage from the Bible on deck. He never forced anyone to attend, but they all came to the weekly service, regardless of their religious beliefs. Nor would he ever resort to physical punishment for any transgression. He tried to treat the crew with kindness and courtesy. He suspected some men attended the Sunday reading out of respect for him.

The next few days passed in relative calm. A few gray clouds developed into short squalls, slowing progress. *Cruzador* entered the area around the equator where the northeast and southeast trade winds converge. Winds were light to nonexistent and seas glassy. Becalmed in The Doldrums, the men climbed the ratlines and altered the sails to catch the slightest breeze. Exhausted and frustrated, they wet the decks endlessly with salt water to prevent the planks from drying out. Oppressed by the sweltering heat, the crew stripped down and looked for shade when unoccupied. A few men leaned on the rail and fished, hauling in good-sized catches, and adding some variety to the meals, which the cook and crew appreciated. William wrote letters to Padre Esténega, María, and Abel Stearns, ordering three shirts from the merchant. The letters would find their way to Alta California on the next ship going north.

Several days passed until the sails caught a stronger wind to carry the *Cruzador* down the coast of Peru.

✠ ✠ ✠

The *Cruzador* reached her destination, the port city of Callao, and dropped anchor in the harbor among ten whalers and trading ships. The wharves were noisy with shouts of men and cries of gulls in counterpoint. The air reeked of old fish and sour sweat.

At the wharf, the ship's supercargo oversaw the dock workers and crew who unloaded the cargo into a warehouse. He traded hides and tallow for credit with the American and British agents located in the port. The credit could be exchanged for merchandise, but it might take weeks for agents and brokers to gather and arrange the purchase of return cargo.

William was relieved to leave the business side on this trip to the supercargo. Scanning the ships, he spied the sailing vessel *Leonor*, his friend Henry Fitch as master, as well as the *Volunteer*, the *Ayacucho*, and the *California* bobbing in the harbor. He looked forward to meeting up with their captains in the city.

William and some of his crew marched to a well-known tavern for a hot meal and drinks. There he found Henry Fitch and another friend John Wilson, captain of the brig *Ayacucho,* each enjoying a tot of rum. Since John had completed business in Callao and would make sail the next day, he agreed to carry the *Cruzador's* sack of mail to San Pedro.

The soothing buzz of talk and laughter filled the tavern. William gradually relaxed with food and rum that warmed his limbs. He joked and laughed at the antics of his crew and other men and even danced a jig with his first mate and two other captains letting off steam.

Eventually, Henry, John, and the other captains called a goodnight and returned to their ships. As the night wore on, William drank his rum and watched sailors drift away to find recreation in other taverns. Some walked off with women who offered themselves for an evening of sweet company. He knew the danger of men jumping ship when in port. He'd done it himself many years ago. Short-handed ships were also known to kidnap sailors for their own crew. William encouraged his men to take their company to the ship for the evening. He relied on his first mate to herd the crew aboard each night they were in port.

William finished another tot of rum and considered what to do next. A barmaid was watching him, her luminous dark eyes sparkling in the firelight as she cleared the dishes and empty mugs, wiping down the table with a filthy rag. William wondered what María was doing, but his eyes wandered over the barmaid's soft, plump arms and the smooth exposed skin of her rounded bosom. She smiled at him invitingly, straightened up, and pushed back her loose dark hair with one hand. *Oh, hell, why not,* he thought.

CHAPTER 25

THE PETITION

To ease his conscience about his brief affair in Callao, William returned home bearing gifts—a fine wool shawl for Mariana, a hunting knife in a leather sheath for Francisco, a wooden top for Esteban, and for María a necklace of red coral and shimmering pearls with matching earrings. During dinner with the children, William related an abridged version of his adventurous voyage.

After the children were in bed, William lit a cigar and sat with María to hear her tale about the glorious Pío Pico wedding she had attended with the children. The celebration had lasted a week with all southern California aristocrats in attendance at the evening balls, dressed in their finest. María had relished the dinners of rich foods and fine wines, followed by music, dancing, and magnificent fireworks. Though Esteban was left with Lucia at night, during the day, María and the three children enjoyed mixing with the other guests at picnics and horse races, but avoided the bull fights.

"I heard much gossip," María said, "especially about the missions. The friars are enraged with the secularization edict. They hate to give up what they worked so hard to build. Many of the aging Franciscans decided to leave their missions and return to Spain, feeling no loyalty to the Mexican government."

"What about Mission San Gabriel?" William asked quickly. "What does Padre Esténega intend to do?"

María reached out to touch his arm. "Since the friars will soon be forced from Mission San Gabriel, Padre Esténega intends to slaughter thousands of cattle and sell the hides and as much tallow as he can. The cattle and wild horses are starving anyway all over Alta California because of this long drought. So, there will be many more shipping voyages." She tightened her grip on his arm and looked around the main room of their little adobe. "Our life here is not secure, *mi amore*. There will be no mission, only a parish church, and our adobe will be sold."

William envisioned their future there. He felt unsteady, as if the ground beneath him was rolling in an earthquake.

"The new governor José Figueroa might be our best chance to claim land and a home of our own," María said. After the chaotic year of three governors, the Mexican president had appointed him to govern.

The following day at the mission, William met Joseph who told him many people considered Figueroa a capable governor because of his successful dealings with the native people, the rancheros, and the friars. Polite and fair, he treated officials, rancheros, and mission neophytes with the same courtesy. To calm the citizens of his new territory, Figueroa granted amnesty almost immediately to all Californios who participated in the altercation at Cahuenga Pass.

"Because of his generous pardon," Joseph said, "citizens are beginning to trust his governing ability. He's trying to make the transition at the missions as easy as possible for the padres as well." After hearing how just and reasonable he was, William was hopeful his petition would be granted.

✠ ✠ ✠

Following a chance encounter with Governor Figueroa at Mission San Gabriel, William returned to the adobe, burst through the front door, and said to his wife, "This governor is a man I can deal with!" They sat down together to strategize

William's approach with the governor and for their return to Yerba Buena.

Whenever William was in port at San Pedro or at the mission during the next month, he sought out Figueroa for further discussions about the future of California. The stooped-shouldered, dark-haired man, part Spanish, part Aztec, and proud of his heritage, was well educated, friendly, and practical. Sitting with William under the vine-covered colonnade outside his mission headquarters, the new governor offered him a glass of wine and began to explain how complicated secularization would be.

"Although the Mexican Congress passed the law calling for secularization, political disagreements are continuing in the Mexican capital." Figueroa poured the wine and continued, "I'm confident these squabbles will be settled soon. So, I am moving ahead on my plan. There must be a slow transition of mission lands and cattle to their rightful owners, the native people of California. I have traveled throughout California from Monterey to the San Francisco Bay missions. Also, to San Diego. I met the people and learned about the land. To organize the transition from the friars' hands to the people, I will appoint more administrators to take inventory of each mission's property."

"When I was last in Yerba Buena," William said, "I learned my father-in-law Don Ignacio Martínez was named administrator for Mission San Rafael. Padre Esténega told my wife Mission San Gabriel will have a similar transition."

"Yes, my administrators are just the beginning. Much more must be done. The mission churches will become parish churches for nearby pueblos. Some pueblos must still be established. Mission lands and herds will be distributed among neophytes over twenty years of age, the ones who tended the fields, vineyards, and orchards for the friars. The rest will be reserved for the government. I will then grant tracts of mission land to applicants deemed worthy of such rewards."

William flashed a look at the governor but quickly pulled his gaze away to contemplate the trim Mission San Gabriel garden. *Ah, yes, granting lands to those deemed worthy. I should plow ahead with my request*, he thought.

"Governor," he said, "I am interested in acquiring a tract of land near Yerba Buena Cove as well as some land across the bay from the San Francisco Presidio. In February I submitted a new *diseño*, a map showing the boundaries of Rancho Saucelito." He paused but continued, "What would you have me do to help you with your plans? My skills, my crew, and I are at your service."

"I have seen the petition you sent Governor Echeandía and will examine the one you just submitted." The governor paused and studied William's face. "You've been an asset to the missions and the Mexican government. A trustworthy man, I think. Honest and ambitious. I'll keep your offer of aid and your request in mind." Figueroa stood. "There is much yet to do. Let's continue our discussion soon."

✠ ✠ ✠

At home, William and María strolled outside, enjoying the cool evening and breathing in the fragrance of orange trees in bloom. William related all he had learned from the governor.

"Your father and I discussed this possibility last year, when he received his commission as administrator for Mission San Rafael. More grants will soon be doled out, no doubt to the governor's special friends and relatives. I must persist and keep putting my hand out."

"But you must add some oil to smooth the way," María said. "Perhaps you can offer your services in some specific way to help the governor with his plans. Can you suggest something to do with trade on the bay? You were so successful helping the missions and the Presidio before. I do so want to live near my sister Juana again."

"I didn't want to tell you this. When I was in San Francisco Bay last year, I saw the Presidio. It was almost deserted. You wouldn't recognize it. And few Ohlones are living in the *ranchería*. Mission Dolores will soon become just a parish church, the lands and stock given away to the remaining neophytes." William frowned. "And to loyal friends of the governor."

María abruptly stopped walking. "We couldn't possibly live at the Presidio then! I'd hoped to live there with Juana and have our children grow up with their cousins." María looked at her husband, despair in her eyes. He stretched an arm over her shoulders and hugged her.

"Do not give up hope, *mi alma*! I talked with your father about the need for a custom house in Yerba Buena Cove so that the Mexican government can collect fees from trading vessels. There are many successful rancheros around the bay, and they must sell their hides and tallow as before. I'll convince the governor that Yerba Buena could grow into a prosperous port, a center for this trade. We will make it prosperous! I have not forgotten our hopes for a home there." William looked at María's troubled face and smoothed away the worry lines on her forehead with his fingertips. "Yes, Yerba Buena for a custom house as well as land for a house for us. I'll present my proposal to the governor."

"Such a project will take time," said María. "We must live there together. I do not wish to be away from you for so long."

"Of course! If he sends me, you and the children will come, too. And I'll build you a house in Yerba Buena, a beautiful *Casa Grande*! It will be the first of many grand houses. There will soon be other houses and many neighbors." William hugged his petite wife. "And we'll claim the land for our Rancho Saucelito, too."

✠ ✠ ✠

A few days later, when he walked into the governor's headquarters at the mission, William learned that Governor Figueroa had similar plans in mind.

"Captain Richardson, I would like you to help the Mexican government establish the pueblo at Yerba Buena," began Figueroa.

Trying to hide his surprise at the governor's statement, William said, "I would be honored to help you with this enterprise. As you are aware, my wife and I lived in the San Francisco Presidio and know the area well. I am at your service."

"I remember you lived there, and believe you are the right man for this assignment. Since I am not that familiar with the area, the first thing I want you to do is draw me a map. I want to see the best site for the pueblo. It must have a plaza for government buildings. The first should be one for a customs officer who will collect duties and fees."

Figueroa pushed paper, pen, and a bottle of ink across the table toward William. William did not hesitate. He had drawn so many charts and maps of the bay. Now, he drew the bay shoreline near Yerba Buena Cove, marking freshwater *lagunas* and land features such as the hill called *Loma Alta.* He traced the paths to Mission Dolores and to the Presidio and added a few curved lines to indicate higher land.

That, he thought, *is where I will build my first house, María's* Casa Grande.

BOOK 3

STAKING A CLAIM

1835–1846

El Pueblo de Yerba Buena and

Rancho Saucelito

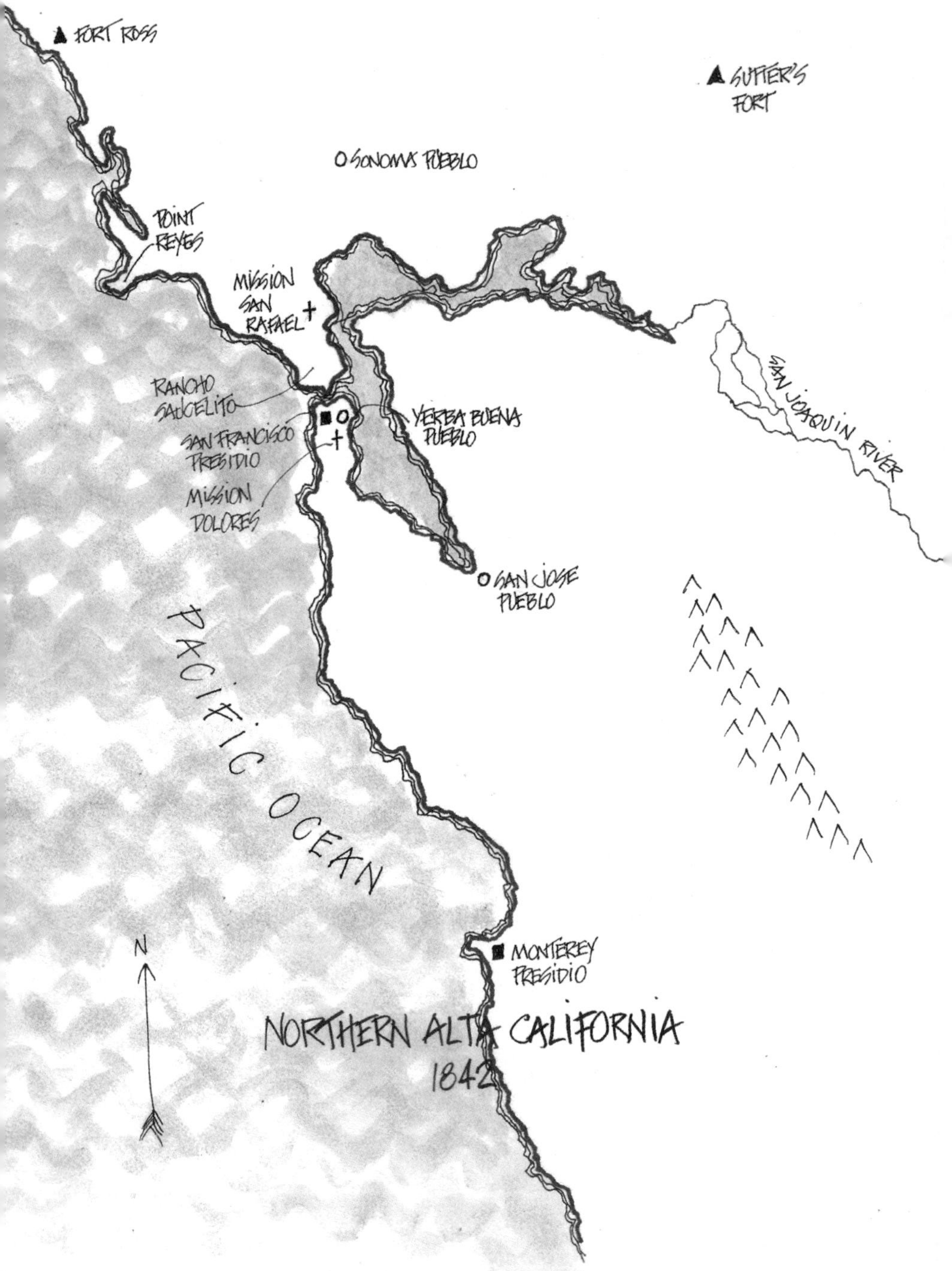
FORT ROSS
SUTTER'S FORT
SONOMA PUEBLO
POINT REYES
MISSION SAN RAFAEL
RANCHO SAUCELITO
SAN FRANCISCO PRESIDIO
MISSION DOLORES
YERBA BUENA PUEBLO
SAN JOAQUIN RIVER
SAN JOSE PUEBLO
PACIFIC OCEAN
N
MONTEREY PRESIDIO
NORTHERN ALTA CALIFORNIA
1842

CHAPTER 26

A TENT-SHANTY

June 1835

María, seated atop their baggage, shelled peas into a bowl on her lap while she watched William and the men he'd hired from the mission erect a temporary shelter. Before the family started their journey, William had sent a letter to Padre José María Gutiérrez, the padre recently assigned to Mission Dolores. He asked the friar if he would direct neophytes to log four redwood trees for him. When he arrived, his hired men dragged the trimmed redwood logs from the mission to a low hill that overlooked Yerba Buena Cove and pounded them deep into the soft ground for tent posts. They were now adding crossbeams over which William planned to stretch a huge sail and snugly anchor the sailcloth's edges to the ground with heavy rocks. This tent-shanty, four posts covered with canvas, would be their home for a while.

To María, camping in a wilderness and living in a tent was more than unpleasant. Growing up at the Presidio headquarters, she learned from her mother the importance of keeping a tidy household and insisting upon perfection. She would be patient, but if they had to remain here for more than a few months, she would insist on a permanent shelter.

Mariana sat next to her mother with unshelled pea pods on her lap and sulked. She watched six-year-old Francisco run for tools and clear away brush following their father's directions. She grumbled that she could help build the tent, too, but María insisted that she help her shell peas. Pouting, Mariana spilled the shelled peas into a basket and threw her empty pea pods onto the ground.

María knew there was more on her daughter's mind than her frustration of not participating in tent building.

During their long ride to the cove, Mariana had confided to her mother her dream of galloping over the hills on a young, lively pony, instead of plodding along on the horse she rode, dumpy, old Gorda. She pleaded for a horse of her own and promised to take good care of it. To prove she could, she had taken care of Gorda on their journey. María told Mariana to speak with her father.

Setting the bowl of peas aside, María impatiently brushed sand from her hands and skirt. Camping on sand dunes in the open, near the bay, was going to be so uncomfortable. And dangerous. All day, cold winds from the ocean whipped sand into their clothing, their hair, and even their food. Because María had lived at the Presidio, she knew to expect a chilly fog at night. She eyed wolves, coyotes, and other wild animals prowling along the shore in search of a beached fish or an unwary rabbit. She imagined them roaming close to their tent in the dark, only a thin canvas wall to keep them out. Although William said he would post a guard every night to chase these marauders, she felt sure she would remain awake in the tent-shanty listening for huffs or low growls, warning of threats to her family. She remained stoic, though. Complaining would frighten the children. There was nothing more she or her husband could do for their safety and comfort.

Except maybe some tea. Glancing at her moody, restless daughter, María said, "Mariana, a tea party might help us feel warm and cozy here. Please gather a basketful of the *yerba buena* plants."

Mariana rose quickly, almost upsetting the basket of shelled peas she cradled in her lap. Handing the basket to her mother, she rushed to gather up the empty pods from the ground and grabbed another basket to fill with the plants for their mint tea. The mint herb grew wild all around their campsite. It didn't take her long to fill the basket for their cook Sophia, who had a pot of water heating over glowing, hot coals.

María searched in the travel chests for a snow-white linen tablecloth and carefully unwrapped the English china tea set, a present William had brought home from one of his trading voyages. She had Mariana arrange the floral teacups, teapot, and plates on one of the chests. As a refined Spanish lady, María insisted on an elegant table, even when camping.

She watched Mariana set the table and reflected on the family's long journey from Mission San Gabriel to this beach at Yerba Buena Cove. Although parting with Aunt Rafaela had been sad, María was elated to return to the San Francisco Presidio area and her family. William was happy, too, because this move brought them one step closer to achieving his quest for land and a permanent home.

✠ ✠ ✠

Their arduous route north on horseback had taken the family across flat plains, up and over many hills, and through dense forests. They forded swift streams, their vaqueros working hard to keep their string of saddle horses together. For twenty-two long days, they'd ridden, sometimes in sudden rainstorms, sometimes in blistering heat, along *El Camino Real*, the path the Spanish explorer General Gaspar de Portolá and Padre Junípero Serra had traveled more than sixty years before.

From Mission San Gabriel to Monterey, Governor Figueroa and a small band of soldiers escorted them. Whenever the Richardsons and the soldiers reached a mission along the Royal Road, they ate and slept there as guests of the friars in charge. Sometimes they had to camp and sleep in the open, but neither horse thieves nor native people ever troubled them. Mexican soldiers had chased the indigenous people east into the San Joaquín River valley a few years before.

When they reached San José, the family took a break from their journey to visit María's parents in *Pueblo de San José*.

María was overjoyed to meet her new siblings who had been born in the last few years, and her parents were delighted to hug their new grandchild, three-year-old Esteban. María's father, retired now and no longer the Presidio comandante, hoped the Mexican government, in recognition for his military service, would soon grant him a rancho on the *contra costa* side of the bay, the coast opposite Yerba Buena Cove where the Richardsons were destined.

After a few days of a merry family reunion, the Richardsons hugged and kissed the don and doña goodbye to continue their journey. Doña Martina wept as they departed because she would not see her daughter or her grandchildren for a long while. William must settle his family at Yerba Buena and establish a pueblo as the governor had ordered. The mission and the Presidio had been there for many years, but William had assured Governor Figueroa a great port would grow near the cove, and he was determined to establish its beginnings. There would not be time for family visits.

✠ ✠ ✠

Now on the desolate beach, María placed her mother's going-away present of homemade anise cakes on a plate. She brushed away tears and trudged to the tent construction site to tell her husband their tea was ready. She saw her husband's rifle propped up against a post and recalled her apprehension of prowling beasts. She patted the pistol in her pocket for reassurance.

William hugged María and called Mariana over. "Our tent-shanty is finished. What do you think of our new home?" he asked, holding open the flap so they could look inside.

Three canvas sleeping hammocks swung from a crossbeam. A rope bed for William and María stood in one corner, and several cow hides covered the flattened sand. Though pleased with her husband's thoughtfulness, María still wasn't thrilled with the idea of camping in this wild, cold place for weeks.

Silently, María wondered also about protection from wild animals. Coyotes had been known to sneak into dwellings with open doorways even when people were there. A tent flap held closed by a stone didn't seem secure to her.

Francisco stood back to look at the outside. "It looks like a canvas box turned upside down. Will those rocks holding down the tent's sides really keep it from sailing away in the wind?"

William laughed. "A schooner in the sky," he said. "No, Francisco. It's secure." He put a hand on his son's shoulder. "With all that work today, Francisco, you'll sleep soundly tonight. Let's go wash up for tea." Together they rode to the bay's edge to wash in the fresh water of *Laguna Dulce*.

When they returned, Francisco was shivering from splashing in the cold water. Mariana wrapped a blanket around his shoulders.

"Some hot tea will warm you," she assured her brother. María watched her daughter settle him on the sand near the campfire and sit beside him with her arm around his shoulders. Even though Mariana was young, she was observant and concerned about her brother's health. María brooded often about Francisco. He was frequently unwell, more than either Esteban or her daughter. She must discuss his health with her sister Juana during their visit tomorrow. She might suggest a remedy she used for her children.

✠ ✠ ✠

While María was busy with the tea and the dinner preparations, Maruha, a Miwok servant, entertained Esteban. After she washed his little hands in a basin, she walked him over to join the family and sat on the sandy ground next to him.

Maruha had been helping with the youngest members at Doña Martina's household in San José, but she readily joined the Richardsons when María asked her to come with them to help care for her children. At twelve years old she was quick, confident, and decisive, yet stayed calm and loving as she dealt with rambunctious Esteban and fearless Francisco. By moving to Yerba Buena with the Richardsons, Maruha explained she would be nearer her mother who was living at Mission San

Rafael with other Miwoks. Empathizing with her desire for family connections, María had promised Maruha she would have opportunities to visit her.

After everyone had gathered, William reached for his teacup and sighed. "Ah, a refreshing break from our labors! But in your china teacups?"

María ignored his comment except to say, "We are still civilized people though on this uncivilized beach. And even in this wilderness, my Englishman must have his tea!"

William laughed out loud and the children joined in because they all knew how he loved his afternoon tea and how much he loved their mother, even when she teased him. "How wise I was to have chosen this brave lady who can make tea for me anywhere!"

"Think again, *mi amore*," said María with an arched eyebrow, "about who chose whom."

"Oh, Mamá," Mariana said, putting down her cup of tea. "Did you choose Papá? Tell us what happened."

María looked over at her husband whose only comment was, "These anise buns are like manna from heaven! I sing praises to the Lord for your talented mother who made them and graciously gave them to us before we left San José."

María ignored him. "Yes, I'll tell you my story, Mariana," María said. "Before I met your father, I lived at the Presidio with my family because your *abuelo,* your grandfather, was the comandante. There was little for young people to do around this bay, and my sisters and I were often bored." She watched her husband sip his tea. "But sometimes something rare happens in life, something exceptional. I think I was also ready to fall in love.

"When your father landed on our beach, I knew my life would change with him. I said to my sisters, 'Oh what a handsome man that stranger is! He is going to be my husband and I will be his wife!' He and I stared at each other. It must have been love at first sight."

"Oh, Mamá!" Mariana said. "You predicted what would happen!"

William sputtered. "You never told me that!"

"What happened next?" asked Francisco, picking up another anise bun.

María smiled as she thought about that night and told the story of their meeting.

"And I remember that we ate and drank a lot!" William said, putting down his empty teacup. "Ah! That is excellent tea." María poured him another cup and ended her tale, knowing he felt a little embarrassed by her openness with the children.

Francisco finished the last bite of his roll. "What will we have for dinner tonight, Mamá?" he asked. William smiled and tousled his son's thick, dark hair.

"You have just had your tea! How can you think of dinner so soon?" María laughed and said, "Sophia made us a beef stew with peas, onions, and carrots. Even though we don't have our beehive oven yet, we can make stews and barbecue over the open fire. That should satisfy my hardworking, hungry boys!"

William patted his wife's arm. "We'll start to build a beehive oven tomorrow. It will be ready to use in a few days after the adobe clay cures and hardens." To the children he said, "Meanwhile, we have plenty of food and should thank God and your Mamá for that."

Mariana and Francisco scrambled to their feet and kissed their mother on each cheek while Esteban, not to be left out, buried his face in her lap. María laughed and lifted him up to bounce on her knees. She turned to face her husband, "William, is our tent ready for us to move in?"

"Yes, my dear. I will have the men move our boxes and chests in immediately. Would you direct them where you want things placed? I want to take a short ride with the children before supper. They have been helpful today and deserve an outing."

CHAPTER 27

A THIEF

Mariana saddled Gorda with her father's help, and the vaquero Ricardo helped Francisco saddle his. They mounted their ponies and rode north. William, riding his chestnut stallion, hugged Esteban to his chest and followed them. When they reached the top of a high dune, they could see down to the bay, across to the high peak of Mount Tamalpais, and to the headlands, the bay's west entrance, where the sun was dipping into the ocean.

The children watched hundreds of pelicans fly low over the water searching for their dinner before nightfall. Sandpipers and egrets poked around the water's edge while gulls squabbled over a dead fish. Nearby, a doe and two fawns stood as still as stone sculptures, ready to leap away if the horse riders came closer. William pointed to the mountain and told the children that in a few years they might live there below the western slope. They would have a wonderful house, land to explore, and many fine horses to ride. While Francisco chatted away with excitement about his father's promise, Mariana patted Gorda's neck but didn't say anything. William wondered what was on her mind.

✠ ✠ ✠

That night after dinner, the younger children put on their nightclothes and said their prayers with María while Mariana helped Maruha and Sophia clean the dishes. When Francisco and Esteban were asleep, Mariana tiptoed to where her father and mother were sitting, put her hand on her father's shoulder, and said, "Papá, I have a request." She paused, chewing on her lip. "I would very much like to have my own pony. I took care of Gorda during our trip and helped Francisco care for the horses he rode. I've also helped Mamá."

William put his hand on hers and pulled her to his side, holding both of her hands and looking tenderly at her. Her dark gray eyes stared steadily and hopefully into his.

"Mariana, a horse is a big responsibility. You know I think nine years old is too young for you to have a horse of your own. It's customary for boys to wait until they are ten."

Holding back tears of disappointment, Mariana countered his argument. "No one had to remind me to brush Gorda, or feed her, or give her water. I helped Francisco take care of his horse, too. I can saddle my horse with help, and I ride well. Please, Papá, allow me to have a pony."

William looked at his wife, who had been listening and watching. She only raised her eyebrows, but he knew she agreed with Mariana, since she had taught her to ride and was fully aware of her daughter's skill and capabilities. He turned back to look in Mariana's earnest eyes and said, "Well, I'll see, *niñita*. Maybe you'll get a pony for Christmas."

Mariana drew her brows together and pursed her lips. "How long is it until Christmas, Papá?"

"Well, today is June twenty-fifth. In six months, it will be Christmas. So you have just half a year to prove to me that you can care for a horse."

Throwing her arms around her father's neck and kissing his sun-roughened cheek, she said, "Thank you, Papá! I'll look after Gorda until then. That way I'll show you I can care for my own horse."

After he helped Mariana into her hammock, William sat down again near his wife and sighed. "How can such simple things make a child so happy?" He looked at María. "What can I do to make you happy, *mi amore*?"

María put her hand on his knee. "I am concerned about Francisco. He was shivering today. Build us a house. When we planned to move here, I thought we would live at the Presidio." She sullenly looked around her. Children in hammock cocoons, a rope bed, hard travel trunks for seats. "This tent is fine for a little while, but we must have a stronger and warmer home before the rains start. That will make me happy."

William picked up her hand and kissed it. "I know the fog and the blowing sand on this barren beach are a trial for you. For all of us. I promise I'll build you a wooden dwelling before winter. One with at least three rooms." He then leaned over to kiss her.

✠ ✠ ✠

William and María continued talking quietly about their plans to visit the Presidio the next day. During a lull in their conversation, María listened to the hissing windblown sand whispering against the canvas tent. She shivered, praying the noise was not sniffing sounds from unknown nighttime prowlers.

"Both Sophia and I are anxious about the wild animals that roam so closely to our shelters," María said. As if she had summoned her, they heard Sophia's soft voice at the entrance to the tent, "*Capitan y Señora,* may I come in?"

"Yes, Sophia," called William.

Maruha pushed back the tent flap for Sophia, and the cook carried in a wriggling rooster and two docile chickens hanging upside down, their feet bound with string. Maruha held a gunny sack.

"I am sorry to bother you," Sophia began, "but we are worried about the bears and coyotes. Maruha and I cannot sleep thinking they might enter our brush shelter looking for food. Would you keep the rooster and chickens here tonight?"

"Of course. That's a good idea," said the captain. He stood to help them put the three birds in the sack, tied the neck of the bag, and placed it on the ground on the side of the tent opposite where the children slept snugly in their hammocks. Once in the sack the birds remained quiet and still.

When the two women left, María confronted her husband. "This won't do! I don't want those birds in our tent either. How can you ignore our danger! We're just as likely to get a beast entering our tent."

"I think we'll be safe for tonight. Besides, I have my rifle." William kissed his wife before he got into their bed. She was still looking worried, so he said, "I'll build a hen house for them tomorrow. Come to bed."

✠ ✠ ✠

Hours later, snuffling and grunting noises outside the tent awakened William and María. William turned up the light of their lantern in time to see a snout with a shiny black nose poking under the tent edge. Then a coal black paw with three-inch claws reached for the gunny sack with the chickens. The children woke, their eyes widening as they took in the sight of a black bruin trying to invade their tent-shanty.

"*Caramba!*" Francisco whispered.

Before William could yank on his trousers and boots, the bear hooked his claws into the sack and pulled it toward the tent edge. The bag ripped, and the two chickens, squawking and flapping their wings in terror, escaped into the tent, but the screeching rooster didn't. William grabbed his flintlock rifle from under the bed and exited the tent, yelling, "Bear!" He circled the tent, but the black bear had already vanished into the dark with his prize. Two of William's men armed with rifles came running toward him.

"Careful! Don't shoot!" William called out. "The bear is gone."

The men told him the others had gone to the aid of the man guarding the horses to help him calm them. With a lantern's light, William and the two armed men looked around the vaqueros' and Sophia's brush huts, but they found only bear tracks and a few feathers.

"We'll hunt that rogue tomorrow. He can't be allowed to return looking for more handouts," William told the two men. When he returned to the tent to calm his family, he found Mariana had captured the two squawking chickens and put them into another gunny sack. María had the children on the bed with her and was cuddling Esteban, whose dark eyes were still huge. She got out of the bed and put back the loaded pistol she had retrieved from a trunk. He grunted his approval, knowing she had been prepared to shoot the bear if the beast had returned.

"The bear is gone, but so is our rooster," said William. "I'm stunned how easily he moved those heavy stones holding down the tent edge." He looked at María, who didn't upbraid him in front of the children. He would apologize to her later because she had been right to worry about the danger. "I'll be hunting that thief tomorrow. We must not have another nighttime raid from him." He helped Francisco and Esteban into their hammocks. "Go back to sleep, children. All is well."

"Can I hunt the bear with you, Papá?" asked Francisco.

"Me, too!" chimed in Mariana from her hammock. María looked horrified.

"Remember, bears are dangerous, ferocious creatures," William said, watching his wife's face. He'd reassure her after the children were asleep. "We'll be hunting this one at dawn."

He hadn't said yes or no to them, but he was sure they would still be asleep in the morning when he left. Besides, he would never let them go on a bear hunt. They'd face that experience soon enough when they grew up.

CHAPTER 28

LIVING AT THE EDGE OF THE WORLD

By the time the children woke the next morning, William had returned from an unsuccessful bear hunt with only a small deer hanging behind his saddle. Mariana and Francisco were disappointed they had not been awakened to go with him.

"You sleepyheads didn't get up when Mamá and I did," William said. "Well, we didn't catch the thief today, but the men are still tracking him. When they do find him, you will next see that bear in our new house as a soft, warm rug."

William gave Sophia the deer and asked her to prepare it for their evening meal. She and Maruha then served the Richardsons and the hired men a breakfast of tortillas, stew left from dinner, and hot chocolate. After their meal, the children dressed to visit their cousins at the San Francisco Presidio, while Ricardo saddled horses for their ride to the fort. William lifted María into the saddle of her sleek black Arabian, handed her Esteban, and mounted his chestnut stallion. Mariana and Francisco climbed onto their horses, ready to follow in line behind their parents.

The family rode along the same path they took yesterday evening, past the spring and the high hill called *Loma Alta*. When their horses' hooves crushed the *yerba buena* plants along the route, its minty fragrance filled the air. As they trotted up to the fort, William cautioned the children not to comment on the run-down condition of the Presidio nor to stare at the poorly dressed soldiers.

"I hope the fort will soon improve when I begin collecting custom duties from trading vessels for the Mexican government," he explained.

Despite William's warning, María and the children were shocked and saddened to see the Presidio's derelict buildings with crumbling walls and fallen roofs. Only a few soldiers in patched uniforms saluted them. Many of the men had transferred to Sonoma with Lieutenant Mariano Guadalupe Vallejo, the San Francisco Presidio's current comandante. Even the comandante headquarters where María had lived as a child needed repair.

Although the Estudillo family did not live in the headquarters, they awaited the Richardsons there on the veranda. María embraced her sister Juana, and the cousins were reintroduced to Mariana and Francisco, whom they had not seen for five years. They were delighted to meet Esteban.

Mariana stared at her aunt Juana and then her mother. Both had beautiful black hair, dark eyes fringed with thick eyelashes, and similar smiles. "Mamá, you and Tia Juana look so much alike!" María and Juana laughed. Mariana's eyes widened. "You even laugh alike!"

"I don't know why you are surprised, Mariana," María said. "We're sisters."

"I wish I had a sister," Mariana said.

"You have me!" Francisco said with a pout. Mariana hugged him.

Juana's daughters Concepción and Gertrudis linked their arms through Mariana's. "And you now have us!" The three girls giggled together.

María watched William walk away from her happy reunion with her sister to talk with Juana's husband, the acting comandante of the Presidio. Lieutenant José Joaquin Estudillo was also now the administrator in charge of secularizing Mission Dolores. William had been pondering how much his family's world would change in the next year and had told María he would discuss with José how they might prepare to face the challenges.

✠ ✠ ✠

María told Juana that William would be sailing north in two weeks to take soldiers to Sonoma. She complained to her sister how lonely and cold the cove was in the little tent-shanty and told the story of their bear encounter in the night.

"Two men are still hunting the bear, but I won't feel completely at ease even when they find him. There is only a canvas wall between us and the wild beasts! William has promised to build us a proper wooden house before the cold winter rains start."

"Then your life there will be better," soothed her sister. "Though we live near the mission now, José and I hope to build a house at Yerba Buena and move to the cove with our family." Juana sighed as she looked across the parade grounds. "The Presidio is in shambles, and most of the men and their families will be stationed at the Sonoma fort as soon as it is built. I will be happy to have you nearby."

"I wish you lived closer now, Juana. I'm concerned about Francisco. He has started to cough again. Sometimes he runs a high fever. The weather here is so cold and damp and windy. It's as bad for Francisco as the padres found it was for the neophytes. The weather across the bay is much better. I pray, in time, we can move there. We petitioned Governor Figueroa for the land near Whaler's Cove."

The two sisters sat on the veranda and discussed the use of the *yerba santa,* the holy herb, and other remedies for coughs and fevers. They also made plans for a *merienda* after Mass on Sunday when the cousins could see more of each other. Then Juana called the children to her.

"You are visiting on an auspicious day, *niños*," said Juana. "Your cousin Ramón is now ten, old enough to have his own horse, if he can ride him. Come watch him try to earn his horse."

The two families walked to the corral and joined others who had gathered there.

Francisco turned to Mariana, his dark brows knitted together. "You won't have to conquer your horse like Ramón does. Girls don't have to prove they are good riders. But I will have to."

"Don't worry, Francisco," she said. "You have a few more years before you will have such a contest. You will be ready for it by then."

The children stood on the lowest rail of the corral to watch Ramón ride a half-broke, black mustang. His father was mounted on his horse in case he needed to intervene, but the boy proved he could handle his horse. After much bucking and kicking, the horse eventually tired. Crooning soft words, Ramón patted the mustang's neck and climbed down.

"An excellent ride," Ramón's father praised his son. "Let us all celebrate with the delicious lunch your mother prepared for us."

✠ ✠ ✠

The next day, William met with Padre Gutiérrez and asked for help in repairing the two schooners he'd left in Yerba Buena Cove while he lived at Mission San Gabriel. The abandoned ships had become waterlogged during his absence and needed refitting and restoration. The padre approached the few Ohlone men still living at the mission to ask whether they would help William fix the schooners. From the small group of men, Diego stepped forward ready to work with him again. Though surprised he still lived at the mission, William clasped the man's hand, pleased to see him. Marino also offered to help when he could though he and his wife now lived in San Rafael, where he was the *alcalde*, mayor. William would rely on both of them to help train other volunteers. Several other men also agreed to work on repairing the ships. All became members of his new crew to transport hides, supplies, and people around the bay once more.

✠ ✠ ✠

While their father dove into ship repairs, the children busied themselves with chores every morning. “We all must do our part,” William told them. “We need water every day. You must be our water carriers.”

Not wanting to disappoint their father, Mariana and Francisco, with Maruha, carried clay pitchers and jugs to a spring that bubbled out of the ground. They hauled the filled containers to Sophia, who poured the water in a barrel, in wash basins, and in cooking pots. Next the children combed the area for dry wood for the cooking fire, which had to be kept going day and night.

After completing their chores, Mariana and Francisco were allowed to ride over the dunes to explore the shores of the cove. One time when the tide was out, they spied a smooth, curved log sticking up from the mudflat. It was too heavy and too deeply fixed in the sand to pull up, so they asked their father to come help. William rode to the water’s edge with the children and assured them what they found was not a log.

“As a former whale chaser, I can tell you that isn’t from a whale either,” he said to his children. “I think it’s a tusk from a huge mammal that must have lived here thousands of years ago. A woolly mammoth. It looked like an elephant but was much larger and covered with a dark brown woolly coat like a long-haired sheep’s.” He drew a picture in the sand for Francisco and Mariana. “I saw the tusks of one in Sitka when I was trading with the Russians. A very unusual find, Francisco!”

Over their afternoon tea, Francisco told his mother about the tusk. She was as amazed as they were that such an animal might have lived there so many years ago.

William told them about his plan for shipping and trading again on the bay. “I’ll also transport lumber. For our house and for other buildings that I’m sure will be built at Yerba Buena. The mission has fallen into disrepair as well. You will not recognize it, María. Perhaps I can help Padre Gutiérrez restore it.”

✠ ✠ ✠

María saw the state of the Mission for herself on Sunday when the Richardsons, Sophia, Maruha, and a few of the vaqueros rode to Mission Dolores to attend Mass. They carried their picnic provisions for the *merienda* they planned to have with the Estudillo family after the church service. The day promised to be perfect, with the fog already gone and an azure sky overhead. As they neared the Mission, the Richardson party met their relatives who were just arriving from the Presidio.

Before entering the church, William noticed a rough corral set up a short way from the church entrance. With Mass starting, he had no opportunity to talk with María about it.

After the service, as the family left the church, Mariana and Francisco raced ahead to the corral. Two mounted vaqueros had dragged a young bull into the corral toward a bear tethered to a post inside the enclosure. The two animals were quickly tied together, one end of a reata looped around a front leg of the bull and the other end around a rear leg of the bear. They began attacking each other, and roars rose from the onlookers.

The shouts and cheers from the crowd attracted William's attention. When he spied his two children, he frowned. "María, it's a bear and bull fight. I don't want our family watching this brutal entertainment. Please gather them. I'll tell José we'll be going home."

The children were disappointed, but María agreed with her husband's decision. While she had them mount their horses, William walked over to José who was near the corral with his family.

"I'm sorry, José and Juana," William said, "because of this entertainment, we won't be able to have a peaceful family *merienda* with you today. Please excuse us."

"It's just a bull and bear fight," said José, eyebrows raised in surprise. "They happen all the time. We can have our picnic after it."

"No," said William, shaking his head. "No. In my opinion, these animal baitings are barbarous and inappropriate. I don't want our children to witness this cruel sport. We'll return to our tent and visit with you another time."

The Richardsons, Sophia, and Maruha rode slowly back to Yerba Buena Cove. The children grumbled to each other but respected their mother and father's decision and didn't object. They proceeded along the trail to the beach to their tent-shanty. Before long, they heard riders galloping behind them. The Richardsons turned in their saddles and saw José and Ramón cantering toward them. The father and son reined in their horses next to the family, and José swept his hat from his head.

"I agree with your decision, William," José said, "and admire your courage to speak. We Californios are often not sensitive enough about cruelty to animals for sport. If you wouldn't mind, we would still like to enjoy a Sunday *merienda* with you and your family. We would also like to see your unique dwelling. My wife and the rest of my family are following us and will arrive soon."

The two men shook hands and all continued to the shanty. By the time they chose a perfect spot overlooking the cove and shook out blankets to sit on, the rest of the Estudillo family arrived. Hugs and kisses among all made for an untroubled beginning to their feast. The bull and bear fight was quickly forgotten.

Ramón and Francisco immediately began to race their horses over the dunes, Ramón on his frisky mustang and Francisco on his sturdy horse. The girls helped their mothers and the servants set up the picnic. Then Mariana led her cousins Concepción and Gertrudis away to poke their heads into the tent-shanty. The three girls had already planned to have a dolly tea party until their families' luncheon began. So they took their rag dolls out of their saddlebags and spread out a blanket.

Since Sophia had banked the campfire carefully, the new logs on the hot coals were soon crackling, and a meat stew was quickly warmed for lunch. When a cold breeze picked up in the afternoon, everyone huddled closer to the warmth. Maria was especially grateful for the campfire. She glanced at Francisco. *What would they do without a fire in this inhospitable spot?* she wondered.

CHAPTER 29

SURVIVAL ON THE BAY

The next week, the men from the mission repaired the waterlogged ships. Marino and Diego taught the new crew how to caulk the planks with oakum and pitch to make the deck watertight and how to scrape and clean the hulls. The schooners, named *San Francisco* and *Guadalupe,* were made seaworthy to fulfill Lieutenant Mariano Guadalupe Vallejo's request to transport some San Francisco Presidio soldiers, their families, horses, household goods, and supplies to Sonoma.

William learned much about Vallejo from his conversations with Governor Figueroa. A brilliant Mexican soldier, the governor had said. In 1829, he led an expedition to defeat a fierce band of runaway mission neophytes hiding in the San Joaquin Valley. Because of this triumph, he became a military hero, and the governor promoted him to comandante of the San Francisco Presidio.

The Mexican government still feared Russian encroachment into Alta California. To ease the fear of invasion, Governor Figueroa explained to William, he ordered twenty-six-year-old Lieutenant Vallejo to reconnoiter near San Francisco Bay for a suitable location to build a presidio and Mexican settlements.

Vallejo led a military expedition north from San Jose until he reached a mountain ridge overlooking the lush Sonoma Valley. He immediately wrote to the governor and recommended the new presidio be built in the valley near the northern Mission San Francisco Solano.

✠ ✠ ✠

William transported most of the San Francisco garrison from the derelict Presidio as close as he could through the tule marshland to Sonoma. Cargo was unloaded from his ships and hauled to the military camp near Mission Solano where fifty of Vallejo's soldiers were bivouacked in tents and where the new Presidio would be built.

William meandered around Mission Solano but was shocked to see how few of Padre Altimira's converts remained. He remembered delivering the mission's bell in 1825 and seeing the beautiful valley, flourishing with grape vines, fruit trees, and vegetable plots carefully tended by the neophytes. Few Miwoks and Pomos were living there now. Many had died from measles, smallpox, syphilis, and other white man diseases, for which they had no immunity and there was no cure.

A soldier shook William from his gloomy reverie by telling him he was invited to Lieutenant Vallejo's tent for a brandy and supper. When William entered the tent, the lieutenant stood and greeted him with a firm handshake.

"Captain Richardson, welcome to Sonoma. You made good time bringing my troops here from the old Presidio. I thank you. Your services are appreciated, and I'll be sure to mention your efficient delivery to the governor in my report."

Though not quite as tall as William, Vallejo was handsome and imposing with a broad face furred with mutton chops.

"I'm pleased to be of assistance, Lieutenant," William said. "My sailors repaired the schooners quickly. If you need my ships for other duties, I'm happy to be of service."

"I do have another request for your service. But let us enjoy a glass of brandy and our meal before we discuss more business.

Please have a seat. I also want to hear about your family and how you're settling in at Yerba Buena Cove."

During their meal, Vallejo informed William about his new extensive civil and military powers. Now, with the title of Military Commander and Director of Colonization of the Northern Frontier, he oversaw secularization of the Sonoma mission, transferring the lands from the Catholic Church to the Mexican authorities, turning it into a pueblo with a parish church. The Miwok and Pomo workers who had not succumbed to disease had been freed from their mission duties and given land, cattle, and other mission assets. Much later William learned that the governor rewarded forty-four thousand acres and mission assets to Vallejo for a rancho in Petaluma Valley.

Their hearty dinner finished, Vallejo asked William to stay another day to assist him in laying out a new pueblo. The Sonoma mission church was the starting point from which they measured streets running east to west and north to south. Like the valley, the pueblo was called Sonoma, the "Valley of the Moon." William realized staying meant leaving María alone for another day or two, but he felt he had no choice. They had agreed she would take the children to her sister's house at Mission Dolores if necessary. But it was the dry season, so there shouldn't be any problems.

✠ ✠ ✠

Soon after he returned to Yerba Buena, William heard that the English brig *Ayacucho* had arrived in the bay near the Presidio. His English friend Captain John Wilson, whom William had not seen since their meeting in Callao, Peru, was still the master. With one of his vaqueros, William galloped to the beach near the Presidio. Spying William's familiar face on shore, Captain Wilson launched a longboat to pick him up.

When William clambered up the Jacob's ladder to the deck, John gave him a broad smile and a bear hug. William piloted the vessel safely into Yerba Buena Cove, and after the crew dropped anchor, invited the *Ayacucho's* captain for a visit ashore and dinner with his family in their tent-shanty. Over a merry dinner that María set up on the travel chests, William pumped his fellow Englishman about their mutual acquaintances in the British merchant marine and for news from the homeland. Captain Wilson also talked about his concerns with the new Factory Act, now law in England. Although he agreed with the new law that prohibited hiring children under age nine, and limited labor for children under age thirteen to nine-hour days, he wondered how that might affect the production of goods and his trade.

"And if that wasn't bad enough," Captain Wilson flared, "the new law abolishing slavery in the British Empire will ruin my profits from shipments of sugar from plantations."

William nodded his head in agreement. "It'll affect your profits, but slavery is cruel. Mexico outlawed slavery a long time ago. It's in their constitution. I'm glad the mission system is ending. It was slavery even though the friars believed differently."

"But you have worse troubles than that here. When anchored in San Diego, I heard there are rumblings and threats of insurrection from Mexican provinces opposed to the current President, López de Santa Ana."

William frowned and gulped the last of his wine. "The Mexican government has been weak and unstable for years. But California's current governor, Figueroa, is reliable. I have confidence in him. I'm worried how this unrest in Tejas and the other Mexican provinces might affect Alta California and trade." William clapped his friend on the shoulder. "Let's not end this fine dinner on a gloomy note."

While María readied the children for sleep, William lit an oil lamp, rummaged in a trunk for a deck of cards, and moved his guest outside the tent. The wind had dropped, and the lamp, moon, and campfire offered enough light for the card players. The men happily surrendered their attention to a game of whist and many glasses of brandy until Captain Wilson's cheeks brightened to cherry red. He swayed a bit in the saddle when he departed and rode to the launch waiting for him on the moonlit beach.

✠ ✠ ✠

The next project William tackled was building a *temescal*, a sweat house for his Ohlone workers. His vaqueros and sailors dug a two-foot-deep pit about ten feet in diameter close to Laguna Dulce. They bent tree saplings over the pit to form a conical structure with a smoke hole over the center. Layers of brush and earth were used for the roof. A mission blanket covered the open doorway.

Francisco studied the completed building inside and out and watched the Ohlone workers carry in firewood and stones.

"Papá, what will Ricardo, Diego, and the other men do in this house?" he asked.

"They will build a fire in the center of the floor and spend time each night in the heated house until they are sweating. Then they'll go outside and plunge into the cold lagoon water to wash. They say sweating cleanses their bodies of pests and impurities. They believe this cleansing also cures illnesses. The women use the sweat house, too."

Although María objected to the delay, William reassured her that the family's house would come next but insisted that the *temescal* was a priority since it was important to their servants. Soon after the *temescal* was completed, William and his crew sailed to Santa Clara to fell trees and rough cut the logs into planks for their house.

"We'll be gone two days, María," he assured her. "Ricardo will remain to guard the horses. The men have chased away most of the wild animals. You and the children will be safe. Don't worry."

"I'm not happy about living in a tent," she said, "but I can take care of the children, William. I worry about you. Logging is dangerous. What would we do if you were hurt? Do be careful."

But two days turned into four, which would have been worrisome but not disastrous, except on the third morning, the coals in the adobe oven were cold. The habit was to bank a fire overnight to have hot coals to stir to life in the morning. But Sophia couldn't resurrect a spark from the oven ashes.

"I am so sorry, Señora," Sophia said, head bowed. "We have nothing hot to eat for breakfast."

A freezing, heavy August fog hung over the land and the bay. The sun might not break through all day. Chilled and shivering, Mariana and Francisco shrugged on layers of heavy clothes and fetched water from the nearby spring for the cook. After a breakfast of beef jerky and cold water, they raced their ponies over the sand dunes hoping to warm themselves. When they returned from their ride, Francisco was still shivering. María looked at his flushed cheeks and felt his feverish forehead. Though usually confident and serene around her children, María now had a furrowed brow and frowned.

"Francisco, put on your night clothes, wrap this blanket around you, and get into my bed," María ordered. "Maruha, get me water in a basin. I must get his fever down."

"But, Mamá, I am cold!" Francisco said. "No cold water . . . I feel weak."

When Maruha brought in the water, María sat on the bed and alternately bathed Francisco's head to cool his fever and rubbed his hands to warm them. Mariana played clapping games with Esteban to entertain him and to keep them both warm.

"I can't even brew mint tea for my poor boy," María fumed. She turned to Maruha. "You and Sophia must ride to the Presidio to get hot coals to start our fire. I can't leave Francisco. Take an iron bucket with you to carry them back. Ricardo must stay here to protect us and the horses. Go now! Hurry!

"Mariana, help Ricardo saddle two horses."

Mariana left the tent to find Ricardo. Soon after, María heard a shout and ducked outside to see who was there. She heard someone galloping toward the tent-shanty along the trail from the Mission.

"*Hola*, María!" the rider called out.

Someone who knew her. Out of the fog, the rider appeared.

"Don Pedro! *Hola*. Oh, you are the answer to our prayers."

Don Pedro, a retired Presidio soldier, galloped up to the tent-shanty and dismounted. When he heard about their problem, he reached into his saddlebag and pulled out the flint he always carried with him. Within a few minutes he had a fire blazing in the campfire pit.

"I must ride on to the Presidio," Don Pedro said, "but I'll check on you tomorrow on my way back to Mission Dolores and my rancho."

"I am so grateful you came to our rescue," María said. "William should be back today or tomorrow, but we have been miserable without a fire."

María bundled Francisco in a blanket and had him sit near the fire to warm himself while Sophia balanced a pot of water over the flames for mint tea. Mariana, Esteban, and Maruha also huddled close to the fire's comforting heat.

After the tea was brewed, Sophia pulled burning sticks from the campfire and built a fire in the beehive oven. That night they had a hot meal with fresh, warm tortillas for dinner and hot coals in the braziers to warm their tent-shanty. Mariana and Esteban curled up in their hammocks, but María stayed up late to care for Francisco, who remained feverish and continued coughing.

Although she had told Don Pedro that William would return in a day, she worried the delay would be longer. If he had suffered an accident, if the ship needed repairs, she wouldn't know for days and must then carry on here alone with the children. Or she could move to the Mission and stay with her sister.

She prayed to God to keep her husband and her family safe. Although this beach was lonelier than she had thought it would be, she had agreed with William they should move here. And William made a commitment to the governor. But when William returned, she would insist he build their new house without delay.

CHAPTER 30

NEW HOME, NEW PUEBLO

In August, trading voyages around the bay and one to Monterey delayed William's construction plans. He promised his family he would begin their house in early September. He was as concerned as María about his son's health even though Francisco had recovered from his recent illness. The tent-shanty wasn't a suitable dwelling for winter.

During this period, William was deeply saddened to hear his benefactor, Governor Figueroa, was seriously ill due to a heart problem and was not expected to live. The governor was aware of William's medical skills and sent a message asking William to make haste to Monterey in case he could advise or assist him.

William felt shaken. While sailing south to Monterey, he mulled over his discussions with the governor and their long meetings planning the future of Yerba Buena, meetings that took place in Los Angeles and during their ride together when the Richardson family moved north. He admired Figueroa's astute handling of the breakup of the missions and his bold proposals for Alta California. Worried for the man and for his own plans to live in Yerba Buena, William anchored in Monterey Bay and hurried to Governor Figueroa's bedside but arrived too late.

A few days after the official mourning period and Figueroa's funeral, the acting governor, Don José Castro, met with William in the governor's office.

"I know Governor Figueroa appointed you Captain of the Port of San Francisco Bay," said Don José. "He received good reports of your loyalty and dedication, and so I can confidently tell you that you will continue in that capacity."

"Thank you for your kind words," William said. "Governor Figueroa was a fine man and had great foresight about this wonderful land. He will be missed." William rubbed his chin but plunged on. "I hope to help you carry out his plans for a pueblo at Yerba Buena. To make the pueblo a success, the governor had agreed some of the land should be sold to residents. If the Mexican government retains rights to all the land, the town won't grow. And the government won't take in as much revenue."

"The governor and I discussed that," Don José said, examining a drawing lying on his desk.

William recognized the rough sketch of the Yerba Buena landscape as the one he had made months ago for Figueroa.

"To proceed with the plans for Yerba Buena," Don José continued, "I request you work with Don Francisco de Haro, the *alcalde* (mayor) of Mission Dolores, to lay out streets and building lots. Before the governor died, he granted a lot to you as well. Some Presidio soldiers and other *gente de razón* are also interested in buying lots." He smiled at William. "You and your family will soon have many neighbors."

"My wife will be especially pleased to hear that news!"

✠ ✠ ✠

In October, Don Francisco de Haro received orders from Governor Castro to plan and measure building lots for a pueblo at Yerba Buena Cove. The beach area would be reserved for a plaza and future government buildings, and the other lots would be sold to residents. Don Francisco sent word to William that he and three members of Mission Dolores' district council wished to meet with him about planning and mapping the pueblo.

A few days later, the four men rode along the mission trail to William's tent-shanty. Hearing the horses approach, William and María stepped out of the tent to greet the alcalde and councilmen.

"*Buenos dias*, gentlemen," called William. He introduced María to the group and then mounted his horse. María invited them to return for a midday meal. Accompanied by two of William's vaqueros, the group rode the short distance over the dunes to the water's edge.

Land along the cove shoreline had been reserved for the Mexican government as a buffer zone to discourage smugglers and as the site for a future custom house. After some discussion, Alcalde de Haro had the men mark off two hundred *varas* to the top of a small dune. He rode up the low hill, looked in all directions, and pointed northwest.

"Measure and mark off a line here for our founding street," he said. "All land from here to the shore belongs to the government. All lots to the west of this line will be sold to individuals for houses."

William fished out paper, ink, and a pen from his saddle bags and scratched out a rough drawing of the lots and main street. While he drew, he struggled to hold down the paper against the prevailing wind. He quickly figured out his new house should be located on the fifth lot west of the government strip of land.

During lunch at the tent-shanty, William discussed with Don Francisco the lot he wanted to claim, the first lot to be sold in the new pueblo for twenty-five pesos, equal to twenty-five American dollars. All the officials agreed to call the pueblo Yerba Buena.

After the men left in late afternoon, William pulled out fresh paper, a pen, ink, and watercolors. Using a travel trunk as a desk, he drew a map of the pueblo as planned. He made a copy that showed his lot and the founding street and labeled it *Calle de la Fundación,* Foundation Street. Francisco and Mariana looked over his shoulder at the maps while he worked. William pointed to the lot he had claimed.

"This spot is where our first house will be built."

A few days later, he directed his men to dismantle the tent-shanty and move it down the hill to his *solar de tierra,* plot of land. Thankful that he had waited to build his house, he began to mark the perimeters on his new plot.

✠ ✠ ✠

Before winter rains fell, William fulfilled his promise to María of a solid wooden house to replace the tent. It was constructed with the rough lumber planks cut during the San José logging trip that summer. William lined the rustic walls of the house with the tent-shanty canvas to keep out the cold and the windblown sand. The house had only three rooms but felt luxurious and cozy compared to the primitive tent-shanty. The beehive adobe oven was moved to the site also. The Ohlones, pleased that William had built their *temescal* in July, worked diligently to finish the sturdy house before the wet season. After enduring the tent-shanty for almost four months, María and the children were relieved to move into the secure dwelling.

One quiet evening after dinner, María sat next to William to mend a torn shirt while he used rawhide strips to make a chair seat. They talked about their future.

"Even though Figueroa has died, I must continue to press for our Saucelito land grant," he said while weaving a leather strip across the seat frame.

"Yes, you should, *mi amore*," agreed María. "No one has done more for Mexico to develop this forsaken wilderness. You helped Alcalde de Haro. You've taken on the responsibility of captain of the port. We have pleaded for the title to the rancho land for almost ten years."

"The Yerba Buena *ayuntamiento*, the city council, has control of Saucelito and must approve the land grant," William said, "I think they will soon. Your father urged me to make improvements on the land to reinforce my claim. I've cleared an area, as required, and I'll fix up a small shack that's near the beach." He touched María's smooth cheek with his fingertips. "But I will also build a *Casa Grande* here in Yerba Buena as I promised you. This little house is only the first step."

✠ ✠ ✠

Juan Bautista de Alvarado was appointed governor to replace Don José Castro, but he assured William that he also was ambitious to carry out Figueroa's plans and wanted him to continue as captain of the port. William would be paid the equivalent of $60 a month for collecting port fees, checking ships' manifests, which listed passengers and crew, handling trading transactions, and guiding ships into the bay.

William was grateful even though the remuneration was not much. As captain of the port, he supported his family with his own secret trading arrangements, deals with rancheros, and a little smuggling. His ships transported hides and tallow from the surrounding ranchos to the Yerba Buena waterfront where they were hauled aboard foreign trading vessels anchored in the cove. Cargo from the foreign ships was unloaded onto William's launches for a fee, taken to the landing area, and later transported on his schooners to residents around the bay, also for a fee. For his efforts, William collected from the ship captains one peso per bag of tallow and one *real*, equal to twelve-and-a-half American cents, per cowhide, which ensured his family's financial security.

✠ ✠ ✠

Cold winter downpours did not stop the trading vessels. William and his crew sailed all seasons around the bay to collect tallow and hides. He worked as hard as his men, hauling five-hundred-pound *botas,* hide-bags, of tallow from landing areas near ranchos and Mission San José to the launches and unloading them at Yerba Buena. The stacks of hides were often just as heavy. By December, his efforts led to a strained back muscle, and his activity in the cold rain led to a fever. He was forced to stay in bed, nursed by María with help from Doña Juana Briones, who lived near the Presidio with her four children and was known as a healer. Ever since the Richardsons had moved to Yerba Buena, Doña Briones had helped María prepare decoctions of medicinal herbs to relieve Francisco's fatigue and breathing problems.

Worried about their father, the children pitched in, doing their chores without complaint or being reminded. Francisco carried firewood and fresh water to the cook Sophia. Mariana helped her brother, but also churned butter and gathered herbs. Little Esteban carried cups of cool water to his father.

William's crew continued their navigation duties, boarding trading vessels to pilot them to Yerba Buena Cove. From his sick bed, William carried out his duties as captain of the port, checking a ship's docket brought to him by a ship's captain or first mate, who often stayed to share news and entertain him with tales about their voyages.

By Christmas, with Diego's kind help, William struggled out of bed to sit at the table with his family for the fine feast María and the cook had prepared.

He had not forgotten the promise he made to his daughter earlier that year. Mariana hugged and kissed her father and mother when she saw Ricardo walk her beautiful pony to the house on Christmas morning. Looking at his beaming child, William began dreaming of a large adobe, a real house for his long-suffering wife. A *Casa Grande*.

CHAPTER 31

GOOD NEIGHBORS IN YERBA BUENA

July 1836

María stood outside her front door on July fourth, raised her hand to shade her eyes from the blazing sun, and gazed at the cove. Half a dozen vessels, brigs, whalers, warships, and one schooner were anchored in the bay, and wide, flat-bottomed rowboats called lighters darted back and forth like water striders to carry the ships' passengers ashore. Each ship was decorated with strings of colorful banners that fluttered and snapped in the sea breeze, and the flags of several countries—American, Mexican, French, and British—waved from the masts.

A procession of mission Ohlones trudged up the sand dunes alongside oxcarts loaded with wood planks. Jacob Primer Leese, a twenty-seven-year-old American, was building a combined residence and retail store next to the southern boundary of the Richardsons' property. Leese planned to sell dry goods, sugar, flour, nails, European furniture, and other merchandise. The prospect of a local shop delighted María and her friends and relatives. They usually waited months to obtain goods from trading vessels. María listened to the ring of hammers and the buzz of handsaws as men rushed to put up the rough siding and roof on the framework of the new house before the American Independence Day celebration. She watched sandy-haired Jacob bob around, directing the hired workmen, and recalled his visit to the cove the previous summer.

Jacob had sailed into the bay looking for a place to establish a mercantile business for himself and his American partners, Captain William S. Hinckley and Nathan Spear. Their main store, located in Monterey, sold American and British merchandise to the pueblo citizens and the surrounding ranchos. Jacob was convinced Yerba Buena Cove was the ideal location for a branch of their business. William was not. He cautioned Jacob that the lots had not yet been mapped for the pueblo, and he doubted the Mexican government would allow him to build a branch store at Yerba Buena.

Undaunted, Jacob spoke to Alcalde de Haro, who explained that he personally was eager to have a mercantile business in Yerba Buena, but at this time the government was claiming all the land near the cove. De Haro offered him land near the Presidio and another parcel closer to the mission, but Jacob was not dissuaded. To him, the cove was ideal since local launches and the trading ships' longboats could most easily land there. He returned to Monterey where he and his partners persisted in their business plans, petitioning for a land grant, and finally securing an agreement for their venture from the new governor, Mariano Chico.

Now Leese's building was almost complete. To honor their American neighbors, María, William, and other Yerba Buena citizens had planned a Fourth of July festivity.

✠ ✠ ✠

Mariana, Francisco, and Esteban joined María outside on the veranda to watch all the activity. Five-year-old Esteban held Mariana's two hands and jumped up and down with joy although María was sure he didn't know the significance of what was happening.

Mariana smiled at her little brother. "We will see our cousins today, Esteban! Ramón, José, Concepción, Gertrudis. We'll play games together and ride our ponies."

"And eat lots of delicious food!" exclaimed Francisco, taking a deep breath and drawing in the delicious smell of bread baking in their adobe brick oven. "Mamá, can Mariana and I ride to the shore to look at the ships?" Francisco asked.

María turned to her children to consider the request. "You have finished your chores, yes? Good. Wait for your cousins to arrive. They'll be here soon. Then you may all ride to the beach together. But don't wander too far. The celebration will begin early this afternoon."

María scrutinized the skeleton of the Leese house. Would the house be ready for the afternoon celebration? Construction seemed to be progressing swiftly. The guests would eat at tables outside, but dancing was planned for the large *sala* in the new building. Near his house, Jacob had erected small tents as accommodations for the rancheros and their families. For the last few days, William had been dashing around the bay, picking up neighbors and sailing them to Yerba Buena for the first American Independence Day celebration.

María searched the cove again and located William's schooner. A lighter was pulling away from the ship with another group of merrymakers from the local ranchos. Her husband was probably among them. Preoccupied with the dozen things she still had to do, she left the children on the veranda to wait for their cousins and turned her attention to the meal preparations. She also wanted to see how her parents and sisters were settling in their rooms, happy they were there to join the festivities. She silently thanked William for adding an extra room to their house to accommodate her family when they visited.

✠ ✠ ✠

At three o'clock in the afternoon, the first grand celebration in Yerba Buena commenced—the first Independence Day observance and a warm welcoming party for the newcomer

Jacob Primer Leese and his store. His sixty-foot long, one-story building had been completed and decorated inside and out with flags and colorful bunting supplied by the ships in the harbor. Leese's partner, Captain Hinckley, a passionate music enthusiast, brought on his barque, *Don Quixote,* a six-piece orchestra consisting of a violin, flute, clarinet, drum, fife, and bugle. On the beach, the Presidio arranged for two six-pounder cannons to be used in place of fireworks during the feast.

All the principal rancho families—Castro, Martínez, Vallejo, Peralta, De Haro, and many others—had assembled for the celebration as did the ships' officers and the three American store owners. Since the Californios tended to have large families, many children attended the party. The twelve-year-old twins Francisco and Ramón de Haro, their sisters Rosalía and Natividad, the Estudillo sisters and brothers, and María's young sisters joined the Richardson children at the festivities. While the older guests enjoyed mission wine and brandy at tables set up outside the Leese residence, the children played tag and hide-and-seek, raced one another, and rode their ponies over the dunes, screeching and laughing.

Don José Joaquín Estudillo, who had been selected the new alcalde of Yerba Buena in January, rose and clinked his glass of wine with his knife. "I am pleased to see so many of our prominent rancheros gathered here to honor this great occasion. The governor and I, as his representative here in Yerba Buena, salute you!" He raised his glass and all the guests did as well. A thunderous boom from the Presidio cannon punctuated his toast, startling the children and a few adults. Answering salutes rumbled from the ships in the harbor.

Vallejo, recently promoted to general for his exploration of northern Alta California and the establishment of the Sonoma Presidio, spoke next.

"Like many of you, I came to this savage country when it was wilderness. The Presidio and the northern missions were the only evidence of civilization. Through the efforts of Don Francisco de Haro, José Joaquín Estudillo, our current alcalde, and my friend Captain Richardson, we see the beginnings of a new life here in Yerba Buena. We also are fortunate indeed that these Americans, Señor Jacob Leese and his partners, Captain William Hinckley and Señor Nathan Spear, decided to establish their new store in our pueblo." The general picked up his wine glass. "*Nuestras cálidas felicitaciones,* our warmest congratulations, to our new *vecinos*!" The guests again raised their glasses to salute their new neighbors, and another cannon roared, causing the young children to stop their games and cover their ears.

In his position of port captain, William felt it was his duty to address the guests as well. "This celebration is in honor of the American Independence Day and to welcome our new neighbors. I am delighted to see my relatives and my friends around these tables, all dear to my family and me. I thank you for your gracious help in making this day a success and wish you health and good cheer. Raise a glass!" And everyone did, cheeks getting rosier with each sip of fortifying wine.

Other guests delivered toasts to the health of all and to the success of the new mercantile store and the pueblo. At some point, William excused himself and caught General Vallejo's eye. The two men strolled a short distance away from the merry, noisy guests.

"This genial party reminds me how much our lives have changed and how our rancho life will change," William said to the general. "The new store will attract more vessels to our cove. Even now, many more foreign ships enter the bay to trade than they did even a year ago."

"I agree and welcome them heartily!" said the general.

"I welcome the new trade also," William said. "But we'll have to provide more than hides and tallow for trade. Fur trappers, explorers, and adventurers have already entered California. If the American settlers in Tejas win their conflict with Mexico, many more immigrants will cross the mountains. Do you have any current news about Tejas?"

"A few months ago, American settlers and Mexican soldiers fought a bloody battle at the old Alamo mission, but Mexico prevailed. The unrest is continuing," General Vallejo said. "To avoid a conflict, we must work for a peaceful inclusion of new settlers. More people like Leese, Spear, and Hinckley, people who build mercantile shops and increase trade. The Californios have never been farmers or shopkeepers. Spain wouldn't allow it, and Mexico followed the same policy. But now that the missions are no longer thriving, we need businessmen and farmers."

"This bay will attract more and more ships with Americans and Europeans, even Russians," William said, thinking aloud. "They'll want to settle here and mix their lives and fortunes with ours. Not all newcomers should be shopkeepers or farmers, though. As this little pueblo grows, we'll need loggers, builders, blacksmiths, doctors." He took another sip of wine. "Will they be willing to become Mexican citizens?"

The two men gazed at the happy scene of mingling guests and then at the two flagpoles at either end of the peak of Leese's building. One flagpole flew the Mexican tricolor and the other the Stars and Stripes. Both flags rippled in the stiff wind off the bay.

✠ ✠ ✠

The drinks led to a hearty banquet, followed by dancing in the new store until early morning. With so many charming señoritas present, Jacob, Nathan, and William Hinckley cheerfully waltzed with many partners. Jacob danced the most with General Vallejo's sister Rosalía. María and her mother smiled behind their fans as the couple whirled blissfully by, gazing into each other's eyes.

"They will be married soon," Doña Martina whispered to her daughter. "Mark my words."

"He is handsome," said María, "although I wish I could get Rosalía interested in Don Timoteo. He's a good man, a good friend of William's. He often visits us for dinner and a game of whist with William." María pointed out the six-foot plus muscular Irishman in a corner of the room with her husband, both towering over the other guests. "And he's wealthy. He made a sizable fortune hunting sea otters and selling the pelts." María sighed. "I don't know how Rosalía is able to resist his gentle manners."

✠ ✠ ✠

During a break in the music, William's father-in-law, the former Presidio comandante, Don Ignacio Martínez pulled him aside and handed him a glass of wine.

"You certainly know how to arrange a wonderful party," the don said to William.

"This is more your daughter's doing," William said, nodding his head toward his wife. "She and the other women worked on this *fiesta* with my brother-in-law, our alcalde. I just carried out orders!"

The men toasted María and each other's health.

"I have a request, William," Don Ignacio said. "Doña Martina and I plan to move from San José to Rancho Pinole permanently in the fall. Would you be able to help with our move?"

"Of course, it would be my pleasure! You don't even have to ask. María and the children will be pleased to know that you and your family will be so much closer for visits, just across the bay."

"I'll let you know the date we wish to move as soon as possible. I thank you in advance for your help."

The don laid a hand on William's arm and locked eyes with him. "I commend you on your success in our country. From the moment I first met you, I knew you were an honorable man. No bank account, but ambitious and trustworthy. I knew also I could trust my daughter's judgment when she chose you for her husband. Although she was attracted to you because of your worldly experiences and accomplishments, she knew you would be faithful."

Don Ignacio looked over at his beautiful daughter dancing with a guest. "Never forget, though, that proud Spanish patrician stock runs in her blood. If you do not disappoint her, you will never disappoint me."

William proudly watched his beautiful wife dance but remembered his indiscretion and felt unworthy of her.

As the night progressed, María and William danced as much as anyone, happy to see so many friends and family members, secure in knowing that their move was a good choice. While they waltzed, William bent his head to murmur in his wife's ear, "Are you truly happy, *mi amore*?"

"With your arms about me, always," she answered. "I'm content to be here in our new town. For now."

She smiled into William's serious blue eyes and whispered in his ear. "You have begun building a magnificent house here, but please do not forget about our dream of living on our own rancho."

"I know which port we're steering toward," he assured her. "And with your father's help, we'll pick up a favorable wind to get us there."

✠ ✠ ✠

As busy as William was with the transport of hides and tallow and with his official port duties, he had not forgotten about Rancho Saucelito. Before Governor Figueroa died, he had agreed to the rancho land grant with certain conditions. To obtain the title, he stipulated that William gain the approval of the territorial legislature and local authorities, something Captain John Reed had failed to do. Though Reed's application for the Saucelito rancho was unsuccessful, the Mexican government stated it would instead grant him the rancho Corte Madera del Presidio, where he and his wife now resided.

Learning from Reed's mistake, William had surveyed the land and refurbished a two-room cabin Reed had built on it. Now he had to stock the rancho with cattle. After his talk with his father-in-law, he saw his chance to fulfill this official requirement.

Don Ignacio had been awarded Rancho Pinole for his services to the Mexican government. Now that he and his family had decided to move from Pueblo San José to their rancho, the don would be concluding his work as administrator of the San Rafael mission. Some of the mission cattle, sheep, and hogs had already been given to loyal neophytes. As permitted by the governor, the don removed a share of stock to Rancho Pinole and distributed some cattle to General Vallejo for his Sonoma home. At William's request, the don reserved some livestock for

William. Once the vaqueros drove the cattle, horses, and sheep to Rancho Saucelito, William rebranded them "WR" below the mission brand.

However, after stocking Saucelito and getting the San Francisco pueblo *ayuntamiento's* acceptance of his petition for the rancho, William was disappointed and frustrated to discover his application's approval had been delayed again. General Vallejo felt William merited the unoccupied land, but a Colonization Law of 1824 still existed that prohibited foreigners from settling within ten leagues of the coastline unless the Mexican government, not just the governor, approved. William would have to travel to Mexico City and appear in person to request approval.

He tallied his duties on the bay and the needs of his family. His mind whirled. A trip to Mexico would take months. He would have to prepare María for his absence. She and the children would be safe though with her sister Juana now in Yerba Buena and Jacob Leese next door. He would have to be sure his crew could carry on his port duties while he was gone.

CHAPTER 32

UNSETTLED

Whenever William was away, Diego or Monico, a more recent hire with experience sailing a ship for Mission Dolores, took responsibility for piloting ships into the bay. Though Monico's hair was white with age, he carried his six-foot muscular frame as lightly as a much younger man. William was confident in his seafaring ability and his judgment, and all the sailors were at ease working with him. Some Kanakas, sailors from the Sandwich Islands who had jumped ship in Yerba Buena, also worked for William. They were seasoned mariners, used to rough seas and daring, almost to the point of being reckless. They reminded William of his old friend and sailor Marino who had retired a few years ago.

William left the piloting and transporting duties in Monico's hands when he sailed to Mexico to get approval of his application for Rancho Saucelito. He would be away for about five months, but with more people in the pueblo and with his well-trained crew, he believed his family and the port would be secure.

✠ ✠ ✠

During one severe storm while William was away, a foreign trading vessel fired two cannon shots seeking the safety of the bay.

Monico heard the distress call. Shouting to a young Kanaka, he raced with him in the pouring rain to the beach where the two launched a longboat. With water and foam flying from their oars, they sliced through the stormy waves, passed the bay entrance to the floundering ship, and scrambled over the rail. Dripping wet, his chest heaving, Monico pushed past the frantic captain.

"Monico," the captain exclaimed recognizing William's trustworthy sailor. "I'm amazed you're here!"

The skipper was unable to navigate the dangerous gateway and his ship was drifting toward the beach outside the headlands.

"Can you save us?" he asked.

"I will get your ship in safely, Captain," Monico answered flatly.

He and the Kanaka secured their longboat. Then, Monico brushed the wheelman aside and took command of the helm. He proceeded to guide the ship through the treacherous entrance, battling the winds and tide. When they entered the calmer harbor of Yerba Buena Cove and set anchor, the sailors shouted.

"Huzzah! Huzzah!"

Townspeople who had gathered on the beach, worried about the safety of the ship, its crew, and its cargo, joined in cheering.

When William returned to Yerba Buena, Nathan Spear told him of the daring rescue of the ship. "Everyone was standing in the rain cheering for Monico. Me loudest of all, since the ship had valuable merchandise on board destined for my store. Monico just walked across the beach when he landed, never smiling or acknowledging our greeting."

William gazed at the harbor where his launch sat with his men offloading goods from another trading vessel. "That's as it should be," he said to Nathan. "You know, Monico had sailed the bay but had never stepped in salt water until he came to work for me. Of all the seamen I have met, he has no peer. But he and his brethren aren't like Europeans and Americans. They do what they must do, never expecting a reward or recognition. I'm proud of him. Of all my men."

✠ ✠ ✠

The sun, as golden as a fresh egg yolk, was rising over the eastern hills across the bay as William walked out on the *Casa Grande* veranda, a mug of hot chocolate in his hand. He was the first one awake in the house except for Sophia, who had made his drink. He now heard María moving around in their room and singing her morning hymn to rouse the household. The children would be up soon, and the family would breakfast together. He looked to the shore and saw his crew readying the launch for a trip onto the bay if a ship was sighted.

His family was now secure in the new, larger house, the largest in the pueblo. He had built it last year to replace the small wood-frame cottage they had lived in during their first winter. Whitewashed and topped with a handsome tile roof, the eight-room adobe stretched to more than sixty-six feet long and forty-nine feet wide. It boasted several bedrooms, a parlor, a large sitting room, and a dining space large enough to be turned into a ballroom for parties. Under the eaves, there was space for extra furniture and grain storage. The three-foot-thick walls kept the house cool in the summer and warm during the chilly, wet winter. William was pleased with his life and his efforts.

The covered veranda provided a fine view of the cove and bay. While William gazed at the shoreline and the new buildings dotting the land down to Yerba Buena Cove, he felt a slight tremor. Several small earthquakes had occurred during the past week, none causing damage though.

Now his body tensed, alert. He had lived through serious California temblors as well as a few in South America when he was there on trading voyages.

He stared at the bay and saw the tide being sucked back, revealing the mud flats. A rolling action heaved the ground under his feet. He clutched a post to keep his footing. His throat tightened when he saw the hill Loma Alta sway east to west. Dropping his mug, he turned and staggered through the doorway to his family. María and the children had gathered for breakfast but were now huddled under the heavy mahogany table.

"It's safer outside!" William shouted, lurching toward his family. He pulled María to her feet. Another roll of the earth almost knocked them both to the floor. The children scrambled after them. María grasped Mariana and Francisco's hands. William picked up Esteban and led them out the door onto the sand.

The earth continued to roll. Their new house creaked and swayed but did not collapse.

Sophia and Maruha were hugging each other outside on the ground near the adobe oven where they had been baking bread. When María called their names, they signaled they were not hurt. William looked to the cove again to see if his crew was safe. They were sitting on the sand to wait out the continuing tremors. As William scanned the area, he realized the massive dune to the south of the cove had shifted closer to the water's edge. Previously, one could walk or ride around the dune at low tide, but no longer.

An earthquake that can change the landscape, he thought to himself. *How unstable these dunes are!* This temblor was the worst one he had ever felt.

✠ ✠ ✠

Tremors rolled through the area for the rest of the day. Each time, William and María paused in clearing broken dishes and cups to see if the tremor would get worse. They told the children to stay outside. After tidying their house, William and María left the children with Maruha and Sophia and hurried to the Leeses' house to see how they fared.

As Doña Martina had predicted, Jacob Leese and Rosalía Vallejo had married. Engaged on April first of the previous year, they wed on April seventh. Jacob's success with the store smoothed the waters toward his acceptance by Mexican officials and more especially by Rosalía's brother, General Vallejo. The general had confessed to William his desire to encourage Americans to settle in California, so what could be more natural than blessing his sister's marriage to a clever, handsome Yankee with a thriving mercantile store?

María was pleased to see it thrive. Three days after the Independence Day party, Jacob unloaded mounds of merchandise from Captain Hinckley's ship, and the Richardsons and local rancho families swarmed his store. The following year, General Vallejo and his wife Francesca were pleased for the young couple when Rosalie Leese, the first child born in Yerba Buena, was baptized.

Jacob, Rosalía, and baby Rosalie were unharmed during the earthquake, but crockery, glassware, tools, and other items were broken or scattered on the store's floor. Having experienced several earthquakes during their lives, María and Rosalía calmly swept up the debris while the men departed to check on María's sister Juana and her family, other neighbors, and William's crew.

✠ ✠ ✠

When William returned home, he and María decided they and the children would sleep on the veranda, making an adventure of it. To calm them before bed, William told them tales about his trading voyages.

"This rolling earth today felt like a ship in full sail on high seas, climbing waves and then sliding into troughs. How easily fish and whales swim in such a sea!" he said. "Once off the coast of Mexico, I saw hundreds of spinner dolphins on the same course as my ship, gliding through the rough waves. They surrounded the ship, seeming to pull it along with them. Their wet backs glistened in the sun as they leaped and spun in the air, twirling in a dance."

"Will we get to see such a sight someday, Papá?" asked Francisco.

"You very well may," William said. "You're almost old enough to become a cabin boy. I was one at twelve years old."

"If I'm on a ship, I won't be able to ride my pony," reasoned Mariana. "I'd rather stay on land. I wouldn't like to be rolling up and down on the sea all the time like we did today during the earthquake." María covered her smile at her daughter's logic.

After overseeing the children's evening prayers and kissing them goodnight, William and María sat at the end of the veranda, each mulling over their own thoughts about the earthquake.

"I'm of two minds about our future," William began quietly. "On one hand, I'm thinking a house in Saucelito would be more secure than this one built on sand."

María peered at her husband in the fading light. "I wasn't afraid today, William. I prayed to God during the earthquake, and thankfully the shaking didn't harm us or the house. But you're probably right. You know more about buildings than I do."

William gazed at the darkening shoreline and spoke his thoughts aloud. "During the last few months, almost thirty foreign trading vessels, whalers, and naval warships with exploratory expeditions visited the bay. As port captain, it's more convenient to live in Yerba Buena because I work here."

"And there are neighbors here for company," María added.

"However," William said, "word is spreading from captain to captain that they can avoid paying high Mexican duties for their cargo by steering left when they enter the bay. They sail to Saucelito to offload and hide cargo from Yerba Buena customs officers. And pay me when they refill their barrels with our fresh spring water. That brings in more cash for us than my port captain salary."

"True. If we move there and start a garden, we could sell vegetables, too. We would have more money to spend in Jacob's store. And," María paused to gaze at her oldest son, sleeping peacefully, "living here is still not healthy, especially for Francisco. His colds with fever get worse each year."

"Do you remember how glorious our days were after our wedding?" asked William as he looked in his wife's dark eyes in the dwindling light. "The breezes at Saucelito were so mild. The redwoods and the meadows of spring wildflowers were so beautiful. No one for miles around. I feel it's getting too crowded here." He looked out at the shadowy shapes of their neighbors' new constructions, most of them for businesses. "We need more privacy and elbow room. I've dreamed of our children living on our land, in open country every day, not growing up on a beach."

María placed her hand on her husband's arm and smiled, her dark eyes glowing. "Yes! Yes, William! I want that, too. If we live there, we can sail across the bay to Yerba Buena to see friends and purchase goods we need. And now that Mamá and Papá have settled at Rancho Pinole, they are closer too. I agree with you, *mi amore*. We should live at Rancho Saucelito."

✠ ✠ ✠

The next year, an unsettling incident delayed the move to Saucelito. William regretted disappointing María, but their plan would have to wait. As captain of the port, William had to help General Vallejo deal with a new settler. "A Swiss adventurer," according to General Vallejo, who had applied to Governor Alvarado for a tract of land in northern Alta California. To choose his land, he required transport around the bay.

CHAPTER 33

CAPTAIN JOHN AUGUSTUS SUTTER

On July 1, 1839, the *Clementine* dropped anchor in Yerba Buena Cove. William wasn't in port to meet the vessel because he was collecting neighbors for the American Independence Day celebrations, now a yearly event. Instead, a Presidio lieutenant boarded the ship and addressed the ship's master Captain Blinn.

"You are in Mexican territory here and are not allowed to land," the lieutenant grumped. "You must sail to Monterey at once and pay duties there. Then you might be permitted to enter our bay again."

Ever charming, John Augustus Sutter, the supercargo, nudged the ship's captain aside and stepped forward to introduce himself as "Captain John Sutter." His military bearing and gentlemanly manners lent credence to his claim. "We apologize for our irregular entry. Our ship suffered severe weather as we sailed down the coast from Sitka and needs some repair. Also, we need provisions and fresh water desperately."

Captain John Wilson and shopkeeper Nathan Spear who now boarded the ship interrupted this unfriendly exchange. To soothe

the prickly reception, Sutter introduced himself and produced several letters of introduction from imminent men stationed at Fort Vancouver, Honolulu, and Sitka. One letter addressed to General Vallejo was from the United States Consul of Honolulu, who called him "a Swiss gentleman of the first class among men of honor, talent, and estimation."

The Consul's fine words impressed Captain Wilson, who was Vallejo's brother-in-law, having married Vallejo's wife's sister Doña Ramona. Wilson was master of the brig *Ayacucho* which was in the harbor unloading cargo destined for Spear's store. As a fellow sea captain, he was in sympathy with Captain Blinn.

"We must make allowances for the difficulties this ship has endured," said Captain Wilson.

Nathan also spoke up. "The ship is obviously in distress, Lieutenant. We cannot turn them away until repairs and supplies are provided."

Pressured by the other men, the lieutenant bowed to the arguments. "Very well, Captain," he muttered. "Your ship can remain here to make repairs and get provisions before you set sail for Monterey."

"And, Captain Sutter," Nathan said, "I can provide overnight accommodations for you."

"I plan to build a farm in California, so eight Kanaka laborers and their wives from the Sandwich Islands are also on the ship," Sutter said.

"I can accommodate your workers and their wives as well."

The ship's captain pushed his crew for speedy repairs to the sails. Although Jacob Leese and Nathan Spear urged him to stay for the Fourth of July celebrations, he declined and sailed the *Clementine* to Monterey with Sutter onboard for his audience with Governor Juan Alvarado.

When Captain Sutter met Alvarado in his Monterey headquarters, the governor read the glowing letter of introduction addressed to Vallejo and frowned because the letter should have been addressed to him, the governor. Alvarado, the nephew of General Vallejo, had little familial love for his uncle because the two had become rivals for control of northern California.

"I arrived in San Francisco Bay by a roundabout route," Sutter explained to the governor. "After crossing the northern Rocky Mountains, I learned the overland route from Fort Vancouver to Alta California was too treacherous in winter. I boarded a supply ship headed to the Sandwich Islands, and in Honolulu I picked up passage to Sitka on a trading brig that sailed south from there along the coast. I serve as supercargo aboard the *Clementine*. I'm still in charge of the ship owner's cargo for trading." Sutter went on to explain his grand scheme for land in northern California.

When Alvarado heard his plan for a frontier farm, he flatly stated his position.

"General Vallejo is Mexico's northern frontier commander. Although your venture, if successful, would be of value to Mexico in preventing foreign encroachments, you will find my uncle will keep a sharp eye on you and your rancho. His way, his rules, might not be compatible with your vision."

However, Captain Sutter left Monterey with the governor's provisional agreement to his plan and with high hopes for a cordial meeting with General Vallejo.

✠ ✠ ✠

After the *Clementine* returned to Yerba Buena Cove, William boarded the ship and introduced himself as port captain. Recalling General Vallejo's warning to expect this overconfident Swiss explorer, William was wary and had prepared himself to handle Sutter's requests.

Before their meeting, William had pumped Nathan Spear for information about the man. Nathan described him as a tall, imposing, and ambitious free spirit. He had escaped a tedious life as a storekeeper and set out for America, leaving behind his wife and five children in his native country, Switzerland. When Nathan asked, Sutter claimed he migrated to become a farmer. His family would join him later.

"When I introduced him to my customers," Nathan said, "both men and women were impressed. It must be his slim, handsome appearance. He says he is a former Swiss officer."

William was suspicious of the man's overconfident behavior. When the ship's captain and Captain Sutter consulted with William about sailing north along the Sacramento River, Sutter blustered that their brig would take them. William set them straight, impressing on them the hefty *Clementine* would scrape the river bottom and a local bay schooner should be hired for the journey.

Sutter seemed disconcerted by this change in his plan. William assumed it was because Sutter, the supercargo, would have to release the brig and its cargo to the *Clementine's* captain, leaving Sutter unable to explore the area in a ship under his control.

With this turn of events, Captain Blinn immediately asked William for provisions and fresh water for his swift return trip to Honolulu.

William's crew transferred Sutter, his Kanakas, and their equipment to shore in the lighters. William then offered to take him across the bay within the next few days to meet General Vallejo.

"In the meantime," William said, "Nathan Spear agreed to provide you accommodation again tonight, Captain Sutter. He's disappointed the *Clementine* carried no freight for trading in Yerba Buena, but he's still happy to become better acquainted and have you and your workers stay with him."

Captain Sutter dipped in a short bow from the waist. "I'm grateful for his hospitality. I'm hoping to find a suitable place to settle north of here, and when I do, I'm sure I will be doing business with Mr. Spear."

"I'll leave you now, but I'll join you after supper to discuss your journey across the bay with Captain Wilson and me. We'll arrange for a crew to row us up the creek to Sonoma to meet General Vallejo. I'll be interested to hear your plans for settling here."

The two men shook hands and parted ways at Spear's house, which was situated close to shore. The governor had indulged Spear to encroach on government land at the edge of the bay in light of his lucrative mercantile store. William gave his crew instructions to provision the *Clementine*, and then rode home to share with María his uneasy feelings about the Swiss adventurer.

"I don't trust the man," he told his wife. "He tells a good

story, but somewhat too good. A man who leaves his family?" William shook his head. "His eyes tell me he is a calculating man. I think he is hiding something. He's interested in going up the Sacramento River, but I'm sure he has no knowledge of the wild territory up there. I'll be returning to Nathan's tonight. I'm interested in finding out where this adventurer hopes to put down roots and why."

✠ ✠ ✠

Captain John Wilson's crew rowed the three men, Sutter, William, and himself, slowly up the Sonoma Creek slough to the embarcadero laid out a few years before. General Vallejo had built an L-shaped *Casa Grande* near the Sonoma Plaza for his wife Doña Francesca and their large family. Adjacent to Vallejo's house was the military headquarters in a two-story adobe barracks where the meeting with Captain Sutter would take place. Upon arriving at the embarcadero, the visitors mounted horses supplied by Vallejo and rode along the wide street to the town plaza.

When they walked in, General Vallejo rose from behind his dark, highly polished desk, imported from England. He had been expecting them and warmly greeted his brother-in-law Captain Wilson and William, then shook hands with his guest Captain Sutter who presented his letters of recommendation.

"I have arranged rooms for all of you for the next few days," the general explained, "so you can visit our delightful settlement here as well as Sonoma Valley. Then we'll discuss your request for land, Captain Sutter. But first, my wife has prepared a fine feast for us. Let us not disappoint her by being late for our meal."

✠ ✠ ✠

On the second day, after a morning ride and a trail lunch, General Vallejo led his visitors back to his headquarters. There they dismounted, brushed off their dusty clothes, and followed their host into his office.

"Captain Sutter, I had heard from Governor Alvarado that you wish to farm north of here," the general said. "Now that you have seen our valley, let us sit and discuss how we can help you." The four men sat at a table and refreshments of wine, cheese, and cake were brought in.

During the last two days, the general had gleaned a clear idea of what Captain Sutter wanted. His demeanor cooled as Sutter now launched into his expectations for a farm. William watched the general's face, knowing he was well aware of the need for settlements along the northern frontier as protection. But a huge farm, a colony such as the one Sutter proposed to build, could be a threat to Vallejo and Mexican rule if it attracted hostile foreign settlers.

Vallejo stroked his chin as Sutter spoke. William could see the idea of a power that could rival Vallejo's vexed the general.

"I too was overwhelmed when I first saw the beauty of this valley," the general said when Sutter finished. "As you can see, we have managed to tame the wilderness quite well in a few short years. There are still many fine unoccupied and untamed tracts of land nearby."

Captain Sutter stiffened in his chair and scratched a trim sideburn. "I do appreciate what you have accomplished here, Sir. And I hope to do something similar myself," he said. "I have heard about a bountiful wilderness further along the Sacramento. . ."

"There is no need to go so far," Vallejo interrupted. "It is indeed wilderness on the upper Sacramento. But Napa Valley is closer, has rich soil, and would serve your farming needs."

Sutter considered the general. "That's extremely generous, Sir," he said. "But I have heard so much about the Sacramento area."

William listened to the exchange, knowing how displeased General Vallejo was with the friendly reception Captain Sutter received in Monterey. Governor Alvarado's concession to this foreigner was an insult to the general who was in command of northern California. William didn't put his oar in, but Captain Wilson did at this point, attempting to dissuade Captain Sutter.

"I've shown you my Sonoma cattle ranch and would be willing

to sell it to you, including the stock, for a low price. I'm too busy sailing and trading to care for it properly."

"I thank you kindly for your offer, Captain Wilson, but no, thank you."

Stunned by this blunt rejection of his property, Wilson burst out, "Well, my God! What the hell do you really want?"

Sutter tried to mollify the captain. "I do truly appreciate your offer, but I have a preference to be on a navigable river. I'll then be able to ship cargo in trade to Yerba Buena more easily."

The men could not argue against this.

General Vallejo pushed back his chair from the table and stood, signaling an end to their meeting. "Since I'm more familiar with the Sacramento frontier, I must warn you about the cattle and horse rustlers, hostile natives, and wild beasts. Even some disgruntled neophytes who couldn't succeed on their own after the missions closed."

William then spoke up. "If you intend to farm, be advised that California suffers from severe dry and wet spells. It's plagued with droughts and floods." Nothing seemed to ruffle Captain Sutter.

"I appreciate your concern and your advice," Sutter said standing and bowing to General Vallejo. "I thank you for your offers and your generous hospitality. I must take my leave tomorrow morning, gentlemen. My next stop is Fort Ross on the coast, since I have greetings to convey to the Russian commandant from an admiral in Sitka."

The next day Sutter borrowed horses and a Miwok guide from the general to ride west to the Russian settlement. Somewhat stunned by his abrupt departure, William and John stayed to discuss Sutter's bold demands with General Vallejo.

✠ ✠ ✠

Heavy rainfall persisted throughout the winter of 1839–1840. In January, rain poured every day, causing rivers to swell over their banks. The San Joaquin Valley transformed into a lake. As William and others had predicted, the worst problems arose in the first year of Sutter's settlement on the Sacramento plain.

Sutter had sailed up the river in August into no-man's land and eventually onto the *Rio de los Americanos* tributary.

Over the first six months he faced hostilities from various native tribes, cattle and horse thieves, and severe weather conditions as he worked to establish his farm. Sutter had purchased a Russian ship, and every other week in the fall, he sent it to Yerba Buena. But after the rains began, there was no word from Captain Sutter for many weeks. When the ship did arrive, Nathan Spear shared the news from Captain Sutter's letter with everyone who visited his store.

William relayed the letter's contents to María when he returned home for his evening meal, flinging his wet, wool serape over a bench on the veranda and removing his boots before entering the house.

"Captain Sutter's ship arrived finally, a month late. This wet weather has taken a toll on the man and his settlement. He tells of herds of deer and elk stranded on high points of land that remain above the flooding water. The river flows so swiftly that if an animal slips off an island, it's carried away and drowns."

"How dreadful!" María said. "But the rain is horrendous here, too. No one can go out without being drenched. Our children are cold and bored, the wood is wet, nothing will dry out! I don't recall ever living through such a wet winter."

William stood behind his wife while she lit candles on the table and put his warm hands on her shoulders. "I have never seen you so frustrated, *mi amore*." He bent and kissed the top of her head. Thinking of Sutter and his huge farm, he said, "We should be making plans to move to our farm. In the spring, the grass will be thick and the trees green. Wildflowers will cover the Saucelito hills. We should be there to enjoy them. To take our minds off this rain, let's start after dinner to plan our new home there."

Over supper, María and William discussed their idea of moving to the rancho with the children. The family excitedly shared thoughts about what their life there might be like. And William promised to explain "why we must move soon."

CHAPTER 34

MAKING A CHOICE

While Sophia and Maruha cleared the supper dishes, María gathered a pen, ink, and paper for William.

She sat beside him at the table and said, "I'd like a sunny spot for a large vegetable garden and places for Castilian rose bushes near the house."

"Of course." He smiled and began sketching a layout for the rancho buildings while they talked.

"I remember a conversation I had with Nathan and his nephew Bill Davis. Captain Sutter had hired Bill to guide his ship up the Sacramento River. They had plenty of time to talk during the journey. Sutter told Bill he rejected the lands near Sonoma because he wanted to be absolute master of his own settlement. Independent. His colony had to sit far away from General Vallejo's military governance."

"I'm glad he moved so far upriver then," María said while she studied William's drawing. "I heard his colony is attracting unsavory foreigners already. Fur trappers who came over the mountains, sailors who jumped ship in Yerba Buena. They are all working for him."

Frowning, William drew the outline for the kitchen area and outdoor adobe ovens. "And soon they'll be staking claims, maybe squatting on another's land here, ignoring Mexico's laws. Sutter will encourage them, too. I don't trust him. He has bought all his cattle, horses, food, and tools on credit." He looked at María. "Did you know your father provided him with cattle and grain and has not seen a peso? Only a note for what Sutter owed. Sutter also accused Don Ignacio and your brother Don José of cheating him."

"Cheating? My father? That's an insult!" María fumed. "Captain Sutter is insufferable. But, as for his delayed payment, surely he will pay when he sells the hides and tallow from his herds. All the rancheros buy on credit if they don't have the money."

"I have my doubts about Captain Sutter, María. He may seem charming and honorable, but he's pompous and looks down his long nose at all who live here. Except the Americans. I fear many of these newcomers will follow Sutter's lead."

María looked horrified. "But if they grab land without asking, how will we protect our rancho? The Mexican government is so weak. And our California governors seem to change with the season!"

"From the little news we get from the United States, I think their Congress is very interested in our territory. I have heard vague grumblings from trappers in Nathan's store about starting a revolution like the one just finished in Tejas." William continued to draw a layout for the rancho barns and corrals. He set down his pen, took a sip of wine, and looked at María.

"We might be better off under the American flag, though." He saw María frown. "You don't agree? I know the stories of land grabbing are unsettling. And some of the Americans are rough and arrogant. But the United States government is stable. If a revolution should ever happen here, I want to be in control of my land just as Sutter is, before others move in as squatters."

Rain thundered on the tile roof. William rose from the table and walked to the door, opening it to look out at the current deluge. The downpour was so heavy that he had only a hazy view of his neighbors' houses and the cove. María joined him at the open door, tugging a shawl around her shoulders. Hugging her to his side, William said, "With Saucelito, I will have the chance to leave my family more than footprints on wet sand."

✠ ✠ ✠

Another foreigner who stirred anxiety in William's gut was Isaac Graham, a Tennessee transplant who trapped and traded in the Rocky Mountains and in 1836 drifted into California. He moved into the Monterey area and, with the governor's approval, established a business making whiskey from wheat. His success attracted the attention of many scoundrels and foreigners of similar mind, claiming they would start businesses, too. William had heard complaints about these ruffians stealing and causing other disturbances at nearby ranchos. Although Isaac had Governor Alvarado's support originally, the massing of so many rowdy and lawless foreigners prompted the governor to fear a revolt.

The news spread north that Mexican soldiers raided the Graham establishment, seized the property, and arrested Isaac and a hundred Americans and Englishmen living nearby. When Isaac objected, General José Castro, who was in charge of carrying out the governor's orders, threatened him with death. In the end, all the arrested foreigners including Graham were shipped to Mexico City for trial and imprisonment.

Even though William was a Mexican citizen, María worried he too might be arrested.

"How could the children and I survive without you?" she said, clasping her hands.

Though William reassured her he would never be arrested, he admitted the thought had occurred to him.

"If you were ever imprisoned, I'd rally my father, General Vallejo, the Peraltas, and all our many friends to protest and rescue you."

William knew he had the support of many influential people. Still, the consequences of the arrests caused worry and speculation about their future. When the British and the American governments intervened, the arrested men were released and given free passage to Monterey, with assurances their property would be returned. As a result of the affair, the United States strengthened its Pacific fleet, and Britain sent a warship to Monterey. These reactions from the American and British governments alarmed many rancheros, stoking fears of a revolution.

✠ ✠ ✠

From January through May in 1841, William took time away from his port duties to stock his land with more cattle and horses and to supervise construction on the rancho. Ohlone and Miwok laborers on loan from General Vallejo followed William's drawing for his family's house, split-rail corrals, barn, and fenced-in vegetable garden. They built small houses, a bunkhouse, and a *temescal* for the indigenous people—servants, sailors, and vaqueros—who would move from Yerba Buena with the Richardsons. Since little rain had fallen in the spring, the work was completed quickly, and the Richardsons moved to Saucelito in June.

The Ohlone and Miwok laborers begged to stay with the Richardsons rather than return to the general. They said they had never been treated so well and promised to do any kind of work. William chose five men, whom he trained as sailors, while the rest returned to Sonoma.

To finish the land grant process after moving in, William and five of his neighbors, along with the Sonoma alcalde, rode for two days around the edges of Rancho Saucelito. They traveled from the Saucelito hacienda north along the bay shore, across to the coast, and south along the Pacific Ocean, camping overnight. The next day, the group returned to Whaler's Cove, finishing their ceremonial ride of possession. The alcalde signed legal papers stating all required steps were concluded, William received his grant from Governor Alvarado, and it was noted in the *toma de razón,* the book of grants, in Monterey.

William sold his Yerba Buena lot and adobe house for $5,000 to a new Yerba Buena resident. He was sure the pueblo would grow into a magnificent port city, but he rooted his future in Rancho Saucelito, where he owned everything and where he could just as easily fulfill his duties as captain of the port. During the past year, even though it was dry, he had made more money from his rancho than from his port job because of an excellent grain harvest. Most trading ships and whalers, before anchoring in Yerba Buena Cove, continued to swing over to Saucelito to purchase his spring water. Now he checked ship manifests and collected government fees in Whaler's Cove while also selling ships his grain, vegetables, cut and stacked dry wood, and barrels of corned beef. To avoid Mexico's duties, the ships' supercargoes asked to unload a portion of their cargo and store it in Saucelito before sailing to Yerba Buena. For small anchorage and storage fees, William happily accommodated them. Merchants and rancheros sailed into Whaler's Cove to conduct surreptitious trading there, avoiding the higher prices charged in Yerba Buena.

✠ ✠ ✠

By midsummer, bright orange poppies and other wildflowers had bloomed and died on the Saucelito hillsides. From a cloudless cerulean sky, the sun toasted the waist-high wild oat grass to gold.

The fragrance from sun-scorched grass and bay, madrone, and redwood trees perfumed the dry, fresh air surrounding the Saucelito hacienda nestled near Whaler's Cove. The two-room house was much smaller than their *Casa Grande* in Yerba Buena, but William promised to expand it soon. María stood on the veranda and paused in her work to inhale deeply. Home! Yes, this place was their home at last. She admired her Castilian roses blooming next to the house and watched a family of California quail march quickly in a line to hide under the bushes. Blue jays squawked and songbirds sang to claim their territory. María sighed contentedly, then vigorously shook sand and dust out of the small rug she held and slipped back inside.

Francisco was waiting there, bursting to talk with his mother. Even when standing still, he seemed to be moving, like her husband. He had grown taller in the last few years, and María had to look up into his merry, chocolate-brown eyes. She marveled that this thirteen-year-old was once her little baby lying in her lap.

"Mamá," Francisco said, "Esteban and I want to ride over the hill to the hidden pond. We promise to be back at midday." Esteban stood next to him, rising up and down on his toes, impatient to hear their mother's answer.

"Since you have done your chores, I'll let you go," said María. "But watch out for each other. Be sure to stay together. And take your rifles. Try to bring home a few ducks for dinner."

"Try?" Esteban said with a laugh. "We won't have to try, Mamá. We'll have no trouble shooting ducks for you."

María smiled at her youngest son and ruffled his light brown hair. He looked so much like William. He too seemed always to be in motion, trying to keep up with Francisco.

María watched her boys sprint to the corral. Two of the family mutts jumped about them and barked at their heels. Francisco's mustang nickered. The boy saddled his horse himself while Ricardo, the vaquero who still worked for William, helped Esteban saddle his. The two boys mounted and tore over the hill, whooping and yelling, racing through the high grasses.

While María watched until they were out of sight, the memory surfaced of the day Francisco earned the right to have his own horse, a California tradition for all ten-year-old boys. Just as his cousin Ramón had won the right to own a horse, Francisco had tamed his half-broke horse a few years ago. William had arranged the contest between boy and horse with his brother-in-law, Lieutenant José Joaquin Estudillo, who hosted the event at the San Francisco Presidio.

✠ ✠ ✠

When they had arrived at the Presidio, María's younger sister, Juana, rushed to embrace her and kiss her cheeks.

"Let's go, *niños*," said Juana to her children who crowded around to greet them. "Your cousin Francisco is old enough to have his own horse. But he must ride him. Come watch."

The two families walked to the corral and joined others who had gathered there. The handsome two-year-old mustang snorted and shivered as he stood in the enclosure, saddled and blindfolded, his bridle held tightly by Ricardo, who murmured to him to calm the animal. The horse was only half broken, and Francisco would have to conquer him in this battle of wills between boy and horse.

William and Francisco's uncle José were mounted on their horses ready to pull the mustang down if he should rear and try to fall backward, but they would do nothing unless the boy was in danger. When Francisco mounted the mustang, Ricardo pulled off the blindfold and quickly stepped out of the way.

Feeling the weight of the boy on his back, the half-wild horse bucked and tried to shake him off. Francisco, who had been riding for years, was fearless, confident he could master his horse. To prevent the mustang from bucking, he hauled on the reins, just as Ricardo had taught him, keeping the horse's head up. Then he kicked the horse with his spurs to get him to move forward.

The horse neighed loudly, frantic with fear and anger, took a few steps, reared, and tried to buck. He kicked fiercely again and again. This action was repeated many times, the horse rebelling and Francisco firmly imposing his wishes through reins and spurs. The test of wills continued for almost an hour with the families and vaqueros watching from outside the corral, cheering for the boy.

Finally the horse, flecked with sweat, began to tire and then stood still, head drooping. Talking softly to his mount, Francisco patted his neck and climbed out of the saddle to stroke the mustang's forehead and quivering flanks. Ricardo took the reins from Francisco and led the horse out of the corral to wipe him down at the Presidio stable. William dismounted and hugged and congratulated his son, proud of his achievement. "You'll make a fine ranchero!"

✠ ✠ ✠

When María continued her housekeeping chores, she realized Esteban would earn his horse soon. She was pleased her sons were growing up, ready to take on responsibilities. Francisco got along well with people and made sound decisions. He rode sometimes with the vaqueros to round up horses and to lasso cattle for slaughter. Esteban was beginning to learn. Both boys were suited to the outdoor rancho life, well trained by William and the vaqueros. Her husband soon would have Francisco managing more of the rancho since William would be dividing his time between port duties across the bay and welcoming ship captains in Whaler's Cove.

Two American ships were now in Yerba Buena harbor, María remembered, which meant William would most likely bring naval officers home for dinner. She must remind Mariana to kill the bullock early so their cook could begin roasting the beef.

✠ ✠ ✠

Upon hearing her brothers' joyful shouts, fifteen-year-old Mariana frowned as she continued churning butter in the kitchen. She yearned to ride with the boys on such a glorious day, but her mother needed her help with household chores and the evening meal. Papá might bring home guests. Ship captains and supercargoes were often invited to the house for dinner and dancing. Although these guests might be strangers, Mariana enjoyed helping her parents entertain them. Besides bringing fine gifts such as elegant shawls, silk shoes, and necklaces, sea captains relayed news from the rest of the world. If her father did invite people to their house, he might also ask Señor de Haro and his handsome twin sons Francisco and Ramón. She began to sing a Spanish folk song, smiling to herself. She would very much like to dance with them, especially Francisco.

CHAPTER 35

A DINNER, A DANCE, AND A CONTEST

A dinner at the Richardsons' home was always a boisterous and generous affair. Platters of freshly roasted beef and duck, chicken tamales, mutton, potatoes, lima beans, peppers, and Indian corn filled the linen-covered tables set up in front of the two-room house. Nearby, barrels of wine and casks of *aguardiente* guaranteed glasses would never be empty. A wooden platform for the evening dancing was set at the side of the house. Since it rarely rained at this time of year, no one worried that the weather might spoil the party.

When USS *Vincennes* and *Porpoise* anchored in Whaler's Cove, María and the children stood on the veranda to greet their guests. William introduced his family to Commodore Charles Wilkes and Lieutenant Cadwalader Ringgold of the United States Navy. He explained to his children the Commodore's scientific expedition for the United States government included surveying the bay and gathering specimens of California's native species. María gave a stiff, brief curtsy to the American officers and said in English, "Pleased to make your acquaintance, Commodore. And Lieutenant."

Although a stern and thoroughly scientific explorer, the commodore bowed slightly to acknowledge her greeting. The younger Lieutenant Ringgold bowed and said, "At your service, Señora."

"I've brought a surprise guest," William said, clasping Don Ignacio around the shoulders.

The children gathered around their grandfather to hug him, and María kissed both of his smooth-shaven cheeks.

"Since your father is the alcalde of Yerba Buena this year," William said, "he toured the Commodore's ships with me today. They are as impressive as their ambitious expedition."

Several more expedition officers, skilled, learned men well suited to carry out the work assigned, came ashore to join the commodore and the Richardsons. These naval officers extended compliments to their gracious host and hostess as they arrived, eagerly anticipating a dinner party on shore after so many months at sea on naval rations.

Besides the Americans, neighbors had been invited to the dinner. John B. R. Cooper, whose rancho to the north bordered the Richardsons' land; handsome, blond, blue-eyed John Reed with his wife Doña Hilaria Sánchez from Rancho Corte Madera del Presidio lying to the east; and the giant Irishman Timothy Murphy, the current administrator of Mission San Rafael, all arrived on horseback.

When Mariana saw the De Haro twins, their sisters, and their father sail into the harbor, she skipped down to the beach to meet them. She had time for only a short greeting and promised to dance with the twins after the meal. During the dinner, as daughter of the hostess, she would ensure every guest's plate remained full and every glass never dry.

Mariana returned to the house to help Rosalita carry more platters of hot food to the table outside. When she finally appeared to take her seat, all of the men stood up as one, in tribute to her. Mariana nodded modestly and lowered her eyes, acknowledging their courtesy and admiration.

✠ ✠ ✠

During the dinner party, William encouraged his guests to elaborate on their expedition. Commodore Wilkes and Lieutenant Ringgold, the master of *Porpoise*, obliged with enthusiasm. Their ships had sailed to the South Sea Islands and other lands, allowing the explorers to meet many different peoples and become familiar with their customs, character, and ways of living. Naturally, the naval officers engaged the Californios in polite conversation, inquisitive about the California climate, resources, and fashion of living.

Wine and brandy flowed even after the tables were cleared, but when the musicians began to play their guitars and violins, all adjourned to the outdoor dance floor. Several couples formed two lines to dance "La Jota," which charmed the Americans. María danced with her father, the aging Don Ignacio, who had lost none of his wit nor vitality. Many glasses of wine and aguardiente later, William started to sing a boisterous sea chantey "The Drunken Sailor" to the tune of an Irish dance song, and Timothy Murphy soon joined in.

The American officers knew the song well. They stomped to its strong rhythm and joined in the chorus, often sung by sailors as they hauled up sails together.

After a pause, Mariana whispered to the musicians, walked to the middle of the floor, and began a solo dance while the spectators gathered around to watch. She locked eyes with Francisco de Haro, affectionately called Chico. Then as she held out the sides of her full skirt, sweeping it back and forth, she gently tapped her feet on the floor in time to the music. Her long brunette hair, usually bound in two braids, cascaded over her shoulders and down her back, and swayed with her every motion. When she danced slowly up to a man among the guests, he attempted to toss his hat or sombrero on her head. The naval officers followed their lead. Commodore Wilkes cast a critical eye on this forward behavior, but the junior naval officers were undeterred. So many times Mariana seemed to give up the fight, coming so close to accepting a hat, but suddenly she would swing and twirl away before the hat could settle.

Lieutenant Ringgold had not failed to notice Mariana's sparkling gray eyes and creamy skin with the bloom of youth on her cheeks. Although he tried his best to anchor his hat on the captivating girl's head, his effort seemed pointless. Then he watched Mariana smile and approach young Chico who easily dropped his sombrero on her head while he sang the words to the Spanish song, asking her to take his sombrero. Mariana sang that she liked his sombrero more than a crown and danced away with it.

When the music faded away, everyone shouted and applauded the dancer, who curtsied, and the young man, who bowed to her. To reclaim his hat, Chico reached into his pocket and presented her a customary token, a ribbon for her hair. He then escorted Mariana from the dance floor.

✠ ✠ ✠

The next morning, the shore surged with early activity. The ships' cooks baked bread in the rancho's beehive ovens, and Maruha and Rosalita helped Esteban collect eggs for the ships' crew. Francisco directed sailors to spots where they could fill barrels with spring water and collect dry firewood. After their chores were finished, he and Esteban thundered into the hills on horses with the De Haro twins, who had stayed overnight.

After breakfast, William boarded *Vincennes* to consult with Commodore Wilkes and Lieutenant Ringgold and provide them maps and information about the bay. Both men pegged William as a consummate mariner and appreciated his generous, agreeable nature.

"This bay is truly a remarkable harbor," said Lieutenant Ringgold. "I'm sure other nations have recognized its strategic importance and that it is the entryway to a rich and glorious land."

William knew of the United States government's keen interest in the bay and all of California. He surmised these American officers weren't here on a strictly scientific expedition. He was also aware that ever since Nathan Spear had established his profitable mercantile business, he had flooded his brother and friends in the East with letters extolling California's virtues and bountiful resources, and these letters had found their way into the hands of the American government's leaders.

Nathan divulged to William that Commodore Wilkes had interrogated him about the foreign trading vessels, whalers, and the visiting Russian and English warships. When Wilkes met with General Vallejo, he had seen the dilapidated condition of the old Presidio and the battery atop the headland—buildings deserted, cannons rusting, a bare flagstaff sprouting from crumbling adobe walls. William understood that Nathan, as an American, believed California at some future date would become part of the United States. According to Nathan, Governor Alvarado agreed and confided to him it was only a matter of time before Alta California would belong to the Americans.

Standing in his cabin with William and Lieutenant Ringgold, Commodore Wilkes looked up from the maps and out an open window at *Isla de Nuestra Señora de Los Angeles*, where hundreds of pelicans and gulls were calling to the cloudless sky as they flew low over the gentle waves washing into Whaler's Cove.

"There is no question in my mind that this bay will be of great scientific and commercial importance to my government."

✠ ✠ ✠

Francisco, Esteban, and the De Haro boys returned from their ride in time for their midday meal and a rest. Later, while Francisco and Esteban attended to afternoon chores, Chico and Ramón de Haro asked permission to set up targets for a shooting contest. William had agreed and his sons helped arrange things for their guests. Don Ignacio would preside as judge. The young men pinned small squares of paper about the size of a silver dollar to wood boards that they leaned against stacks of hay in a field.

"Each contestant will have one shot to hit his target," ruled the don.

The officers were not trained sharp shooters. Most were pleased when they nicked the edge of the target, and a few strutted about when their shot was close to the center. The De Haro twins took their turns and did about as well as the rest.

Hearing the boys and a few naval officers laughing and having a riotous time, Mariana and the De Haro sisters wandered over to watch. After Mariana's brother Francisco shot and proved his skill, he urged his sister to join them.

"You should take a turn, Mariana!"

Don Ignacio agreed. The American seamen paused to watch, murmuring among themselves and wondering about this next shooter's prowess. Francisco pinned a new target on a board and strolled back to the others, winking at his sister. Only her brothers and the De Haros had seen her shoot before. Although conscious of all the young men watching her, Mariana confidently stepped forward.

All talking ceased when the don handed her a loaded rifle. With practiced ease, she raised it to her shoulder, coolly sighted along the barrel at the target, and squeezed the trigger. Don Ignacio walked to the target, put his hands on his hips, and raised his bushy gray eyebrows.

"*Dios mío,* my Lord!" he gasped. "She hit the pin head at the center of the paper!"

✠ ✠ ✠

After the American scientific corps spent two months exploring the bay, *Vicennes* and *Porpoise* sailed to Monterey. Life at Rancho Saucelito returned to its usual bustling pace. Whalers and trading vessels, as many as thirty or forty at a time, regularly anchored in Whaler's Cove for provisions and refit, with repairs to decks and sails or repainting. In October, a visitor to the Cove stirred unpleasant memories of shipwrecks for William but offered Francisco an adventure.

CHAPTER 36

THE CRUEL SEA

In Whaler's Cove, sailors from the anchored ships refilled their empty barrels with fresh spring water and bought barrels of the rancho's beef. The soft fall weather produced bountiful vegetable crops to sell to the ships there and to those in Yerba Buena. Wheat fields ripened, ready for harvest.

"Rain is coming, Captain," Monico predicted in early October. "I see the signs. The animals wear thick coats, the plants are heavy with berries. We will have a wet season soon."

William trusted the old man's forecast and began to prepare for the storms, harvesting the grain as soon as possible. Afterward, the field hands burned the stalks and acres of dry grass and underbrush to encourage new growth the next spring and to rid the rancho of fuel that could feed grass fires. Maruha and Rosalita helped Sophia make mounds of dried beef, *carne ceca,* which would be eaten during winter when it was too wet to slaughter cattle. Other workers living on the rancho harvested and stored apples, winter squash, and dried berries. Francisco and Esteban hunted ducks, rabbits, and small deer, providing variety from the usual roasted beef dinner.

"Maybe Papá will go with us soon to shoot an elk," said Esteban. "What a treat that would be!"

✠ ✠ ✠

As Monico predicted, stormy weather soon swept in from the Pacific, soaking the hills and whipping up high seas. One October day during a morning rainstorm, four drenched riders galloped up to the hacienda. William and Francisco stepped onto the covered veranda to meet them.

"Captain Richardson," the lead rider shouted over the roaring downpour, "I am José Yves Limantour, the owner and captain of the schooner *Ayacucho*. We desperately need your help." The man dismounted and stood, dripping hat in hand, under the veranda roof to plead his case. "While searching for the entrance to San Francisco Bay, I made a grave error and steered the ship into a bay farther north. The *Ayacucho* is now wrecked on the rocks along the coast."

"Of course I will help," William replied. "Come in to dry off. We'll decide what to do."

The riders tied up their horses, left their soggy hats, coats, and boots on the porch, and entered the warm hacienda. William poured each man a glass of brandy and sat at the table with them. He introduced María who served them hot food. Each murmured their thanks and began eating eagerly. Between mouthfuls, José filled in details about himself and his ship.

"I am French by birth," he began, "but I've been working as a navigator and trader in Mexico City. The Mexican branch of the French trading firm Bizat and Russell hired me for their venture into the Pacific trade market."

"Ah, yes, I know the firm. I know your brig too," William replied. "My friend John Wilson used to be its captain."

"A good ship. I agreed to sail as supercargo in charge of the freight. The California rancheros crave our luxury goods. Mexican law dictates that the ship have a Mexican captain, and I chose the *Ayacucho* and its captain. However, I wasn't pleased with the man and let him go after we stopped in Monterey to pay customs duties. I regret that decision now, for several reasons.

By stopping in Monterey, I did what few captains do . . . I paid the duties in advance."

William glanced at María who raised one eyebrow but said nothing. María had made her thoughts on smuggling clear to him. She worried William would be caught and arrested for helping smugglers from the trading ships that moored in their harbor. But José reaffirmed what William had told her—few sea captains paid the duties before selling their goods. The *Ayacucho's* shipwreck showed how expensive a mistake that could be. William thought of all the money this man had paid and would lose because of the lost or ruined cargo. He could have saved him quite a bit in duties if Limantour had skirted Monterey and sailed to San Francisco Bay and Saucelito. If he had kept his captain and found the entrance to the bay, that is.

José continued his tragic tale, explaining how, unknowingly, he'd sailed past the bay and mistaken a point of land for the bay entrance when he saw breakers.

"I had been told to expect breakers before entering San Francisco Bay. But the vessel was suddenly aground on a sandbar. We took a skiff ashore to look for Yerba Buena but found no town. Then that southeaster blew in a few days ago, and the ship bilged. We threw much of the cargo overboard and dragged it to shore, but seawater filled the ship's hull and soaked much of the remaining cargo. We camped on the beach in the cold and wet until a native came upon our party and guided us to a nearby rancho."

Limantour recounted how they'd borrowed horses from the ranchero who directed them to Rancho Saucelito and William for help.

"At this point," William said, "the best course of action is to go to Yerba Buena and arrange for a ship to sail us up the coast and pick up the remains of the cargo. Captain John Paty's bark *Don Quixote* may be available. First though, you, Captain Paty, assuming he's willing, and I would ride north to locate the wreck and see what more can be salvaged."

As port captain and a seaman, William was eager to help a fellow ship captain in distress.

✠ ✠ ✠

When José and William arrived in Yerba Buena later that day, Captain Paty agreed to help them. Within two days, Paty organized a search party to sail across the bay and ride overland to find the *Ayacucho*. They anchored at Whaler's Cove. María and Mariana packed food for the riders, and Francisco lashed medical supplies for the shipwrecked survivors onto pack horses.

Not wanting to miss out on the excitement, the thirteen-year-old boy pleaded with his father, "May I ride with you? I'd like to help."

William studied his son's hopeful face and then looked at his worried wife, before he replied, "You'll be a great help to us, Francisco. Saddle your horse."

After kissing his mother, Francisco grabbed his poncho and hat and rushed out the door to the corral before his mother might object.

William, Francisco, Monico, and three Saucelito vaqueros mounted their horses and rode off with Captain Paty, José Limantour, and the rest of the search party.

✠ ✠ ✠

After two days of riding in wind, rain, and hail, with poor directions from José Limantour that caused Captain Paty to fume that his navigation on shore was as bad as it was on the sea, they reached the site of the wreck on the Point Reyes sandbar. The scene at the beach was worse than William had imagined. The rain had stopped, but the relentless sea slammed into the tipped brig on the rocky shore, breaking parts of its masts and further caving in its side. The beach was strewn with crates, barrels, torn sails, and knotted rigging. He had seen many shipwrecks, but he was saddened to see the proud *Ayacucho* in such ruin. He recalled his loss of the *Josephine*, but shook off the memory to focus on the scene before him.

A few members of the crew were still pulling cargo out of the sea, floundering against the push of the waves surging onto the beach that was littered with sharp, broken shells, seaweed, and detritus of other ill-fated ships. The exhausted men, sinking and stumbling in the wet sand, struggled to prevent the backwash from reclaiming their prizes. William instructed his vaqueros and Francisco to salvage whatever cargo they could. He turned his attention to the wounded crew members who needed medical care.

Vaqueros never did anything with their boots on the ground that they could do on horseback. Francisco joined them lassoing pieces of cargo near the shore and riding their horses up the beach, dragging behind them sacks of grain, barrels of cheeses and condiments, kegs of brandy, and crates of Italian silks and French silk brocades.

Monico threw his reata around the ship's deck rail and backed up his horse to hold the reata taut. Then he and José grasped the taut safety line, staggered through the waves, and clambered aboard the wreck. They climbed below deck into cold water above their waists and threw more of the cargo out toward shore where men rescued it from the sea's grasp.

After tossing all the cargo they could overboard, José and Monico fought their way through the surf to land. Bedraggled and exhausted, José approached William. "Captain, I thank you and your son and your men for helping us rescue so much of this valuable shipment. I am in your debt."

"I'm glad we arrived in time. Due to this sad calamity, I urge you to negotiate with Monterey for the return of some of your customs duties, even though most of your salvaged merchandise might still be sold. We can't take much out of this cove today, only what our pack animals can carry. When the weather takes a turn for the better, Captain Paty will sail you here in his ship to retrieve the rest. Meanwhile, you'll be a welcome guest at my rancho." William scratched his chin and then added, "I might have space in Saucelito and in Yerba Buena where you can store and sell your cargo."

José bowed his head. "You are most generous. I can never fully repay you, but perhaps your charming wife and daughter will accept some of the fine silks and perfumes I have. As a token of my gratitude."

"I'm sure they will be most happy with that."

José shook William's hand and walked over to direct the loading of the pack animals. William turned to pack up his medical supplies and then scanned the beach for Francisco. He was sitting on a crate talking with the vaqueros but appeared exhausted. María will be cross with me if Francisco is ill, thought William. He knew the boy was eager for adventure, and he was proud of Francisco's work today but hoped he had not made a mistake in bringing him.

✠ ✠ ✠

While José stayed with the Richardsons at Saucelito, he arranged to store the goods they had brought on the pack horses and to sell them at a discount to William's neighbors. María and Mariana were delighted with the many treasures they were offered from the stored cargo and excited to have such luxurious fabric to sew new silk dresses in time for holiday celebrations. After the new year, José settled in Yerba Buena, but the Richardson house was not free of visitors for long.

CHAPTER 37

LIFE IN PARADISE

February 1842

On a chill evening, María stood on the veranda and watched William and a stranger beach the launch. A guest for dinner. The aroma of roasting beef and baking bread wafted in the breeze. As always, there was plenty of food for a visitor. She went inside to tell the cook they would have a guest this evening.

When the door opened a few minutes later, William entered and María turned from setting another place at the table to meet the young man accompanying her husband.

William took her hand and kissed her on the cheek. "María, I'd like to introduce you to John Bidwell, who just arrived in Yerba Buena." He continued in English. "John, my wife, María Antonia. I have invited him to dinner, *mi amore.*"

John removed his hat and said, "I'm sorry to interfere with your evening meal, Señora. But I'm most grateful to the captain for inviting me to your home."

"We are always happy to meet travelers and welcome them," replied María. An American but not a naval officer or a sailor. *Why is this dark-haired visitor in California*? she wondered.

"John is now working for Captain Sutter, María," William said. "Sutter made a deal with the Russians when their governor in Sitka ordered the navy to abandon Fort Ross. Sutter bought all the livestock and the buildings. John will be overseeing the removal of Fort Ross and Bodega structures to Sutter's settlement."

María was not pleased to learn this. Many foreigners who worked for Sutter spread out in the hills and just took land, not waiting for a land grant from Mexico. *This man has a job now, but what will he do when that work is finished?* she wondered.

John met Mariana, Francisco, and Esteban and sat down with the Richardson family for dinner. Maruha and Mariana brought in platters of hot food while William poured the wine. Observing that all were served, María, who was intrigued by their handsome, well-mannered American guest, asked John about his arrival in California. He seemed more refined than other Americans she'd met in Yerba Buena, especially the sailors. She wanted to draw more information from him to find out why he came and what he planned to do.

"You are a long way from your home, Señor," she started.

"That's true, Señora. I *am* a long way from home." John paused and fingered the stem of his wine glass.

"What drew you to Alta California and Yerba Buena?" María coaxed him.

"Well, more than two years ago, I got an itch to travel," John began. "I longed to see the prairie, so I left Ohio to go west. I carried only a pocketknife, seventy-five dollars, and a knapsack of spare clothes. When I arrived in Missouri nearly penniless, I was offered a teaching job in a small town. They had a new school and desperately needed a teacher. I gratefully accepted even though I had no experience."

"It must have been difficult for you to move that far, no family or friends with you. We know so many people in California, relatives as well as friends, that we feel welcome everywhere." María remembered the early days spent at Mission San Gabriel. Lonely at first, but her cousins smoothed her way. What kind of man would travel alone, just to see prairies? Men do take chances though. She glanced at William. After all, he did.

"The people in Missouri made me feel welcome as a teacher, I assure you," John said. "But I started to yearn for a place of my own to farm. After a year of teaching, I had enough money to stake a claim on 160 acres, which I did."

"Then why didn't you stay? What pushed you to move on?" asked William.

"Someone jumped my claim while I was away in St. Louis for a couple of weeks."

"The bastard!" exploded William, thinking of the troubles his neighbors were having with squatters.

María glanced at her husband but didn't admonish him in front of their guest. The children lived around sailors and had heard worse language. But John's experience raised her worries over the security of their rancho, even though they had filed their land grant with Mexico. She would talk with William and her father about that.

John continued his story. He had worked the land a bit, but when he returned from St. Louis, the claim jumper was living on it and would not leave. The law took his side because John hadn't truly lived on his land. When he was teaching, he lived in the town where the school was. The result was the scoundrel got the land. John resolved to move on then, but he had to continue teaching because all his earnings had gone into the land.

"During that miserable winter, a Frenchman named Roubideaux, who had been to California, convinced me and some townspeople that it was paradise. Fertile, hospitable to strangers, millions of cattle and horses. A land of perennial spring. Some town folks and I made up our minds to move and formed the Western Emigration Society. None of us had an inkling of how to equip ourselves. All we knew was that California lay west.

"Then we heard the other side of the story from the newspapers. Reporters described the unfavorable feelings toward Americans in California because of the war with Mexico in Texas. An article also gave an account of the Graham Affair. That news troubled a lot of folks.

"I argued that most of those Americans were ruffians, fur trappers and adventurers. Peaceful, law-abiding farmers and settlers would be welcome, I reasoned. Even so, I found myself alone in the Society and no one else wanting to go west."

"Ah, yes, Isaac Graham. That was all resolved, though, and the Americans and other foreigners were freed," explained William. María remained quiet, remembering how upsetting the Graham Affair had been for her and her family, how afraid she'd been that William would be arrested.

But there it was, she thought. *What John would do*. He planned to settle here on a farm.

The children hung on their guest's every word. When they didn't understand what John said, they asked their father to translate.

"Did you cross the plains and the mountains by yourself?" Francisco asked.

"No, no. I bought provisions, a rifle, and a wagon, so others would see I was determined to go. When a few others decided to join me, I got a team of oxen for my wagon. We met up with other families in another town who were set to emigrate. One man, John Bartleson, was elected captain of the group—sixty-nine men, women, and children. By a stroke of luck, a missionary party led by an old Rocky mountaineer passed through the town just as we were ready to leave. We had the benefit of safety with them until they split off at Soda Springs in Idaho Territory. We learned a lot from that old mountain man. I don't think I'd be here today if we had never met that group." John folded his napkin slowly and placed it on the table, a grave look in his eyes.

"At times I didn't think I would make it. Especially when half our party refused to continue on the trackless path over the mountains to California. They decided to follow the more-traveled route to Oregon."

Giving his hosts a satisfied smile, he said, "But I am here. We made it. The first emigrant wagon train to arrive in California."

The first! María tensed and drew in a breath but said nothing. She looked at John's thin face. Such a difficult trip, and yet more would follow? A chill of fear slid down her spine. Would they be squatters or claim jumpers, stealing their land just as one did to John?

By this time, a curtain of dark had crept up behind *Isla de Nuestra Señora de Los Angeles,* and the moon had risen behind the island. When Maruha cleared the dishes and Mariana lit more tallow candles for the table, John rose from his seat to thank his hostess for his meal.

"*Muchas gracias,* Señora," he said to María.

"*De nada*, Señor," she replied. "You are welcome to stay with us tonight, of course. We often have guests stay. Please sit and tell us more about your journey."

William offered tobacco and a pipe to John, and María poured glasses of aguardiente for the two men. Esteban and Francisco never stirred from their seats. María was charmed by this serious, polite young man, but the more John spoke, the more she became alarmed, imagining how many *americanos* might soon invade their peaceful territory. Because of the Graham Affair, many Mexican women were already fearful of the uncivilized adventurers from the "States."

"The journey was perilous," continued John, taking a puff on his pipe. María looked at William, a man who had faced many dangers himself. She could tell he admired this man's fortitude. "Some families turned back. We dealt with Indians, tremendous herds of stampeding buffaloes, hailstorms, lack of water and food. We made it, though, all thirty men and one woman with her baby daughter. In November last year, we staggered out of the mountains into California. We were starving, having eaten only mule meat for days."

"Such a dangerous journey!" María said. Yet more would come.

"When we stumbled upon Dr. John Marsh's ranch near Mount Diablo," John said, "we felt we were saved. He killed two pigs and had his servants make tortillas. We later found out he had to use some of his seed wheat to make them. When he grumbled about his loss of one prize beef that some men in our party had killed for food, we gave him gunpowder, a knife, and such in payment. He didn't seem mollified. But we had only a few dollars and little to trade. We resolved to leave Marsh rather than stay where we weren't welcome. At first we had thought him generous, but later we came to see his true stripes."

"We know John Marsh from his brief stay in Yerba Buena," William said slowly. "Not the most charitable neighbor."

"Ah, so we agree," John nodded. "We wanted to leave but needed passports. So Marsh traveled to Mission San José to get us passports into this territory. When he returned, he charged five dollars for them! Later we discovered the passports cost him nothing. Those of us who didn't pay, or couldn't pay, decided to leave anyway, prepared to plead with the Mexican authorities. When we arrived in San José, we met Comandante General Vallejo who, to our surprise, welcomed us."

"Yes, he admires the United States and its democratic values," William said. "He'll be sympathetic to your settling here. And with other Americans who venture over the mountains. Though the territory of Texas broke away in '36 and now hopes to join the Union, Mexico still owns California. Here you must become Mexican and respect Californios and their customs if you wish to stay."

María relaxed her tense shoulders. William had made Mexico's requirements clear to John. He seemed decent, lawful, but Captain Sutter, who lived by his own rules, might soon influence John's behavior and expectations.

✠ ✠ ✠

In the morning, William, Francisco, and Esteban gave John a tour of Rancho Saucelito, riding past the fields being tilled for wheat, and up the slopes of Mount Tamalpais, above the early morning fog to look out over the bay. On their way, they passed large herds of elk, antelope, and deer and frightened ducks and geese into flight from small ponds. When they rode along a path through the cool dense redwood forest, the trees dripped with the water collected in their crowns from the fog.

John craned his neck to look to the tops of the magnificent trees. "On my journey, I passed through a stand of mammoth trees like these. They seemed to block out the sun. More than ten men with their arms outstretched would be needed to encircle the base of one."

"Those gigantic trees are a relative of these coastal redwoods," William said. "This forest runs down to the bay shoreline. Redwood trees were used to build the missions and presidios. I used it for some parts of my house. Good soft wood, easy to cut. The buildings at Bodega and Fort Ross are redwood."

"I'm eager to start removing those buildings to Captain Sutter's farm. He calls his settlement New Helvetia, in honor of his homeland, Switzerland. Did you know that?"

"Yes, Nathan Spear told me. When do you plan to start the move?"

"As soon as possible. I must ask a favor of you, though. I must check on the fort's current state. Might you loan me horses and a guide to help me find my way? I'm willing to pay."

"I can arrange that. You probably should wait a few days or even a week. Due to the rain, the trails will be mired in mud. The rivers are probably overflowing their banks. A treacherous ride."

"That's a most generous offer," John said. "I appreciate your hospitality."

William reined in his horse and watched Francisco and Esteban race their horses downhill to the shore. "While you remain with us, I would ask a favor in return. You said you'd been a teacher. I'd like you to give my sons reading and writing lessons in English. They speak mostly Spanish, but they can also jabber away in the language of the vaqueros and sailors. As you know from talking with them, they can bumble along in English. But I haven't been home enough to teach them much, especially reading and writing. With more Americans settling around here, they must learn English."

"I'll be happy to teach your boys," John said.

✠ ✠ ✠

Later that night when they were alone preparing for bed, William told María about his arrangement with John.

"Our sons must be equipped to run our farm, María, and deal with Americans in the future," William said as he undressed and pulled on a nightshirt. "It's becoming more apparent that it's not only our splendid harbor that is attracting attention. Commodore Wilkes's visit to the bay last year will increase the United States' interest in California. President Polk already offered once to buy this territory. Maybe he will again. John's emigrant party will not be the last."

"I agree, *mi amore,* that our sons need education," María said. "I'm not happy, however, to hear that more Americans will come." She began to brush her loosened hair fiercely. "I know you and General Vallejo would welcome them. But I feel uneasy with them. Many seem sly and condescending. Some treat us as if we are dull-witted or ignorant. In *our* homeland! We open our doors, offer food and drink and shelter, and they insult us and our generosity with their rude behavior. My friends said that they overheard some call us lazy because we never started businesses like those now in Yerba Buena." María got into bed and hugged the covers to herself, scowling. "Enterprising Yankees! They do not understand or appreciate our happiness and satisfaction with our way of living."

"I see their faults too," William said. "But they're here and more will be coming. Many will be settlers wanting farms or ranchos, just as it happened in Texas. There'll also be more merchants like Abel Stearns and Jacob Leese. Americans aren't blind to the profitable trade with the Sandwich Islands and China. More trade is better for us as well." William climbed into bed next to his wife and gave her a kiss. "Don't worry, María. If Mexico can avoid a war with the United States over the Republic of Texas and come to an agreement for that territory, perhaps an American acquisition of Alta California will work out also. I believe that would stabilize our governance, a blessing for most of us Californios."

While her husband snored beside her, María lay awake and thought about her daughter going to Yerba Buena to sell their produce. She must warn her again about strangers and forbid her to go alone. Fewer friends and more unknown foreigners might be roaming the streets soon.

✠ ✠ ✠

While awaiting dryer weather, John began lessons with Esteban and Francisco. The boys sat at the dining table bent over slates writing English words with chalk while John stood opposite thumbing through books for passages they could read aloud to him. William had purchased the books in English from trading ships for the boys' lessons.

When a horse in the corral neighed, Esteban lifted his head from his slate. Then he asked John, "What was it like to ride near stampeding buffaloes?"

John looked up from his book and gazed over the boys' heads. "Honestly, it was frightening. But also thrilling. They are huge animals, many larger than your father's largest bull, with massive shoulders and shaggy heads with horns. You first knew they were coming by the shaking of the ground. We pulled the wagons together then quickly to form a square, and some men rode a mile or so back to meet the herd and to shoot rifles in the air to frighten the lead buffaloes away from our wagons. If the head buffaloes weren't turned in time, the herd would overrun the riflemen and our wagons."

The boys stared wide-eyed at John.

"As the herd surged by, their power and wildness was overwhelming. The trembling ground, clouds of dust, the thundering noise—it's hard to describe the rush I felt."

"Like being in an earthquake!" Francisco said. "Did you ever kill one?"

"Oh, yes, I killed some. We killed buffaloes for food around the Platte River. The Indians eat them and skin them for their woolly hides. There are so many in a herd—as far as the eye can see! The plain was sometimes black with them for several days as our wagons journeyed by. I saw in one day more buffaloes than I've seen cattle in my whole life."

"I hope to see them one day," Francisco said.

"I'm sure you will. More people are traveling west and people will be traveling east as well," John said picking up his book. "Let's get back to our lesson now. Start with reading this page, Francisco."

While the boy read aloud, John's mind drifted to his dangerous journey. How often he himself had come close to death.

He shivered, remembering with horror that one burning hot day, when he was riding alone on the plains, searching for his wandering oxen. Fearing a heat mirage he'd spied was hostile natives following him, he panicked and plunged his horse into a stream that became a quagmire. He pulled himself out, but his horse sank down over his head. He managed to drag his mount out and wiped mud from his horse's nostrils, eyes, and ears. With great relief, he saw the mirage turn into two riders from his emigrant party, out looking for him.

When his party finally made it to the mountains, narrow trails forced them to abandon the wagons and turn their mules, horses, and oxen into pack animals carrying provisions and only necessary tools. Hunger, thirst, dying animals. Nothing went as expected. But they came out of the mountains alive. He was thankful but also pleased with his achievement. He closed his eyes briefly to shake off the distressing scenes and concentrate once again on Francisco's reading.

✠ ✠ ✠

Over the next few months, John Bidwell traveled between Saucelito and Fort Ross to check on Captain Sutter's investment. To move the entire fort, he began dismantling buildings and arranged for the pieces, as well as the old brass cannons, oxcarts, wagons, and farm implements, to be shipped up the Sacramento River to Sutter's New Helvetia. Hundreds of horses, sheep, and cattle would be herded there also.

After a few weeks at Fort Ross, John returned to the Richardson hacienda to purchase more provisions and continued teaching Francisco and Esteban. Occasionally, Mariana listened to their lessons to improve her English, but only when María allowed her. She had too many household duties, which left little time for lessons.

As summer approached, John proposed bringing the boys with him to Fort Ross and Bodega where he could tutor them and oversee the dismantling of the buildings at the same time.

"Frankly, it's lonely up there. I'd appreciate their company," he said to María and William. "I'll be sending weekly reports to Captain Sutter and the mail sack to you to ship to him. I'll send you letters about the boys' lessons, too."

María was not ready to trust this stranger. Francisco was just thirteen and Esteban only eleven. Would they watch out for each other and not take foolish chances? She knew Francisco was growing up and eager to adventure on his own, to challenge himself. On the rancho, William allowed him to ride with vaqueros to round up cattle. She worried always about his safety. Would John? Was he responsible enough to discipline and take care of her boys, alone? In the last few weeks, she had only seen evidence of a polite, cheerful, and capable young man so perhaps all would be well.

Her concerns were overruled by her husband's opinion and the boys' excitement. Trusting John and their boys, William agreed to let them go.

"You can go, but you must write to me every week," María told her sons. "And John, I'd like a weekly note from you to report on their behavior please."

"I'll include their letters to you with mine in the mail sack," John said with a smile.

✠ ✠ ✠

John sent regular reports to the captain on the boys' progress, promising to bring them home in late fall. He didn't allow them to shirk their lessons, but they had time to enjoy exploring the wilderness near the fort and Bodega Bay. As he promised, before he would sail with provisions and equipment to Sutter's Fort, he brought them home for the Christmas hunt and the holiday celebration.

CHAPTER 38

A CHRISTMAS HUNT

María rose at first light and, while she washed and dressed, sang a morning hymn, her wake-up call for the household. The December chill had invaded the house, but Rosalita placed hot coals in braziers which would soon warm the main room. When María paused to look through the window at the foggy gray winter sky beginning to clear over *Isla de Nuestra Señora de Los Angeles,* she heard William's tenor voice joining in her song while he dressed. Besides the excitement of the season and the celebrations soon to come, María was elated to be in the adobe house that William had completed that year with the help of the rancho workers. It wasn't as large as their Yerba Buena *Casa Grande,* but he promised to add rooms in the future.

When María heard Mariana begin to sing, but not the boys, she walked into their room and over to their beds. She looked down at the two burrowed in their blankets, remembering how relieved and delighted she'd felt when they returned home safely after their months with John Bidwell.

"Get up, sleepy heads! Today is the day you will hunt for Christmas dinner!" she said as she shook their blanket cocoons. "Dress warmly. It will be cool in the ravines."

Francisco and Esteban sat up, untangled themselves from their bedding, and threw on their clothes.

Mariana helped her mother stretch a fresh tablecloth over the table and set it for breakfast while Rosalita and Maruha brought in mugs of hot chocolate. Soon steaming dishes of beef, eggs, and fresh hot bread were arranged on the table, and the family gathered, eager to begin their day.

"I think we will go north this morning," William said to María. "Ricardo reported seeing a herd of elk in one of the valleys. I'm looking forward to elk venison this year."

The boys rushed through their breakfast, excited to be on their way. "*Muchas gracias, Mamá*," said both boys in chorus and they hurriedly left the table. Grabbing their rifles, ponchos, and hats, they called to their father, "Hurry, Papá!" and scampered to the corral.

"Well," William said, wiping his mouth. "I guess we are off on our hunt!"

Rising from his seat, he leaned over his wife and kissed her. Entering their bedroom, he pulled two rifles from under their bed, picked up his poncho and hat, and followed his sons.

Esteban, Francisco, and four vaqueros were sitting in their saddles, their horses dancing under them, sensing their excitement. Several of the rancho dogs were pacing in circles and barking, ready to go. Ricardo had saddled William's black horse as well as a horse for the American Commodore Thomas ap Catesby Jones who would join them. His sloop-of-war USS *Cyane* bobbed in the swells in Whaler's Cove, anchored there since mid-December.

✠ ✠ ✠

Commodore Jones was commander of the United States Pacific Squadron in 1842. William had heard the story about how the United States fleet came to be on the California coast. The commodore had received false information that the United States and Mexico were at war and that a British ship was sailing off the coast looking to take control of Alta California. The commodore immediately sailed the *Cyane* with two other sloops ready to claim Monterey for the United States of America.

In October, despite seeing no signs of war preparations, he sailed into Monterey harbor and raised the United States flag. The next day, Thomas Oliver Larkin, an American merchant residing in the town, set Jones straight, telling him the two countries were at peace. Realizing he had been misinformed, Commodore Jones apologized to the bewildered residents and sailed *Cyane* to Los Angeles to apologize officially to Brigadier-General Manuel Micheltorena, the recently appointed governor, who demanded public satisfaction for the commodore's outrageous action. After accepting the commodore's sincere regrets, the governor gave the commodore permission to visit Yerba Buena for refitting his warships. Naturally, the three American ships had anchored in Saucelito.

✠ ✠ ✠

Commodore Jones, a dark-haired, middle-aged man, experienced in naval combat, command, and diplomacy, was also a capable rider and marksman. When he walked up the beach from the *Cyane's* longboat, William greeted him and handed him a rifle, saying, "We'll be looking to bag an elk for Christmas dinner. But a deer or antelope as well wouldn't go amiss. And maybe even a grizzly. There are plenty of them skulking about where we are riding."

"I'm delighted to be here and experience a California hunt," the commodore said. He slipped the rifle into the scabbard on his saddle and mounted his horse. "Let's go!"

The party rode north for a short time and then turned west along a trail that led to a bush-covered ravine. Herds of elk and deer were browsing on the steep hillsides and in the valley near a lagoon. The grazing animals jerked up their heads upon hearing the intruders, ears alert, but the prey stayed stone still. The hunters halted to confer about how to proceed and agreed to follow William's plan of attack.

"Watch out for bear, Commodore," William said. "They are mean when hungry, worse when angered. Be sure you have a dead shot, otherwise get the hell out of there."

Three hunters rode quietly to different places in the ravine and waited to ambush the deer and elk. Two vaqueros quieted the dogs, led them to the far side of the ravine, and began beating the bushes to chase the herds toward the hunters.

A bull elk bugled the alarm. Soon the dogs were baying and the noise of panicked animals crashing through bushes reached the men waiting for a good shot. Warning his sons to stay back, William moved slowly down the center of the ravine away from the other riders. Raising his rifle and spurring his big black horse, he charged ahead, shooting a magnificent bull elk. A few more shots were heard from the other hunters. William returned to the waiting group dragging his prize at the end of his reata. His men hung the elk from a manzanita tree and dressed it, leaving it to drain the rest of the blood.

William heard another shot. A few minutes later, Commodore Jones walked his horse through the bushes with a deer draped over its rump. After the men relieved him of his prize, the riders started to return to their stations. The dogs were still yapping and baying, and without warning, more frightened antelope, deer, and elk rushed headlong into the waiting hunters.

Catching glimpses of silver-tipped brown fur darting through the thick brush, William shouted, "Bear! Watch out!"

Concealed among the fleeing deer and antelope, an enraged grizzly pushed through the bushes and swatted at one of the savagely barking dogs. Growling, the bear lunged forward toward a rider, but without urging, the man's wily horse jumped aside and out of reach. When the furious beast stood to face his enemies, William fired a bullet through the bear's throat. A volley of shots from the commodore and two of the vaqueros smashed into his chest, belly, and a rear leg, dispatching the bruin.

"You certainly know how to organize an exciting hunt, Captain Richardson!" said the commodore, reining in his agitated horse.

Two of the vaqueros dressed the deer and the grizzly. They stuffed the rump and other choice cuts of bear meat into canvas sacks that held about fifty pounds each, and threw in the paws to be taken to the Richardson hacienda, along with the elk and deer.

✠ ✠ ✠

While the men were on their hunt, María and Mariana decorated the house with garlands of ivy, toyon tree branches with red berries, and bay branches, filling the air with a tangy, woodsy fragrance. Tallow candles were set in every window and on tables to keep the dark winter night at bay and to welcome the arrival of the Christ Child on Christmas.

"I can't wait for Christmas Day," Mariana said, pulling a garland of ivy from the pile of vines. "I'm excited to see all our friends here around our table."

"There'll be a pageant on Christmas Eve also, like the one we saw at Mission San Gabriel," María said as she watched her daughter drape the garland over the doorway. "And we'll sing hymns at the San Rafael mission church, *cariño*, with our family and dear friends." María studied her daughter and said, "Don Timoteo will be with us then and here too for Christmas dinner. The De Haros accepted our dinner invitation also."

Mariana's bright smile and sparkling eyes told María all she needed to know about her daughter's reason for eagerly anticipating their Christmas celebration.

CHAPTER 39

A CHRISTMAS CELEBRATION

In the afternoon on Christmas Eve, the Richardsons rode to San Rafael to dine with their good friend Timothy Murphy. When Timothy's thirty-five dogs—beagles and greyhounds—announced their arrival at the Murphy adobe, the owner himself stepped outside to greet them. William and the children dismounted, and the two men shook hands.

"We're grateful for your invitation," William said to their host and then turned to help his wife from her saddle.

"The least I could do for such good friends," said Timothy. "You know I love celebrations. Especially with children." Mariana beamed and curtsied to him, and the boys shook his hand. "And good food!" He patted his belly to emphasize his words.

"You are looking very fine indeed, Don Timoteo," María said, admiring his coat and polished leather boots.

Timothy bent his six-foot-two frame to kiss María's hand, taking it gently in his huge paw. "Always a pleasure to see you and your family, Doña María."

María smiled down at the old friend's curly gray hair. "And we are happy to be here with you." She sighed softly as he ushered them indoors, wishing once again that General Vallejo's sister

Doña Rosalía had accepted the marriage proposal of this big-hearted man instead of marrying Jacob Leese.

After an evening meal followed by a brief rest, the Richardsons and Timothy rode the short distance to the San Rafael church for Midnight Mass celebrated by Padre José Lorenso Quijas, who had replaced Padre Altimira when the old friar died years before. Padre Quijas, a Mexican priest, oversaw this church and the San Francisco Solano church in Sonoma now that the mission chapels had been converted into parish churches.

The modest San Rafael church was alight with dozens of tallow candles, and lanterns illuminated the courtyard. Some neophytes who remained, living in the diminished mission *rancheria,* were established members of the mission choir. They sang sacred music in Latin during the service, accompanied by a string and reed band that played flute, guitar, cymbals, and violins. All the worshippers sang the well-known hymns along with the choir. While the church bell rang joyfully at the end of the Mass, the attendees spilled out on the plaza to watch the shepherds and the archangel drive away the Devil in the play *Los Pastores*.

During the Christmas pageant, María recalled another pageant in this church, not long ago, when Francisco had boldly played the sword-wielding Archangel Michael and chased off Satan. How he had glided and danced around the plodding devil actor, just as his father had taught him to do in a fist fight. María had laughed aloud and felt so proud of him. But he was no longer that boy. Now he was almost a young man, beginning to take his place in the world.

On the ride back to the Murphy house where they would sleep, María gazed at the clear night sky sparkling with hundreds of bright stars and whispered to her husband, "A most wonderful start to our Christmas celebration, thanking God for our family and our fine life together."

✠ ✠ ✠

After breakfast with Timothy, the Richardsons rode along the trail to Saucelito with the chilly ocean fog pouring over the hills like thick clouds of smoke. At the rancho, they found the servants making tortillas, churning fresh butter, and plucking feathers from fat chickens that would be served that evening. Everyone sang as they bustled around preparing for a splendid dinner. By afternoon, the good smells of corn fritters, roasting beef and venison, and *Dulce de Calabaza,* a candied pumpkin dessert, wafted throughout the hacienda. María and Mariana dressed up in the silk dresses sewn from Limantour's fabric, and William, Francisco, and Esteban polished their boots and brushed their black velvet jackets.

Guests arrived in the late afternoon. Neighbor John Reed and his wife Doña Hilaria Sánchez Reed from *Rancho Corte Madre del Presidio* rode up first, bringing a basket full of sweetmeats for the party. Timothy arrived close behind, leaping from his fine horse and grasping John's hand, the two, tall Irishmen, like bookends, equal in height and girth. María greeted Doña Hilaria on the veranda and helped her inside with her basket. Seeing Timothy, María returned to the veranda steps. He swept off his wide-brimmed hat and reached out to kiss her hand.

"Thank you for including this old bachelor in your celebration," he said.

"You are always welcome in our home, Don Timoteo."

Timothy lifted his saddlebag filled with bottles of wine and brandy he had brought for the celebration and walked in with John, arms draped over one another's shoulders. Commodore Jones arrived on the shore at the same time that a small boat pulled up on the beach. Mariana's gray eyes lit up when she saw Don Francisco de Haro disembark and stroll up with his daughters Rosalía and Natividad on either arm and his twin sons Ramón and Francisco. María smiled as she watched her giddy daughter run to meet them.

"A fine celebration indeed," William said coming up behind his wife and encircling her waist with his arms. "Will we be having a wedding party soon?"

"Not quite yet," said María, hugging his arms. "There is still time. She's only sixteen. A bit too impulsive, I think. And these two boys as well. At least, Chico is, not Ramón. But I could not ask for more handsome, amiable, or mannerly young men to court our daughter."

✠ ✠ ✠

Tallow candles were lit and the table was set with sparkling glasses ready for the ruby red mission wines. A pitcher of wine sat at each place setting allowing guests to help themselves. After William gave thanks to God for their bounty and the chance to share it with family and friends, Timothy pushed back his chair and stood, a glass of wine in his hand.

"Raise a glass to our wonderful hosts! May the roof of your house never fall in, and may those below it never fall out!"

"Here, here!" the company called out together.

Because Maruha had requested to visit her mother at the Miwok settlement for the holiday, María and Mariana helped Rosalita serve. They carried platters of venison, juicy roast beef, and stuffed roasted chicken to the table, and the guests helped themselves to a portion of each delicacy.

"Try this bear meat," William said as he offered the hot platter to Timothy. "The Commodore and I shot this bruin a few days ago. But I hear you like to dance with a bear before bringing him to your table."

The big man poured himself some wine. "Well, you have to show these brutes who's boss. Although I didn't bring the bear I met to my table, he won't be messing with me again." After a swig of wine, Timothy proceeded to tell the tale of his encounter with a bear.

"My friend Domingo and I were riding along a trail—I was leading—when out of the bushes, rose a huge cinnamon bear in front of my horse. The horse reared, I lost my seat, and the horse bolted. The bear stood to its full height right in front of me growling, and then roared. So, like any good wrestler, I tucked my head down and charged into him before he could take a swipe. I wrapped my arms around his middle and tried to squeeze the life out of him as I kicked him with my knees. Domingo rode up and started whipping the bear across the eyes and nose with his reata, making him angrier it seemed to me. The beast clawed at my back, but fortunately I had on my heavy leather coat. It will never be the same." Pausing to shake his head and sip his wine, he continued, "Well, the bear and I fell down and rolled around a bit on the ground. But I guess he finally had enough. He pushed me away and scampered off."

Looking around the table, Timothy saw guests with wide eyes and dropped jaws. "When I got to my feet, I told Domingo he might be a well-meaning Spaniard, but he should never again get mixed up in an Irishman's brawl." The party roared with laughter.

When the dishes were cleared away, the friends distributed themselves in seats around the main room, smoking their preferred tobacco and sipping glasses of wine or aguardiente. Francisco and a rancho hand began to play Spanish love songs on their guitars. Someone joined them on a violin. María charmed the guests by singing the lyrics in her sweet voice, her thick hair hanging loose over her shoulders and her dark eyes shining in the flickering candlelight.

William took his turn entertaining them with a spirited English sea chantey, "Wild Rover," that started guests stamping their feet and clapping. Timothy joined in singing, and William, with a glass of aguardiente in one hand, put his other arm around his wife, and changing the words in the last verse, sang:

"I'll return to my wife, tell her that I am done.
I'll ask her to forgive her roving husband."

María made a face at William, and the audience roared, knowing the truth of the lines for any seaman. After the singing, the floor was cleared of table and chairs for dancing. William invited his wife to dance a waltz, and the Reeds followed their lead. Francisco and Don Timoteo gallantly asked the De Haro girls to dance. Chico de Haro bowed to Mariana, who looked into his eyes, laid her hand lightly in his, and waltzed onto the floor. María stared thoughtfully at her daughter, and William followed her gaze.

"They make a fine couple," María said.

William chuckled. "Ever the matchmaker! You are just like your mother."

"I did not make the match. Chico set his cap for her a long time ago. And she accepted. Do you remember when Mariana danced to entertain Commodore Wilkes and his officers? She knows who she wants."

"He's a decent young chap. He might be an acceptable son-in-law." William whirled María around the floor, wondering again at the thought of his daughter getting married. He agreed with María. Not quite yet.

The celebration lasted well into the night as was usual at the Richardson hacienda. The gentlemen played cards, Mariana danced an old Spanish dance, and finally Timothy sang an Irish melody. By two in the morning, the De Haros sailed home and the commodore returned to his ship. The Reeds and Don Timoteo stayed over, and the hosts provided them with comfortable places for sleeping. After all settled down, María wrapped a wool shawl around her shoulders and walked outside to stand beside William on the veranda. The two of them contemplated the starlit sky, the sliver of moon overhead, and the shadowy bay hugging *Isla de Nuestra Señora de Los Angeles*.

"*Contento, mi amore?*" she whispered to him.

He kissed her gently on her lips. "Very content," he murmured. He looked out again at the darkened landscape and tranquil bay. "I could not ask for more. I am a lucky man to live in this Eden with you and our children. At last, we are home."

✠ ✠ ✠

Life at Rancho Saucelito brought freedom and joy, but also grief. No matter how hard William and María worked to protect themselves and their loved ones, the unpredictable, the unexpected, happened and ripped apart their hearts and dreams.

CHAPTER 40

DEATH IN PARADISE

A few weeks after Christmas, many people on the rancho developed coughs and sniffles, spreading the illness from one to the other, especially among the Ohlones and Miwoks. Because they believed sweating would cure them, they brought the sick to the smoky *temescal* William had built for them. Many improved, but more became ill because those who were well stayed in the same confined space with the sick.

Although fourteen-year-old Francisco didn't join in this cure, he too became weak and feverish. Despite María's constant care, serving him mint teas, blackberry syrup for his wracking cough, and willow bark tea for the pain, his condition worsened. She tried to cool him with spring water, but his fever spiked. He became weaker and weaker, not eating, his arms and legs thinning to just skin stretched over bones.

In the evening, worry creasing his brow, William hovered at the boy's bedside with his wife. Standing behind her, he placed his hands on her tense shoulders.

"Come, María," he urged. "I'll take over for a while. You need rest."

His wife sighed, her hand shaking as she removed the damp cloth from Francisco's burning forehead and placed it in the basin of water. The feverish boy moaned and tossed his head on his damp pillow. "He is no better," she said in a quivering whisper. "What can we do?"

William felt helpless as he took over the care of his suffering child. None of his medical knowledge could relieve or cure him. Padre Quijas visited to bless the boy because he lay near death. He performed the last rites for the dying and the dead according to Roman Catholic tradition.

By the end of January, on a cold rainy day, Francisco, one of the heirs to William's paradise, struggled to take in one more breath.

Then he let it out and lay still.

María crossed his hands on his thin chest and collapsed in tears at his bedside, hugging his wasted body as it turned cold. Esteban, frightened and crying, clutched a sobbing Mariana. Doña Martina, who had come from Rancho Pinole a few days before, hugged both children, who had never faced a family member's death. William carried his shattered wife to their bed. He returned to comfort his children while he tried to hide his own overwhelming grief.

✠ ✠ ✠

Tears blurred María's sight as she and her mother washed the boy's body in the morning and prepared him for his final rest. She looked at her lifeless Francisco who had brought them such happiness. Whom she had taught to walk, to talk, to ride, to swim. Who had performed chores without protest and teased his brother and sister with an impish smile. Who had eaten her meals with relish. Who had yearned to explore the seas and foreign lands as his father had. God had snatched him away from her, her son, her joy, his body soon to be laid in the cold ground in a simple redwood coffin.

✠ ✠ ✠

On the day of the burial services, sorrowing family members and close friends gathered at the Saucelito Rancho. Besides María's parents, sisters, brother José, and their families, the De Haros,

Peraltas, Timothy Murphy, and many others arrived to support the Richardsons in their grief. As customary for all Californios of the Roman Catholic faith, the remains would be laid to rest in "*Campo Santo*," sacred ground. For the Richardsons, that sacred place was near Mission San Rafael.

The vaqueros who knew and loved Francisco carried his casket, draped with a pure white cloth, from the house. They placed it in an oxcart that would bear it to the church for a funeral Mass, a fitting celebration for the young boy's return to God. Since the Church forbade riding to a funeral, the solemn procession of mourners, dressed in somber clothing, walked the muddy trail to San Rafael behind the slow-moving cart pulled by a black ox. The misty gray sky wept over the loss of the wild, carefree boy who once rode joyfully over the golden California hills.

For an hour, most of the mourners remained quiet while they walked. Then a few spoke to others in low voices, remembering stories of their time spent with Francisco.

"He was a clever boy and as good a horseman as any *caballero* or vaquero," his uncle Don José Martínez said. "I taught him to pick up a peso from the ground on his galloping horse. Do you remember his first time trying that trick, Vicente?"

Don Vicente Peralta smiled and nodded his head. "I do. The horse was standing still and Francisco slid off its back. He dusted himself off, mounted, and tried again and again, even though we laughed each time he failed. He did master the trick at a gallop. He became one of our best riders when we had riding contests."

The De Haro twins walked with Esteban. "Francisco was a great friend, Esteban," said Ramón. "We enjoyed visiting you and him because we could ride and hunt together. And have wrestling contests. Then my brother and I didn't have to wrestle each other." Ramón punched his brother Chico's shoulder.

"Francisco didn't give up easily," Chico said. "So many times I thought I had won, and then suddenly he was on top and I was pinned to the ground!"

With a rueful smile, Esteban clapped his friend on the shoulder. "He liked boxing even more. Papá taught him and me." Esteban paused. "Francisco was proud of our father. When we lived in the tent-shanty all alone at Yerba Buena Cove and a bear stole our rooster, he told me, 'Don't worry, little brother. Papá will get that bear. He can do anything. Build ships and houses, pilot any vessel including warships, kill a bear, and defend us. Always. Everything will be all right.'"

✠ ✠ ✠

Many old Californios recognized death as part of God's will, the natural way of life, and felt sad but at ease when an old friend or a parent, after a long, fulfilling life, was carried away. Reuniting with God was a consolation to the dying, and in a way, a joy, something to be celebrated. However, the living, even with the comfort of faith, found it hard to accept the death of a child.

After the mourners laid Francisco to rest, María spent hours lying in bed or sitting wrapped in a blanket on the veranda, staring into space, barely eating, ignoring all around her. Although William tried to be stoic, having seen death many times, he wept. After the funeral he spent days alone, riding in the hills or rowing on the bay, grieving for his son for whom he had had so many plans and hopes.

Doña Martina stayed with the Richardsons for several weeks to try to comfort her daughter. One day, hoping to help her come to terms with her loss, she sat beside her on the veranda. Doña Martina could share no clear path or map to guide María through her valley of grief. She would have to find her own way, but children imitate their parents and need them to model how to rise above their sorrow.

Holding María's two hands in hers and looking into her sorrowful dark eyes, Doña Martina said, "María, your children need you. Your husband needs you. It is not our way to grieve forever over a loved one, even a child. Yes, we have lost our beloved Francisco, but he will live on in our memories. You must pull this family together and get them back into their usual way of life. Because they are living and need you to help them understand, to comfort them in their grief. Then show them how to move on. Take off this melancholy mask and be your loving self. As a mother. As a wife."

María lifted her head and looked at her concerned mother and then out at the beach where Esteban walked alone, chin pressed to his chest, kicking pebbles. Mariana silently walked past her, carrying a bucket of water to the kitchen, trying to be a dutiful daughter. María shifted her focus to the bay, catching sight of her husband, his back muscles straining as he rowed to shore.

"Yes, Mamá, you are right." María hugged her mother and kissed her cheek.

Doña Martina watched her daughter step off the veranda and walk to the beach where she gathered Esteban in her arms. Together, mother and son went to meet William. After Esteban helped his father haul the skiff onto the sand, the two men hugged. María placed her hands on her grief-stricken husband's cheeks and kissed him. They embraced, clinging tightly to one another.

"Please, God," Doña Martina prayed, "ease their sorrow. Help them move on with their life together."

CHAPTER 41

GRAFT AND SMUGGLING AND POLITICAL UNREST

William looped and knotted a rope around a water barrel, and a crewman tied it to other barrels. All would be floated together and towed to a whaler anchored in Whaler's Cove. When the two men heard shouts, they turned to watch Benito Díaz disembark from his launch at the wharf William had recently built, and jump to the shore.

Straightening to his full height, William greeted the Mexican administrator of the port while the man plodded over the sand to his side. "Good day to you, Señor Díaz! What brings you here across the bay?" he asked, knowing full well what his mission was.

Díaz regarded the crates, sacks of grain, and numerous barrels scattered on the beach. Sailors were filling the barrels with water from a twenty-foot square cistern William had constructed close to the water's edge. A wooden flume now carried fresh water from the hillside springs to the cistern where the barrels could be filled quickly.

"Captain Richardson, I see you are providing the whalers and trade ships with supplies as well as your water. You have been warned many times about snubbing the government's trade regulations for foreign vessels. These ships should have anchored in Yerba Buena before coming here for water or trading." Díaz walked to a huge blackened iron kettle sitting on the sand. "Where did you get this? And why?"

William ignored the comment about trade regulations and crossed his arms over his chest. "A whaling ship captain was short of money. He gave it to me in trade for provisions."

"The Monterey custom house will decide whether this should be in payment of customs duties. These ship captains are all in flagrant violation of the rules. This is illicit trading."

While the angry Díaz stomped around the beach, William grinned, knowing this little man was bluffing as usual. He had weathered this scene many times in the past two years. While the administrator ranted, William glimpsed action in the harbor. The current San Francisco alcalde, William Hinckley, was transferring several barrels aboard his schooner anchored between two whalers.

"And what is happening there?" shouted the irate official, pointing at the schooner.

"That's my brother-in-law taking aboard some salt pork and a few sacks of ship bread from a whaler. He said it was all arranged with you."

Díaz gritted his teeth. "I'll deal with him in Yerba Buena. But you . . . you are making up rules to your own advantage, Captain Richardson. As Captain of the Port, you are responsible for allowing this illegal trading in Saucelito and will be held accountable. I'll be sending my complaint in a letter to the Monterey customs administrator. And I'm confiscating that cauldron." Díaz directed his sailors to load the kettle on his vessel.

Eyes narrowed, William stared at the back of the pompous official marching to his launch. "We'll see about that," William said under his breath.

He was not about to change his trading policies. Captains of whalers and trade vessels preferred to lighten their load in Saucelito before visiting Monterey or Yerba Buena to avoid paying the full tax on their goods. As long as they agreed to split the difference with him, he was fine with that. There were plenty of places at Whaler's Cove to hide liquor, fine silks, clothing, and household goods from prying government eyes. His conniving with hardened ship captains eager to avoid high port duties was too lucrative to give up, not only for himself but also for the merchants and local rancheros preferring to barter for cheaper goods on this side of the bay.

✠ ✠ ✠

Over the next few months, William received several letters, all claiming he was abusing his duties as captain of the port and stating he will be called to account for illegal trading. He knew why Díaz was interested in his business. Díaz's officious letters to Monterey espoused virtue for selfish reasons. As administrator of the port in Yerba Buena, this mid-level official was authorized to tally and tax the value on all goods traded and to keep twenty-five percent of the receipts in compensation. He wanted his money!

Finally, in October 1844, after sending letters in answer to Díaz's accusations, William wrote his bureaucratic response, "This Captaincy is not responsible for anything you may do regarding the whaling ships anchored in Saucelito, because of their having anchored by arrangement with orders which the Custom House gave; this is my answer to your Official Letter dated today."

María leaned over him at the table, her hand on his shoulder, while William read her his letter in response to the administrator. She squeezed his shoulder and drew her brows together.

"Are you sure you wish to make him an enemy, William? You are taking a huge risk. Think of the consequences. At the very least, you might lose your position as port captain."

"You know I have always sailed close to the wind." William patted her hand on his shoulder. "Díaz will be replaced within a year. Remember, *mi amore,* fortune favors the bold."

The next summer, construction of a new adobe custom house began on Yerba Buena Plaza. Díaz hired William and a crew of his men to dismantle the derelict Presidio adobes and move lumber, roof tiles, and other reusable materials to the plaza to construct the government building, which was completed in a year. A receiver, two revenue guards, and a boat crew were assigned to the new custom house to increase surveillance of all vessels entering the bay as well as to collect the fees. Even before it was completed, William was relieved of his duties as captain of the port on San Francisco Bay. He cared little about losing his position since he hadn't been paid a peso for his labors. His true income flowed from selling water, beef, and produce to the ships anchoring in his harbor.

✠ ✠ ✠

When he was relieved from duty, William wrote to Governor Micheltorena petitioning for his back pay. He knew it was unlikely he would receive cash since Yerba Buena officials, the Mexican soldiers, and even General Vallejo hadn't received pay from the Mexican government for years. Vallejo had told him he was paying Sonoma Presidio soldiers out of his own pocket, from his sale of cattle, hides, and wine. Still, hoping to get something for his service, William offered Governor Micheltorena an alternative. In lieu of pesos, he would settle for a tract of land on the Mendocino Coast. He was familiar with the coast from his many sailing journeys north. With new construction ratcheting up in Yerba Buena, William wagered that the dense redwood forest in the Mendocino area would be perfect for logging, and a sawmill there would provide lumber for a building boom. Shipping the lumber to San Francisco Bay would be easy.

The governor's reply in October was as William had hoped. The Mexican treasury was impoverished, payment for his employment was impossible, but two leagues of land on the northern Pacific Coast could be granted in recognition of his invaluable services. The governor added a stipulation in the land grant document. If William chose to take possession of the land, he must protect the indigenous people from unscrupulous individuals who might kidnap their children to sell them. He must also teach these native people useful work skills and guard against invasion from foreigners. William readily agreed.

✠ ✠ ✠

Weeks later, William rode along a narrow deer trail that passed through a dense forest of ferns and fragrant redwoods on the Mendocino Coast. He had sailed north on a schooner he now owned to perform the ceremonial ride of possession as he had done for Rancho Saucelito. After his ship dropped anchor near the river *Grande,* he and two of his vaqueros disembarked with horses and supplies to inspect and survey the land he had been granted as payment. He felt in his gut it would do nicely as compensation for his almost eight years of service to Mexico as captain of the port.

Reining in his large black stallion at the edge of the redwoods, William paused with his vaqueros Felis and Juan to regard the peaceful scene of deer and elk grazing in a meadow. The morning rain had stopped and sunlight broke through the rags of clouds overhead.

"Felis, we'll bring a hundred head of cattle here from Saucelito," William said. "I want you and Juan to guard them. Do you think you can manage living here?"

"Captain, we'll be happy to do as you say," Felis replied while Juan nodded his agreement. "May we have our families join us after we build some suitable shelters?"

"Of course, and I'll pay both of you extra for your duties. We might get a few local people to help you, too. But you'll have to instruct them."

While Felis and Juan made camp, William started to draw his *diseño* of the land he was claiming, marking off the rivers and the latitudes on his map. When they returned to the rancho, he would send a copy of it to the governor to finalize his title to the land. He would also send a signed receipt to acknowledge his acceptance of the title to the Mendocino land in payment for his services as captain of the port. By signing that receipt of title, he renounced all his previous requests for cash from the Mexican government.

✠ ✠ ✠

Several days later, William arrived at Rancho Saucelito and strode in the door with a wide smile on his face. Surprised, María dropped her sewing and stood to greet her husband. Tossing off his hat, he grabbed her around the waist, lifted her off the floor, and swung her around in a circle.

"María, I made an excellent deal with Mexico for my back pay! Our Mendocino rancho is magnificent. Much grander than I expected," he said as he lowered her to the floor.

María kissed her husband warmly, happy he was so satisfied. He had worked hard for so many years, relying on his skills and enterprise to take care of his family since the government offered only promises. After their deep sorrow over Francisco's death and the annoyance of the Yerba Buena customs receiver Díaz, they merited some joy in their lives.

"We'll continue to live at Rancho Saucelito to be near family and friends," he said. "I believe you would prefer that. But the new rancho will bring in cash from lumber as well as from the cattle I'll raise on it." Chuckling, he looked deeply into her eyes. "It seems you have made a ranchero out of me."

María laughed with him. "I'm so happy to hear this good news, William. And, yes, I would prefer to live here than anywhere else. What will you call your new rancho?"

"I thought about that on the way home. Rancho Albion. Long, long ago, my home country was known as Albion. Yes, Rancho Albion it is."

✠ ✠ ✠

William was grimly happy that he had negotiated his arrangements for pay so promptly with Governor Micheltorena. Things were not going well with the governorship.

In 1841 the Mexican government had installed Brigadier-General Micheltorena as governor, replacing Governor Alvarado, to strengthen its control of Alta California from invasions of lawless, foreign settlers and in anticipation of war with the United States.

Talking with his friend Timoteo over a game of whist one evening, William commented, "The general promised order and safety, and secured friends among rancheros, but he lacks the shrewdness of a good governor. Many of his troops were ex-convicts who deserted the battalion and now roam the countryside, spreading fear among the Californios."

"I've heard the rumors, too," Timoteo said, putting his hand on William's sleeve. "Be on guard here at your rancho, William. Previously the missions furnished food, drink, and other supplies to the presidios, but no more. Even the remaining troops have little to sustain them at the presidios. They forage for food at night, stealing provisions from civilians and anything else they want."

Over the next few years of Micheltornena's governorship, Alta California sank into chaos.

In 1845 the general faced retaliation from the former governor Alvarado. With reinforcements from Captain Sutter, John Bidwell, and other settlers, Micheltorena rode into battle with Alvarado and General José Castro for control of California. Although Micheltorena had a superior force of skilled troops, he was unwilling to kill or injure Californios, the people he had been sent to protect. The clash ended in two days, a bloodless conflict.

Governor Micheltorena prevailed, but he realized it was wiser to capitulate his governorship and return to Mexico, rather than kill those who opposed him and make survivors despise him as governor. Don Pío Pico was appointed provisional governor, the presidios remained understaffed and in ruins, and California stumbled on, defenseless against a foreign invasion.

✠ ✠ ✠

Over the next two years, William traded and smuggled goods with little interference from the new custom house guards or the latest administrator, Díaz's replacement. His Mendocino rancho flourished, stocked with cattle and horses he had driven there for Felis and Juan to oversee, and the lumber operation was beginning. He was on his way to becoming one of the richest men in Alta California.

When the end of the year approached, William and María looked forward to joyous Christmas and New Year celebrations. Trading vessels brought in French wines, cheeses, and other special foods that they purchased for the holidays. As in former years, they anticipated a full house and would be expected to entertain lavishly.

CHAPTER 42

AMERICANS AND RUMORS OF WAR

Chico, his brother Ramón, and their uncles Francisco and Ysidro Sánchez were drinking in the sole saloon in Yerba Buena when Captain Elliot Libbey strolled in. He stood at the doorway, thumbs hooked in his belt, and scanned the room. The twins glanced up from their table at the visitor and recognized the coarse-looking man with the crooked nose immediately. Mariana had told Chico how uncomfortable she felt with this captain in her house.

In a low voice, Chico said to his uncles, "He sails his American bark along the California coast and frequently anchors at Whaler's Cove. When he dines with the Richardsons, he stares at Mariana, following her every move. She avoids him and retreats to the kitchen as soon as a meal is over."

Chico covertly watched as the bartender stepped forward to meet his customer.

"Welcome, welcome, Captain Libbey! May I offer you a glass of aguardiente? The best in Yerba Buena, young and vigorous!"

"Exactly why I came. Thank you kindly," Captain Libbey said.

The captain claimed his glass at the bar and turned toward the young men and their uncles. He raised his glass. "Good evening, gentlemen."

After a couple of glasses of brandy, the captain, oblivious to his cold reception, approached the men at their table.

"Well, gentlemen, mind if I join you?" Without waiting for an answer, he pulled up a chair to sit near them. His presumptuous behavior irritated Chico all the more. "This is fine aguardiente, wouldn't you say? I've just been at Captain Richardson's and I do believe this brandy is better than the stuff he gets." He downed his glass, got up, grabbed the bottle from the bar, and offered more to all at the table. "But there are other attractions that make up for his choice of liquor. Such as his fine buxom daughter. I wouldn't mind a roll in the hay with that young wench."

The captain refilled his glass, but Chico slammed his empty one upside down on the table. "Curb your tongue as well as your thoughts, Señor, about the captain's daughter," he growled, staring coldly into Libbey's eyes.

Captain Libbey tried to make a joke of it. "Oh, ho, I see where your interest lies! I had no idea you had staked a claim on the girl. So, you want to bed her yourself!"

Chico was out of his chair, his long-bladed knife in his hand. Ramón grabbed for his brother's arm. Slightly tipsy, Don Ysidro tried to hold back Captain Libbey who was now standing. Words, shouts, and curses filled the air, sending the bartender running out of the saloon. When he returned with the alcalde William Hinckley, Libbey lay on the floor bleeding and groaning from a stab wound. The alcalde immediately arrested Chico, Ramón, and their uncle Don Ysidro while the bartender arranged care of Captain Libbey's wound.

✠ ✠ ✠

William heard about the incident a few days later when he sailed to Yerba Buena. He returned home and relayed the grim tale to his family after dinner. He tried to break the news gently, conscious of Mariana's feelings, but he wanted his children to know the consequences of rash actions. His wife, daughter, and son were shocked at the violence that happened in sleepy Yerba Buena.

"Libbey recovered from his wound, and Hinckley held a swift trial to calm the pueblo and stop the gossip." He watched Mariana as he said, "Don Ysidro was released, but the De Haro brothers were sentenced to prison for six months."

Mariana cupped her face in her hands and cried out. "My Christmas celebration is ruined," she whined. "Now I won't have a chance to talk to, dance with, or even see Chico until June."

Weeping, she fled to her room. William watched her go, and then turned back to María and Esteban, both stunned by this story.

"The brothers were taken to the San José calaboose because there's no jail in Yerba Buena," he said. "That will be a hardship for their father. But I hope the punishment will teach Chico a lesson. I feel sorry that his brother was dragged into it."

María agreed Chico's punishment was fitting for such a violent action and hoped it would teach the headstrong youngster self-control.

"I'm not pleased with Mariana's infatuation with Chico," William said. "She is so young. The boy can be reckless."

"Libbey's crass talk about our daughter also proves my point about Americans," María said to William and Esteban. "Many are like Captain Libbey. Rude and with no respect for Californios. Be on guard when you deal with them, Esteban."

✠ ✠ ✠

In the spring of 1846, unexpected hoofbeats drew William away from his midday meal. He stepped onto his veranda, pulling his napkin from his shirtfront. The rider was their former Yerba Buena neighbor Jacob Leese, who now resided in Sonoma with his wife Rosalía.

"Jacob! What are you doing in these parts?" William asked evenly. Although the two men were no longer friends due to a financial disagreement, the captain did not forget his manners. "May I offer you a meal?" He then noticed his visitor's grim face.

"Thank you, William," Jacob said, dismounting. "I have disturbing news to impart."

"Come in, come in. You've had a long ride this morning."

The two men entered the house where María greeted Jacob and offered him a cup of tea and a plate of hot food. The three gathered at the table, and Jacob began.

"As you know, the United States President James Polk made overtures a while ago to the Mexican government, hoping to purchase California."

"And many Californios say they would be happy to be under that more stable democratic government," William said. "We've had seven governors since Figueroa died. Eight, now that Don Pío Pico is governor."

"Very true," Jacob agreed. "Many rancheros as well as merchants—and even unpaid soldiers!—are disenchanted with the current state of affairs. The United States Consul Thomas Larkin in Monterey wrote me that Polk is impatient. He's floating the idea of the United States becoming an advisor to California, should the citizens wish to separate themselves from Mexico. Mr. Larkin made it clear that does not mean the President is urging a revolution. Larkin has contacted prominent people—Abel Stearns, me, and several rancheros. And now you. He wanted all to be aware of what is being discussed."

Unsmiling, María looked at her husband and then clasped her hands in her lap. William saw her reaction. He knew how she felt about Americans. They had heard Governor Pico and General José Castro, Vallejo's replacement, were struggling with a plague of foreign explorers and settlers swarming over the Sierra Mountains. María wouldn't speak her mind about these American invaders in front of their visitor, who was from the United States. Although Jacob was now Mexican and married to Don Vallejo's sister, William knew which side he was on.

"I speak with many ship captains, Jacob," William said. "They bring rumors of war between Mexico and the United States."

"No, no, nothing like that is being discussed," Jacob assured him. "At the Monterey *junta,* the political council, last week, some members told General Castro we should align with France or Great Britain. My father-in-law, Don Mariano, strongly supported connection with the United States. A few men encouraged independence from Mexico. However, there was no consensus by the end of this council meeting, and Governor Pico was not even there. I wanted to warn you to be prepared, though."

"I'm sure it won't be smooth sailing ahead. Pico will be outraged when he hears of Castro's *junta*. And what about this hot-head Frémont?"

"Oh, yes, that American army officer. He says he's leading a Topographical Engineering Corps' expedition. He entered Mexican territory without permission and arrived at Sutter's New Helvetia with sixty armed civilians and some Delaware Indians. Frémont claims his mission for the United States is to survey the unexplored West for routes to the Pacific."

"Where is he now?"

Jacob told William what he had heard. Frémont had traveled south from Sutter's and camped for a time near Monterey. But Castro sent him packing. He had told Frémont to have his expedition remain northeast of Monterey, away from the coast. Instead, the American wandered all over the countryside, to the coast and back, as if he were searching for a rancho of his own. Frémont then refused to leave and boasted that his explorations would bring in ten thousand settlers in the next six months.

"That wild comment led to a foolhardy standoff in Monterey at Gavilán Peak. Frémont actually raised the American flag there! All Castro had to do was wait and starve them out. After three days, Frémont and his men slithered away at night, taking their flag with them. They're traveling north now to Oregon Territory," Jacob finished.

William glanced at his wife and saw fear mixed with anger in her eyes. "Let's hope that's the last of those invaders." Turning back to their guest, he said, "I'll keep my ears open, Jacob. Thank you for the news and the warning."

✠ ✠ ✠

Whaler's Cove was busy as usual providing foodstuffs and water to trading vessels and to the warship USS *Portsmouth,* which had been moored there several days. During their stay, the warship's captain, John Montgomery, became friendly with William and invited him to dine aboard the ship frequently. William trusted the captain because he had been polite and conciliatory in his dealings with all Californios.

From his conversations with Don Mariano, merchants, and other rancheros, William could conjecture what might happen in Alta California in the near future. During one midday meal with Montgomery, he broached the subject of American interests in the territory.

"I've lived along this bay and sailed the California coast for more than twenty years," William began. "I've shared my detailed charts of the bay with Commodore Wilkes, you, and many other American ship captains. As the port captain of San Francisco Bay for almost ten years, I've piloted whalers, schooners, warships, and frigates safely into and out of the bay. If you or the captain of any American frigate on the coast need my piloting services, I'd be happy to assist."

William observed Captain Montgomery study him from across the table. They were about the same age and respected each other's abilities as seamen.

"I'll keep your sentiments in mind, Captain," the officer replied. He wiped his mouth with his dinner napkin and placed it on the table. "I agree that the Pacific fleet may need your talents."

Before leaving the ship, William asked permission to visit the ship's surgeon for a minor issue, which Captain Montgomery agreed to. William asked the surgeon for an ointment to treat a recurring rash.

"I've used it before," he said to the medical officer, "but my supply has run out. The mercury in it seems to do the trick." Opening his medicinal chest, the surgeon reached for a bottle of the blue ointment.

"That should last you a while," he said. "Use sparingly. This drug is powerful."

As William was rowed to shore, he tucked the bottle of ointment in his shirt. *No need to alarm María with my inconvenient issue*, he thought. He also mulled over his conversation with Montgomery and wondered whether his piloting skills truly would be needed. On such a glorious day, a light breeze ruffling his hair, sun warming his shoulders, how could war come to their peaceful bay, he asked himself.

CHAPTER 43

THE BEAR FLAG REPUBLIC

By June 1846 Captain Frémont and his followers left Oregon Territory, fiercely chased out by the Klamath people when the expedition invaded their lands. The Americans retreated south and encamped near Sonoma, the largest border town in northern Alta California.

Campfires glowed in the dark, chilly night. Frémont stared into the flames of one fire, contemplating his next move. President Polk and Frémont's father-in-law Senator Thomas Benton believed California should be theirs. If he moved their agenda forward here, they'd be in his debt. A decisive man, he wasn't one to wait for orders from Washington. Here in the wilderness, he was the leader and his men would follow him.

Hearing loud talk on the fringes of the campfire light, Frémont raised his head and put his hand on his pistol. He stood when one of the camp guards approached and said, "Captain, some American settlers want to meet you. They have information about General Castro."

Three men came forward and poured out their complaints about General Castro's hostile actions. He was trying to drive them out of the country by enforcing Governor Pico's decree threatening to take away their land and to expel foreigners who were not naturalized. They also said the Mexicans were encouraging local native people to burn the American settlers' crops.

"What would you have me do?" Frémont asked. "I have no enforcement power here. My expedition is not a fighting force."

The men continued to grumble but eventually left dissatisfied that this American army captain would not support or defend them.

A few days later, a small group of the American settlers stole one hundred seventy horses that were to be delivered to General Castro. These settlers had never pledged allegiance to Mexico, though by living in California, they should have. The men, led by a rogue named Ezequiel Merritt, drove the herd to Captain Frémont's camp for safety.

This might be a turning point, Frémont thought. He urged them on to further action against the Mexicans but said again, "I'm a United States army officer. My men and I cannot join you."

The next day, June fourteenth, in the early morning hours, Merritt and his American followers invaded Sonoma. They pounded on Don Mariano Guadalupe Vallejo's door and declared he was under arrest.

✠ ✠ ✠

The retired don, no longer a general, had no soldiers to protect the pueblo, but he didn't bolt his door when threatened by armed, hostile men. Following the usual Spanish custom, he calmly welcomed a few of the leaders into his office and said he would like to dress before discussing the issue with them.

"And since it is a chilly morning, gentlemen, I will arrange for my servants to bring wine and aguardiente to warm you while I change."

The intruders drank quite a few bottles before he finally reappeared in his full dress uniform, his sword at his side, and asked what he could do for them. Merritt laid out their demands.

By midmorning, a scruffy scoundrel, William Ide, became impatient. He had spread the lies about Mexicans burning American crops to stir up the American settlers in Alta California.

When he entered Vallejo's house, he found several men lying about snoring and one at a table, a glass of brandy in his hand, trying to write. Don Mariano was sitting at his desk, relaxed and smoking a cigar. He told Ide he was waiting to read and then perhaps sign this document. Tearing the document from the hands of the brandy-soused scribbler, Ide finished writing it and had Don Mariano sign it.

After he grabbed the document from the don, Ide marched outside and addressed the crowd of townspeople and the other American settlers waiting for news. He declared California was a new nation, not part of the United States. He read the articles of capitulation, the document the don signed. Cheers and shouts rose from the crowd. A murder of crows flew from their perches in the trees, echoing the cheers with raucous caws.

"We need a flag for our new country," one man in the throng yelled.

"I'll make one," an American volunteered. Stealing a large white cloth and paint from a Sonoma house, he drew a grizzly bear and a five-pointed red star on the cloth, and painted a stripe of red at the bottom edge. He explained he chose the bear because it always stands its ground in a fight, and he and his rebel settlers would not back down either. Under the bear, he painted the words "California Republic."

✠ ✠ ✠

A few days later, two men galloped onto Rancho Saucelito. The riders reined in their horses at the wharf. William rode from the hacienda to the wharf to meet them. One courier leaped into a longboat to row to USS *Portsmouth*. The other rider looked worried. William invited him into the hacienda to impart his news.

Once inside, the man blurted out, "Americans captured Sonoma and declared California a republic!"

William stuttered, "W-what? Tell me how. Who's involved?"

The man related what he knew, from the early morning raid to the flag-raising event. "The don's wife, Francesca, and his servant heard or witnessed the whole thing. They told me."

"And where is Don Mariano now?" asked William, stunned by this story, thinking of the danger this action might bring to his doorstep. "And his wife?"

"The last I heard the don, his brother Salvador, Jacob Leese, and a colonel who was visiting the don were arrested and sent to Frémont's camp. The don's wife was in tears when I saw her, but she and the six children are unhurt. Frémont sent the messenger who is now on *Portsmouth*. I was told to guide him here."

"So who's in charge at Sonoma if not Frémont?"

"That wild man Ide and his group of rogues. They are calling themselves the 'Bear Flaggers,' or just the Bears."

After the messengers left, María hurried to her husband who was looking across the harbor at the anchored trading vessels and *Portsmouth,* a somber look on his face. He held her hand and told her what had happened.

She gasped and put a hand to her throat. "What will happen now?" she asked. "I fear for the don's safety and his wife's! And ours! Will they invade San Rafael and here next?"

To reassure her, William put his arm around her shoulders and pulled her to his side. He was in a quandary now. As a Mexican citizen, he should oppose these American rebels, but personally, he leaned toward an American annexation of Alta California.

"If Don Mariano prevails and keeps the temperature down, things might be all the better for us," William mused. "But with General Castro and Governor Pico as well as Frémont in the mix, who knows how the winds will blow. We can only prepare as best we can to protect our small patch of land from this storm."

✠ ✠ ✠

Although Governor Pico had been incensed when General Castro called a *junta* without him, the threats of a foreign invasion united the two leaders to a common goal of defending Alta California. Governor Pico and General Castro joined forces in Monterey, and the general led an expedition north to attack the Bear Flaggers and reclaim Sonoma.

Meanwhile, William heard of another incident north of Saucelito. At Rancho Olómpali, one of Frémont's soldiers led twenty Americans in a confrontation with fifty Mexican troops commanded by Juan Padilla and Captain Joaquin de la Torre. After the skirmish, the Mexican soldiers retreated to Mission San Rafael, and the Americans returned to Sonoma. Now Captain Frémont was helping the Bears and leading one hundred and thirty men to San Rafael to hunt down the Mexicans.

Frémont's camp in Sonoma and stories of armed men roaming the countryside raised alarm among the Californians. The fighting at Olómpali stirred up panic, and about a hundred people, mostly Miwok and Pomo women and children, fled to Rancho Saucelito for protection. The refugees camped close to the hacienda, and the Richardsons made them as comfortable and as secure as they could, providing food for all.

✠ ✠ ✠

Two days after the Olómpali fight, at midnight, the Rancho Saucelito dogs set up a racket of howling and barking. Riders with somber faces thundered up to the hacienda. One dismounted from his spent horse and pounded on the door. With fifteen-year-old Esteban at his side, William leaned his loaded rifle against the wall next to the door and cautiously opened it to face the tense Juan Padilla and Captain de la Torre.

"We learned Frémont is leading a formidable group to engage us at San Rafael," said Captain de la Torre. "Once they find we are gone, they will follow our trail. They can only be a few hours behind us. As a loyal Mexican citizen, you must help us escape."

William heard the desperation in the officer's voice and saw his ragged, exhausted soldiers standing behind him. With all the women and children on his rancho, he didn't want a bloody battle to take place on his doorstep.

Wanting to help but not wishing to be accused later of being complicit, William said, "My schooner is at the wharf. I don't see how I can prevent you taking it. I would be overpowered by your troops. Resistance would be foolish."

The men took the hint. A few horses were loaded on the ship, the rest let loose to mingle with William's herd. Fresh horses would be rounded up where they landed. Diego and a few more of William's sailors were called on to sail the schooner. William and Esteban watched them depart and returned to the hacienda.

"We will be meeting Captain Frémont in a few hours, Esteban," William said as he fastened the door. "Go back to sleep so you will be ready. I've depended on you to manage the rancho when I'm away. Now we must be ready to defend it."

But would they be ready? William drew his brows together and considered his choices. Like Vallejo, he had to remain cool-headed with the Americans. Frémont sounded unreasonable and eager for an excuse to fight. William was determined to prevent bloodshed on his rancho.

CHAPTER 44

THE END OF AN ERA

Captain Frémont and his band, one hundred thirty strong, stormed into San Rafael late Friday evening to battle the Mexican troops, but only a swarm of grasshoppers rose from the grass to greet them, pelting their faces in retaliation. Although they discovered the trail Captain de la Torre and his soldiers had taken, Frémont and the Bear Flaggers chose to rest their horses and camp at the mission for the night. They pressed on to the Richardsons' place the next day, galloping to Rancho Saucelito, flying an American flag, and craving a fight.

When the riders approached, the rancho dogs yowled a warning, compelling the occupants in the house to abandon their morning meal and throw open the front door. Restraining two dogs by the scruff of their necks, Esteban stood beside his father on the veranda when Frémont reined in his horse next to it. He brusquely introduced himself and told them his mission. William introduced himself and his son and made it clear that Frémont was on their property.

To Esteban, the handsome, dark-haired Frémont sat astride his horse with an impressive soldier-like bearing, but what a cold, unforgiving eye he had! He was a wild cat ready to pounce on unwary prey. For one of the first times in his young life, Esteban felt true fear.

When Frémont learned De la Torre had escaped by sailing across the bay, his stony face radiated anger and frustration, but he contained himself.

"We will rest here for a few hours today, Captain Richardson," Frémont said to William. "The horses need to recover."

Esteban saw his father bristle at this uncivilized demand but knew he was at a disadvantage with this officious man and his surly followers.

With an order from Frémont, his men dismounted and made themselves as comfortable as they could on the bare ground outside the house.

Hungry men are often quick to cause trouble, so William told María to have food prepared for the horsemen. Such hospitality would be customary for guests in a California home, except these hostile visitors were not guests. When Esteban followed his mother inside to shut the dogs in the house, he heard her complain furiously about so many ruthless men carrying pistols and rifles near her home. She warned Mariana to stay inside, out of sight, and with a loaded pistol in her pocket. She directed Sophia, Rosalita, and Maruha to gather and boil as many eggs as they could. María and Mariana made tortillas and porridge and found whatever could be served to the unexpected and unruly crowd.

"Esteban, you must help Rosalita and me distribute the eggs and porridge."

When food was ready, Esteban brought it out on a tray. The five Delaware men in Frémont's group preferred eating dried venison which they pulled from their saddlebags. The boy tried not to gape at the brutal short-handled maces studded with spikes that each carried. These powerful, muscular men, dressed in buckskin coats similar to the Americans' jackets, also carried long knives in their belts. They acted like Frémont's guardians, as did the other riders, aware of his every move and gesture. Their leader's commands were never questioned.

Esteban overheard Frémont talking with a man he called Kit, short for Christopher Carson, a well-known wilderness guide. This buckskin-attired adventurer clearly admired the captain. A short, stocky man with blond hair worn to his shoulders and a bristly chin, Carson mirrored his leader's stern expression when he heard De la Torre had escaped.

✠ ✠ ✠

The hungry, impatient soldiers settled themselves in small groups on the ground and stared at María and Rosalita as they handed out food and drinks. When Rosalita offered tortillas to one group, a smirking soldier grabbed her wrist, upsetting the platter on her tray as he pulled her into his lap. The other men in the group laughed as she tugged and pleaded in Spanish to be released.

Seeing the scuffle, William advanced on Frémont. "You can stay here for now, but I beg you to command your men not to bother the women and children. They were already terrified by the incident at Rancho Olómpali."

When Frémont growled a sharp reprimand to his troops, the soldier released Rosalita, who rushed to the house for refuge, rubbing her bruised wrist.

"I will assure the safety of the women and children," Frémont said. "So you have heard about the battle at Olómpali? The cause was the vicious killing of two Americans.

"After the Bear Flaggers captured Sonoma, two of their members were sent to a nearby rancho, Sotoyome, for a keg of gunpowder. We heard Don Vallejo had stored gunpowder there. The two Americans, Cowie and Fowler, never reached their destination. Juan Padilla captured them, tied them to trees, and tortured them to death. Their jaws were broken—torn out—and their bodies dismembered."

Overhearing this description when she walked back to the veranda, María gasped.

"Captain," William said between gritted teeth, "please spare us these gruesome details, especially with my wife present!"

"I do beg your pardon, Señora," Frémont grunted, bowing slightly. "Padilla and his group rode to San Rafael to join forces with De la Torre. Since Cowie and Fowler were American citizens, I agreed to aid the Bears and their new Republic and to bring the murderers to justice. We learned that Padilla and De la Torre had fled to Saucelito."

"And what of Don Mariano and Doña Francesca?" María asked staring into their invader's cold eyes. "Where are they now?"

"Vallejo, his brother, and the other captives are prisoners of the Bears," Frémont said, "and being held at Sutter's Fort. His wife and family are in Sonoma and unharmed."

After eating his meal, Captain Frémont had William show him around the rancho. He strolled past the butchery and the vegetable plot and then lingered near the corral as if thinking of buying the place. Seeing the uniformed army captain, the Miwok and Pomo children who had sought refuge at the rancho scurried away from the corral.

Surveying the band of horses in the corral, Frémont said, "Captain Richardson, my men need fresh horses. I'm requisitioning thirty of your saddle horses."

Stunned by this brazen appropriation, William's eyes blazed. He bunched his fists, ready to argue or punch Frémont. He swore liberally. "You bastard! You arrogant blackguard! How dare you come on my land and make demands! You're stealing my horses, just as those American swine stole horses meant for Castro's army."

His heated words carried beyond the corral. The children's mothers called them from their play. William's field workers looked up from the vegetable garden toward the confrontation, hoes and shovels in their hands.

Frémont's cold blue eyes echoed William's glare. "I'll write a voucher for payment from the United States government," he snarled, "when you deliver the horses to San Rafael. Tomorrow." Reaching for the pistol on his belt, Frémont added, "I need provisions for my men. I'll take those with us today."

Shutting out thoughts of risks to his family and workers, William took a step closer. He grasped Frémont's hand on his gun and drew back his fist, prepared to throttle the man. Riding past the corral, William's ranch hand Ricardo overheard the exchange.

In a split second, his lasso hissed through the air and dropped over Frémont's head, its noose settling past his shoulders. Pulling it tightly, Ricardo pinned Frémont's arms. Vaqueros carried no weapons other than lethal long-bladed knives and reatas, but they were expert in using both.

Shouts and clicks from pistols froze everyone on the scene. William became aware of those around them. He loosened his grip on Frémont's arm and stepped back.

Five of Frémont's soldiers, hearing the commotion, had rushed to the corral. With a nod from William, Ricardo flicked the reata and freed the American. Frémont tugged off the noose and signaled his soldiers to stand down.

"Damn your eyes!" William said under his breath. "I'll order provisions be gathered for you today. And horses delivered tomorrow. But I'll be keeping a tally of the costs to demand payment from the American government."

This impudent firebrand was not like the reasonable American naval officers he had dealt with previously. Frémont made it sound as though the Bear Flag revolt was the motive for his armed support, but was it actually a veil hiding the true event—the United States' annexation of California? Did he know more than he was ready to reveal? Or was he overstepping his command, making decisions and taking actions beyond his orders? Such cocky young men were dangerous, often interested in making a name for themselves. In William's mind, either explanation meant Frémont could not be trusted.

The next day, Esteban and two rancho vaqueros rounded up thirty half-broke horses to fill Frémont's requisition. With so many armed men on their beach yesterday, he agreed with his father's decision to comply, though his Papá was obviously furious. By late afternoon, still remembering that chill of fear he experienced looking into Frémont's icy eyes, Esteban warily drove the string of horses to San Rafael with the vaqueros.

✠ ✠ ✠

The same day Esteban was rounding up horses for Frémont, the twin De Haro brothers, Ramón and Chico, who had been released recently from prison, were visiting their elderly uncle,

Don José de los Reyes Berreyesa, on his rancho. Distressed by the seizing of Sonoma, their uncle prevailed on the two young men to accompany him across the bay that morning to find his son, the *alcalde* of Sonoma. Not knowing that Frémont occupied the mission buildings, the three sailed a small boat from San Pablo across the bay and up San Rafael creek, intending to borrow horses at the mission and ride on to Sonoma. They disembarked and trudged along the trail to the mission.

Kit Carson and two American soldiers on horseback blocked their way.

Carson rode back to Frémont, who stood on the mission veranda, and asked, "What shall I do with these men? Should I take them as prisoners?"

Still seething over the savage deaths of the two Americans at the hands of the Mexicans, Frémont waved his hand in callous dismissal and answered, "I have no room for prisoners. Do your duty." Then he turned and walked away.

Carson galloped back to the orchard where he relayed Frémont's orders to the soldiers. Then he and one rider dismounted and drew their pistols.

"Stop! Stop! Don't shoot! We have no weapons!" The two young men kneeled, held up their hands, and pleaded for their lives.

"We are not soldiers!"

"My uncle is looking for his son. Don't shoot!"

Two shots cut the air and pierced the hearts of the kneeling twins. Their uncle raved on in shock, "*Madre de Dios*, Mother of God, kill me too!"

Frémont's soldier coolly obliged with a single shot.

✠ ✠ ✠

Esteban arrived in San Rafael just after his two dear friends, one being Mariana's beloved, had met their tragic fate. He saw their bodies still on the blood-soaked ground where they had fallen. Flies buzzed loudly all around them. Turkey vultures flew in circles above, waiting to descend.

He screamed out their names, jumped off his horse, and knelt to touch the faces of his friends. Stunned and shaking, he yelled at a bystander who had been going through the pockets of the dead men to tell him what had happened. Although he was enraged, Esteban was afraid and knew he was helpless. If he protested, this arrogant Frémont might just as coldly shoot him and his family! He couldn't just leave their bodies here but felt humiliated even asking Frémont for permission to move them.

After covering their faces with his jacket and Don José's with a bandana, he dragged himself and the requisitioned horses to the mission to face the heartless man lounging on the veranda. "Your horses," he said. He must not show fear or anger. He looked back down the trail. "Why were those men killed?"

"They were enemy spies," Frémont said dismissively.

Esteban hung his head and shook it, knowing they had just been released from prison. How could they be spies? Instead of protesting, he only asked, "Can I notify their families so they can claim their bodies and bury them?"

"Do as you wish."

During Esteban's long ride home, he thought bitterly about the senseless deed and wondered why his two good-humored, generous friends and their kind uncle were killed. How would he tell his sweet sister her handsome Chico, the love of her life, her future husband, was dead?

CHAPTER 45

CONFRONTING A BRUTE

The shocking deaths of the De Haro twins and their uncle unnerved the entire Richardson family. When Esteban stammered through his appalling story of the event, Mariana froze and her eyes brimmed with tears. She fled to her room and lay on her bed sobbing into her pillow. María followed and tried to comfort her daughter while William hugged Esteban to console him over the loss of his close friends.

William was outraged at the Americans' actions, the murder of two unarmed young men and a defenseless old man, and frustrated that he couldn't retaliate. Somehow war had come to his peaceful home, and he couldn't prevent it. Nothing he could say would soothe his family or lift the gloom that settled over his home. With a wretched heart, he sent word to the Yerba Buena alcalde to warn him about the tragedy and to Don Francisco de Haro so he could arrange for someone to collect the bodies of his sons and Don José.

✠ ✠ ✠

When William and María sat alone that night on the veranda, they grieved together over the loss of the twins and worried about what it meant for their family. This brutal act was so close to their home, only a few miles away. And how it pierced the hearts of their children and them!

"Will the Americans attack us next?" María fretted aloud. "Will they set fire to our home?" She plucked at her shawl, pulling it tighter around her shoulders, her dark eyes round with fear. "Will we ever feel safe again?"

William took her hands in his roughened ones. He would give his life to protect his beautiful wife and his children. "I'm furious about this hothead Frémont. And anxious about what he might do. I've posted watchers above the trail to San Rafael and near the harbor. We arranged a warning signal if strangers approach. We must be on our guard."

"What will we do if the Americans take away our land? Our harbor? What will happen to our servants?"

William could tell her mind was spinning in circles, but he had no answers. He hated this feeling of helplessness and tried to reassure his wife, to calm her. "I have faith in the American naval officers I've dealt with. They know my sympathies lie with them and the American government. But Frémont must be put on a leash. I pray that will happen soon." He had hoped for a peaceful merger with America, but they might be facing a storm.

María made the sign of the cross. "I can only pray tonight for the souls of those poor boys and Don José. And for the safety of our family including my mother and my father. And all our Californio friends."

✠ ✠ ✠

Mariana couldn't sleep. She paced the floor in her room, grieving for Chico. Thinking of the plans they had made for their future, she moaned in agony. She opened the shutters to look out her window and sucked in the cool night air to calm her shuddering sobs. Chico's face rushed into her mind when she recalled the last ride they had together with her brother and Ramón to the top of Mount Tamalpais. His hat off, his thick, dark hair windblown, his mischievous eyes looking deeply into hers. Chico had surveyed the golden hills and glorious bay below, telling her his dream of a rancho of his own. She was only twenty and he only a few years older. How could their life together be over so soon? Her grief squeezed her heart.

After exhausting herself into a fitful sleep and waking in the morning, Mariana emerged from her room and sat silently at the breakfast table with her family. She looked at Esteban poking at his breakfast, still visibly upset. He had witnessed the gruesome scene and had to deliver the horrific news about her beloved Chico and his twin Ramón. Her brother avoided staring at her red, puffy eyes but glanced at her several times. He said little. Mariana couldn't think of anything to say to comfort him. Her throat tight, she swallowed a cup of chocolate but couldn't eat.

"Mamá, I want to take a walk alone this morning," she said. "I promise to do my chores when I return."

María looked at her heartbroken daughter's face. "Of course, *mi alma*," María replied as she gathered some of the empty dishes. "But don't go far. Coyotes were seen this morning nearby. Take your pistol to scare them away if you see them. We will talk later after you clear your head."

✠ ✠ ✠

Mariana rose from the table to get her hat in her room. She put it on, thinking how she would never again be going for a walk with Chico, never hold his hand. They would never laugh or dance together looking into each other's eyes. She gulped back a sob, finding it hard to breathe. How could she live without him? Her life was worthless. How could she bear it?

Emptiness gripped her like a fever. Her pistol was lying on her bedside table. Picking it up, she loaded it and put it in her skirt pocket.

When she walked up to the corral, Ricardo greeted her solemnly, knowing what had happened to the De Haros. Intending to walk past, Mariana looked at the horses and said to Ricardo, "I don't see either of my horses. Are they in another field?" Maybe stroking them would calm her.

"Many horses were taken to the Americans' camp in San Rafael, Señorita," he said. "These are the saddle horses we have left."

Mariana pressed her lips tightly together and narrowed her gaze on the horses in the corral. Her fury swelled, overshadowing her sorrow and blinding her, blocking thoughts of danger. Frémont took away her Chico, but she would not let him keep her horses. She touched the pistol, the one her mother had given her for protection when Frémont invaded the rancho.

"Help me saddle one of these," she said. Ricardo complied without question.

Mariana gathered her skirt and threw her leg over the saddled horse to sit astride it. Once she was mounted, she jerked the horse's head north and kicked him into a gallop along the trail to San Rafael. As she rode, she steeled herself for a confrontation with Frémont and concentrated on what she would say to this cold-blooded, heartless American. Her rage made her oblivious to potential consequences for her rash action.

✠ ✠ ✠

When she arrived at the San Rafael mission, clouds of dust rose from the trail as she slowed her galloping horse to a walk. Crows flew up cawing a warning, and grasshoppers chirred in the dry, brown grass.

Two American soldiers with rifles advanced toward her on foot. "Halt!" one called out.

The other soldier ordered her to dismount and grabbed for her horse's bridle. Reining in her horse, she alighted, brushing off help from either soldier.

"Who are you and what is your business here?" one of them snapped.

"I am Mariana Richardson," she flared, "and I've come to reclaim my horses."

The loud, gruff commands roused Captain Frémont, who strode out from one of the mission buildings. He sauntered up behind his soldiers.

"Good morning, Señorita," he said. "What can I do for you?"

Seeing his condescending manner, she burned.

Mariana looked over at the nearby corral of horses and spotted her two riding animals. Swallowing her anger about Chico's death and Frémont's attitude, she stepped up to him and glared into his wary eyes.

"Captain Frémont," she spoke up, chin held high. "Two of my favorite saddle horses have been given to you by mistake. They are my personal riding horses. I trained them. I want you to return them to me."

Frémont gazed steadily at Mariana, who stared back.

"How will we know which ones are yours?" he asked.

Mariana stepped closer to the corral, put two fingers into her mouth, and whistled. A bay and a white horse neighed in answer and trotted to the corral gate, ears pricked to her call. "Those two are mine."

When Frémont shouted orders to two of his soldiers to get her horses, several men who heard his command stepped out of the mission buildings to see what was happening. Those lounging on the veranda stood up.

Mariana's heart thumped with terror. It had finally registered with her that she was a lamb in a lion's den. Here she was alone, no other women in the camp.

The men stared at her, but not in admiration, which she would usually acknowledge modestly. At her family's dinner parties, many men respectfully stood or bowed when she entered the room. During those times, she was secure under the protection of her father and mother. Determined not to show fear now, she touched the pistol in her skirt pocket for reassurance. Useless. *Just leave quickly*, she thought.

Snatching the lead ropes of the white horse and the bay from the soldier's hand, she mounted the rancho horse and stared down at Captain Frémont. Worried that these rough-looking men might return to the rancho and perhaps harm the people there, Mariana spoke up again.

"I thank you, Captain, for returning my property." Her throat tight, she paused, her fury rising over this callous man's actions.

"I also implore you to prohibit your men from molesting the women and children on our rancho. They have nothing of value and are helpless and frightened after all that has happened."

Captain Frémont's eyes narrowed as he scrutinized the young woman before him. "You remind me of my young wife Jessie, waiting for my return. She has the same fire and boldness as you." He smiled coldly. "I assure you, Señorita, my men are under my control. They will not harm you or anyone on your rancho."

Mariana jerked her horse's head around toward the trail to Saucelito and cantered away, leading her saddle horses. She was surprised to meet her father and her brother within sight of the mission. Her father was putting his rifle back in its scabbard, which hung from his saddle. His stony face told her of his disapproval of her behavior.

"Ricardo told me you had taken the trail to San Rafael," Esteban said.

"When Esteban informed me, we followed you," her father said with a stone face. "You were foolish to go alone."

"You heard everything?" Mariana asked. "When I rode here, I was angry. Angry about my horses. Furious and heartbroken about Chico." She choked a bit upon saying his name. "When I arrived, though, I realized my risky position among those cruel men."

"Papá was ready to shoot if one of them hurt you," said her brother.

"I had my pistol," Mariana said, eyes downcast, "but knew it would not be of much use."

"Let's go home," William said. "Your mother will be frantic with worry." He stared at his daughter. "You never thought of the possible consequences dealing with a powder-keg like Frémont, did you? What if he had refused you? Or he wasn't there and those boorish rascals assaulted you? Your action was foolhardy." William tugged on his reins to turn his horse around. He paused and looked at his daughter. "But you handled the encounter with Frémont well." He kicked his horse into a canter.

Mariana thought about her mistake, and fear gripped her heart. Not only had she put herself in danger, but also her father and brother. If her father had confronted Frémont with a loaded gun, he might have been killed. And Esteban. A tear slid down her cheek when she realized the risk she had taken with their lives.

✠ ✠ ✠

The next day, William heard from neighbors that Frémont's men had captured a messenger carrying a letter from Captain de la Torre that said he would be attacking Sonoma. Although a detachment of the Bears hurried to defend the Sonoma garrison, they encountered no enemy and their hard ride was pointless.

When an irate Frémont discovered the letter was a ruse, he and his men rode to Whaler's Cove hoping for more reliable information about De la Torre and his soldiers. Although William had no information about De la Torre's plans, the Americans brazenly set up camp at the rancho, forcing the Richardsons to deal with them and feed the rabble once again. Even though the atrocity of the murders of a potential son-in-law, his twin brother, and their uncle Don José was raw in his mind, William dealt tactfully with Frémont and his barbarians to avoid another confrontation.

Deciding to seek De la Torre in Yerba Buena, Frémont commandeered a launch in the Saucelito harbor to take him and twenty of his men across the bay. They first searched the battery *Castillo de San Joaquín*, the fort subordinate to the San Francisco Presidio, built close to the bay entrance. The battery and the decaying presidio, however, were deserted and held no evidence of Mexican troops.

When Frémont returned to the Richardson rancho, his men boasted about spiking the six cannons in the *Castillo* to the other soldiers camped at Saucelito. William knew spiking the rusty guns was futile. Even in their prime, only two of those seventeenth-century cannons could have damaged an enemy ship.

Wearing a smug look, Frémont approached William. "We are leaving tomorrow, Captain, and require more horses. And food. Have them ready by morning."

The following morning, more horses and cattle were rounded up, leaving the ranch with four saddle horses, including Mariana's. William felt relieved to see the Americans gallop away but feared they would return. If these isolated skirmishes escalated into a war, he mused, this intrusion might be only the opening volley of threats to their rancho, to their safety. He had to do something to secure his family and all they owned from the storm to come.

CHAPTER 46

A NEW ERA

By July 16, with Frémont gone, the men, women, and children who had abandoned their homes for the safety of Rancho Saucelito drifted back to their farms to pick up their lives again. William thought his family and rancho were safe from marauding Bear Flaggers, so he sailed across the bay to Yerba Buena, hoping to learn where things stood between Mexico and the United States.

From the boat landing, he marched up the sandy hill past Kent Hall and Nathan Spear's store and grist mill to the custom house on the plaza. Frowning, he paused to look at the flag snapping in the breeze at the top of the plaza flagpole. He had spotted the United States flag from his ship when he entered the harbor. Alta California and his life would soon change. Questions buzzed in his head. Will it be for the better? Will he and María hang on to their rancho?

At the custom house door, William greeted his brother-in-law, Don José Joaquín Estudillo.

"Ah, William, how are you and your wife? Safe? All is well?" the don asked.

"My wife and I and the children are fine," William replied. "I hope you and your family are, too."

After Don José assured him that his family had avoided confrontation with Frémont, William glanced at the flagpole and said, "I've been worried these last few days, so I'm here seeking news. I see the American flag now flies over Yerba Buena. What do you know about the state of things in California? Are we now part of the United States?"

"I do have news," the don said. "Mexico and the United States have been at war since May thirteenth! Battles were fought along the Río Bravo."

"My God!" William's eyes widened in surprise. "So perhaps Frémont did know something about America's intentions."

"Perhaps," Don José drawled. "Captain Frémont celebrated the California Republic on the Fourth and installed himself in his Sonoma headquarters. Then a lieutenant brought him news. The United States Navy had arrived in Monterey on July seventh. Commodore John Sloat, the commander-in-chief aboard the lead warship, had claimed the town." Don José clamped a hand on William's shoulder. "Without firing a shot! The Stars and Stripes now flies over the Monterey custom house."

A ship captain who had recently sailed from Sutter's Fort exited the custom house just then and stopped to talk with the two men. After quickly shaking hands, he added what he knew. "Commodore Sloat had sent the lieutenant to inform Frémont about the navy's arrival and to order him to raise the American flag in Sonoma. Although Captain Frémont outranked him, the lieutenant had pointed at the Bear Flag and stated, 'Get that thing down!'"

"I'll bet that put his nose out of joint!" William chuckled.

"That will be the last place the Bear Flag will ever be flown," Don José said, crossing his arms over his chest.

"When Captain Frémont left Sonoma," the ship captain continued, "and rode to Sutter's Fort, another courier intercepted him and delivered further orders from Commodore Sloat to report to Monterey as soon as possible. The commodore also sent a United States flag and a copy of a proclamation. The flag now flies over the fort." The ship captain thrust out his chest and grasped the lapels of his jacket. "So, gentlemen, all of us are going to be Americans!" He grinned broadly and added, "By the way, Don Mariano Vallejo and his friends were released. When I sailed, they were riding to Sonoma."

"Hallelujah!" William grabbed the don's arm and did a do-se-do dance with him on the veranda. "What a relief! Frémont and his ruffians are gone, and Don Mariano is free. Thank you, Captain, for this auspicious news. I'm hopeful the United States annexation will go smoothly now."

While the men were talking, an American naval officer strode out the custom house door and introduced himself. He promptly handed William a copy of Sloat's proclamation and an American flag to raise at his rancho. William read the proclamation. "Henceforward California will be a portion of the United States."

✠ ✠ ✠

When William returned to Saucelito, he noticed María walking to the wharf to meet him. Leaving his crew with the ship, he jumped to the wharf and gathered her to his chest. Bending low to kiss her, he said, "We are part of the United States now. We'll all be Americans soon."

María caught her breath. "I can't believe how swiftly this has happened!"

William tucked her arm under his and strolled with her, carrying the American flag to their flagstaff. He lowered the Mexican flag slowly, folded it, and replaced it with the American banner.

Looking up at it, he said, "Long may it wave. And with steady hands on the tiller." After enduring the disarray in the Mexican government over the preceding years, he believed there might be hope for tranquility. He told María about the proclamation and the American flags now flying at the Yerba Buena custom house, over the remains of the San Francisco Presidio and *Castillo de San Joaquín*, at the Sonoma Presidio headquarters, and at Sutter's Fort.

"We don't have to worry about Frémont anymore," he assured her. "The American naval commander Commodore Sloat is now at the helm. He's been in Monterey since July seventh and instructed Frémont to report to him there. I know the American takeover isn't what you wished for, but Sloat will bring peace and order to Alta California."

"I pray you are right, *mi amore*," María said. "I don't trust Americans though." Brushing away a loose lock of hair, she gazed back at their hacienda. "Peace may come, but it will last only as long as they stay away from the Californios' ranchos."

William gently turned María's chin toward him and brushed her cheek with his fingertips. To his eyes, she still looked as lovely as the first day he saw her, and yet she had endured so much.

"I have forced so many changes on you. The move away from your family to Mission San Gabriel, the hard life at Yerba Buena in a tent-shanty, and then settling here to build our rancho. We both know some changes can be good and some bad." He looked up again at the flag snapping in the sea breeze. "We've both learned to bend with the winds of change. As always, we'll welcome some and weather the rest."

✠ ✠ ✠

Months before Frémont's intrusion, when USS *Portsmouth* had visited San Francisco Bay and Whaler's Cove, Commander Montgomery had become well acquainted with William, his navigation skills, and his extensive knowledge of the bay and the California seacoast. He remembered William's offer to serve as pilot for the American navy if needed. On July twentieth Montgomery wrote a letter of recommendation to Sloat stating that Richardson "has been, heretofore, pilot and harbormaster of this port, and is desirous to retain the position under the change of government. There is certainly no man so fit for it, and his feelings are right toward us." The United States Consul in Monterey, Thomas O. Larkin, also praised William, calling him reliable, kind, honest, and influential.

At the end of July, Commodore Robert F. Stockton replaced Commodore Sloat, who was in poor health. Armed resistance was still erupting in southern California, and Stockton decided to sail to San Pedro to support American troops there. He needed maritime assistance in the coastal waters, though.

Days later, a messenger arrived in Saucelito to request William sail immediately to Monterey to meet Stockton because his services were needed. William read the message in his hand, and with a joyous whoop, ran up the beach to find María, Mariana, and Esteban.

"María! Where are you?" he shouted. "I have news!"

María and Mariana rushed onto the veranda, anxious looks on their faces. "Is Frémont back?" María asked, gripping the railing.

Esteban sprinted from the corral to his father's side, beaming. "What is it, Papá? Is a trading ship arriving in our harbor?" For his son, a ship meant news of the world as well as many fine things to buy and a chance to sell provisions.

William chuckled and said, "It is a ship, Esteban, but a warship in Monterey. I've been issued orders to pilot the leading ship. I believe this bit of luck will bond us with the Americans."

Hugging his son, he climbed the steps to the veranda to calm his wife and his daughter's fears. He felt confident the American government would do right by them.

AUTHOR'S NOTE

BLENDING FACT WITH FICTION

Because historical fiction is a mix of facts and imagination, I describe my novel as speculative historical fiction. Although Captain William Richardson and his family truly lived in Alta California, many details of their lives are unknown. My extensive research and imagination filled the gaps.

I referred to many first-person accounts, primary sources, and academic books for my research, reading some and skimming through others, dipping in to find interesting daily life details and specific facts as well as differing opinions about the people and the time period. Contemporary writings and historical documents often have conflicting viewpoints about early California. My research revealed distinct cultures with incompatible customs and values that merged and clashed in Alta California. This novel, tinged with historical hindsight, presents my point of view about these events.

Richardson often brushed shoulders with or became a good friend of many famous historical figures. Through American and California history studies, you might recognize names such as John C. Frémont, Christopher (Kit) Carson, Captain John A. Sutter, and Mariano Guadalupe Vallejo. Surnames such as Sloat, Figueroa, Pico, Stockton, and Martinez will sound familiar because California streets and cities are named after them.

Men generally hold a more prominent place in historical memory, especially those who were explorers or victors in wars. In my novel, I added details gleaned from written remembrances about daily life in the 1800s and events that did happen or might have happened to people who are less celebrated. These people include the Spanish and Mexican women, the laborers, and especially the indigenous people who lived in Alta California long before and after the Spanish explorers and missionaries arrived. For these people and the Richardsons, I designed scenes and dialogue to immerse readers in their lives during this era.

Readers will come to appreciate the struggles and resilience of the Richardson family and the human joys and sorrows they shared in their time. This novel is as much a love story about two people as about Alta California. Perhaps a land loved too much by people from so many cultures. I hope my story will captivate both fans of fiction and history.

Book 1: Seduction

- Captain William A. Richardson did leave his whaling ship and lived at the San Francisco Presidio, where the Martínez family was living at that time.
- The Franciscan friars built the twenty-one California missions as described and indeed treated the Native people in their care sometimes fairly and sometimes brutally. The Spanish colonization of Alta California resulted in indigenous people being enslaved at the missions and the ruin of their homelands. Today, we are critical of the friars' attitudes and cruel customs, but they behaved as was generally accepted at that time.
- Information about the Ohlones, Miwok, Tongva, and other indigenous people was gathered from books and websites. A single, haunting line from an Ohlone song inspired my book title.
- Marino was a Miwok leader who worked with Richardson for a time. I hope I treated the view of this original population fairly. Any inaccuracies are mine.

- Women were the backbone of the Alta California settlers. Some wives, such as Doña Martina Martínez, were privileged and had indigenous women and men as household servants. Other wives labored without much help, bearing and rearing children, cooking, cleaning, sewing, doctoring, chopping wood, and looking after domestic animals, as I described in my novel. Women married to mariners were often alone for months when their husbands were at sea. They had to oversee all rancho work themselves or with the aid of a rancho manager.

Book 2: Life on Land and Sea

- The Richardsons lived in southern California for a time, where they met Nathaniel Pryor, the Fitch family, Joseph Chapman, Michael White, Doña Eulalia Pérez, and Abel Stearns.
- Captain Richardson worked with Joseph Chapman, Michael White, and dozens of mission neophytes to build the schooner *Guadalupe.* An anchor commemorating its construction stands in Mission San Gabriel Archangel's garden.

Book 3: Staking a Claim

- The Richardsons rode along the *Camino Real*, the Royal Road, from Mission San Gabriel to Yerba Buena Cove. The *Camino Real* was the trail Spanish explorers traveled and the road that linked the chain of California missions. The Spanish road followed many indigenous peoples' trails. Much of California State Route 101 was built over the same road.
- Captain Richardson constructed a tent-shanty near San Francisco Bay at Yerba Buena Cove and later built an eight-room adobe house there, his *Casa Grande*. His building is known to be the first residence built by a white person in Yerba Buena, later renamed San Francisco. His *Casa Grande* no longer exists, although a plaque on the site in San Francisco commemorates where it once stood on Grant Street between Washington and Clay Streets.

- The Bear Flag Republic of California reigned for a few weeks in 1846, and United States Army Captain John Charles Frémont clashed with Richardson and his family.

Governors of Alta California—1822 to 1846

Pablo Vincente Sola: 1822
Luís Argüello: acting governor, 1822–1825
José María de Echeandía: 1825–1831
Manuel Victoria: 1831–1832
Pío Pico: 1832 (twenty days)
José María de Echeandía: 1832–1833 (only in south Alta California)
Agustín Vicente Zamorano: 1832–1833 (only in north Alta California)
José Figueroa: 1833–1835
José Castro: acting governor, 1835–1836
Nicolás Gutiérrez: acting governor, 1836 (four months)
Mariano Chico: 1836 (three months)
Nicolás Gutiérrez: acting governor, 1836 (three months)
Juan Bautista Alvarado: 1836–1842
Manuel Micheltorena: 1842–1845
Pío Pico: 1845–1846
José María Flores: 1846–1847

GLOSSARY

Aguardiente: A fiery Mexican liquor, brandy.
Alcalde: An appointed official of a pueblo, with the duties of a mayor and justice of the peace.
Asistencia: An outlying location established by a mission; San Rafael was built as an *asistencia* for Mission Dolores.
Buñuelos: Fried honey cakes.
Bota: A bag made of stretched cowhides sewn together with an awl and used to hold tallow, which was rendered from cattle or elk fat; each weighed five hundred pounds.
Caballero: A Spanish-speaking gentleman, usually of the upper class.
Cálidas felicitaciones. Warm congratulations.
Caramba: An expression of surprise or fear.
Cariño: Sweet one.
Carreta: Two-wheeled wooden cart pulled by one or two oxen. The wheels are solid wood made from cross-sections of a tree.
Chumash: A group of native people living in southern Alta California before the Spanish arrived.
Comandante: Commander, or commandant of a presidio.
Contra costa: The other coast; refers to the coast on the east side of San Francisco Bay.
Costeños: The indigenous people living around San Francisco Bay before the Spanish arrived; this term is the name the Spanish gave to the Ohlone and Miwok people.

Deputación: The Alta California board of representatives who report to the governor and the Mexican government.

Diseño: A hand-drawn map of land, marking boundaries for a rancho.

Don, Doña: Polite terms used to address important men and women respectfully, they were often landholders.

Dueña: A guardian for unmarried girls, usually an older married woman.

Gabrielinos: The name the friars gave to the indigenous people who were baptized at Mission San Gabriel. The people living in southern Alta California, near what is now Los Angeles, were the Chumash and Tongva.

Gente de razón: Baptized Spanish or Mexican Catholics, the aristocracy of Alta California, usually the families and relatives of the officers and soldiers who had come in the 1700s from Mexico City.

Laguna: A lake or marsh.

La Jota: A Spanish dance.

Loma Alta: Spanish, meaning "high hill"; now known as Telegraph Hill in San Francisco.

Merienda: Light meal, a picnic.

Mi alma: My soul, my heart.

Mi amore: My love.

Miwok: A group of indigenous people who lived north of the San Francisco Bay. The Spanish called them and the Ohlone *Costeños*.

Monjerio: The women's dormitory at each mission.

Neophyte: A Native American at a mission to learn the Roman Catholic religion and to be baptized.

Niñita: Little girl.

Ohlone: A group of indigenous people who lived around San Francisco Bay. The Spanish called them and the Miwoks *Costeños*.

Peso: The Spanish coin in the early 1800s.

Presidio: A military outpost; a fort.

Pueblo: A civilian settlement.

Ranchería: The village of houses near each mission where the neophyte families lived.

Rancho: The large cattle ranches granted by the Mexican government to worthy citizens.

Real: One piece of a peso that was divided into bits, each bit equal to twelve and a half American cents or one-eighth of a peso. Originally a Spanish coin whose value changed depending on the varying silver content. The English word "dollar" is derived from the Spanish word *dólar*. The *dólar* was divided into eight *reales,* or bits.

Reata: A lasso, in Alta California, a long rope of braided leather strips, used by vaqueros.

Rebozos: Shawls or large scarves worn over women's heads and shoulders.

Señorita: A Spanish-speaking unmarried woman.

Temescal: A conical-shaped smoke house built by Native people. The heat and smoke causes the body to sweat. Used to cleanse and rid the body of pests.

Tongva: A group of indigenous people living in southern Alta California before the Spanish arrived.

Tule: A tall rush, a plant growing on flooded lands or marshy ground.

Vaquero: A ranch hand who herds cattle on a rancho.

ACKNOWLEDGMENTS

Over many years I've researched, written, and rewritten my novel, relying on newspapers, primary resources, first-person accounts, and various nineteenth century sources. I am particularly indebted to the reminiscences of Captain Richardson's children, Steve (Esteban) Richardson (*Days of the Dons*) and Mariana Richardson Torres ("Recollections of Mrs. Torres"). And naturally to Hubert Howe Bancroft and his *History of California* in seven volumes. Other primary sources include William Heath Davis's *Seventy-Five Years in San Francisco,* John Bidwell's "Echoes of the Past," and Mariano Guadalupe Vallejo's "Ranch and Mission Days in Alta California."

I rounded out my research with many contemporary resources such as Robert Ryal Miller's *Captain William A. Richardson: Mariner, Ranchero, and Founder of San Francisco*, Jack Mason's *Early Marin*, Ruth Lescohier's *Tent-Shanty at Yerba Buena Cove,* Malcolm Margolin's *The Ohlone Way: Indian Life in the San Francisco-Monterey Bay,* and Derek Lundy's *The Way of the Ship: A Square-Rigger Voyage in the Last Days of Sail.*

I am grateful for the friends and family who encouraged me in my work. My beta readers helped steer me in the right direction so that Richardson, a key witness to this time, came alive on the page. I want to thank my early readers Inge Roberts, Stephanie

Sigue, Linda Hatch, Rolf Seitle, Jonathon Moses, Renee Zutter, Marcia Caldwell, and my editor Karen Eaton for their insights, support, and enthusiasm, and Linda Beeman for her striking hand-drawn maps. A special thanks goes to my book coach Kathleen Furin, who helped me flesh out my characters' emotions, and my copyeditor Candace Allen, who smoothed my story's rough edges. Bringing my book to the world would not have been possible without the care and guidance of She Writes Press publisher Brooke Warner, managing editor Shannon Green, and SparkPress associate publisher Lauren Wise.

Many people and organizations provided me with a wealth of historical information: Sausalito Historical Society (special thanks to Jan D. Keizer), California Historical Society, Marin Civic Center Library (Anne T. Kent California Room), California State Library (California History Room), San Francisco Historical Society, and the University of California in Berkeley (Bancroft Library).

I want especially to acknowledge my patient, loving husband Peter who allows me to focus and be noncommunicative for hours while I write and texts me when dinner is ready, and my children Chris and Jennifer who read my blog and brighten every day.

ABOUT THE AUTHOR

Author Marianne T. Rafter has always been drawn to historical fiction. When she lived in California, she worked on history and literature programs for a publishing company. Intrigued by California's pre-statehood era, she discovered the land she lived on had been part of a huge Mexican rancho in the 1800s, and before that the homeland of the Miwoks, the original inhabitants. Her research grew, and after the author and her husband moved to an island near Seattle, she wrote this novel and her blog, *Welcome to the Past: Dancing on the Brink of the World.*

Author photo © Peter E. Martin